OTTO

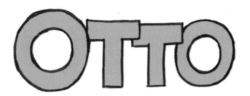

TO DAD

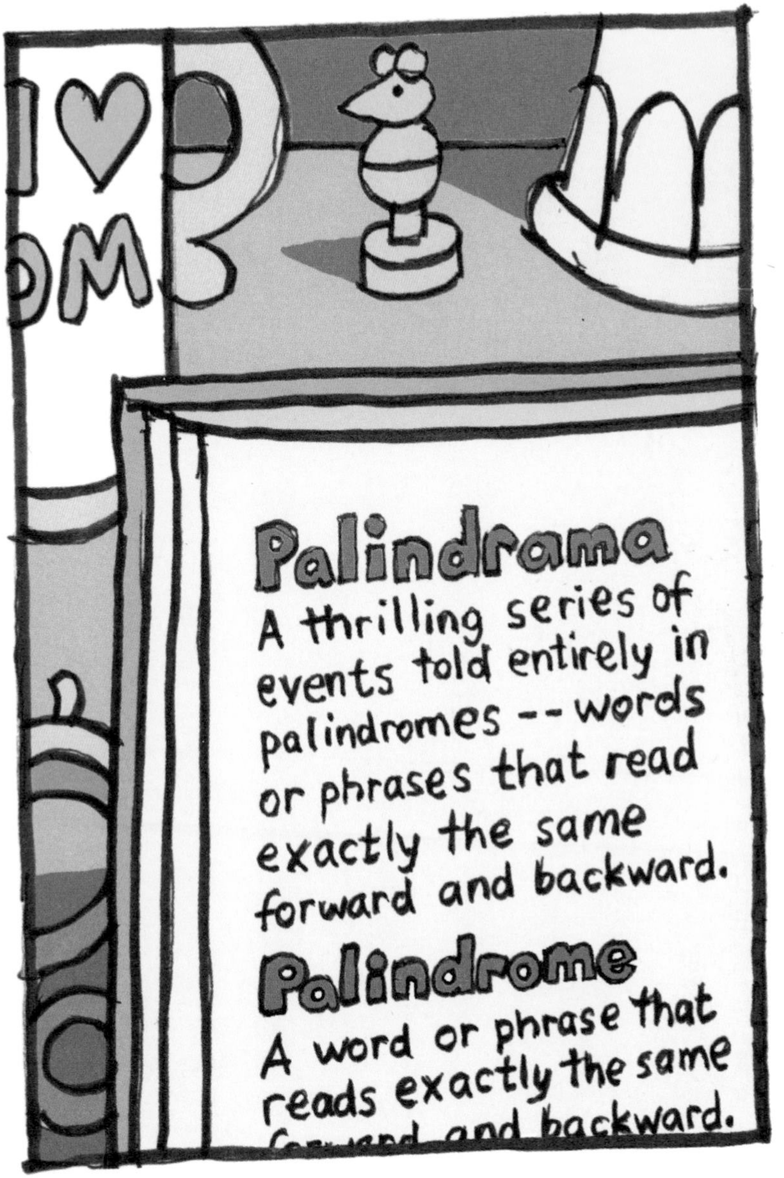
I ♥
OM
Palindrama
A thrilling series of events told entirely in palindromes -- words or phrases that read exactly the same forward and backward.
Palindrome
A word or phrase that reads exactly the same forward and backward.

JON AGEE

OTTO

A PALINDRAMA

DIAL BOOKS
FOR YOUNG READERS

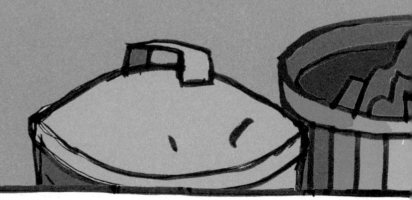

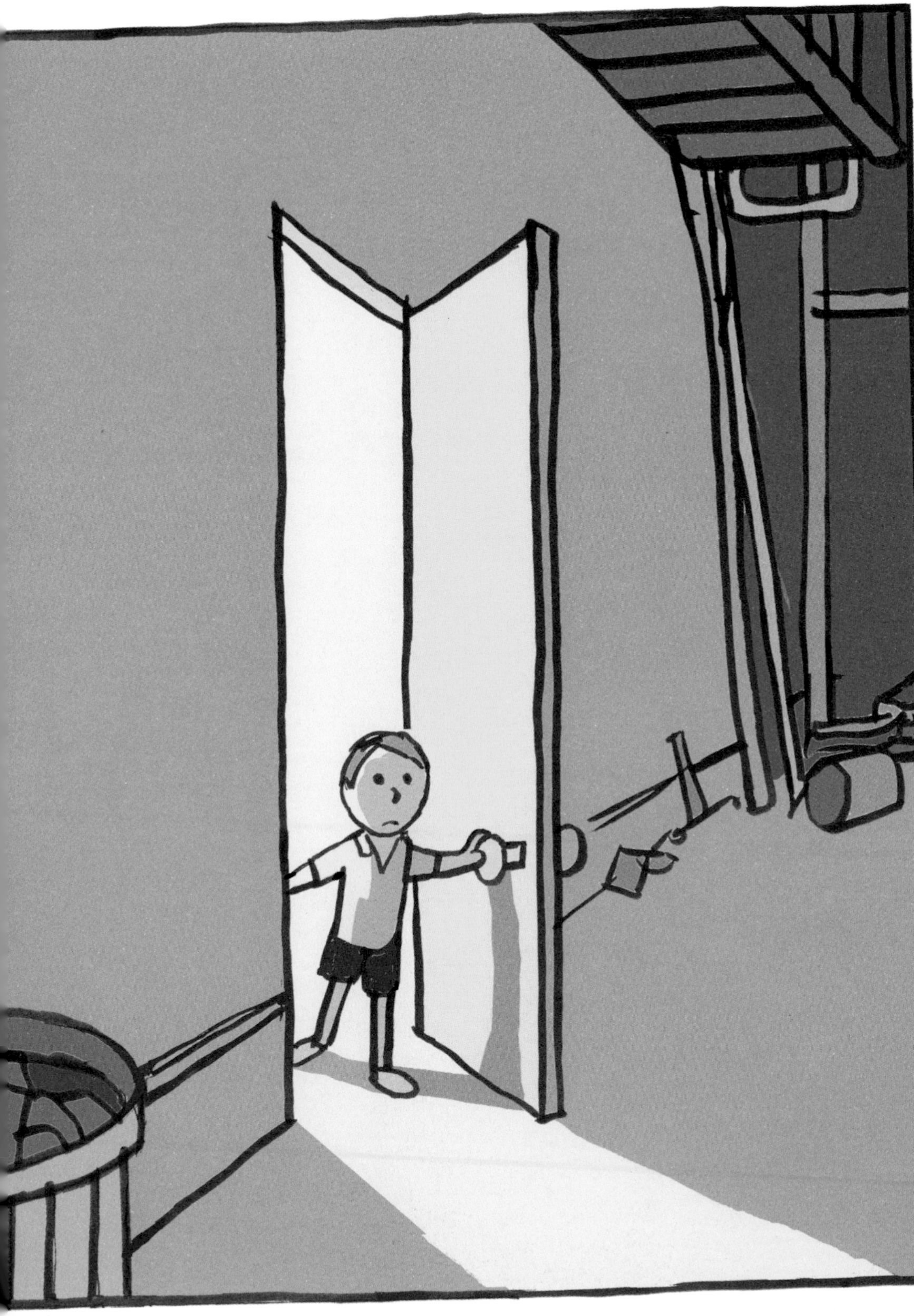

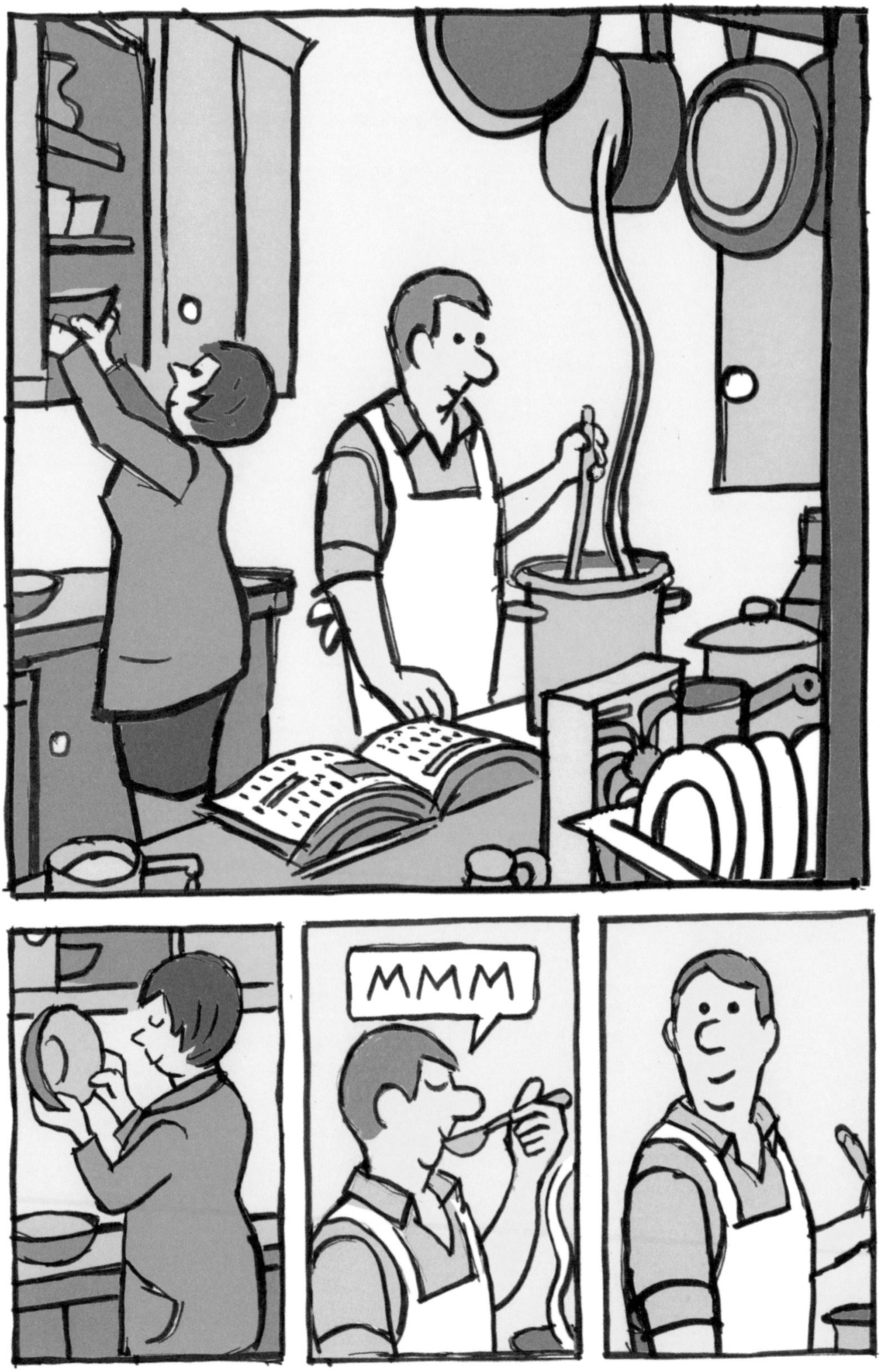
MMM

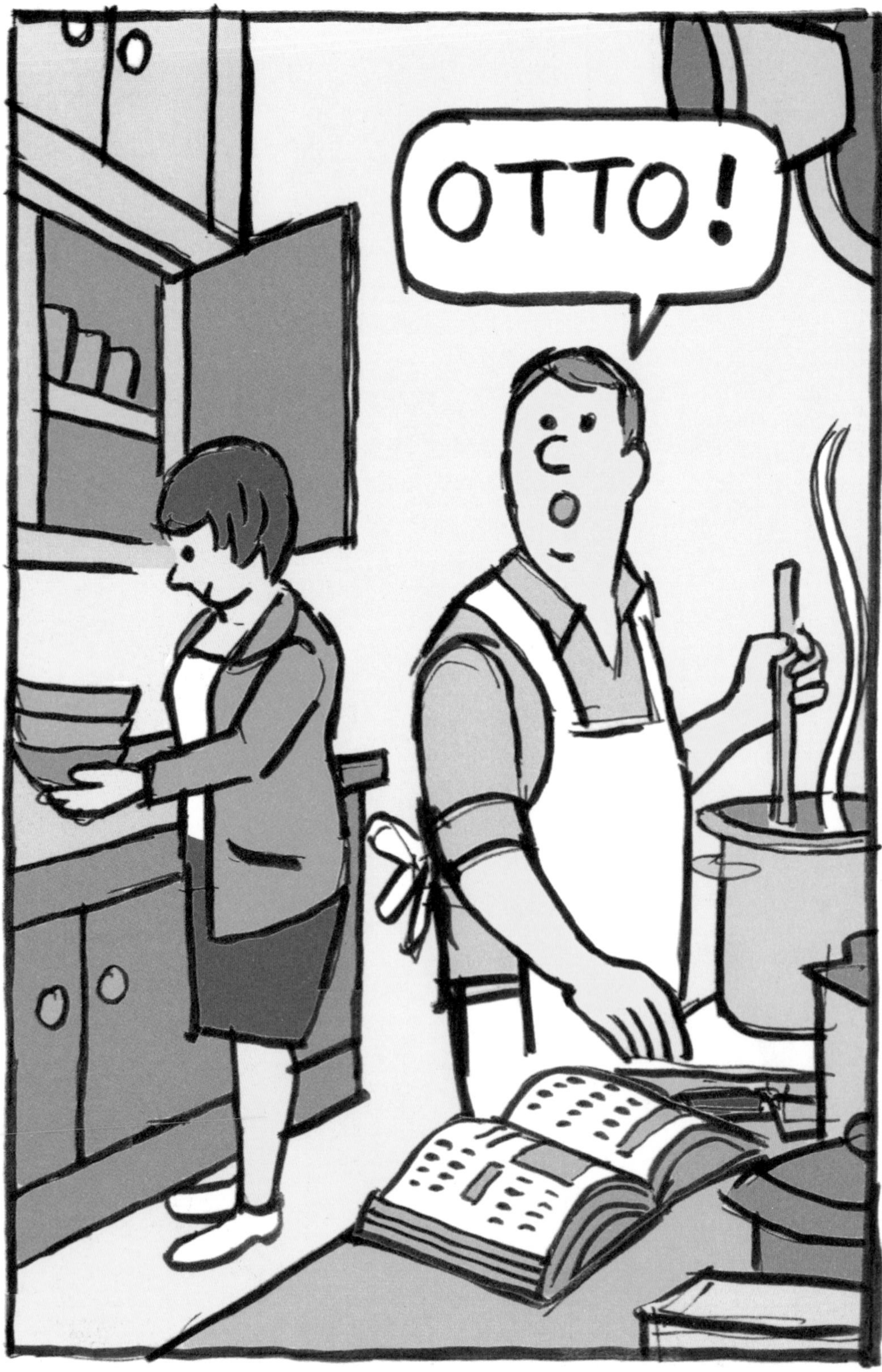
OTTO!

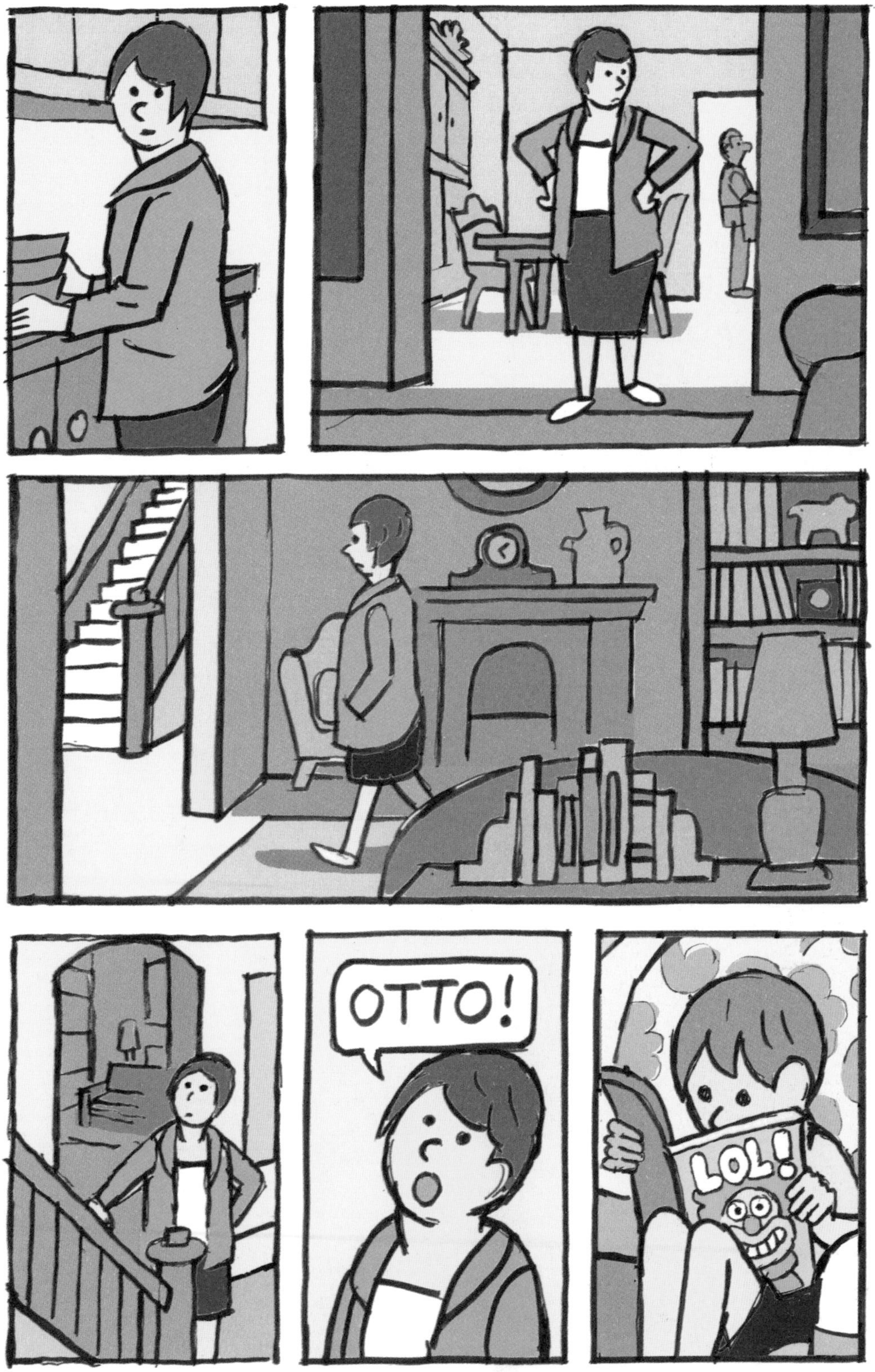
OTTO!
LOL!

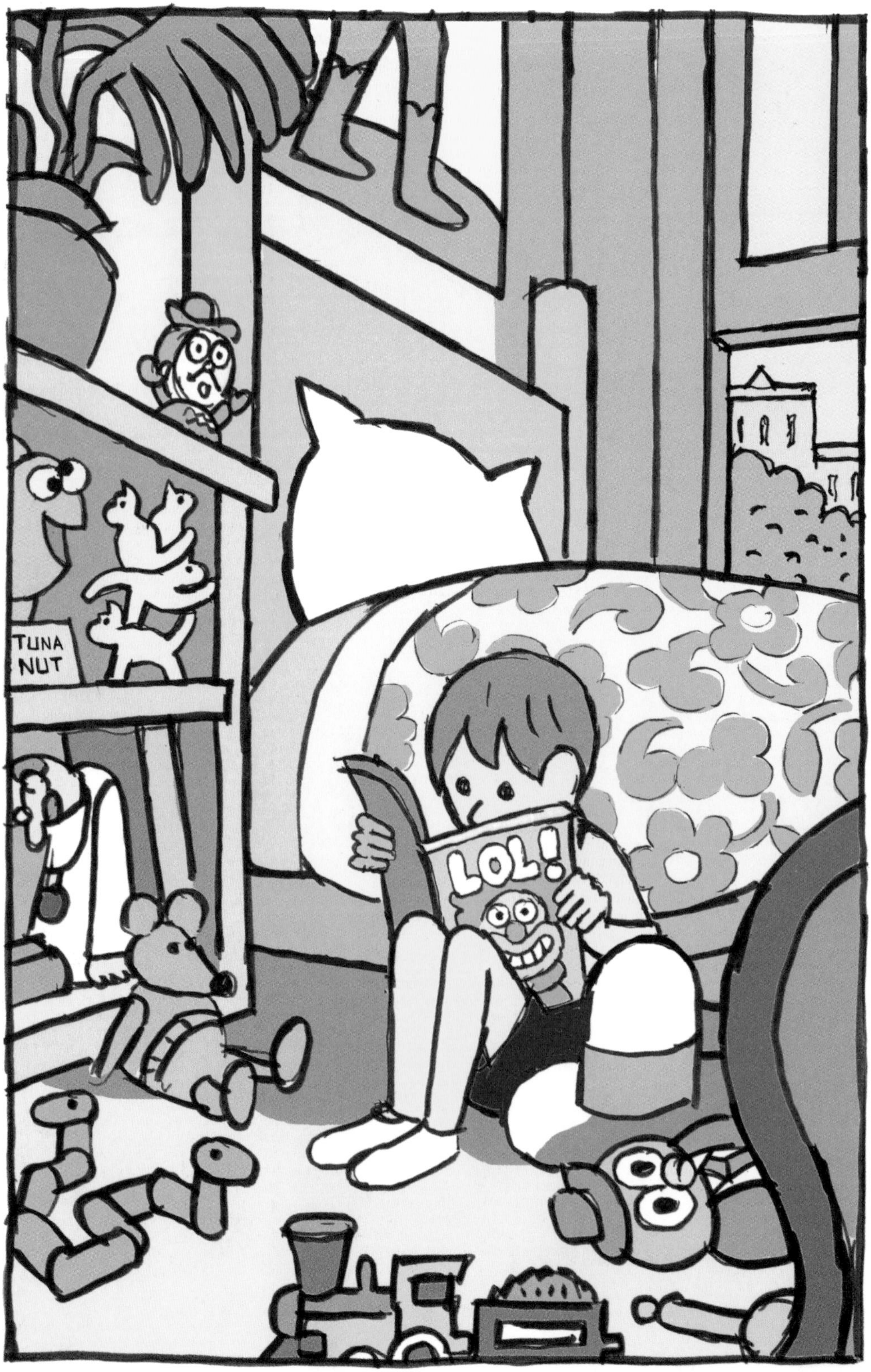
TUNA
NUT
LOL!

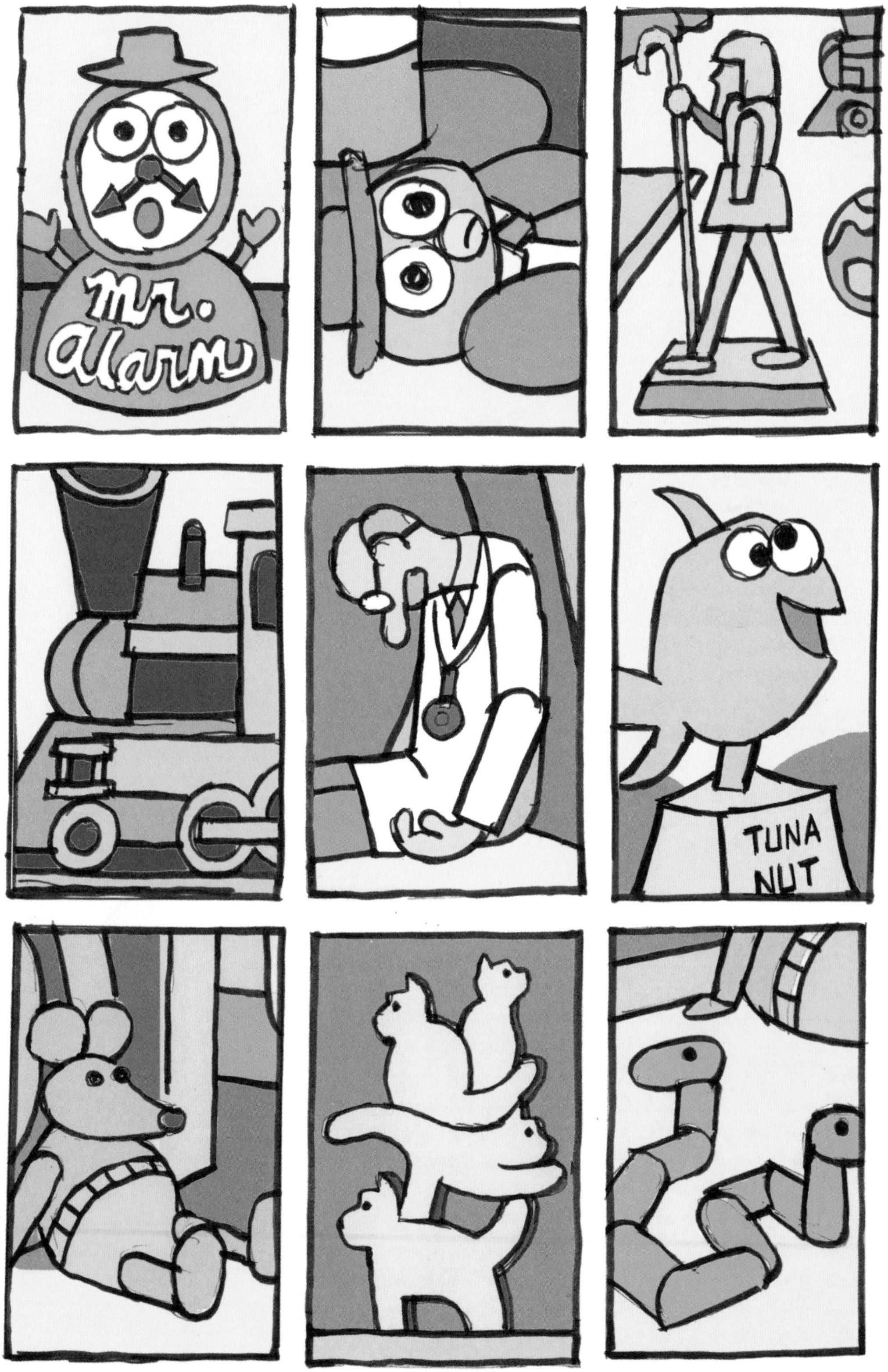
mr. alarm
TUNA NUT

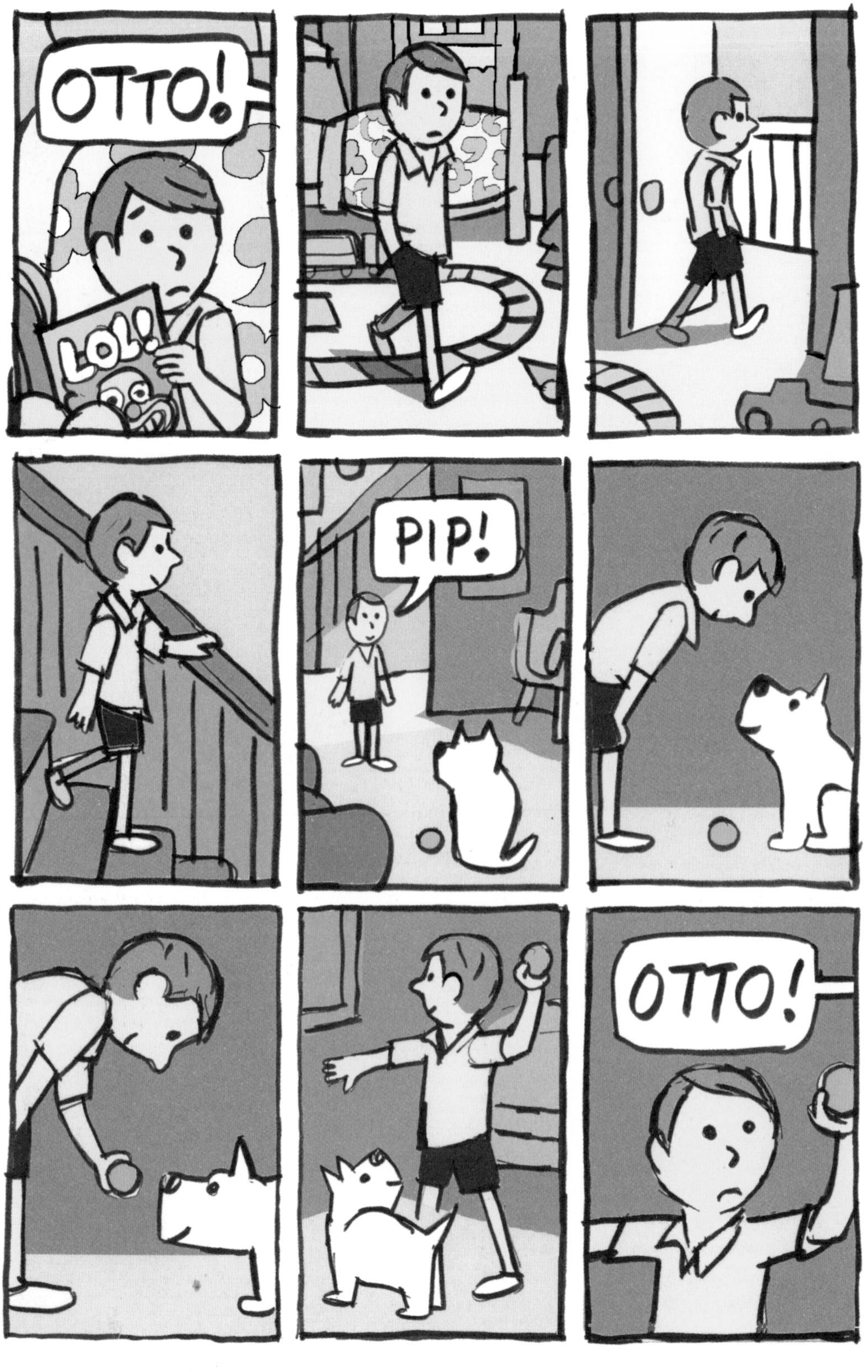
OTTO!
LOL!
PIP!
OTTO!

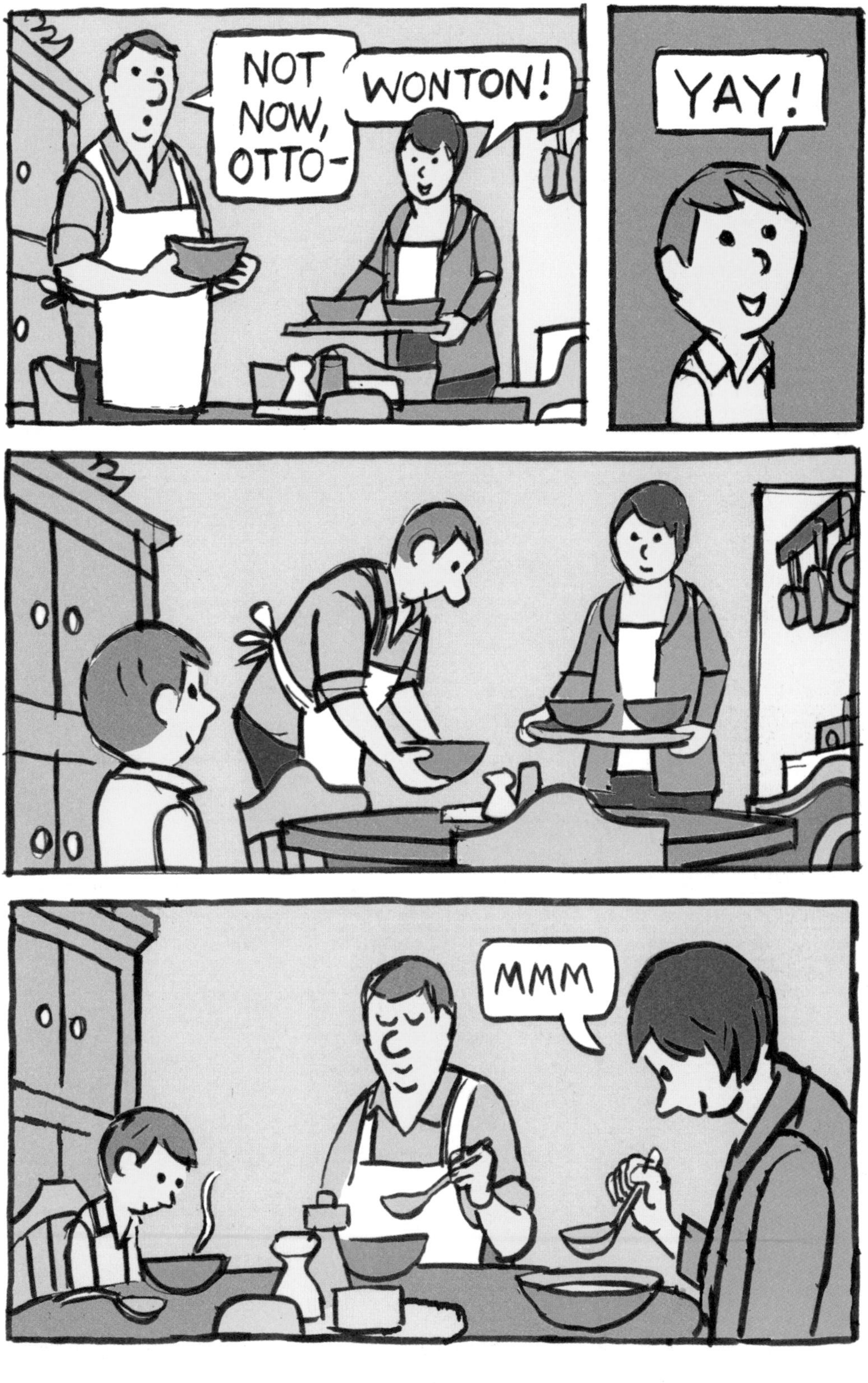
NOT NOW, OTTO-
WONTON!
YAY!
MMM

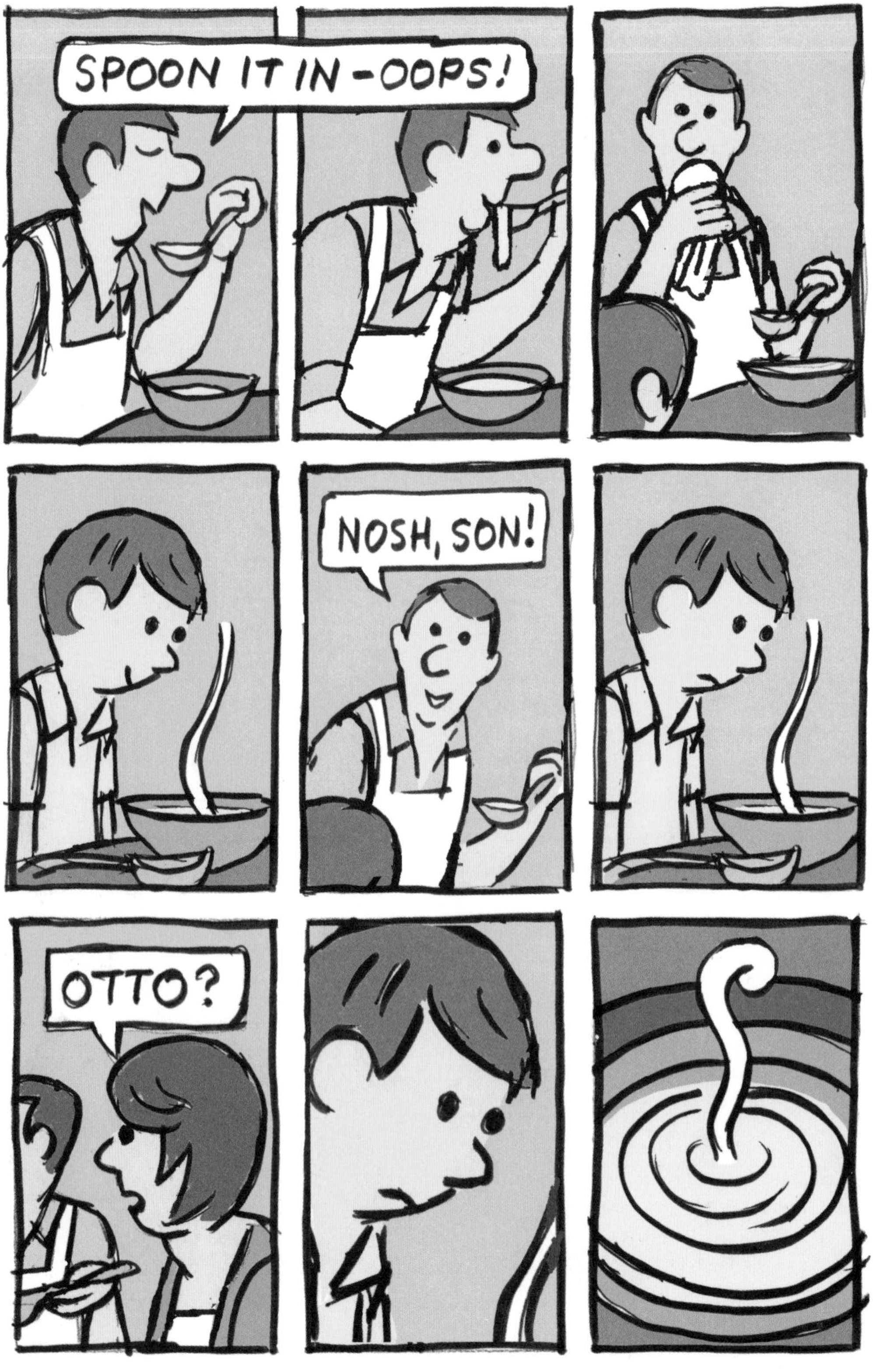
SPOON IT IN-OOPS!
NOSH, SON!
OTTO?

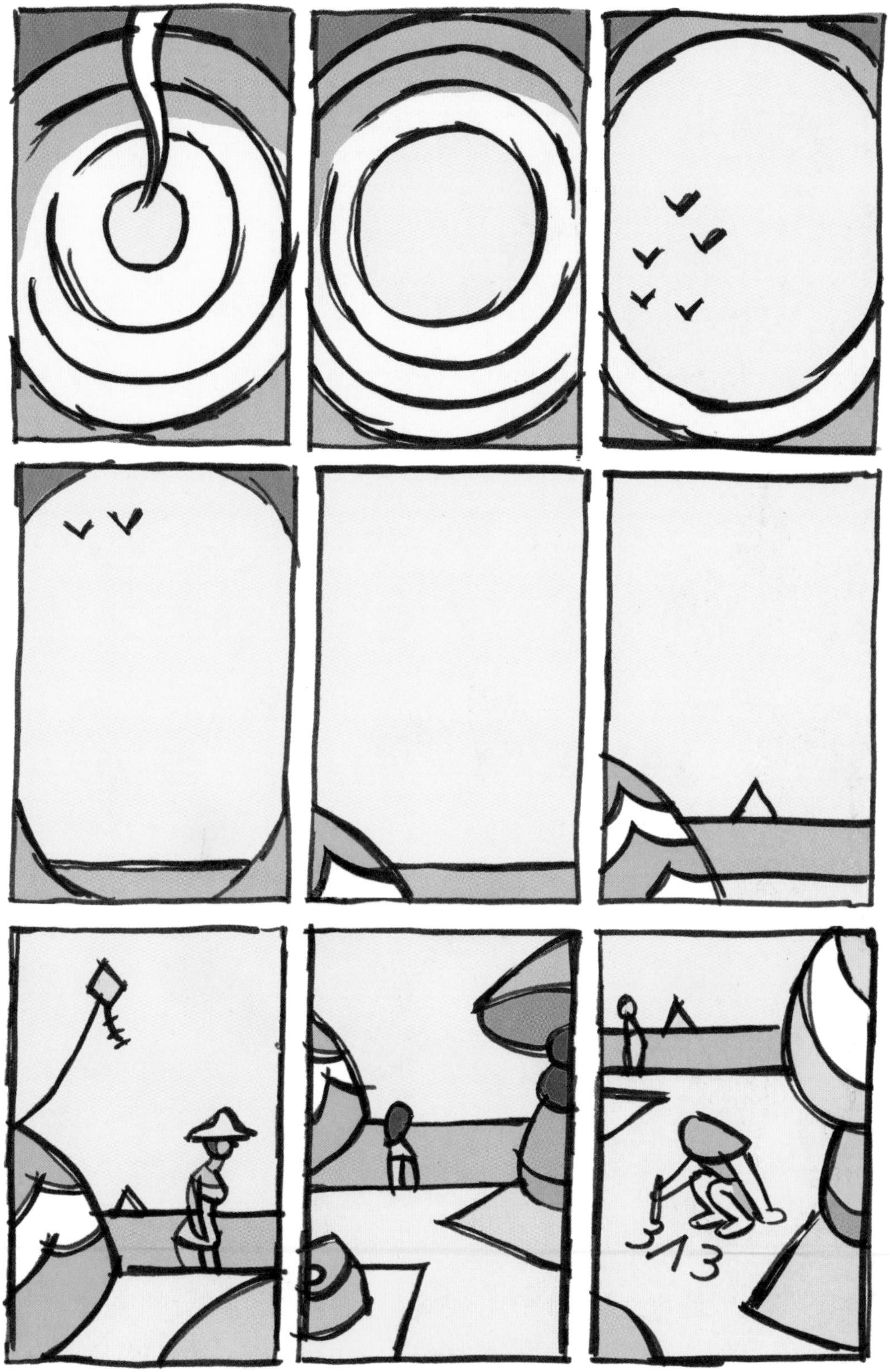
313

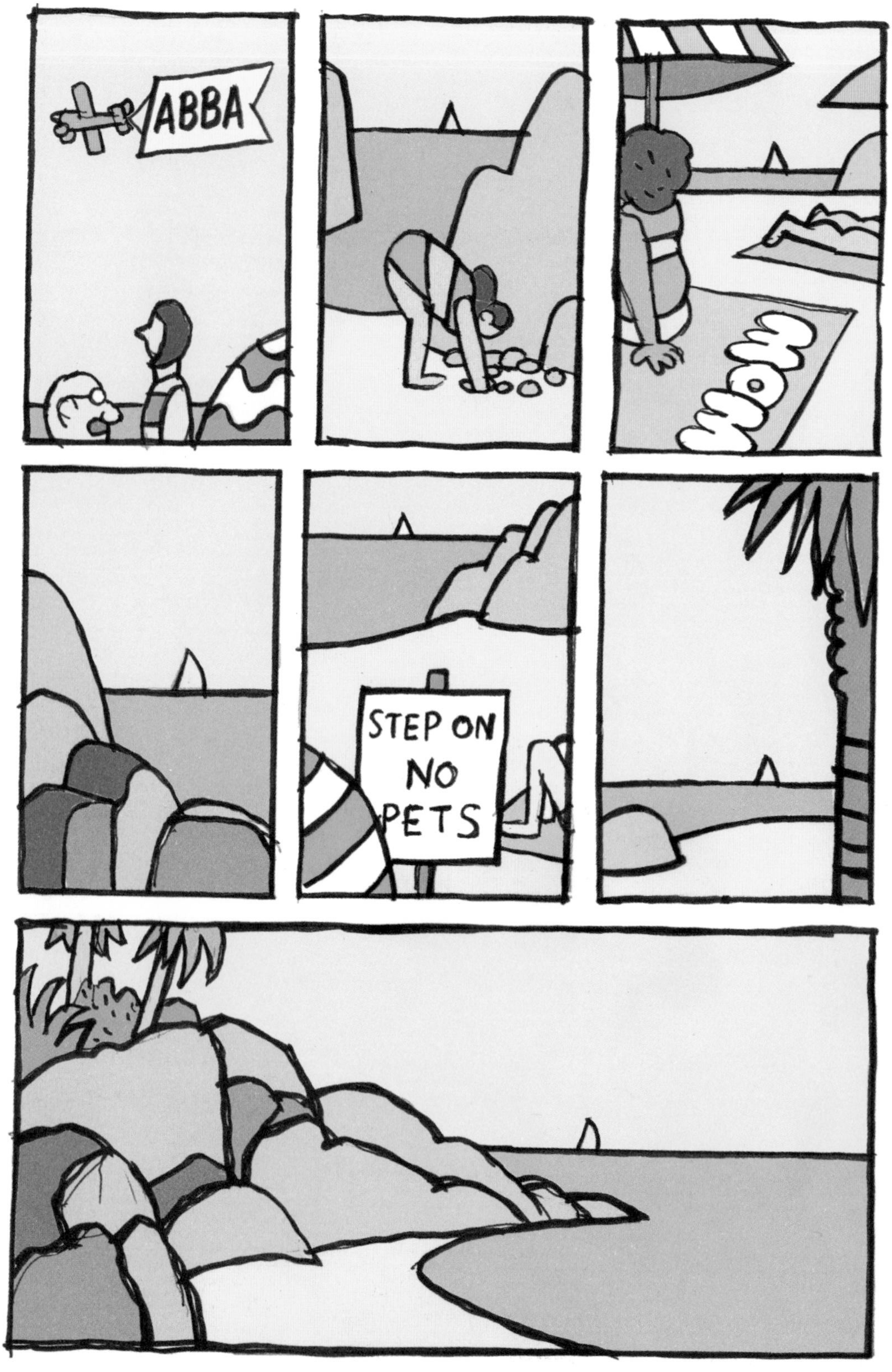
ABBA
WOW
STEP ON
NO
PETS

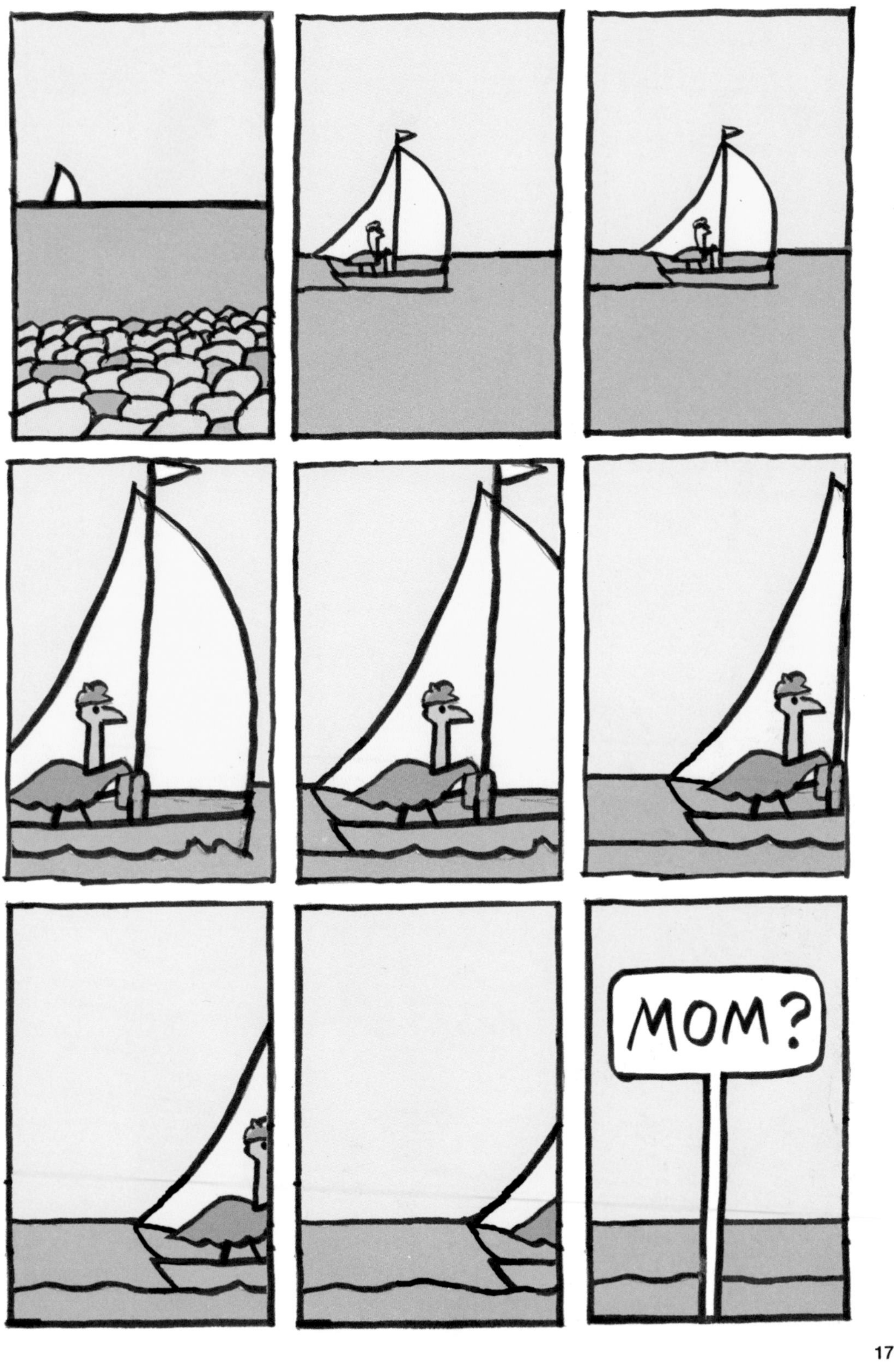
MOM?

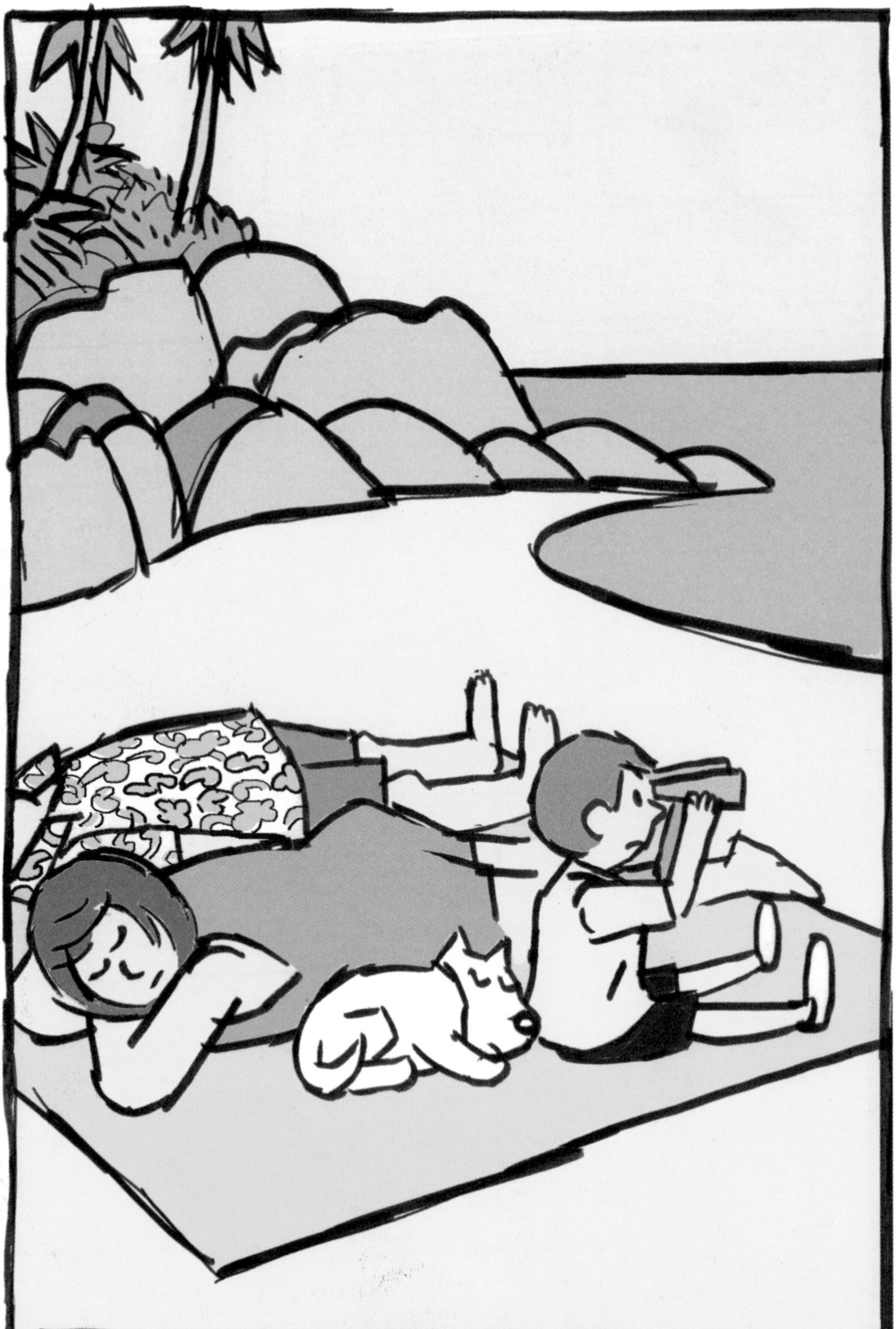

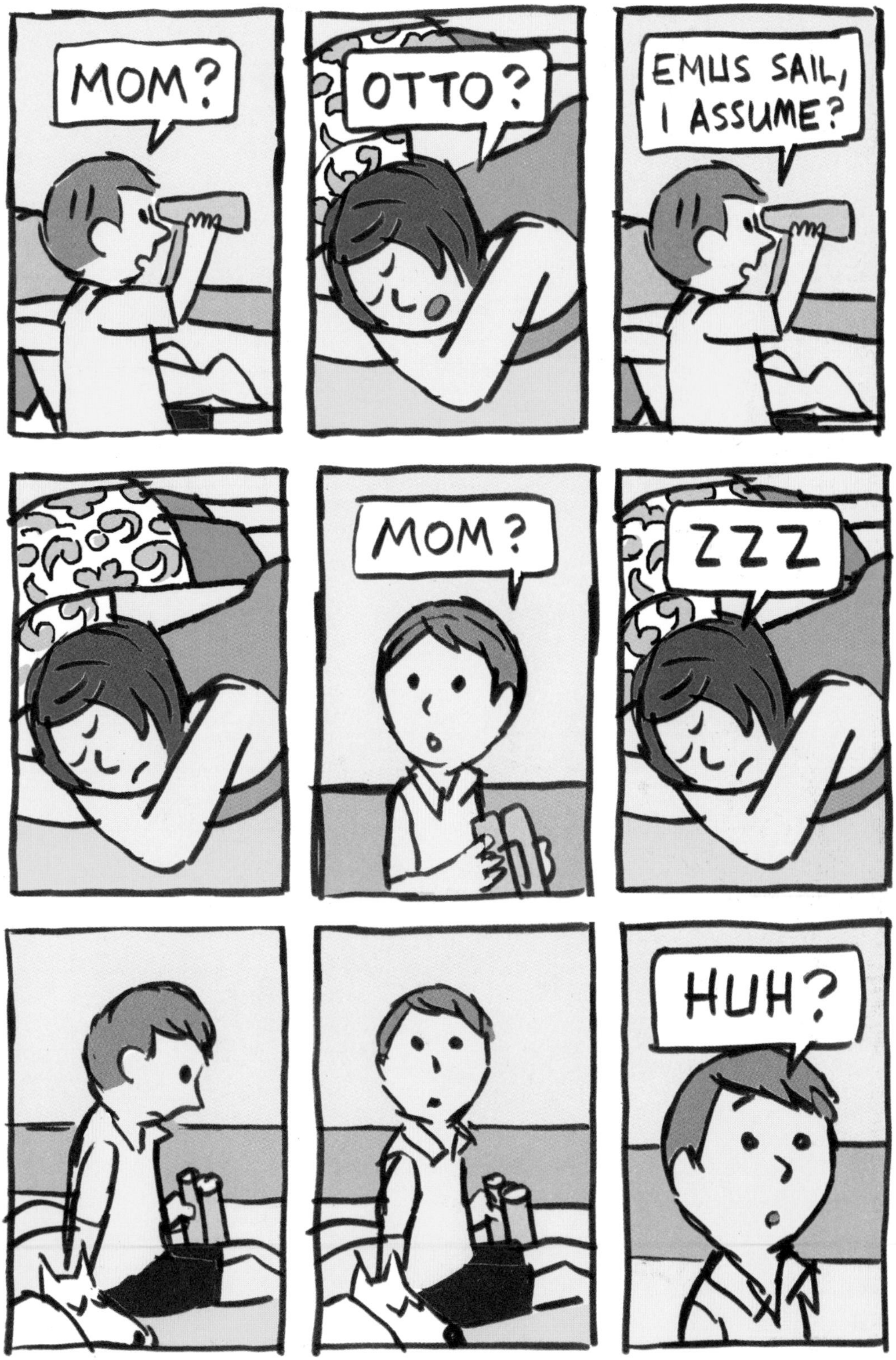
MOM?
OTTO?
EMUS SAIL, I ASSUME?
MOM?
ZZZ
HUH?

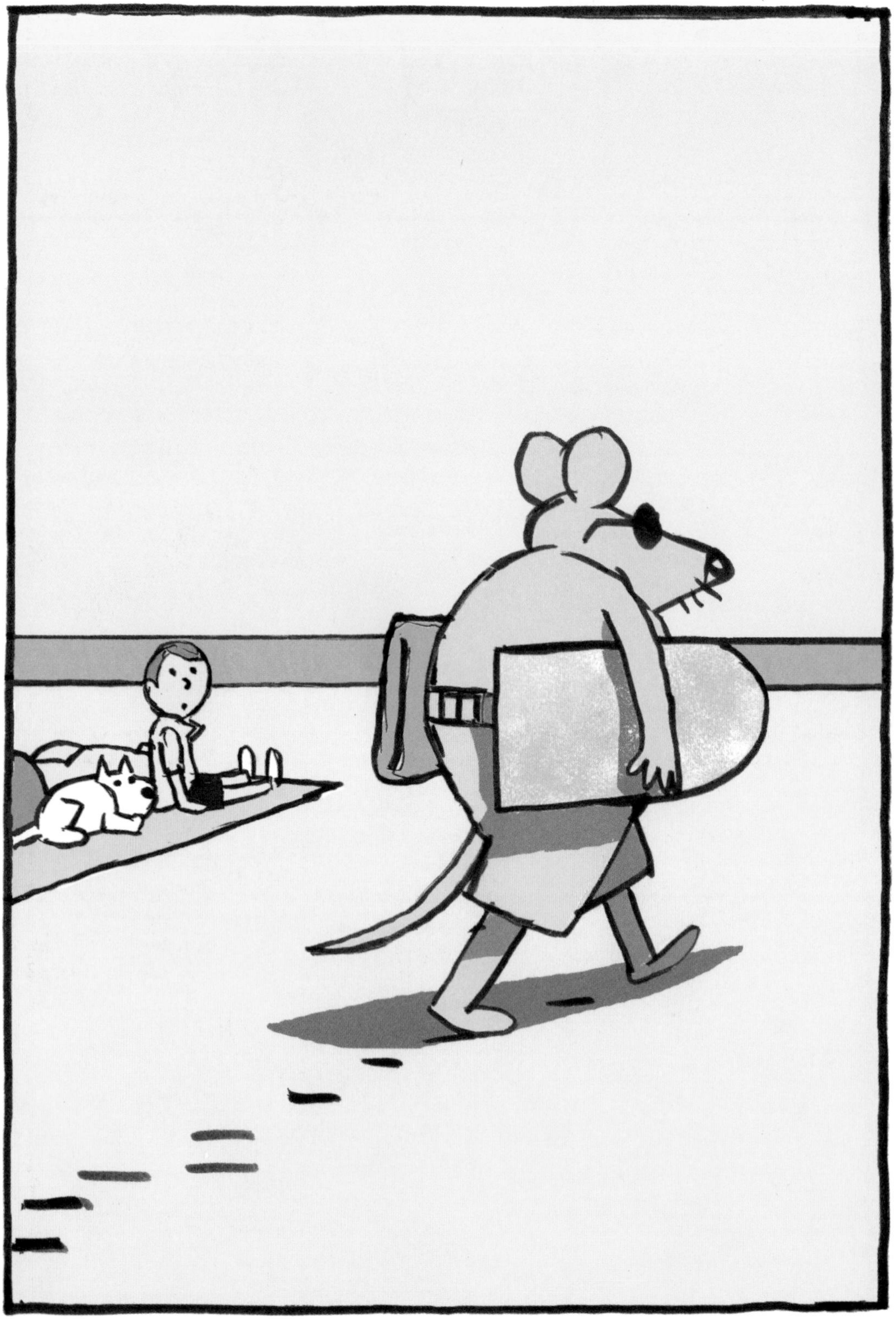

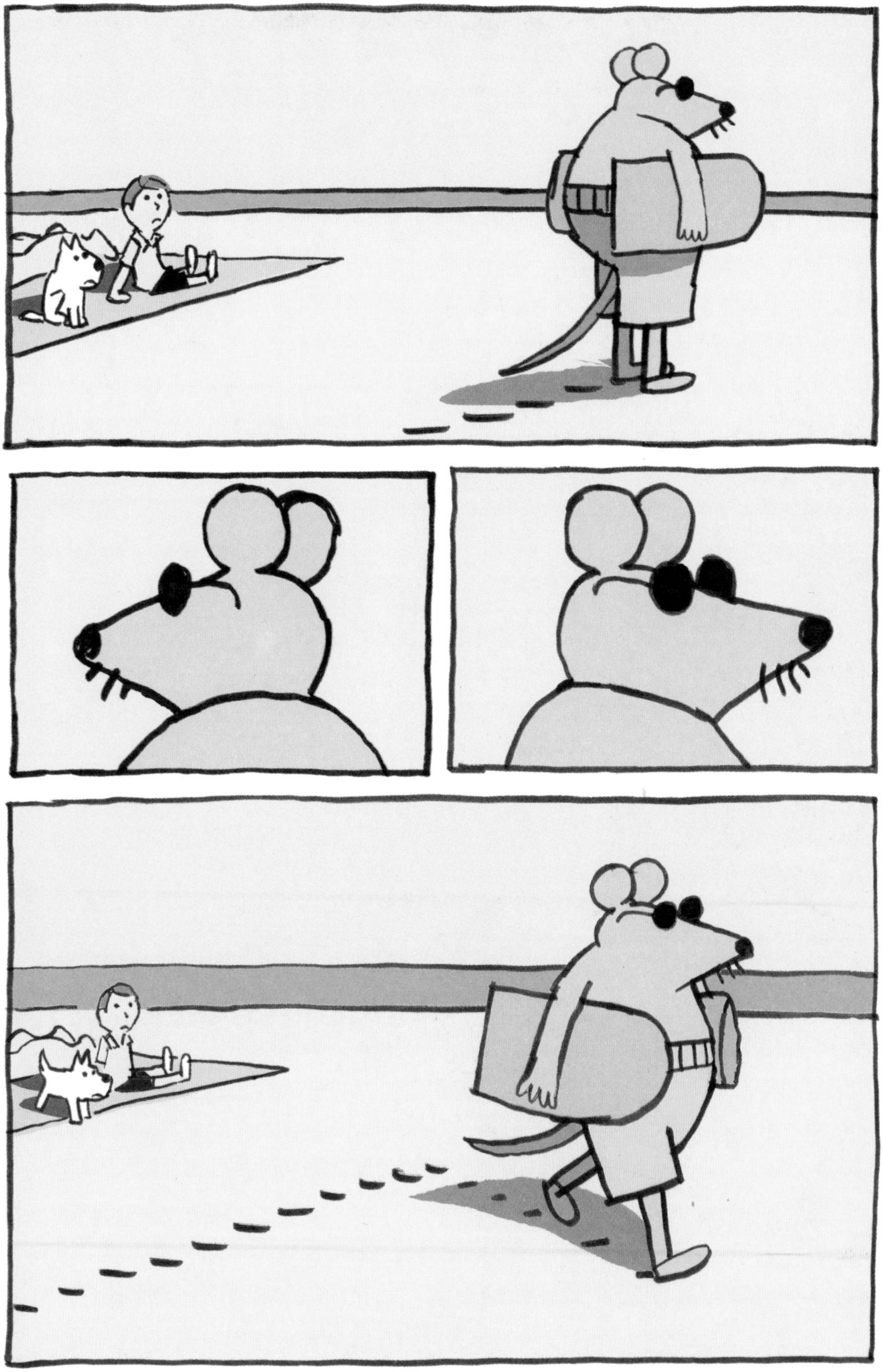

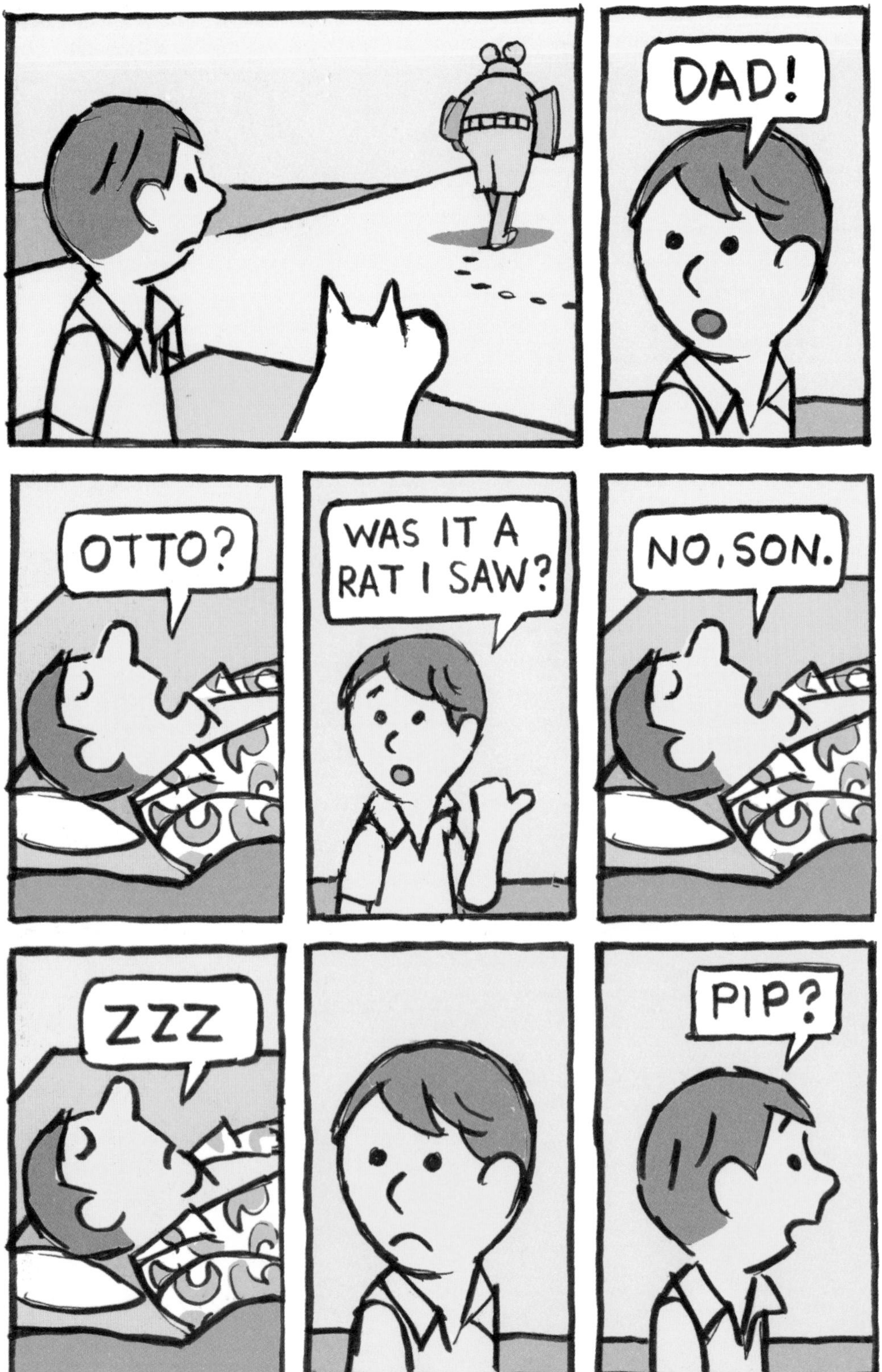
DAD!
OTTO?
WAS IT A RAT I SAW?
NO, SON.
ZZZ
PIP?

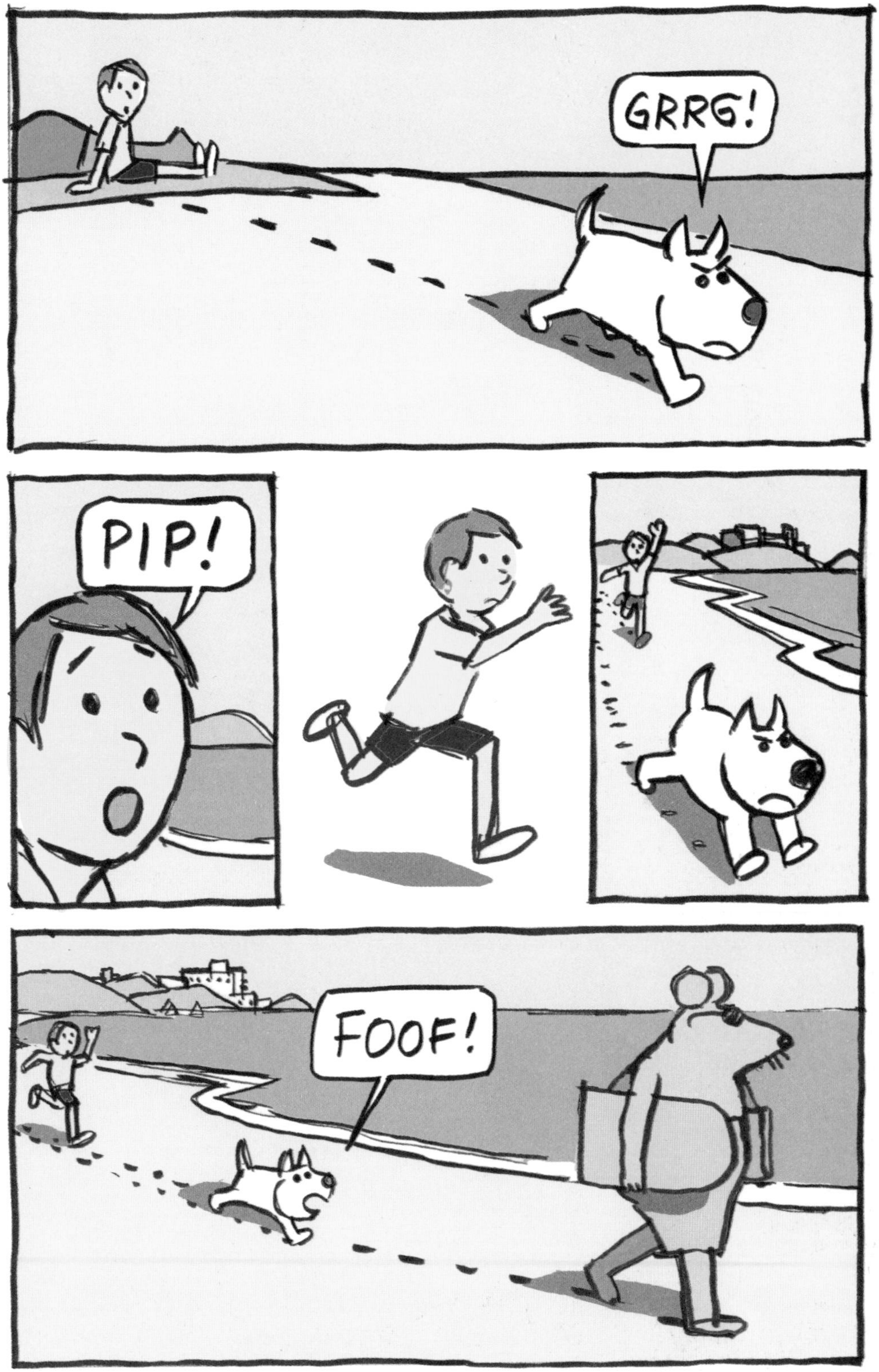
GRRG!
PIP!
FOOF!

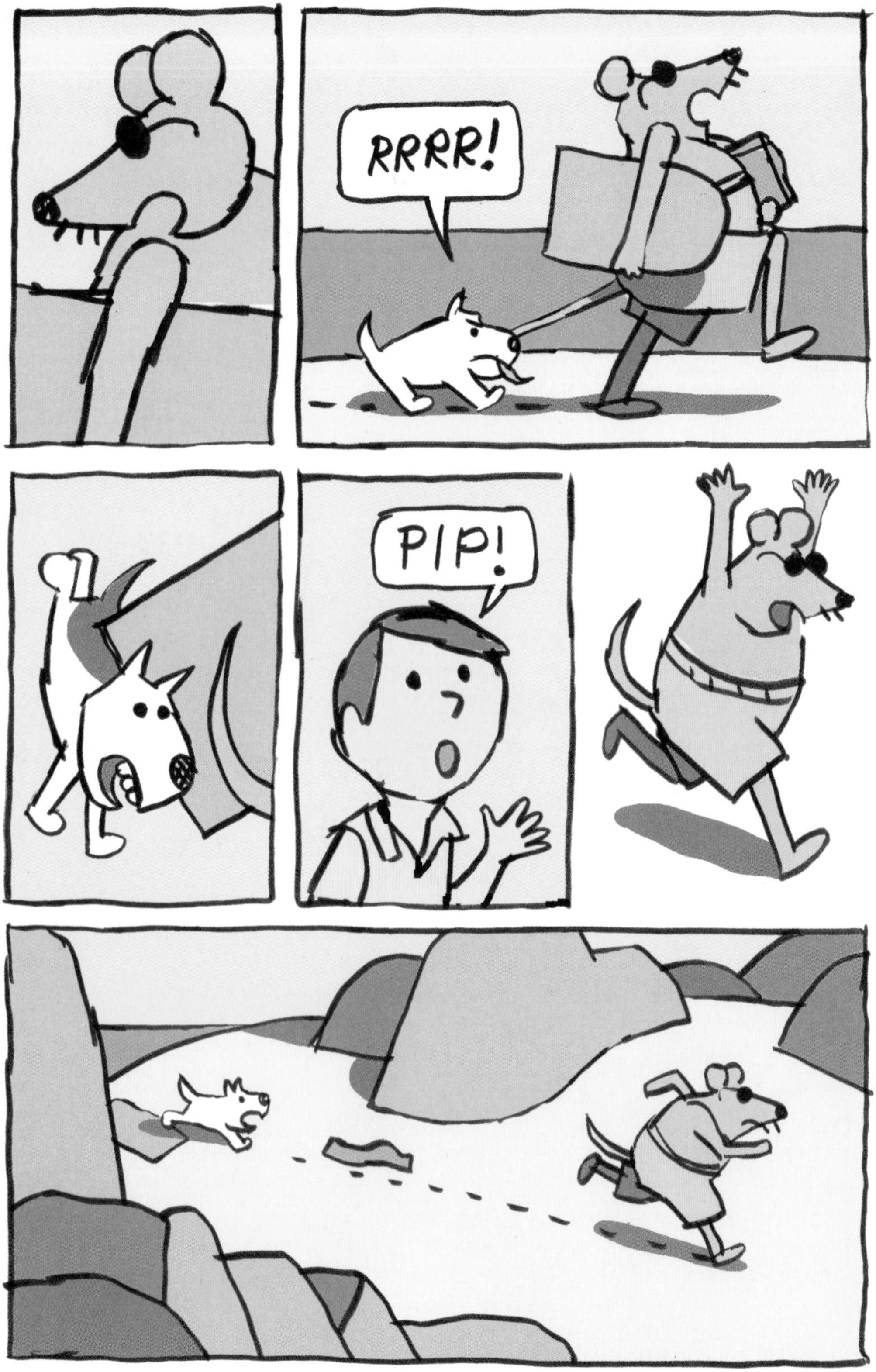
RRRR!
PIP!

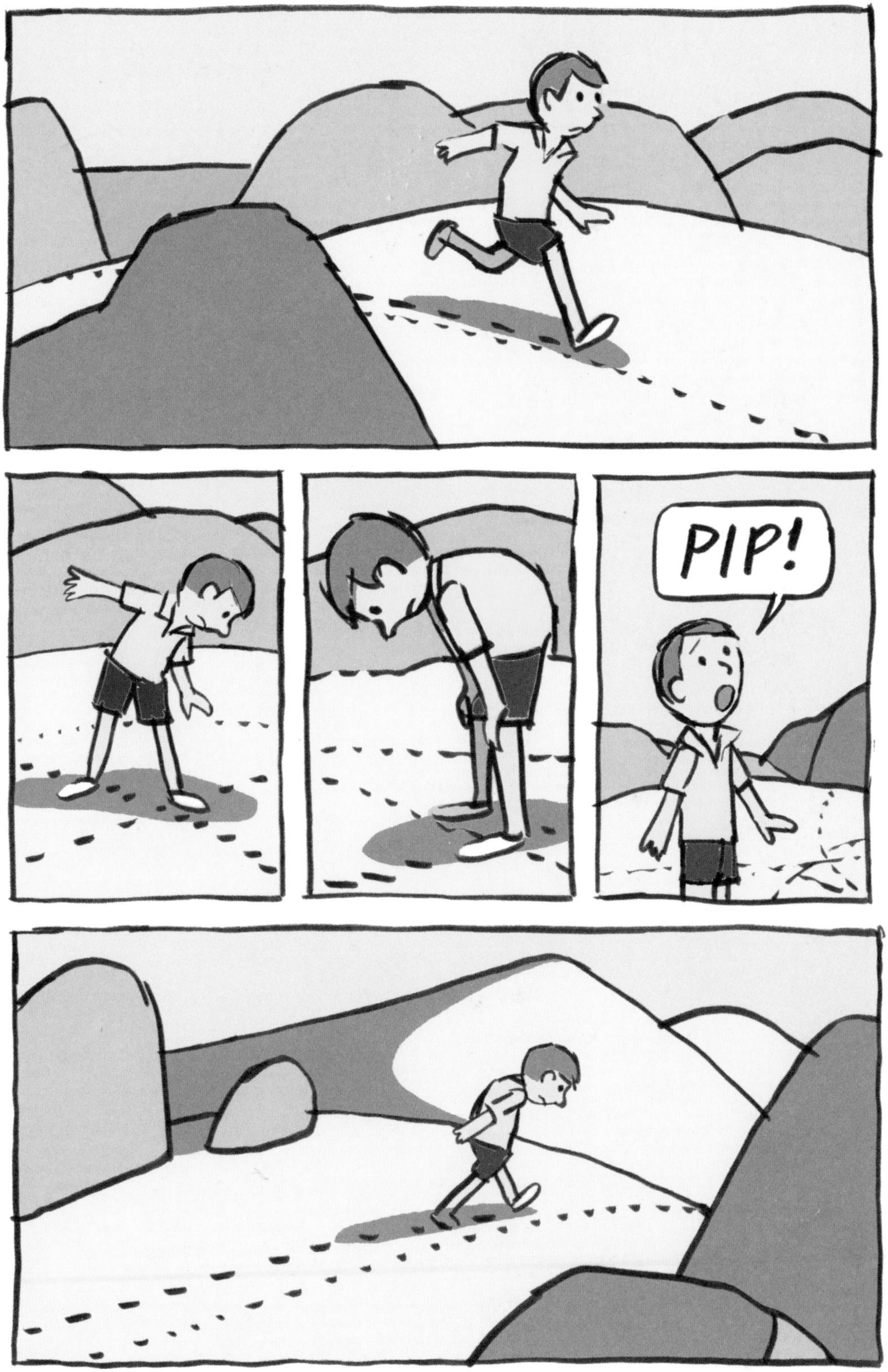
PIP!

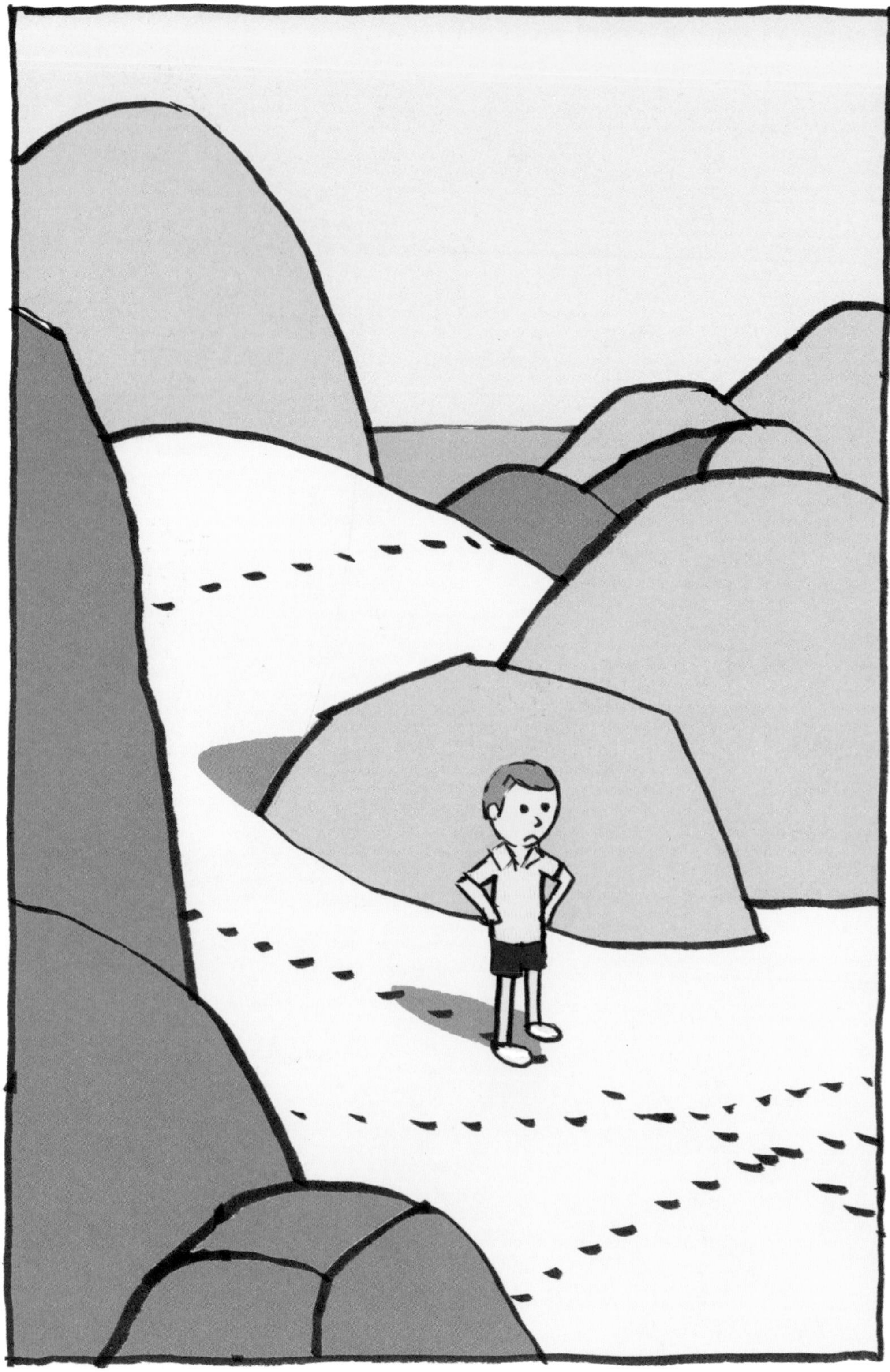

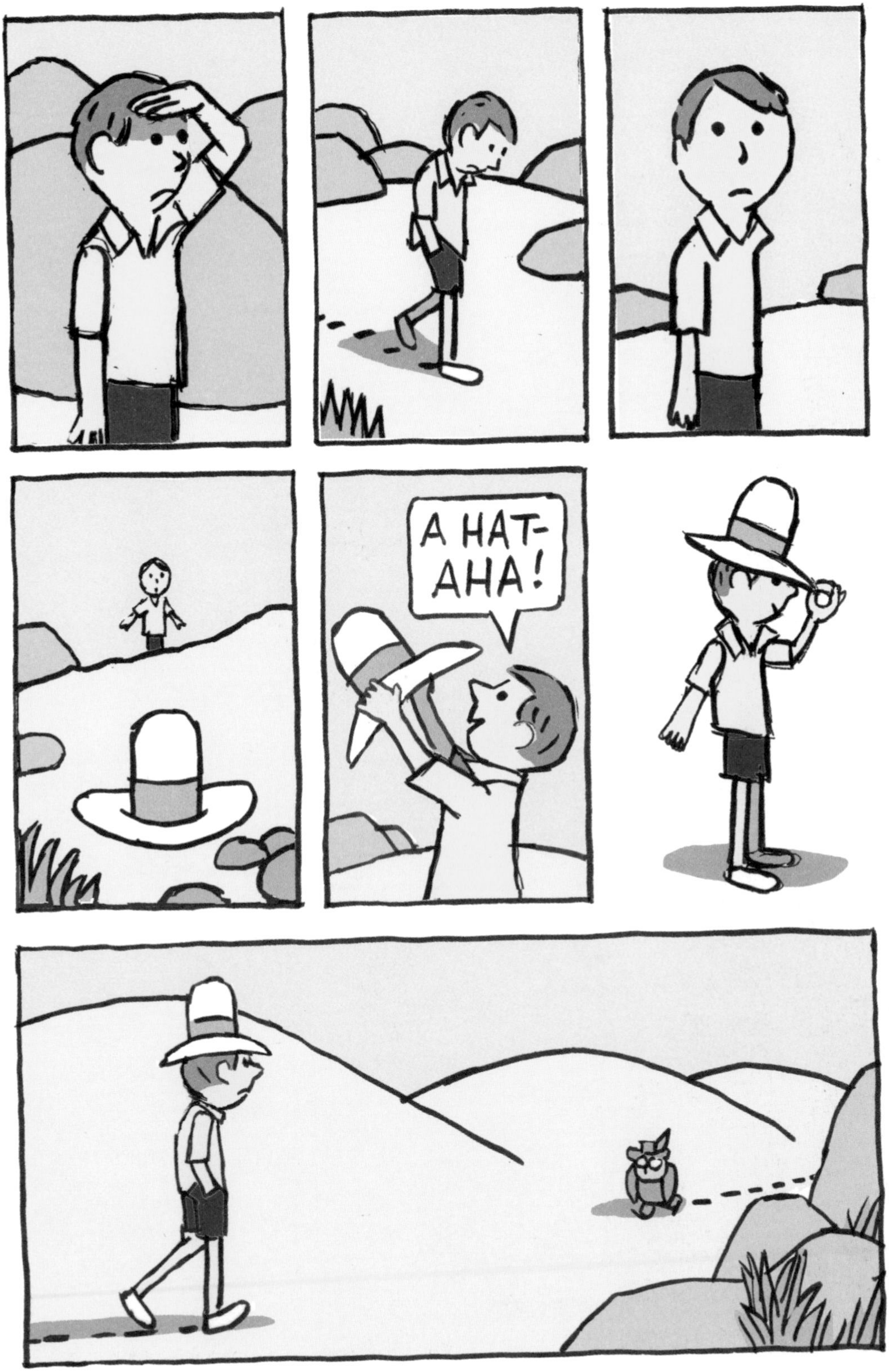
A HAT-
AHA!

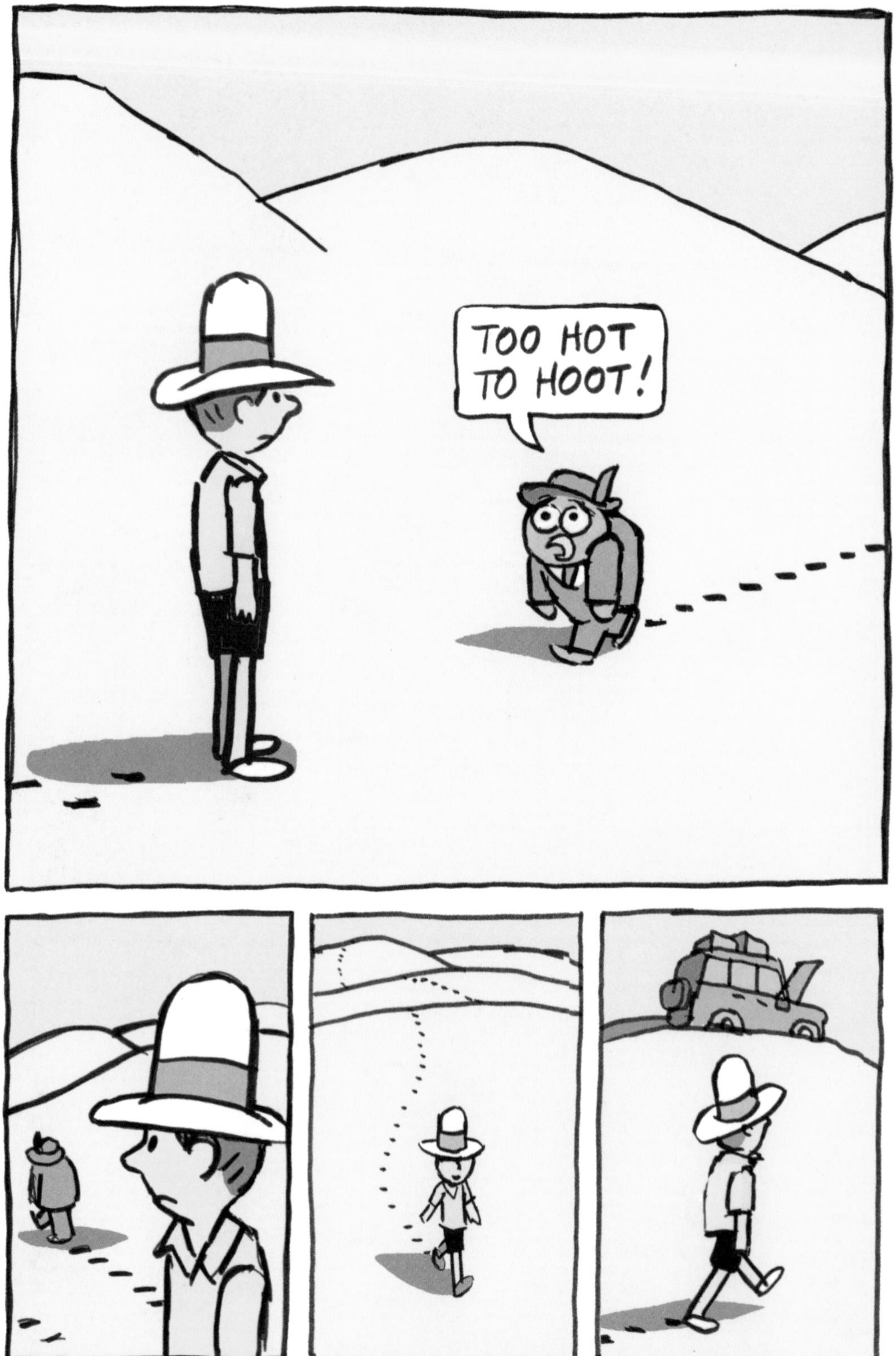
TOO HOT TO HOOT!

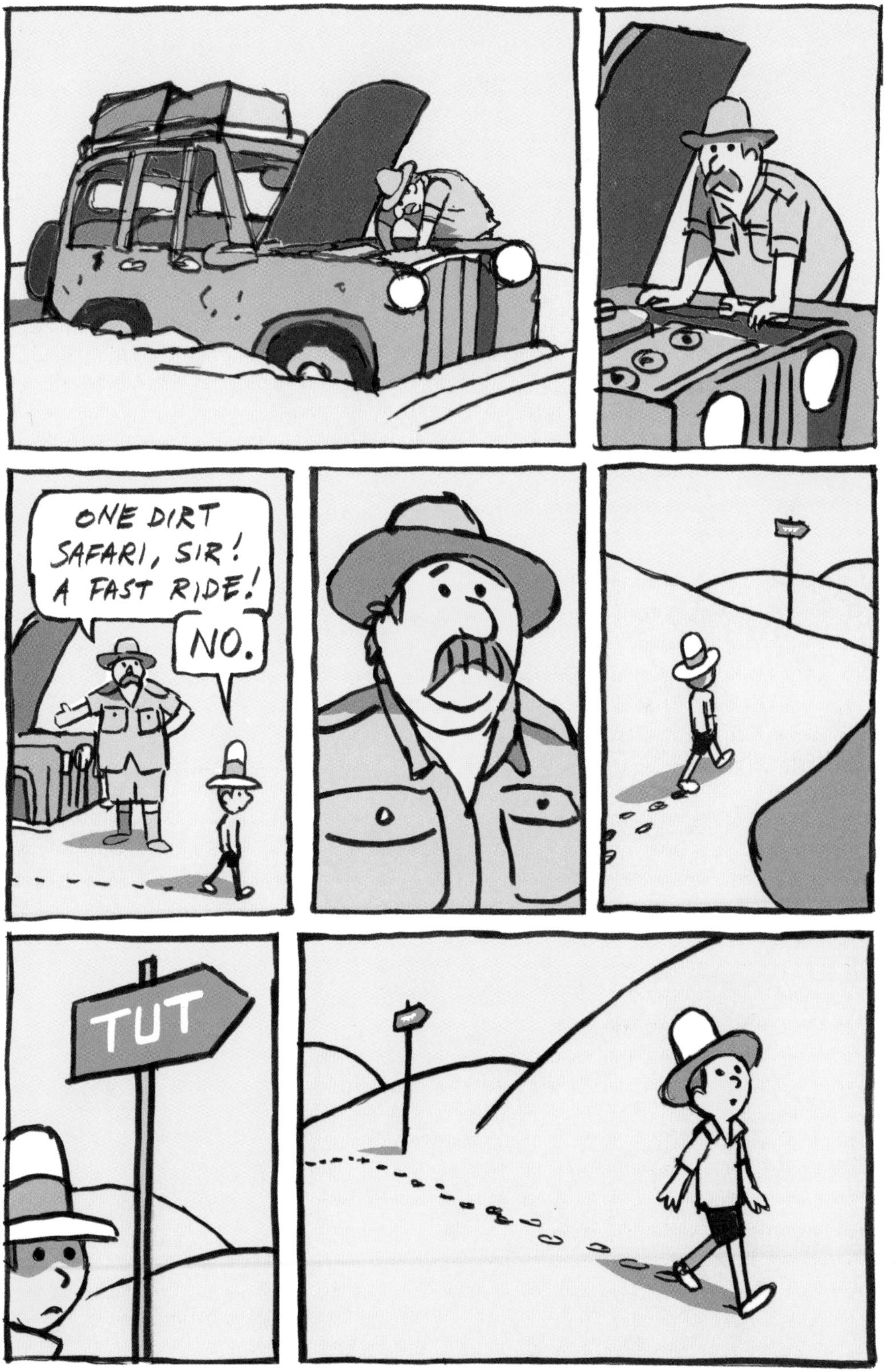
ONE DIRT SAFARI, SIR! A FAST RIDE!
NO.
TUT

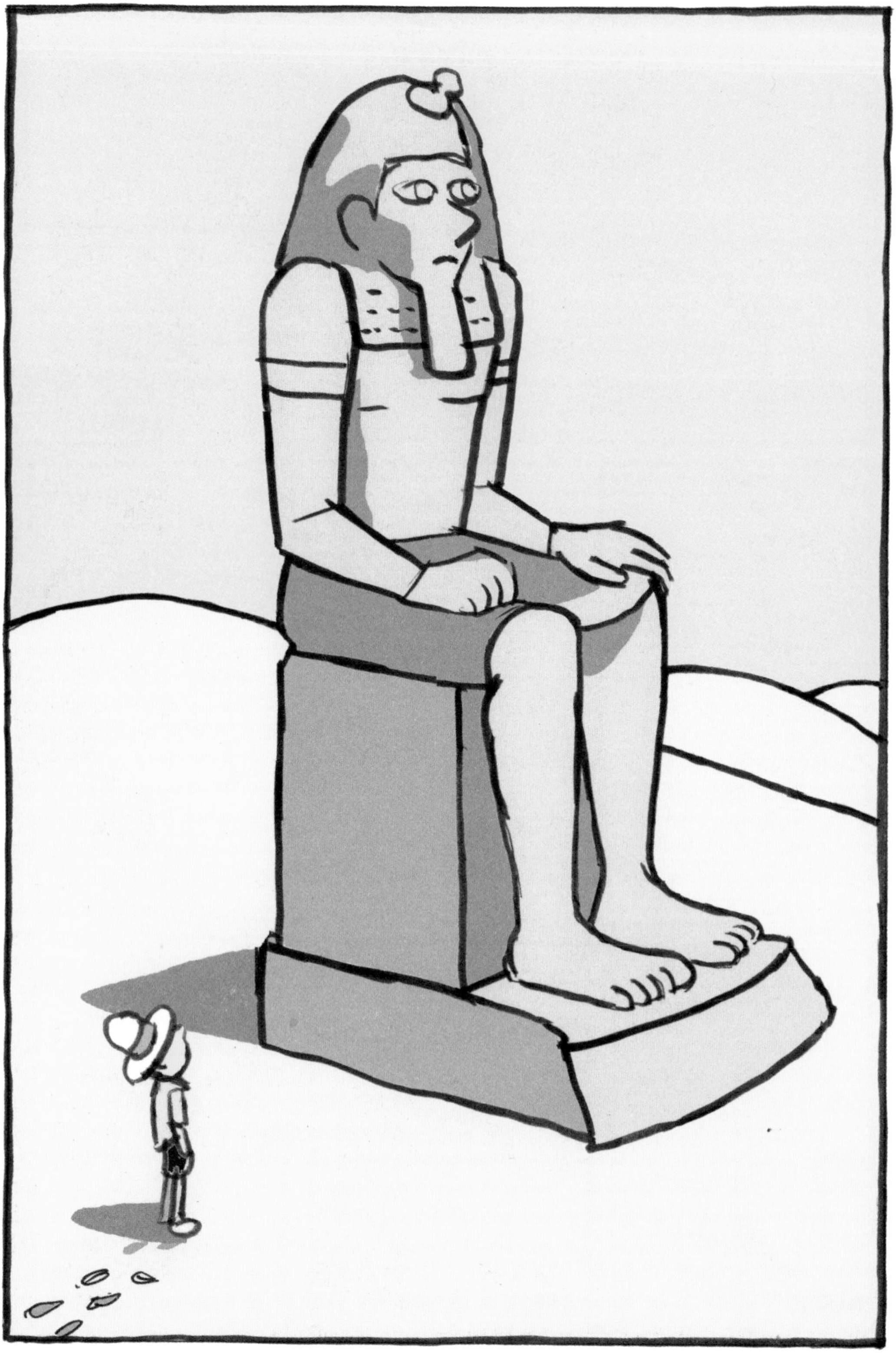

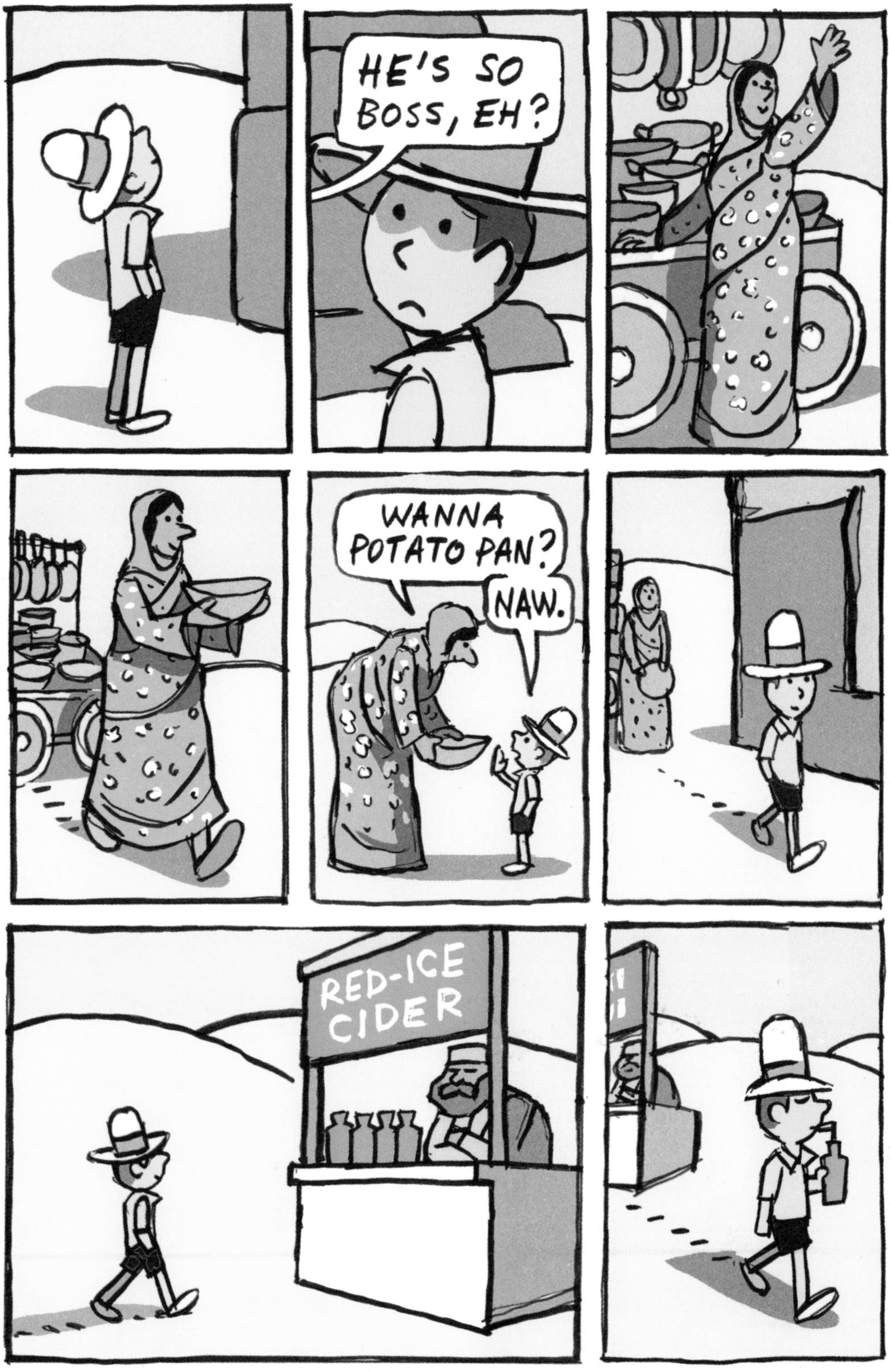
HE'S SO BOSS, EH?
WANNA POTATO PAN?
NAW.
RED-ICE CIDER

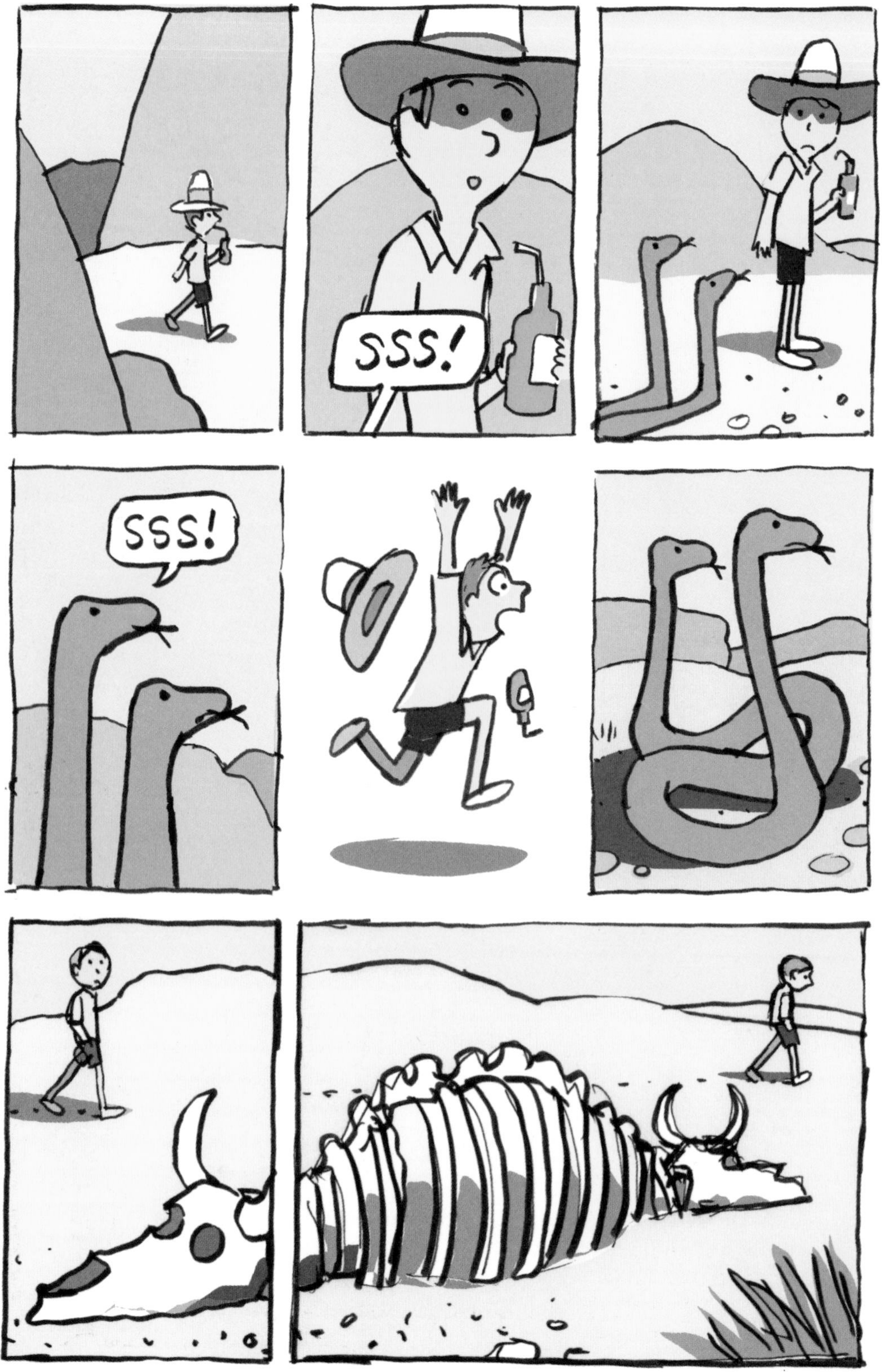
SSS!
SSS!

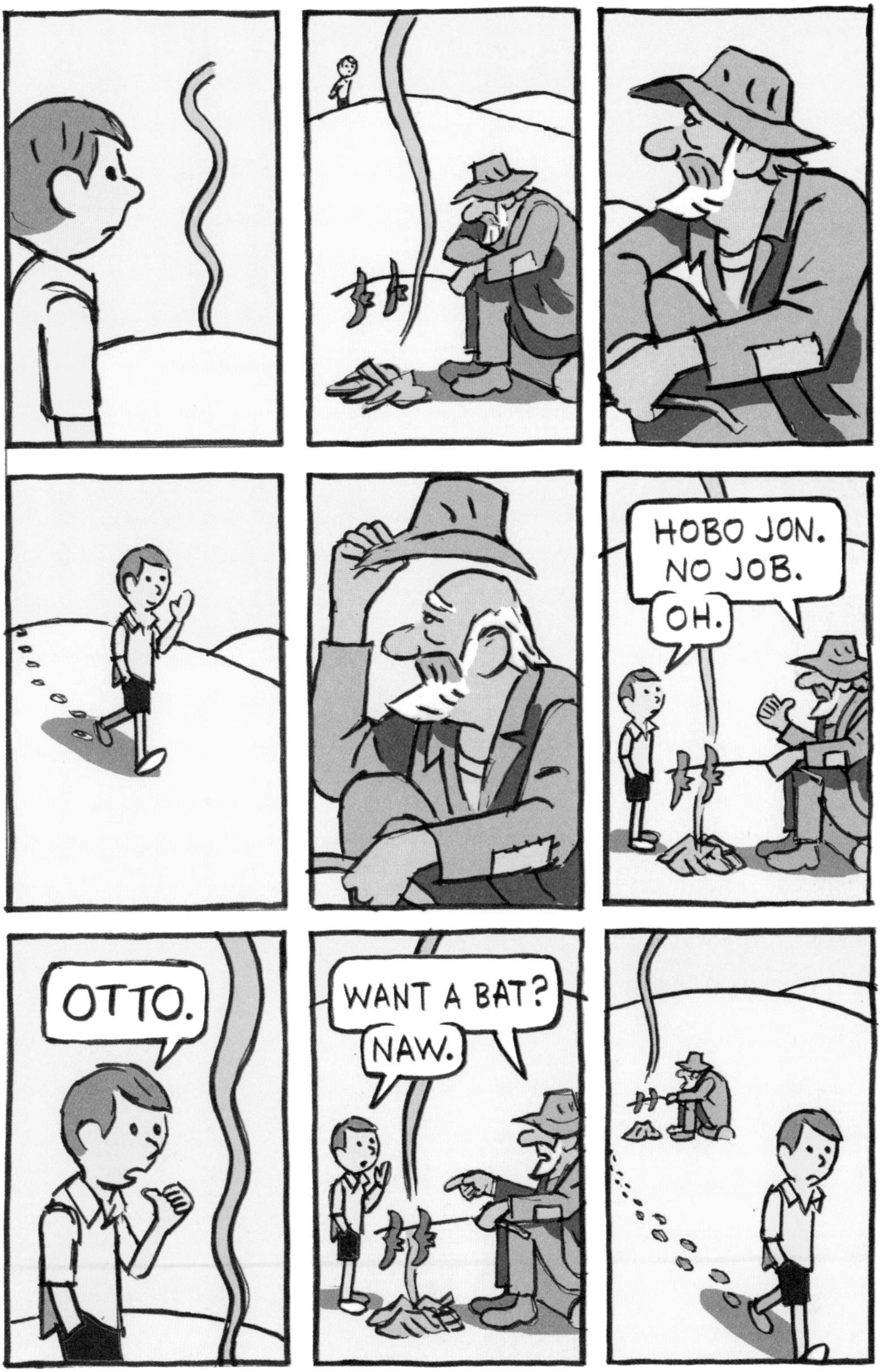
HOBO JON. NO JOB.
OH.
OTTO.
WANT A BAT?
NAW.

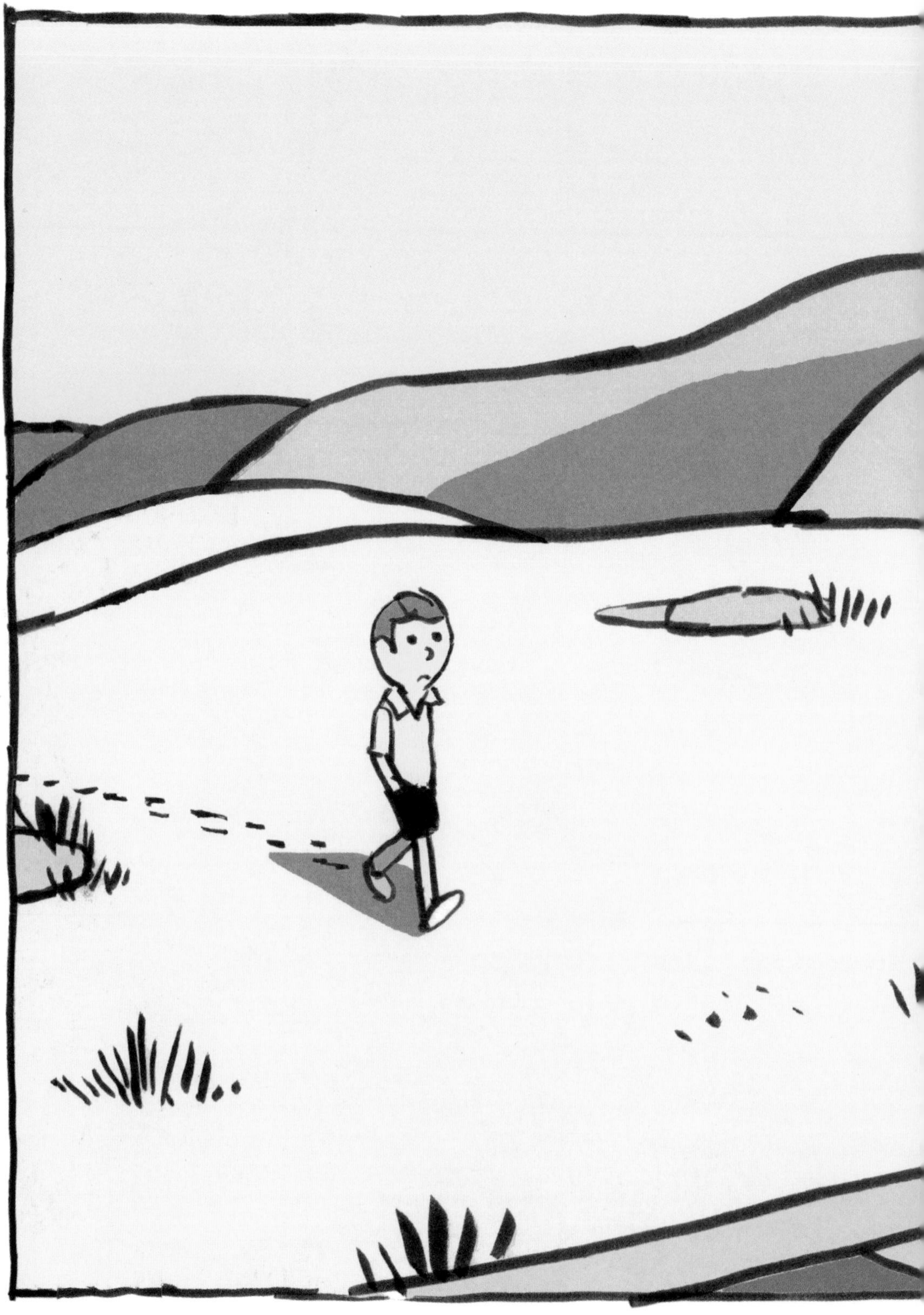

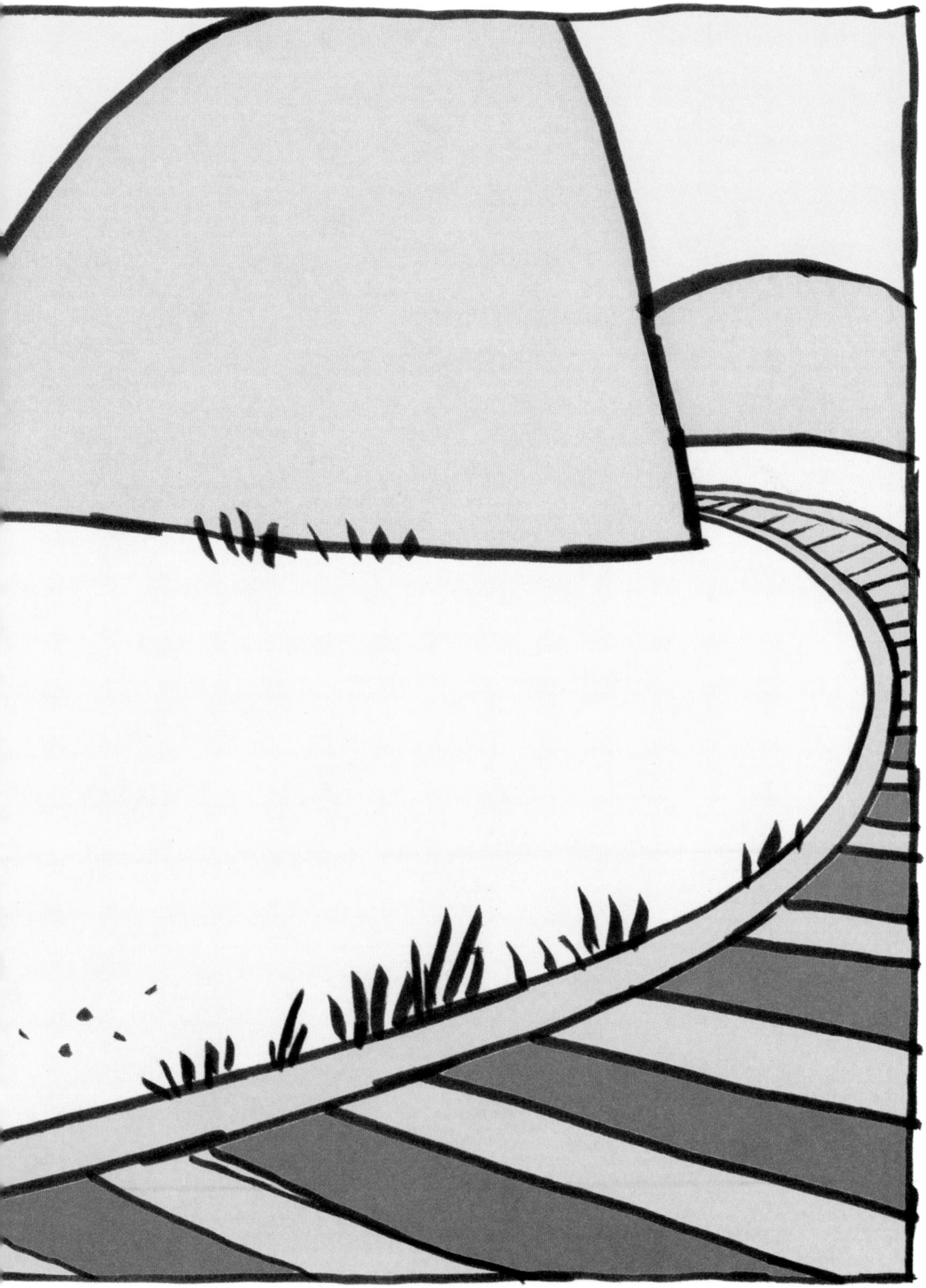

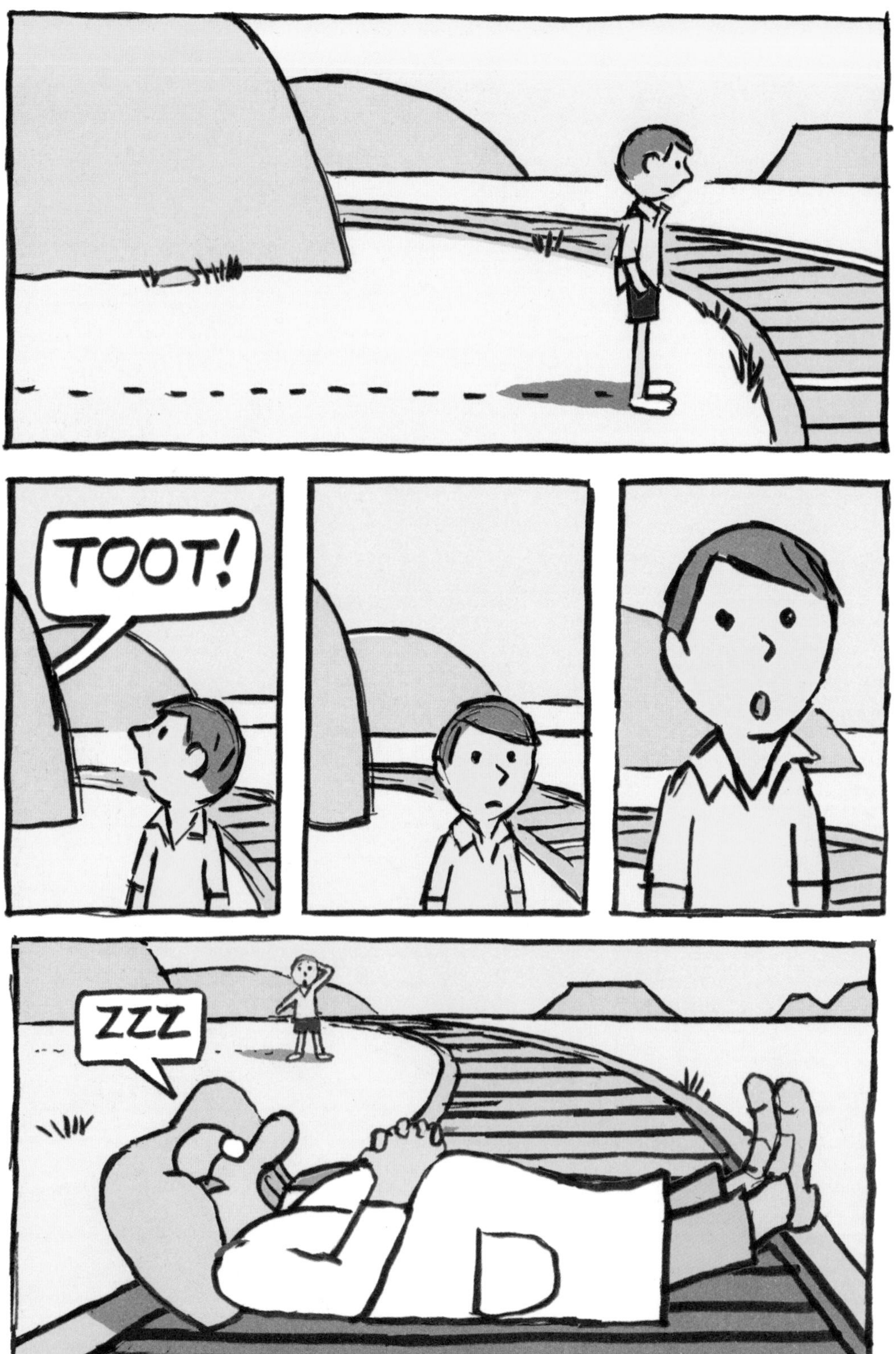
TOOT!
ZZZ

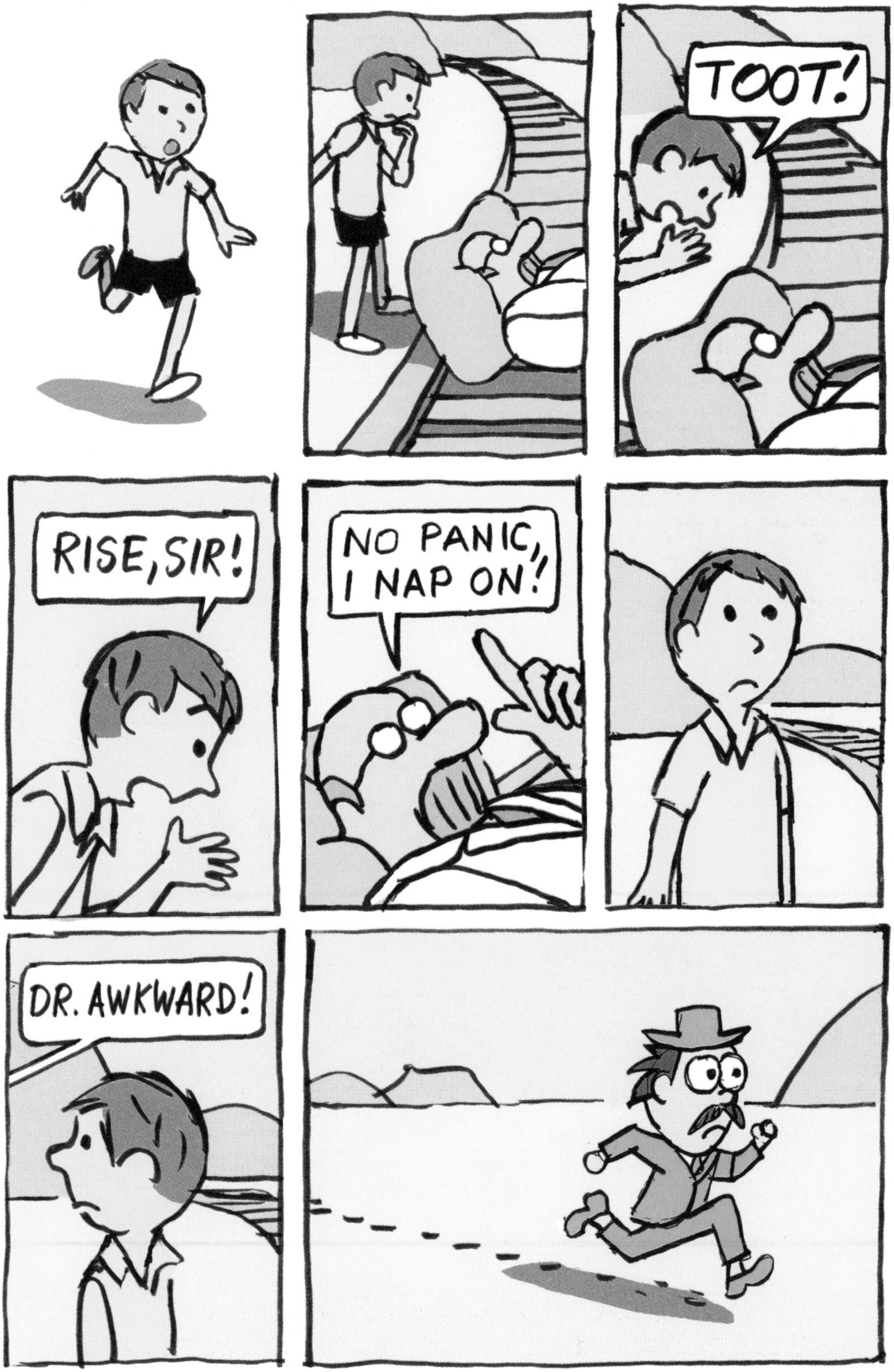
TOOT!
RISE, SIR!
NO PANIC, I NAP ON!
DR. AWKWARD!

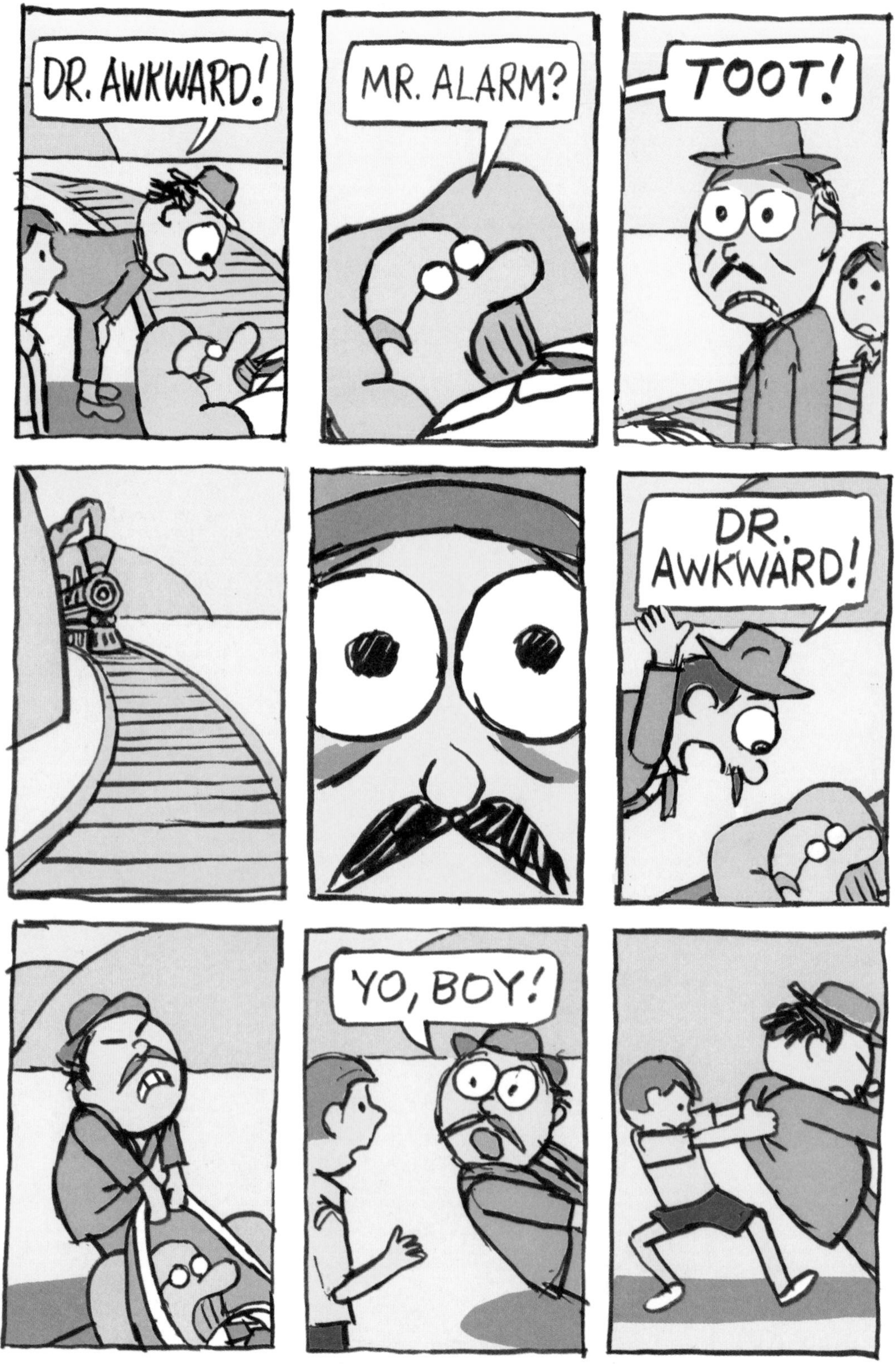
DR. AWKWARD!
MR. ALARM?
TOOT!
DR. AWKWARD!
YO, BOY!

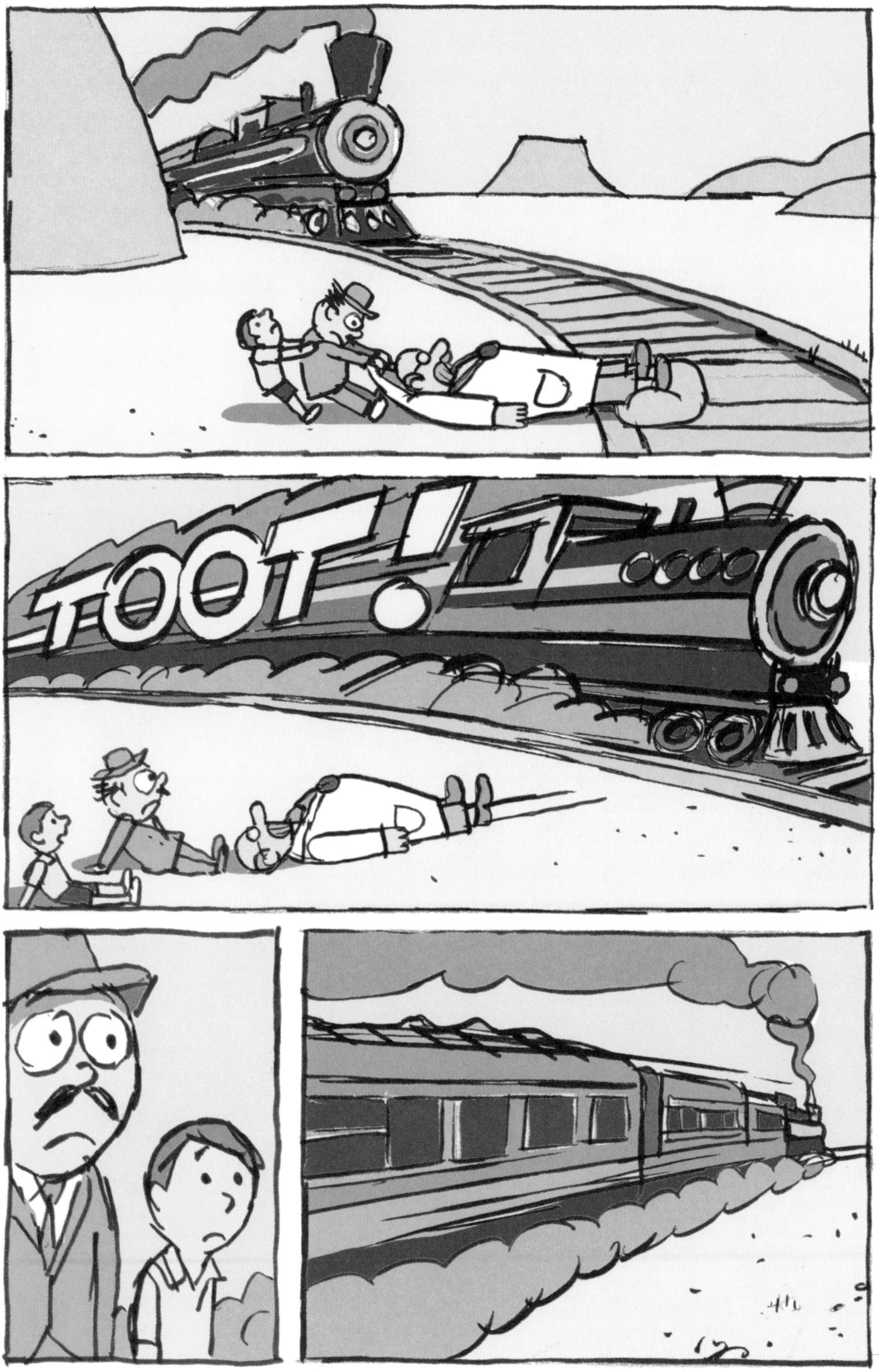
D
TOOT!
D

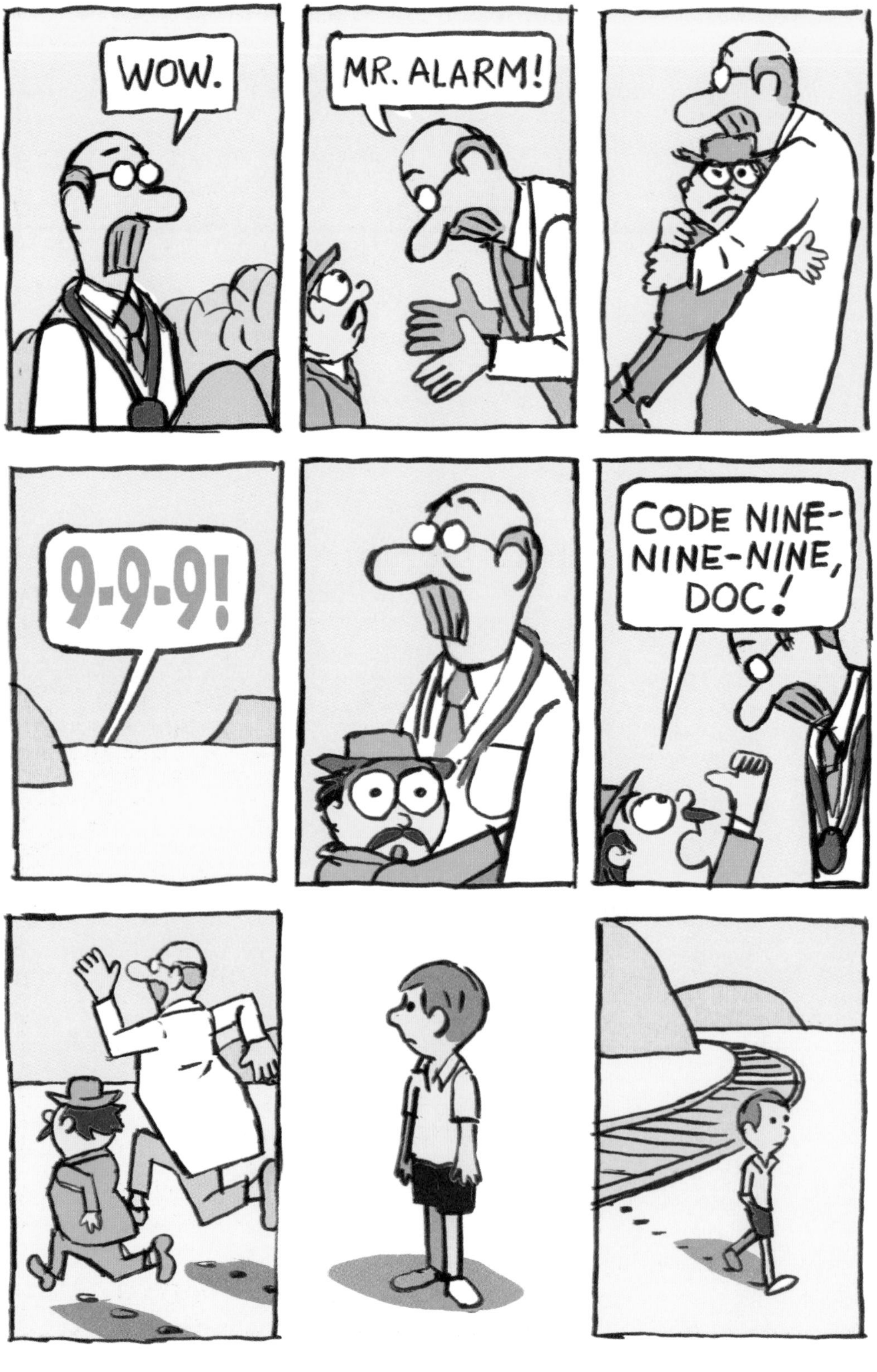
WOW.
MR. ALARM!
9-9-9!
CODE NINE-NINE-NINE, DOC!

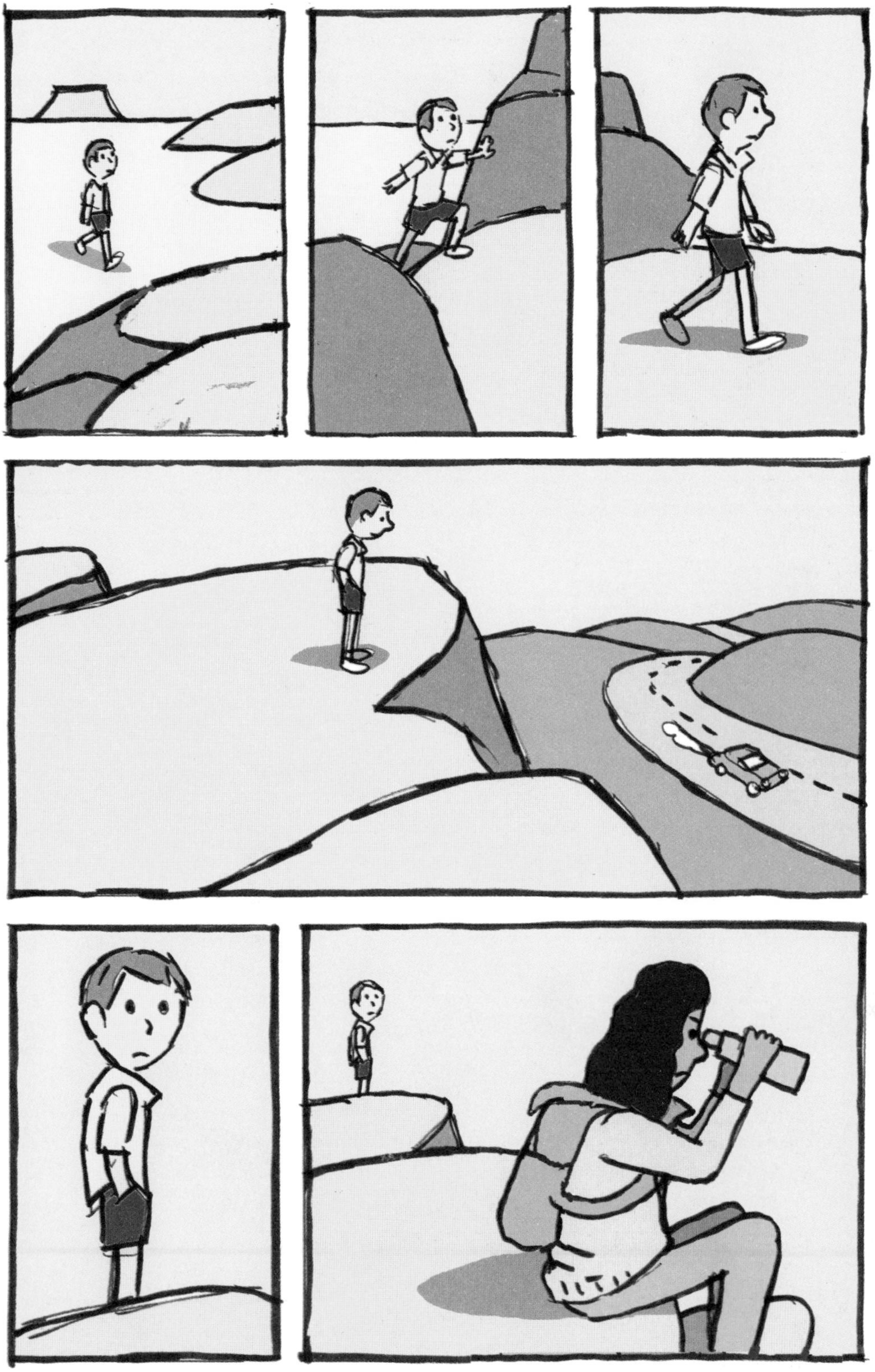

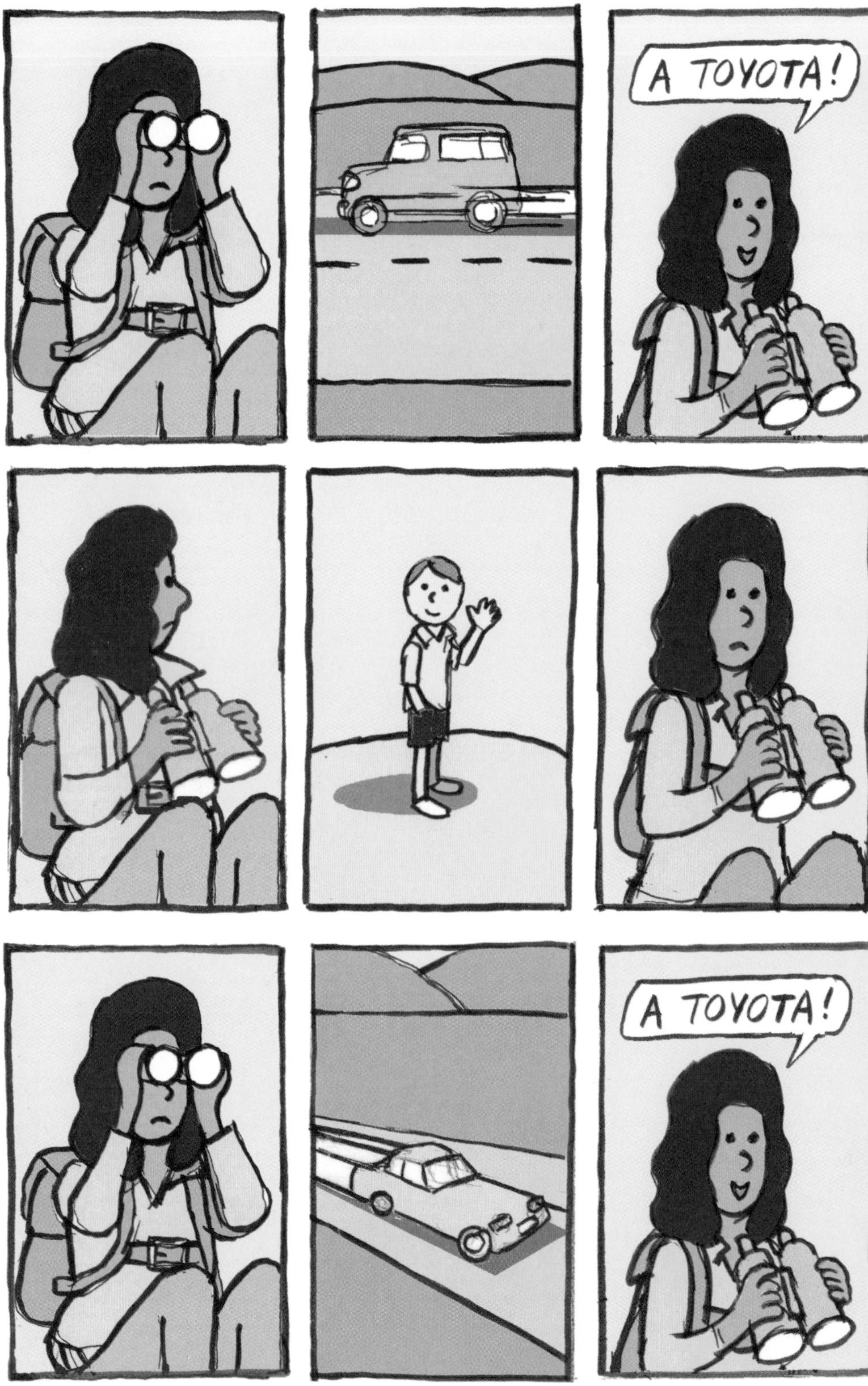
A TOYOTA!
A TOYOTA!

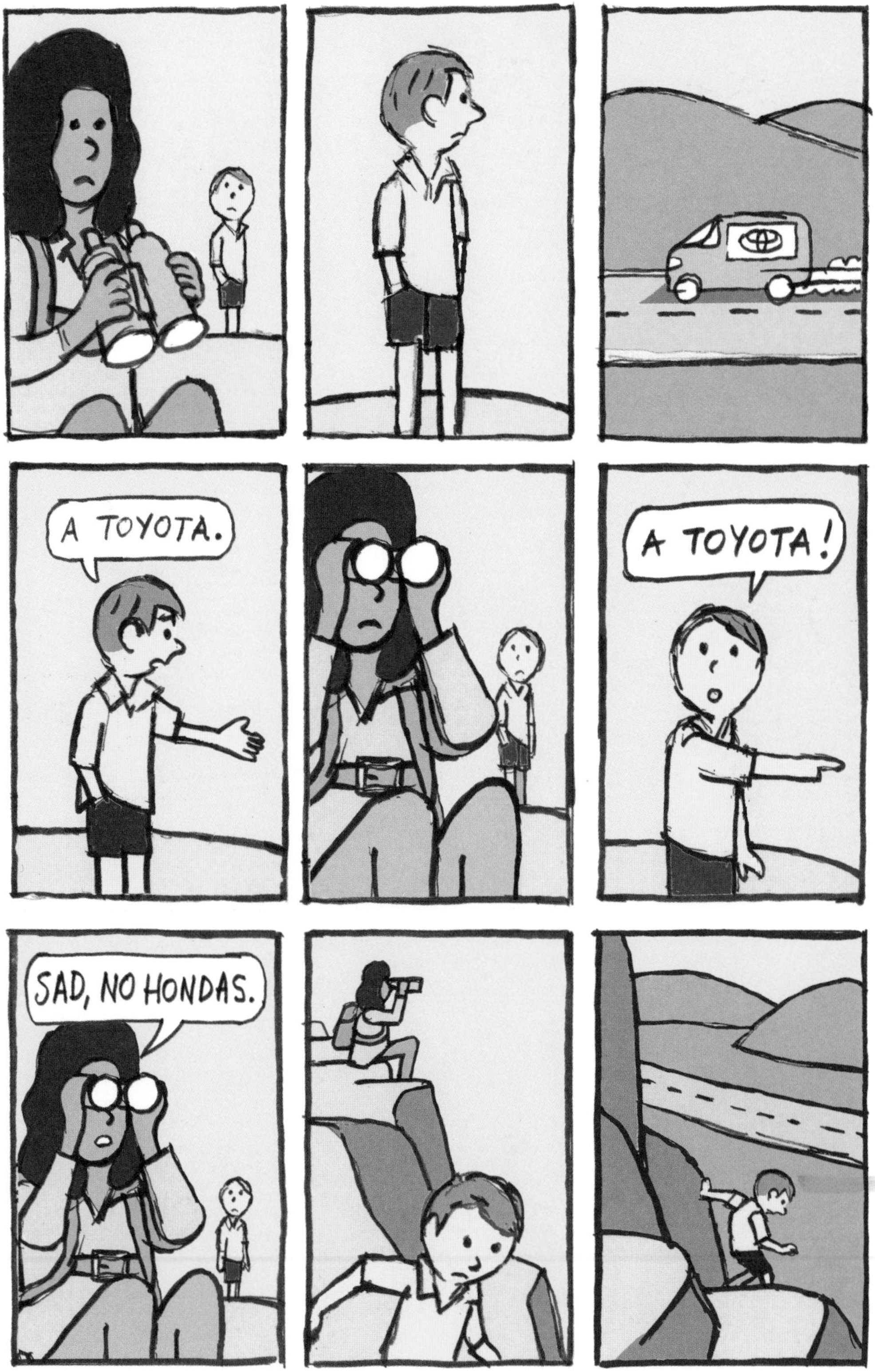
A TOYOTA.
A TOYOTA!
SAD, NO HONDAS.

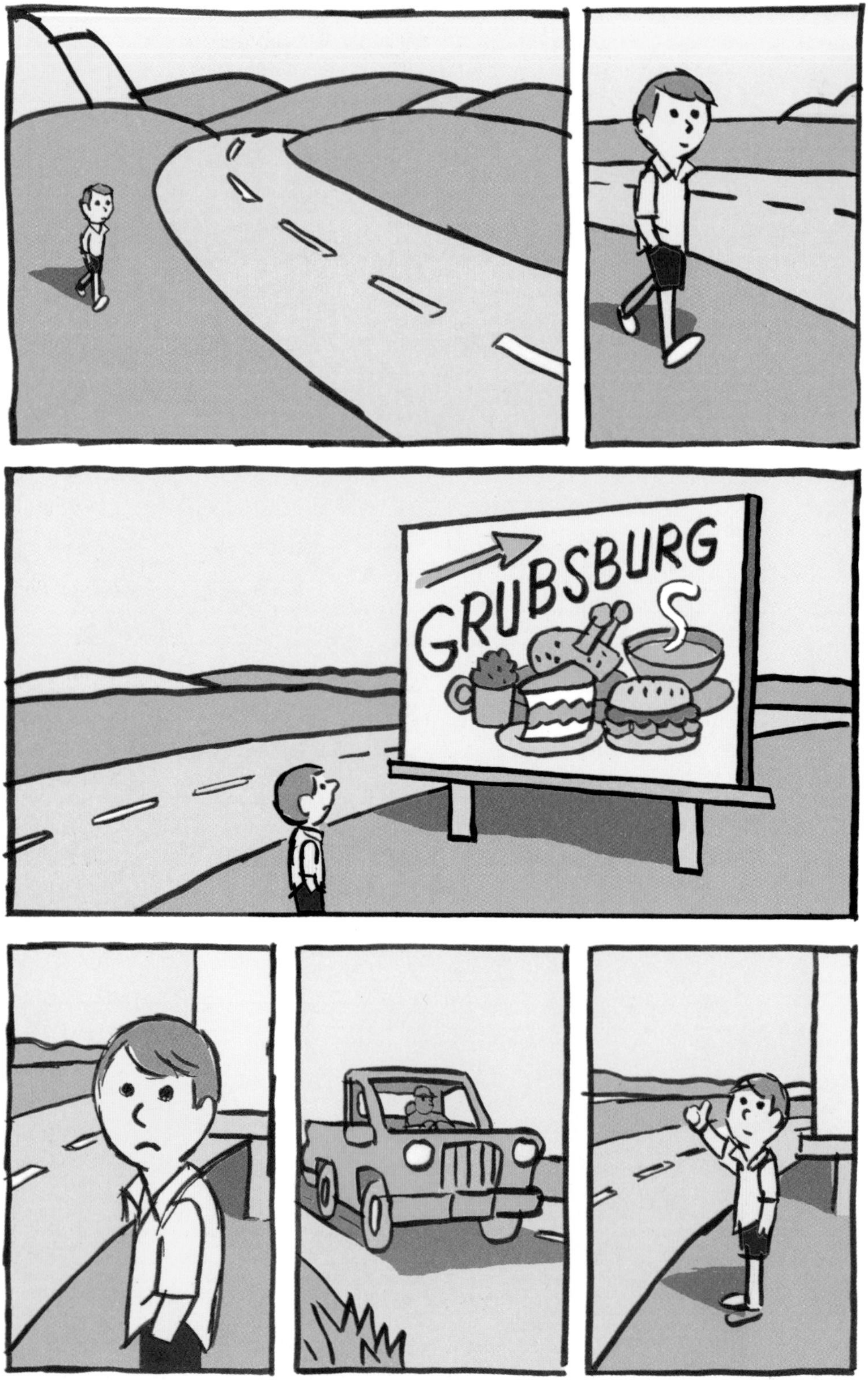
GRUBSBURG

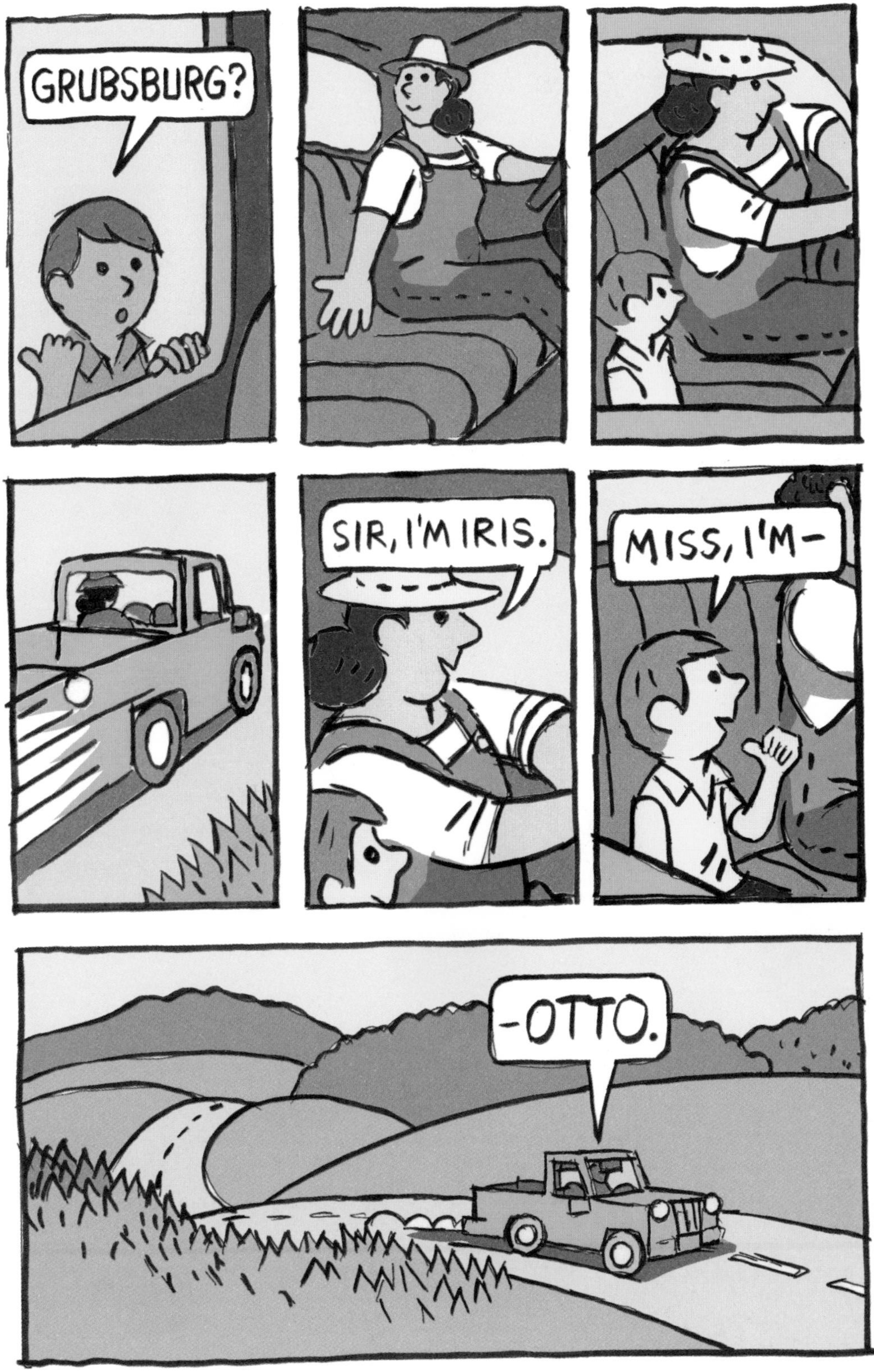
GRUBSBURG?
SIR, I'M IRIS.
MISS, I'M-
-OTTO.

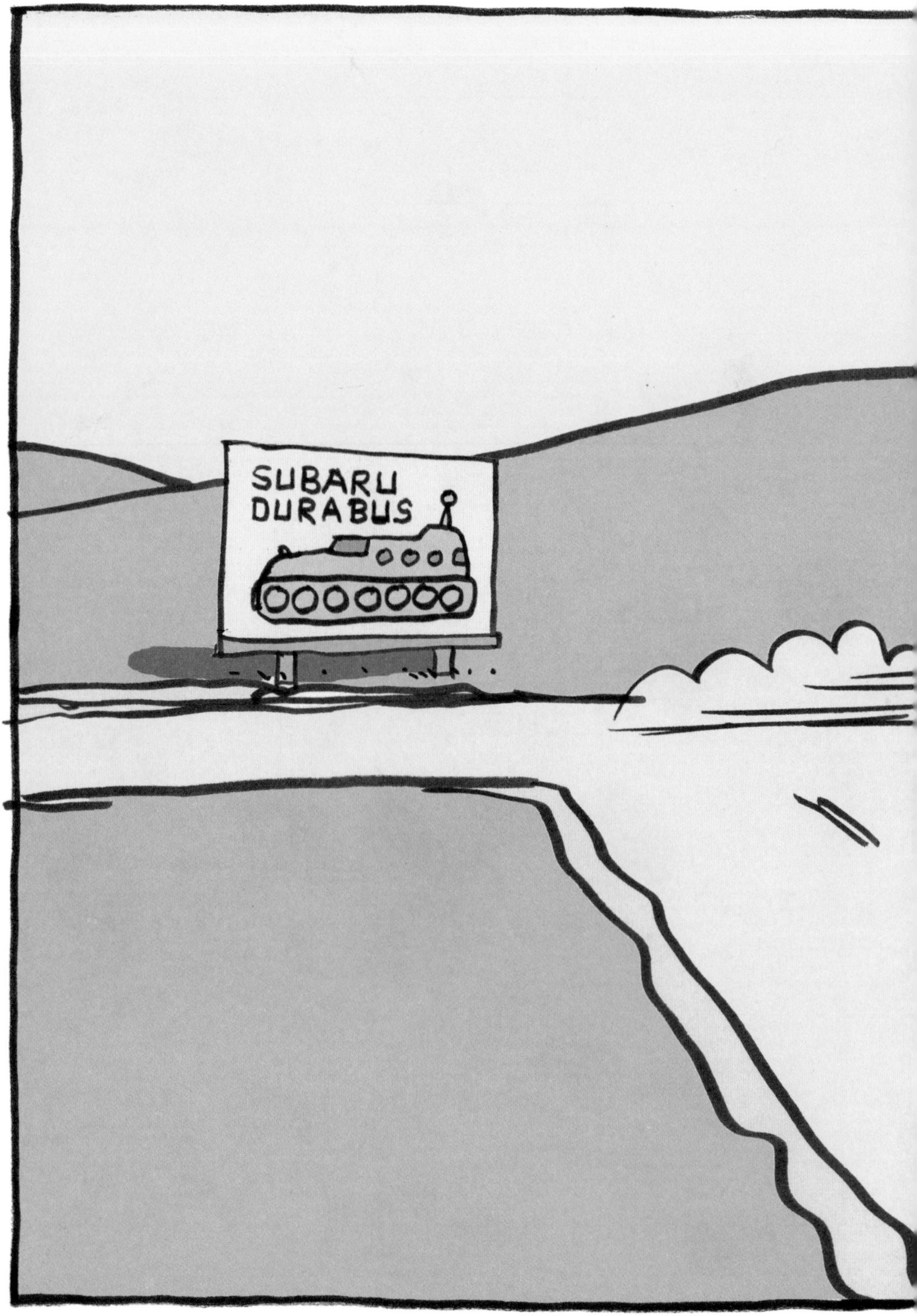
SUBARU
DURABUS

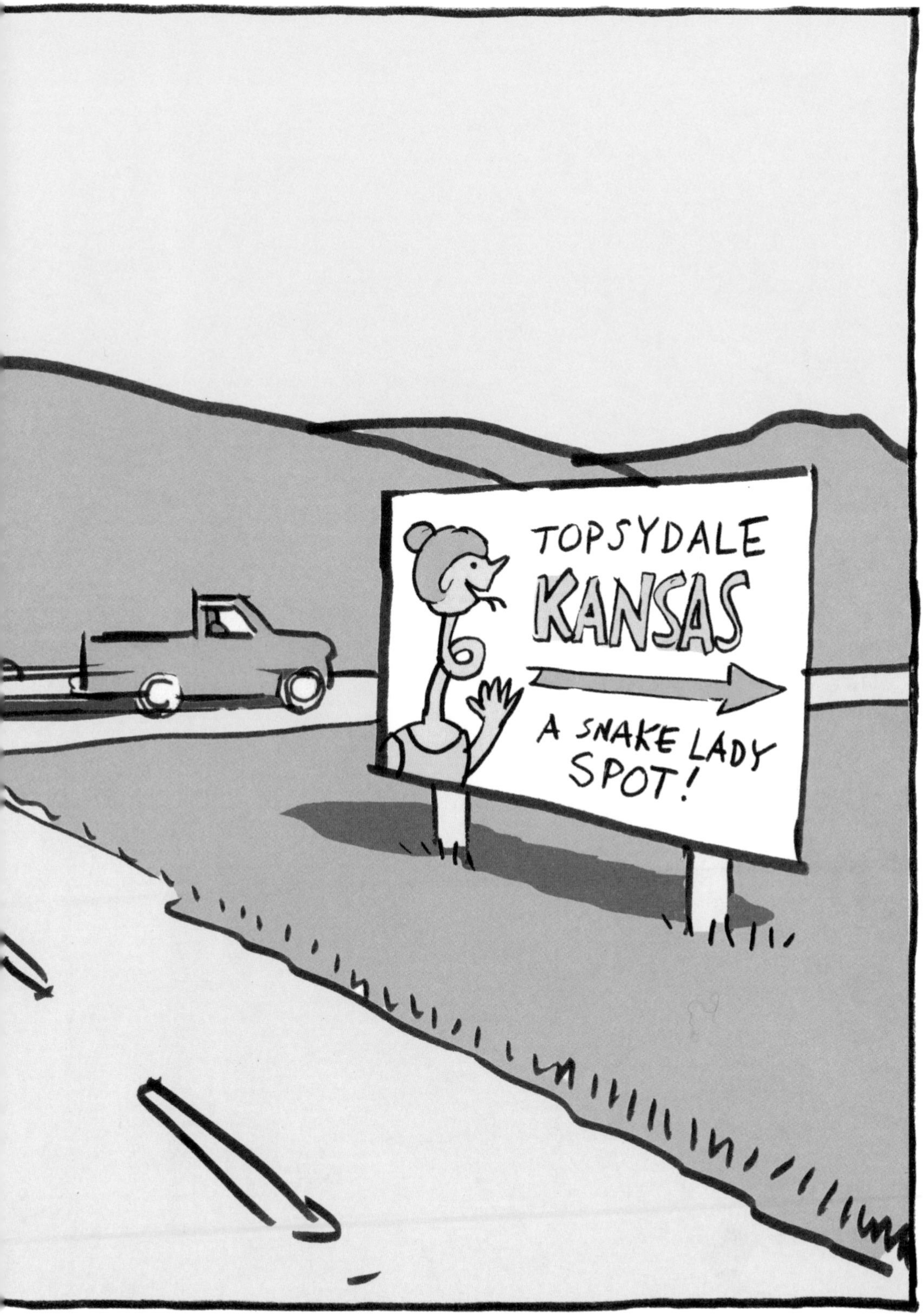
TOPSYDALE
KANSAS
A SNAKE LADY SPOT!

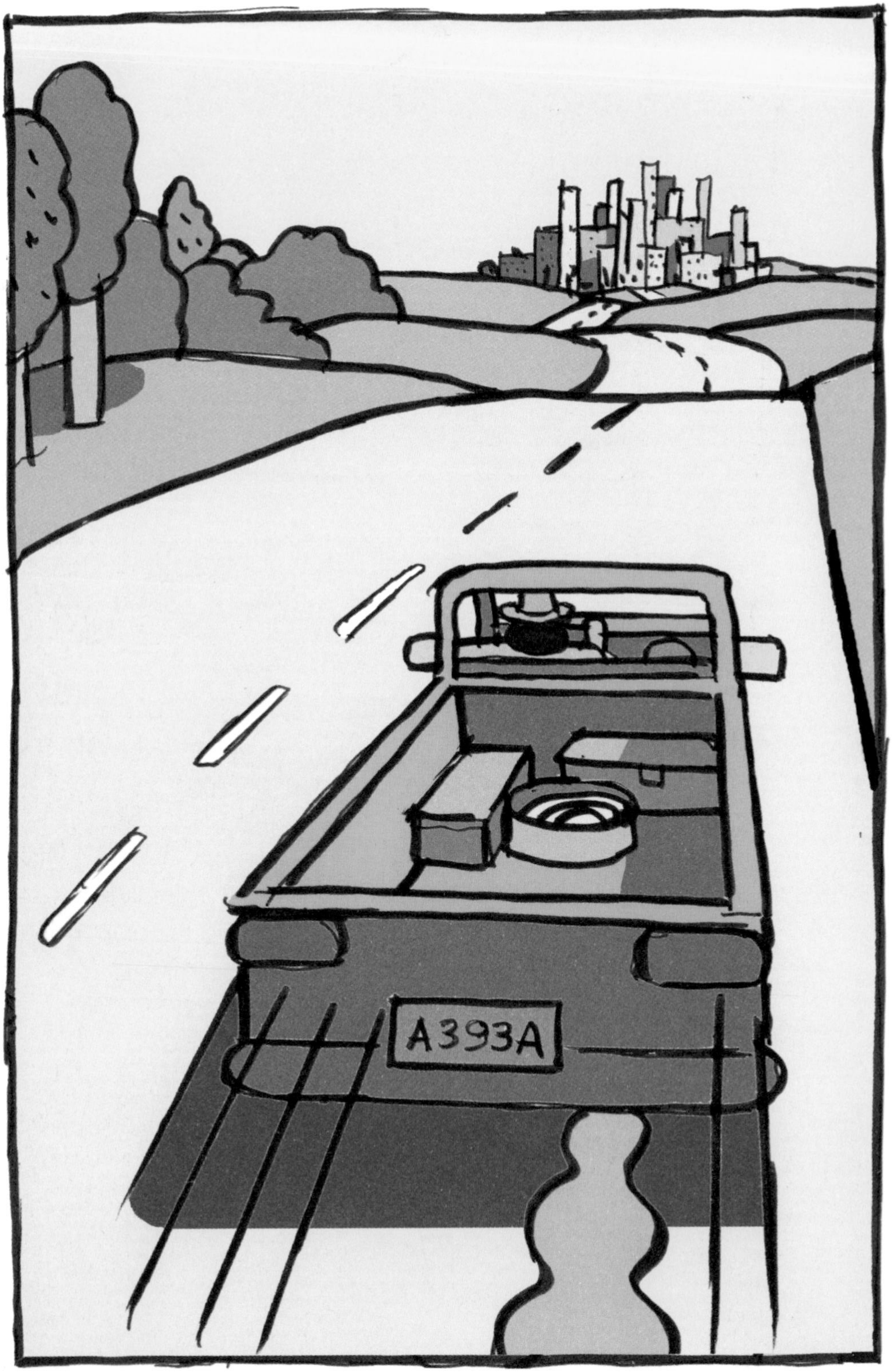
A393A

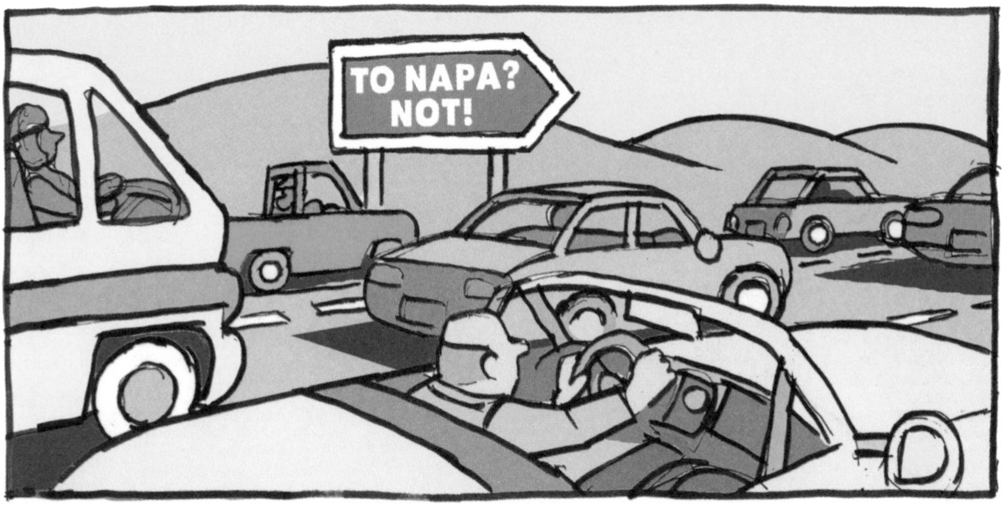
TO NAPA?
NOT!

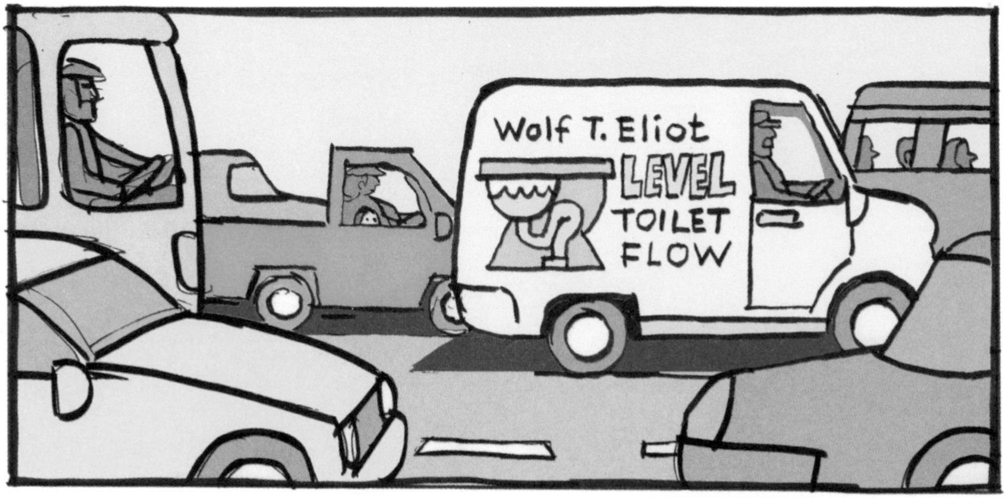
Wolf T. Eliot
LEVEL
TOILET
FLOW

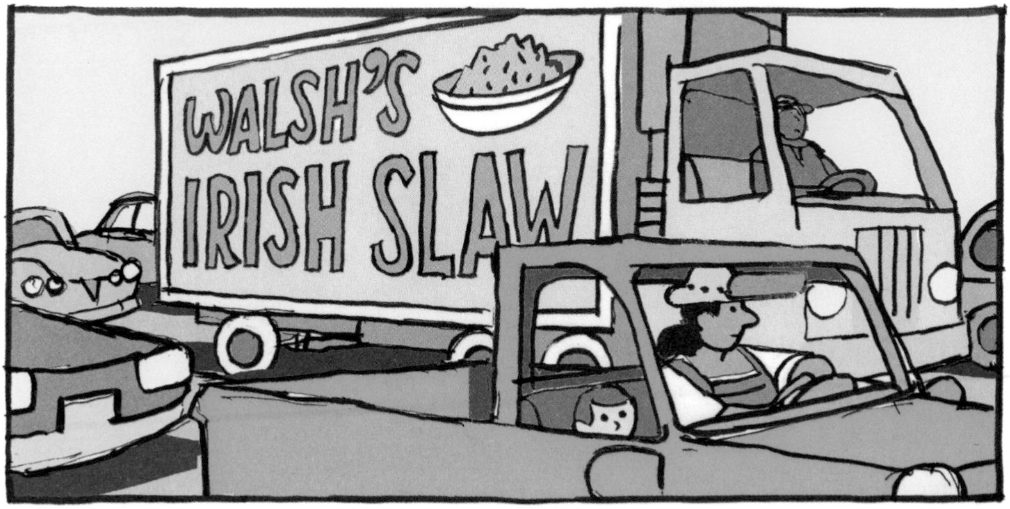
WALSH'S
IRISH SLAW

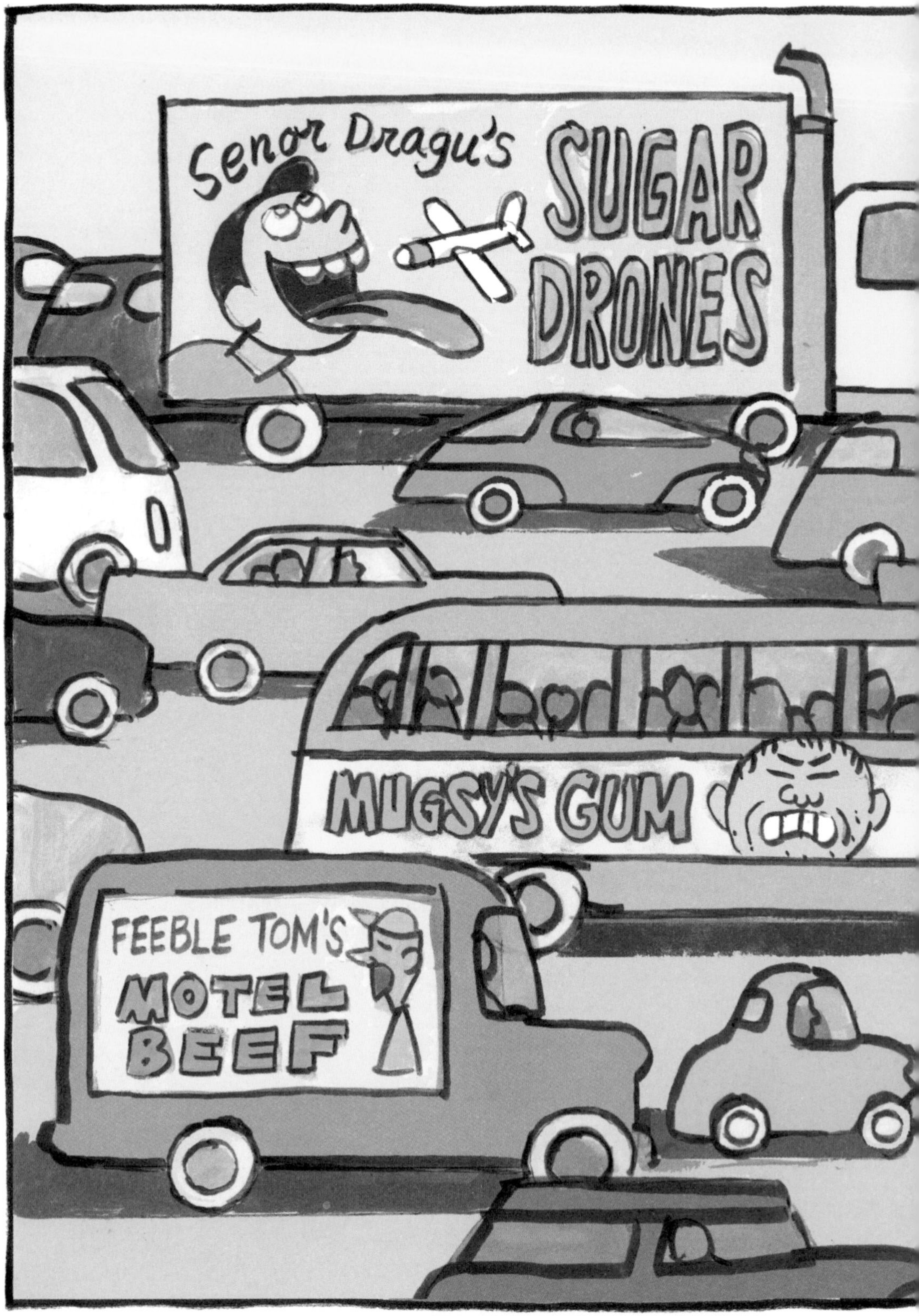
Senor Dragu's
SUGAR
DRONES
MUGSY'S GUM
FEEBLE TOM'S
MOTEL
BEEF

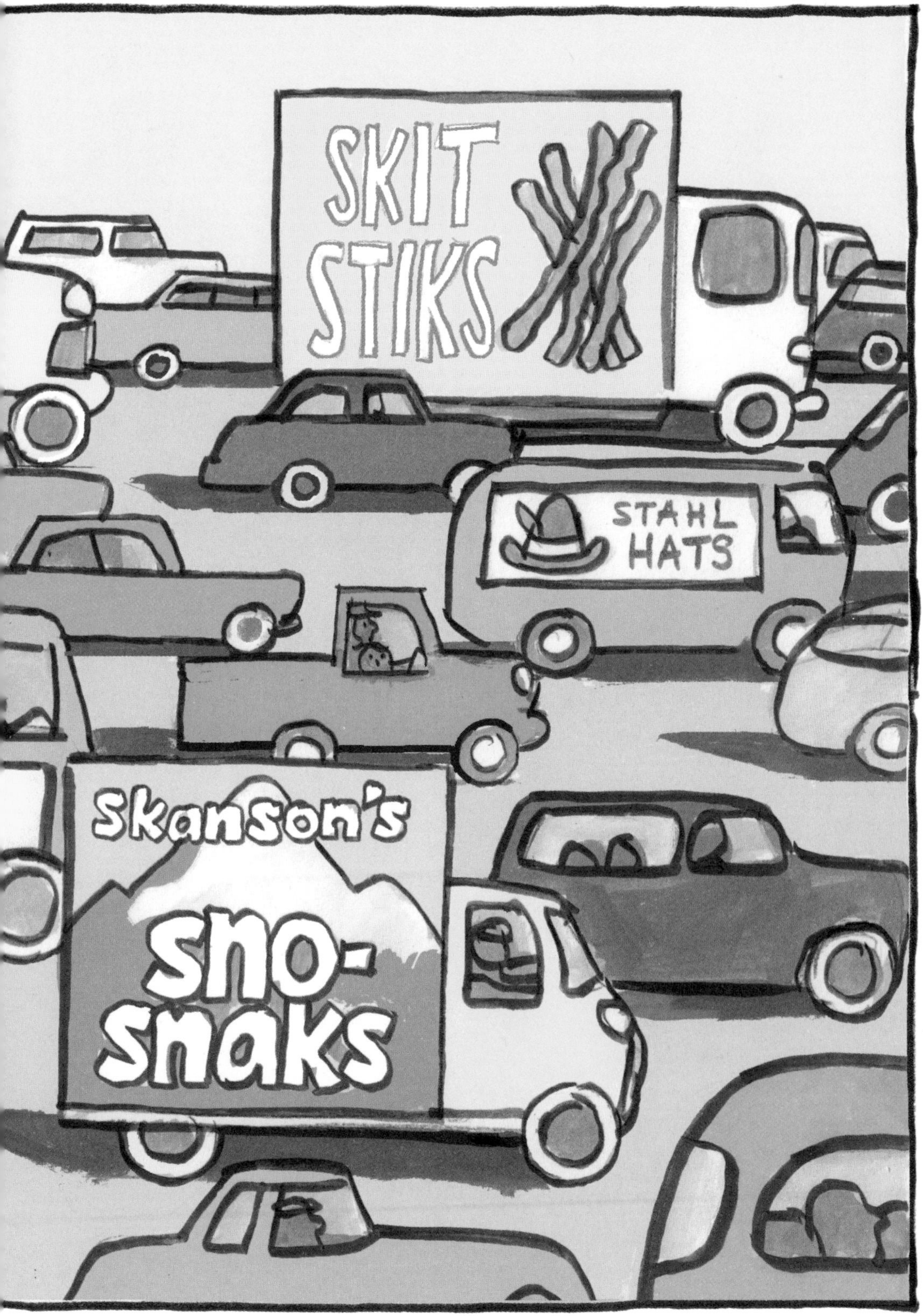
SKIT
STIKS
STAHL
HATS
Skanson's
sno-
snaks

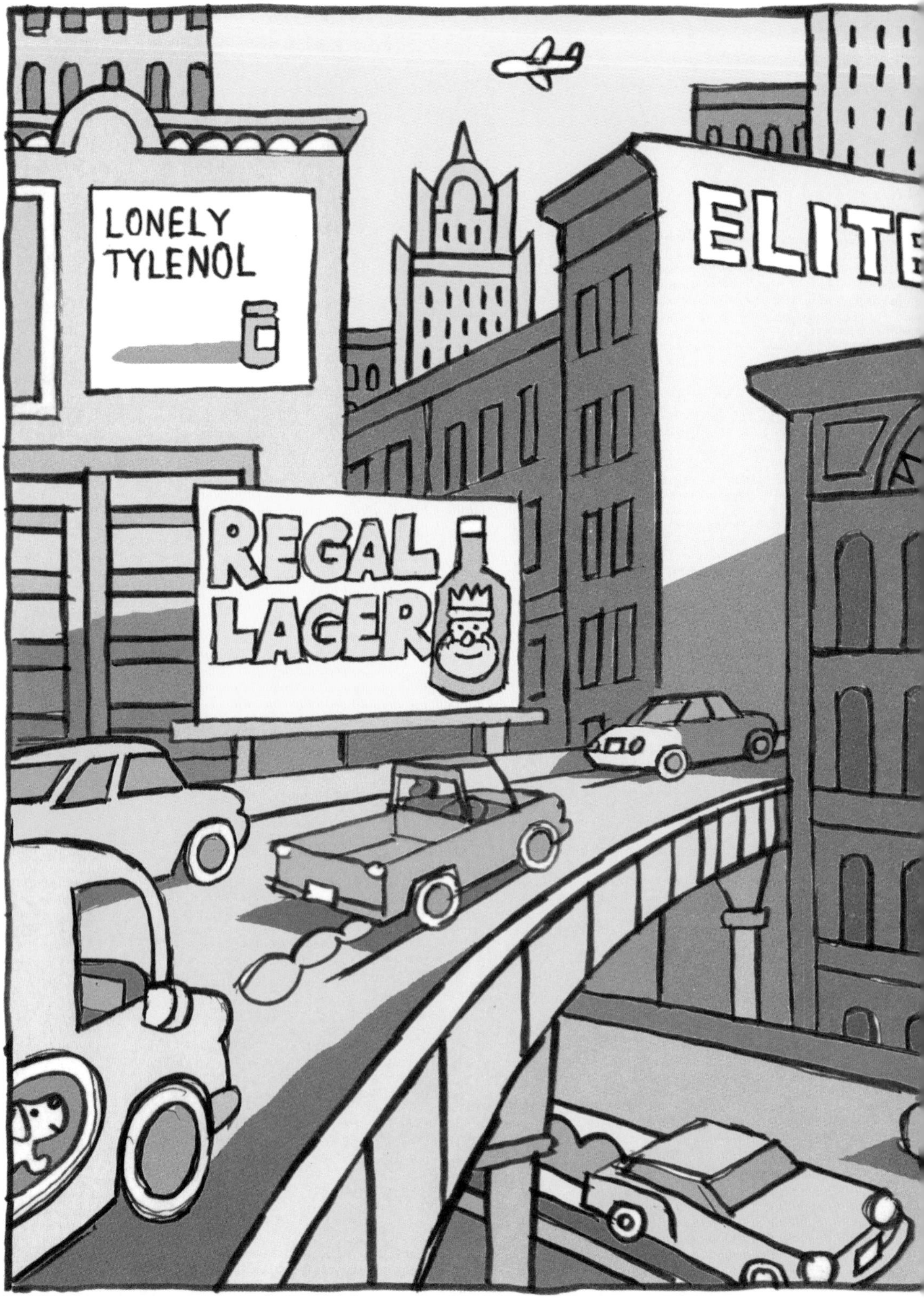
LONELY
TYLENOL
REGAL
LAGER
ELITE

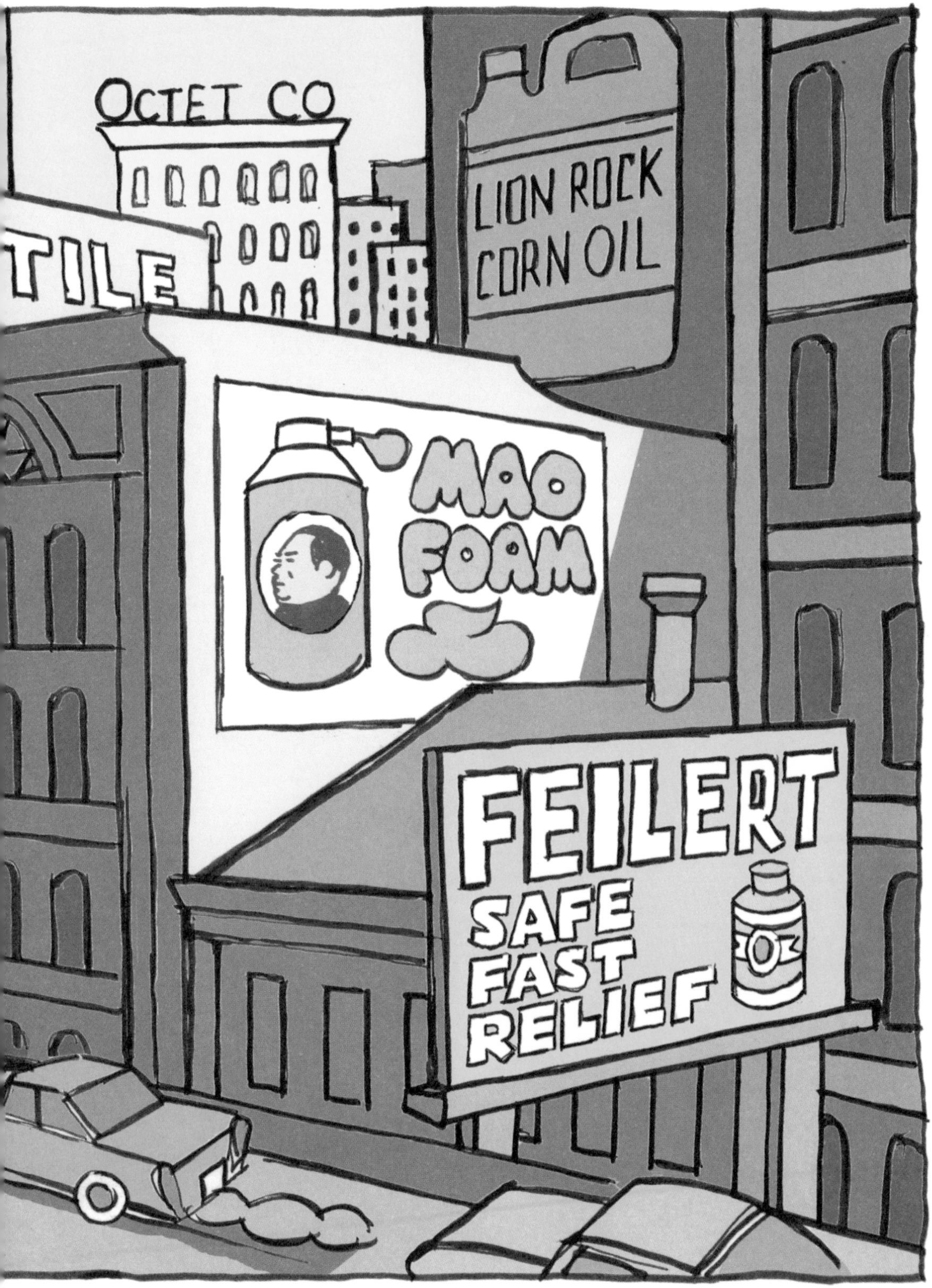
OCTET CO
TILE
LION ROCK
CORN OIL
MAO
FOAM
FEILERT
SAFE
FAST
RELIEF

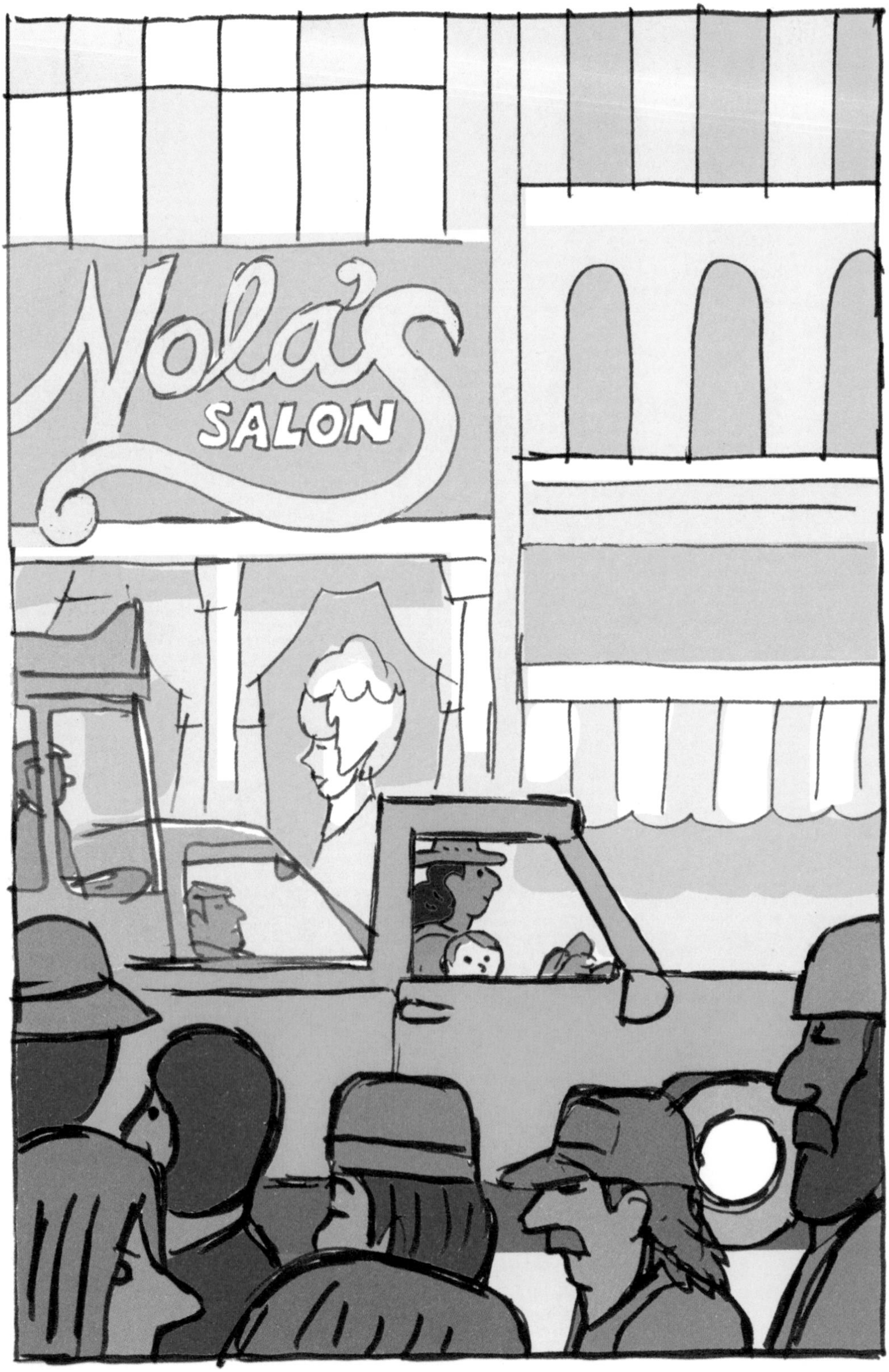
Nola's
SALON

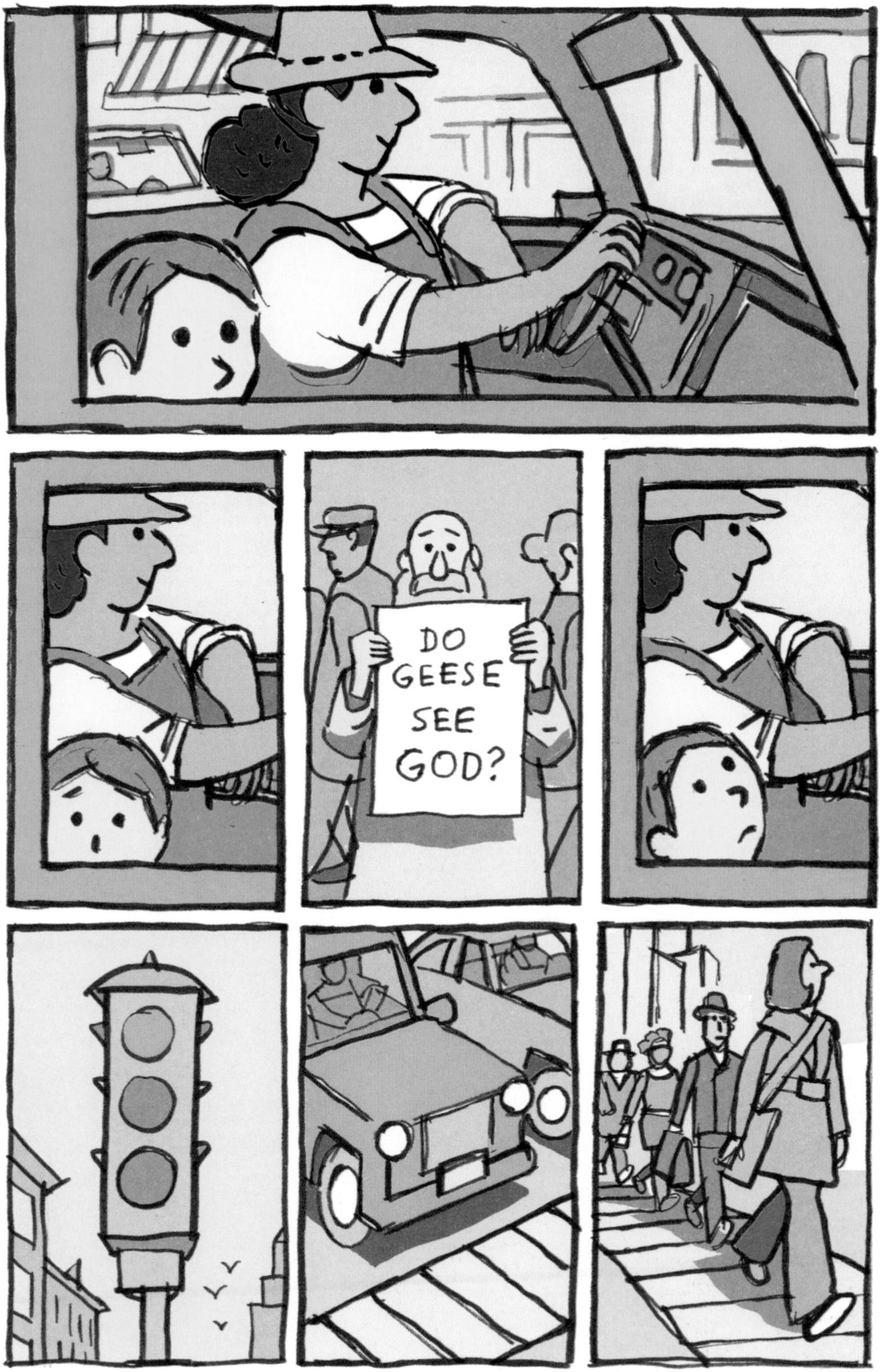
DO GEESE SEE GOD?

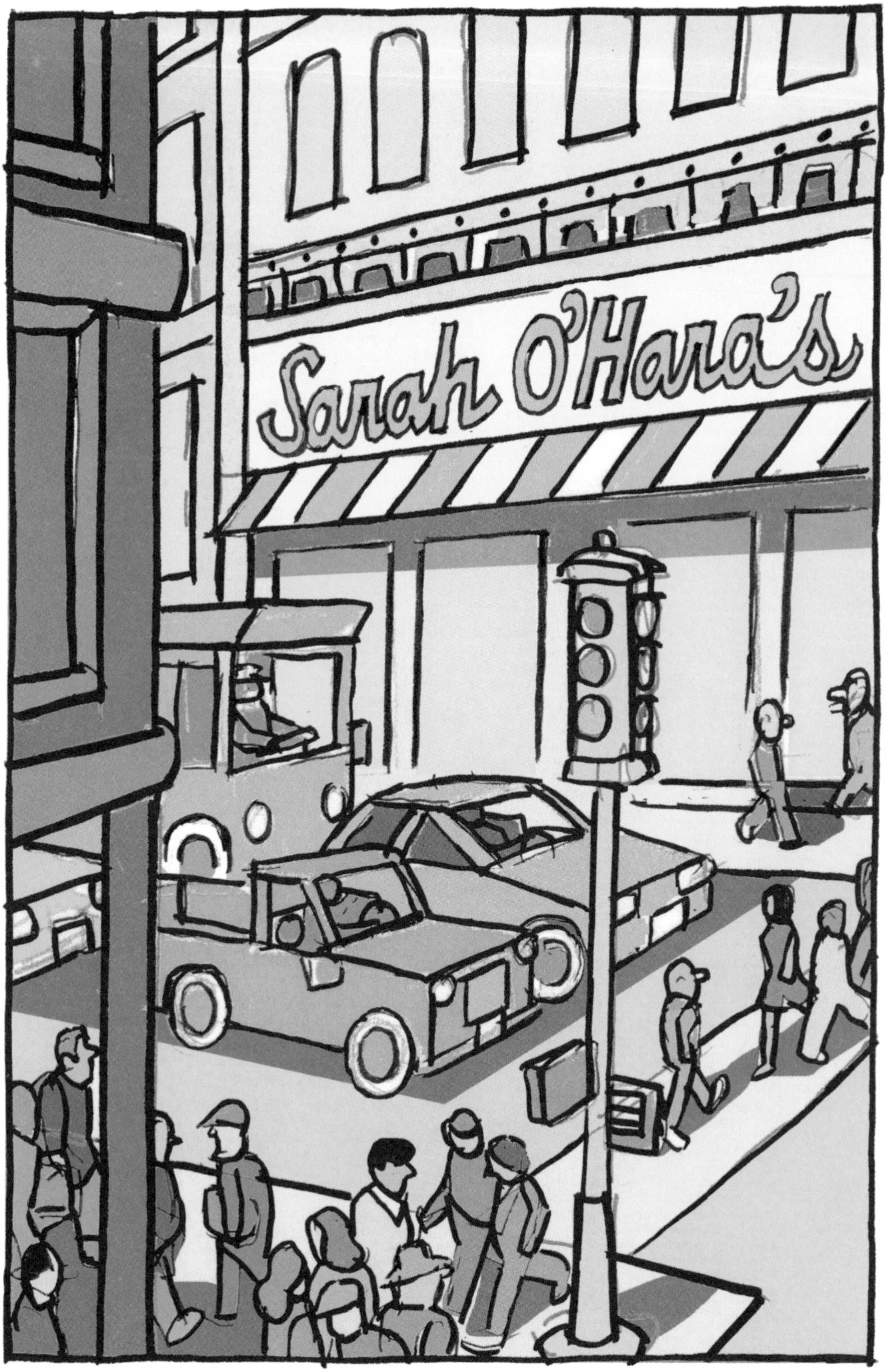
Sarah O'Hara's

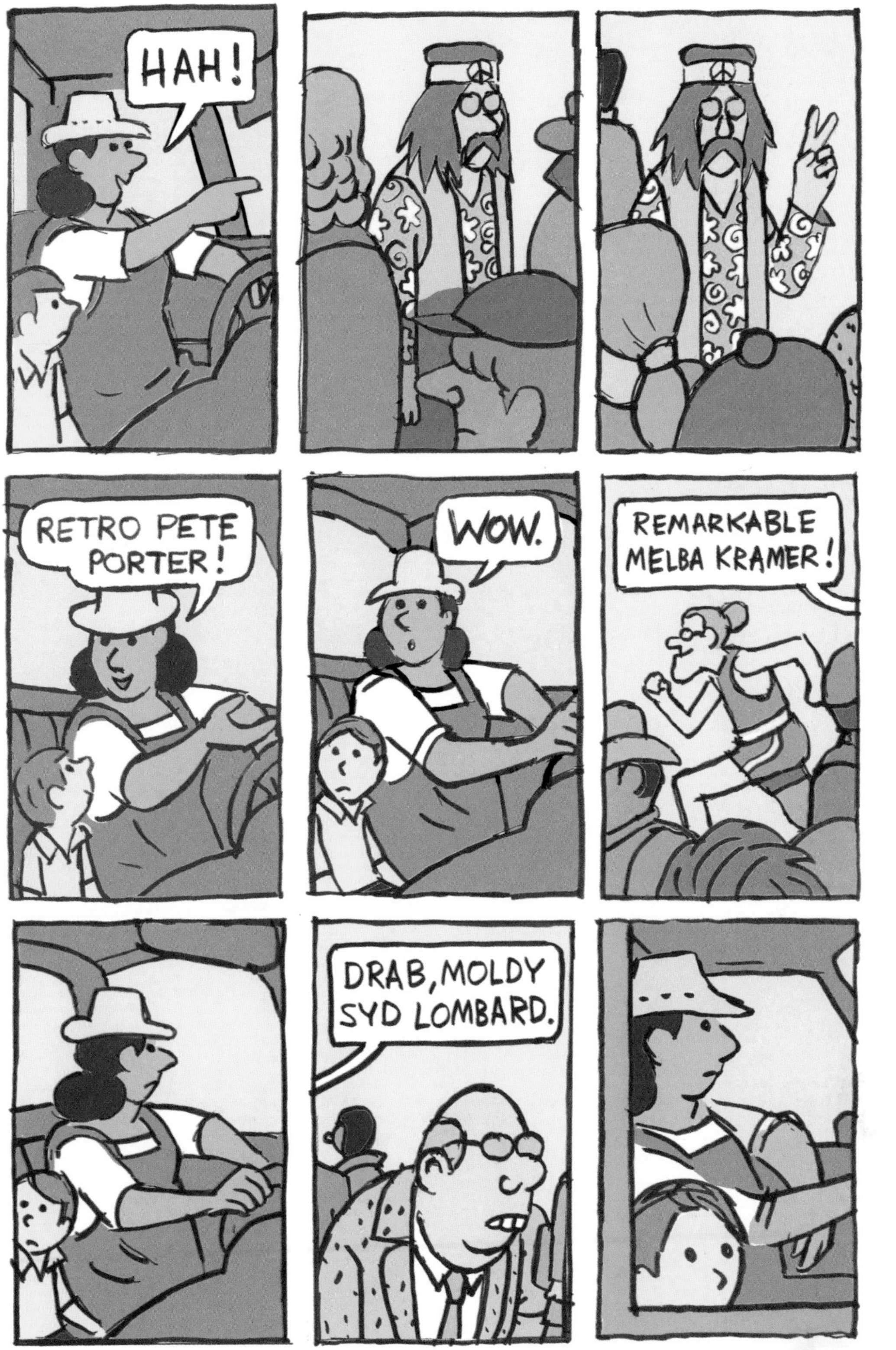
HAH!
RETRO PETE PORTER!
WOW.
REMARKABLE MELBA KRAMER!
DRAB, MOLDY SYD LOMBARD.

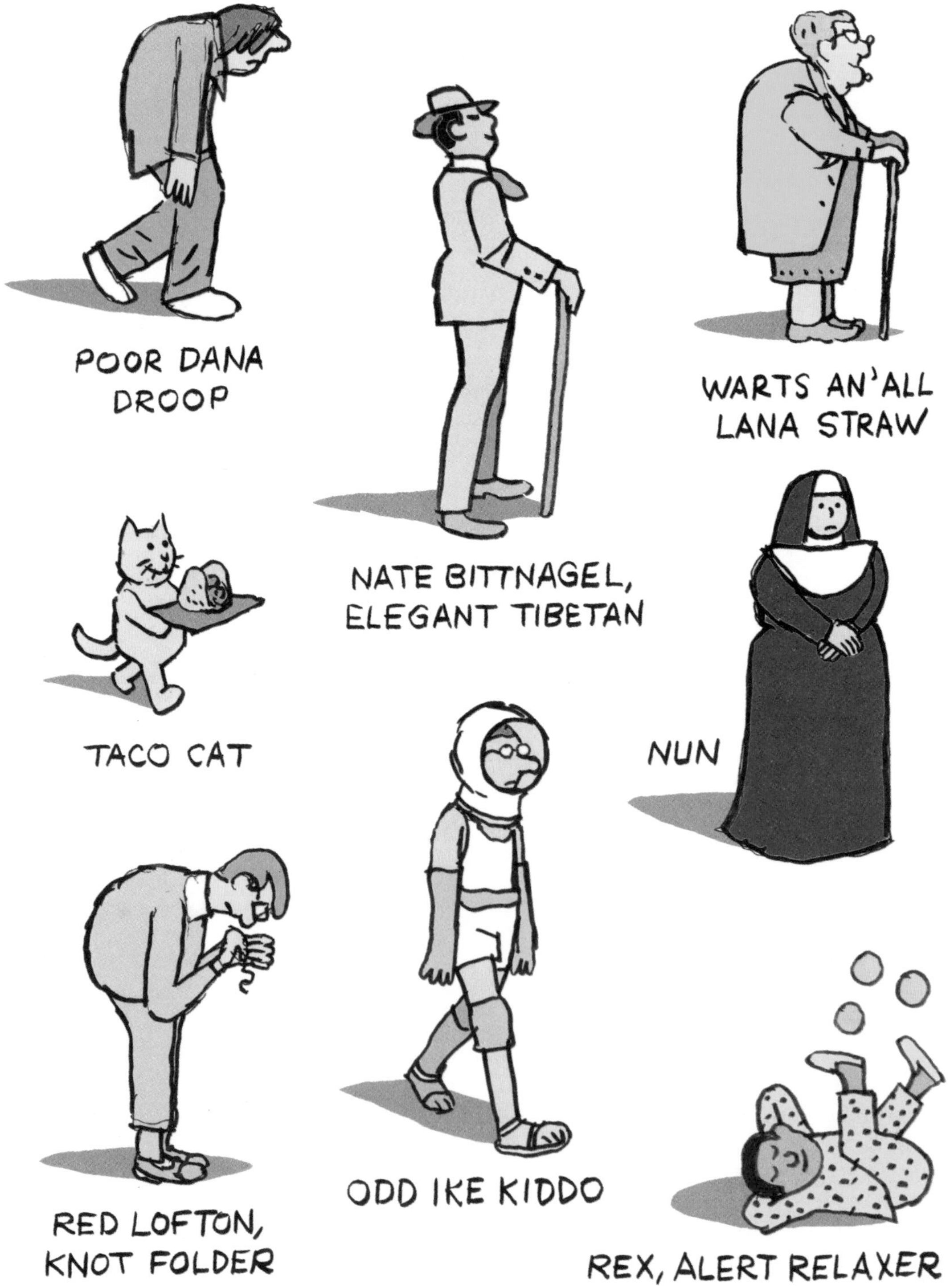
POOR DANA DROOP
NATE BITTNAGEL, ELEGANT TIBETAN
WARTS AN'ALL LANA STRAW
TACO CAT
NUN
RED LOFTON, KNOT FOLDER
ODD IKE KIDDO
REX, ALERT RELAXER

RENE POE,
PIPE OPENER

EVIL CARA
CLIVE

NEIL,
A LI'L ALIEN

REGAN AMY TRAPP,
PARTY MANAGER

SIR RON NORRIS

REG GABLER,
APPAREL BAGGER

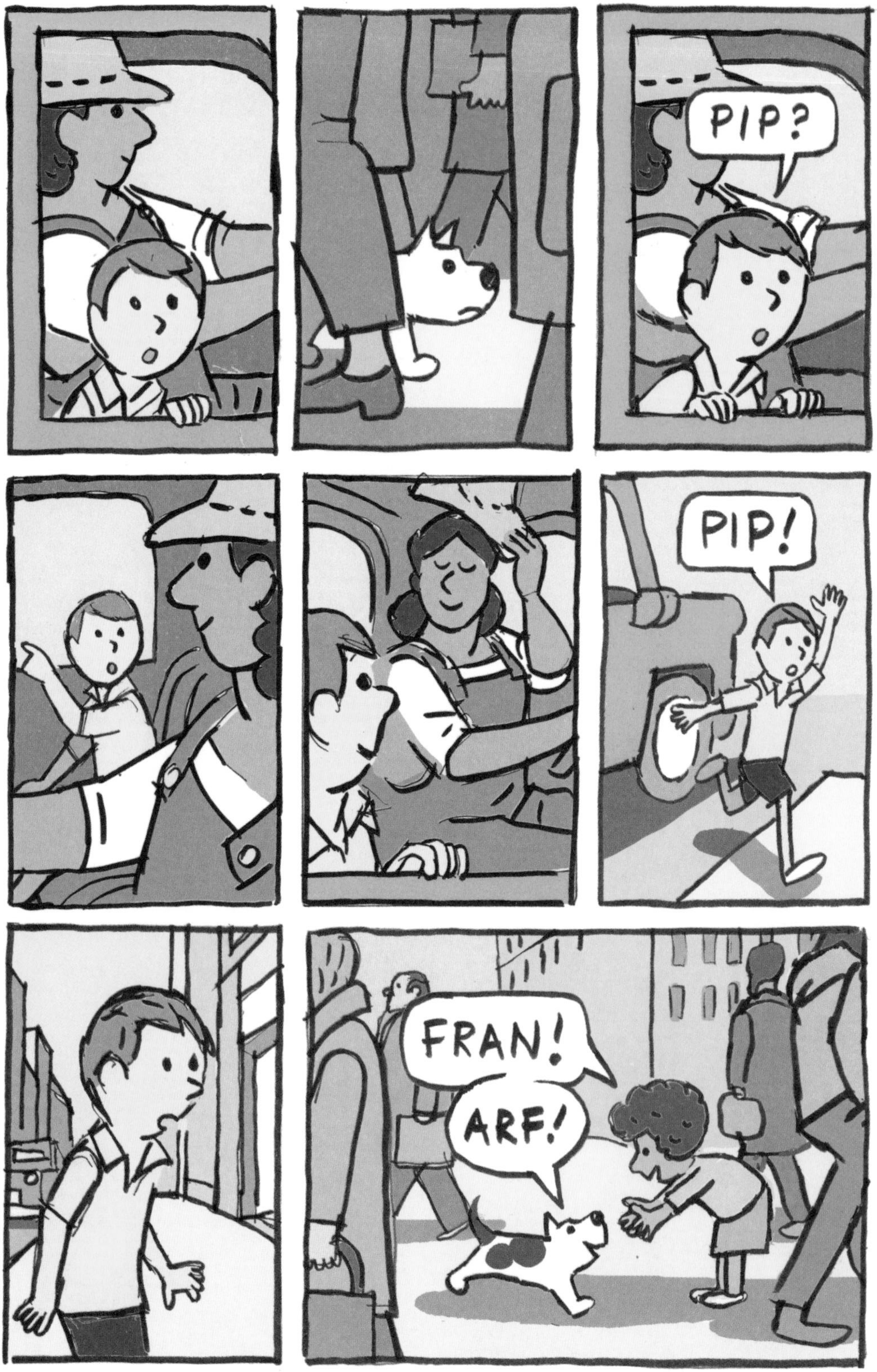
PIP?
PIP!
FRAN!
ARF!

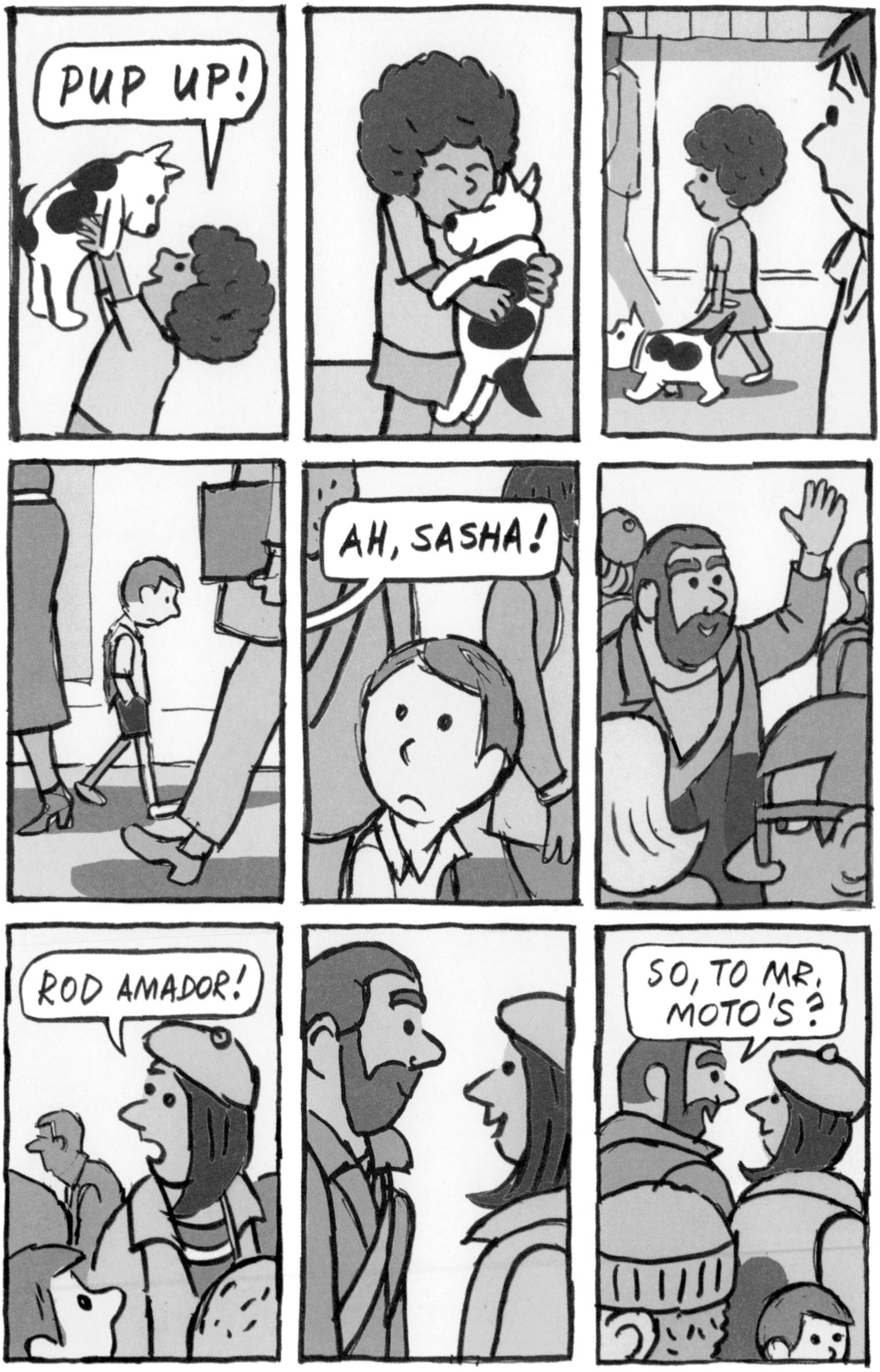
PUP UP!
AH, SASHA!
ROD AMADOR!
SO, TO MR. MOTO'S?

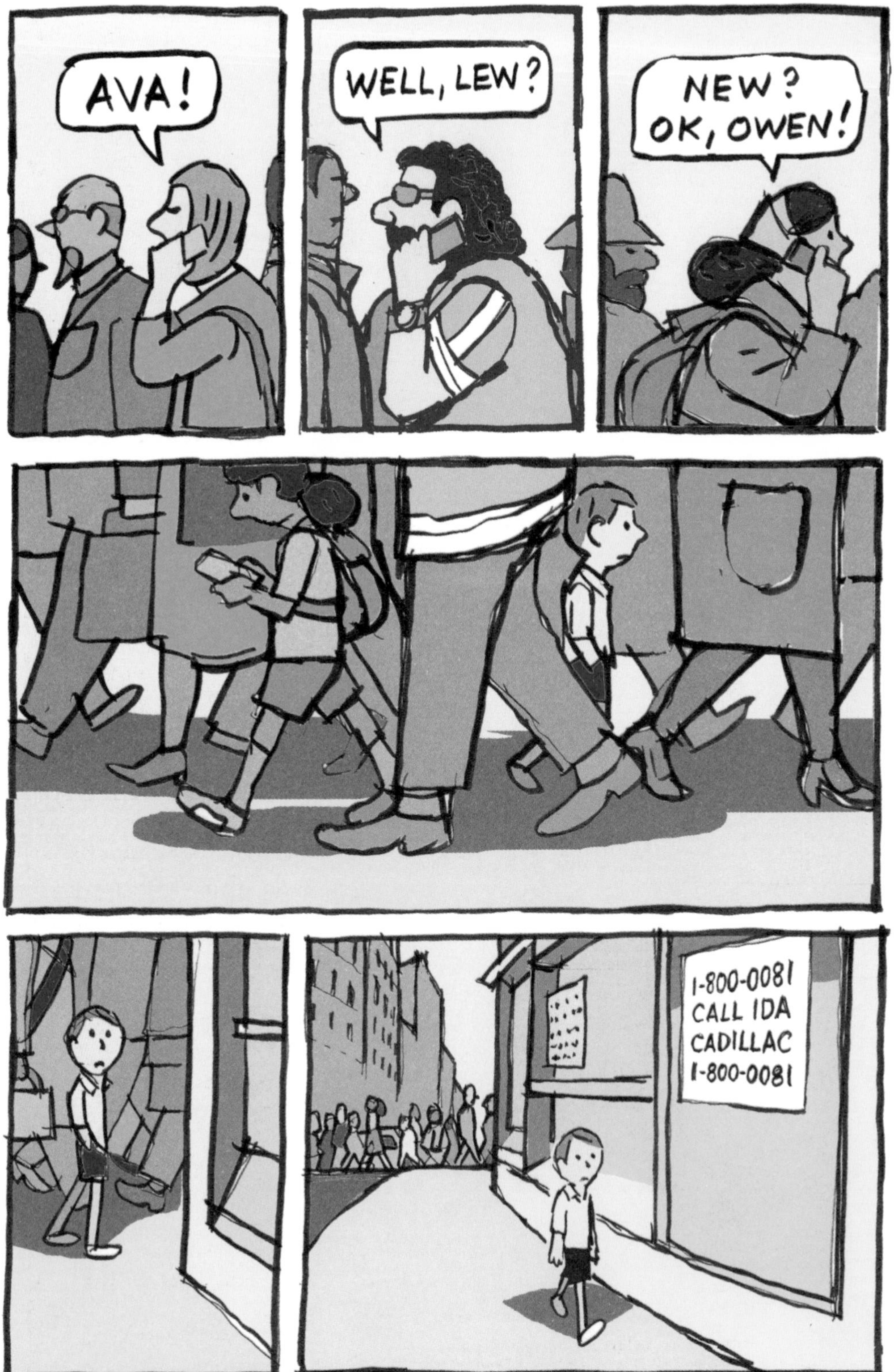
AVA!
WELL, LEW?
NEW? OK, OWEN!
1-800-0081
CALL IDA
CADILLAC
1-800-0081

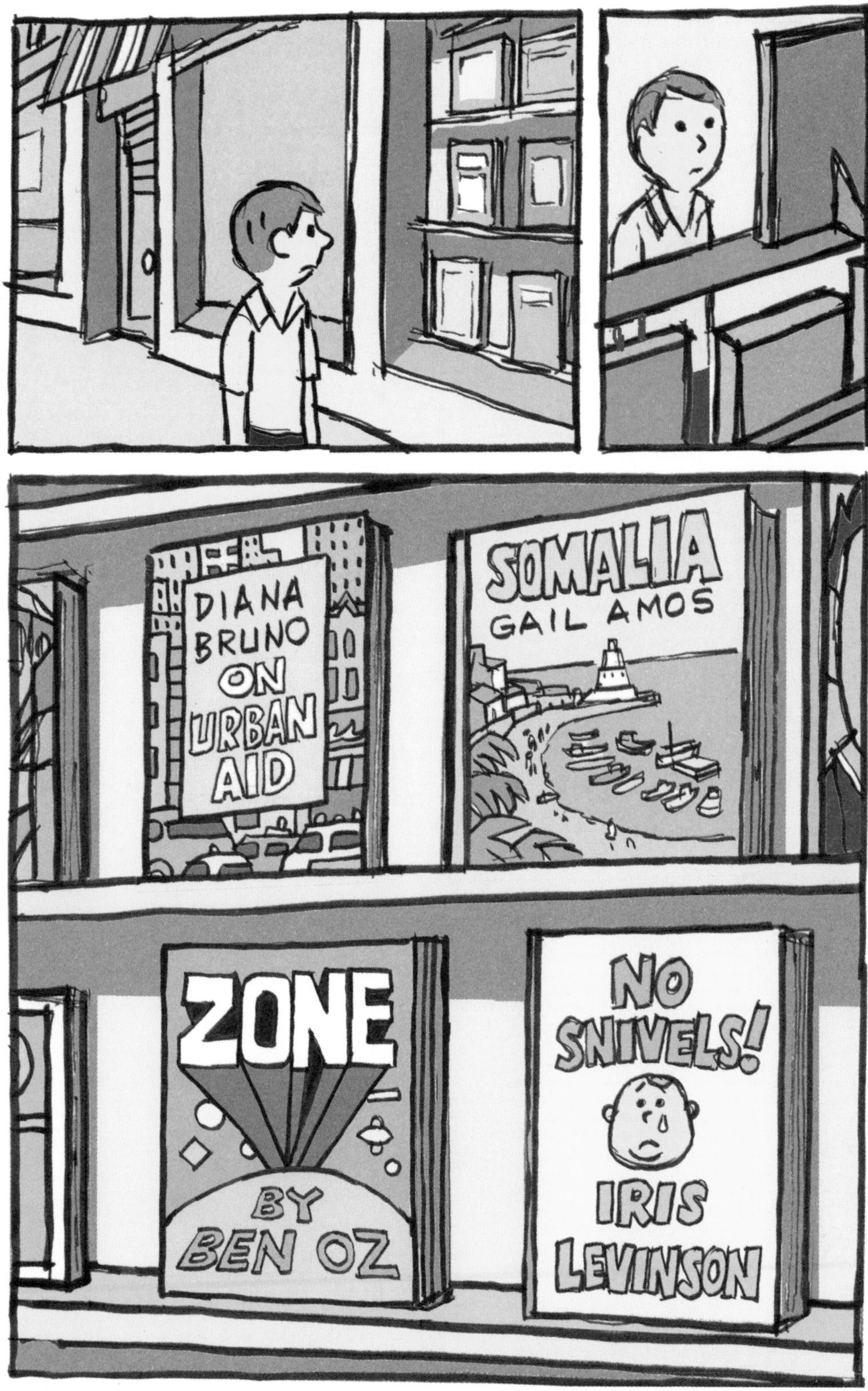
DIANA BRUNO ON URBAN AID
SOMALIA GAIL AMOS
ZONE BY BEN OZ
NO SNIVELS! IRIS LEVINSON

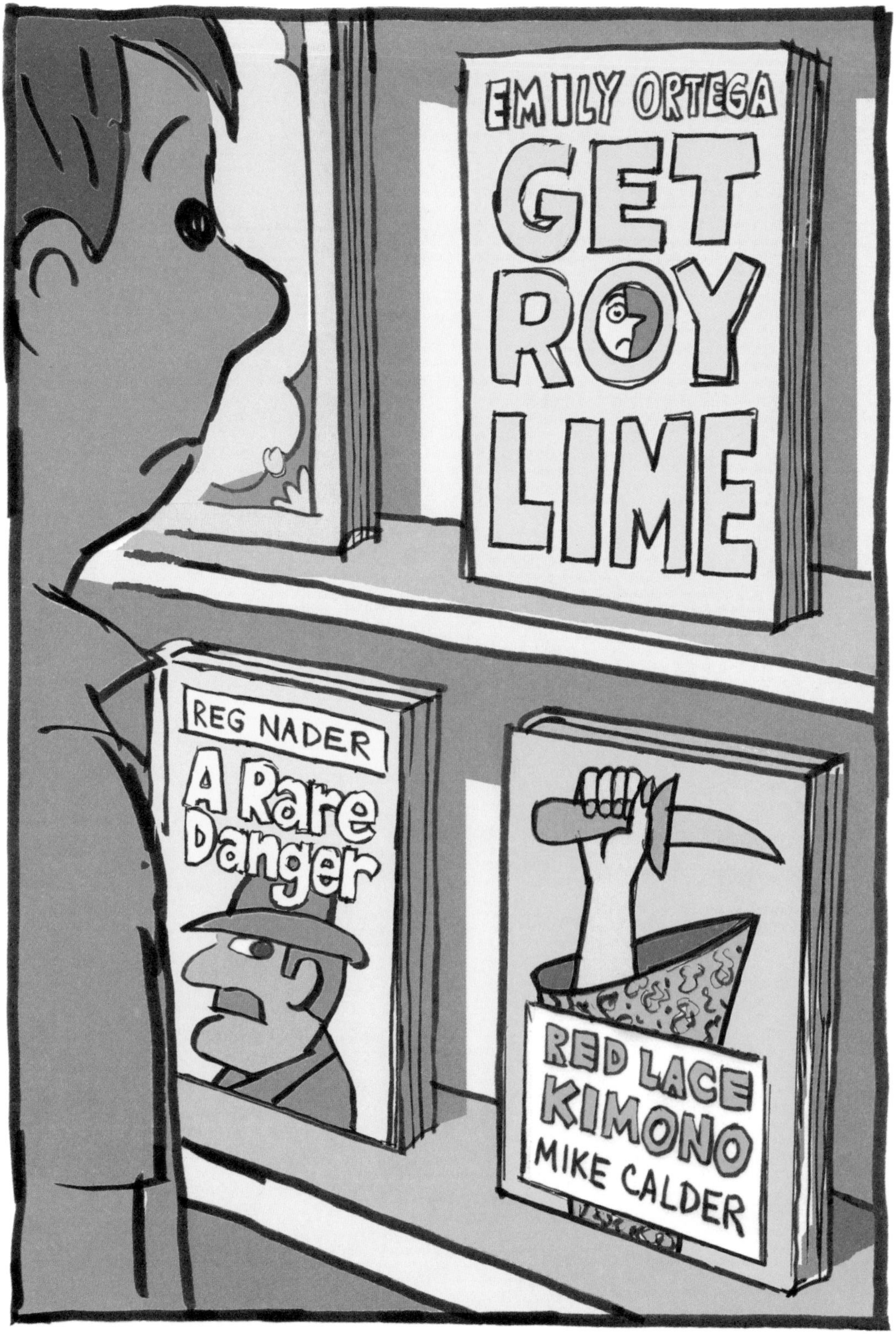
EMILY ORTEGA
GET ROY LIME
REG NADER
A Rare Danger
RED LACE KIMONO
MIKE CALDER

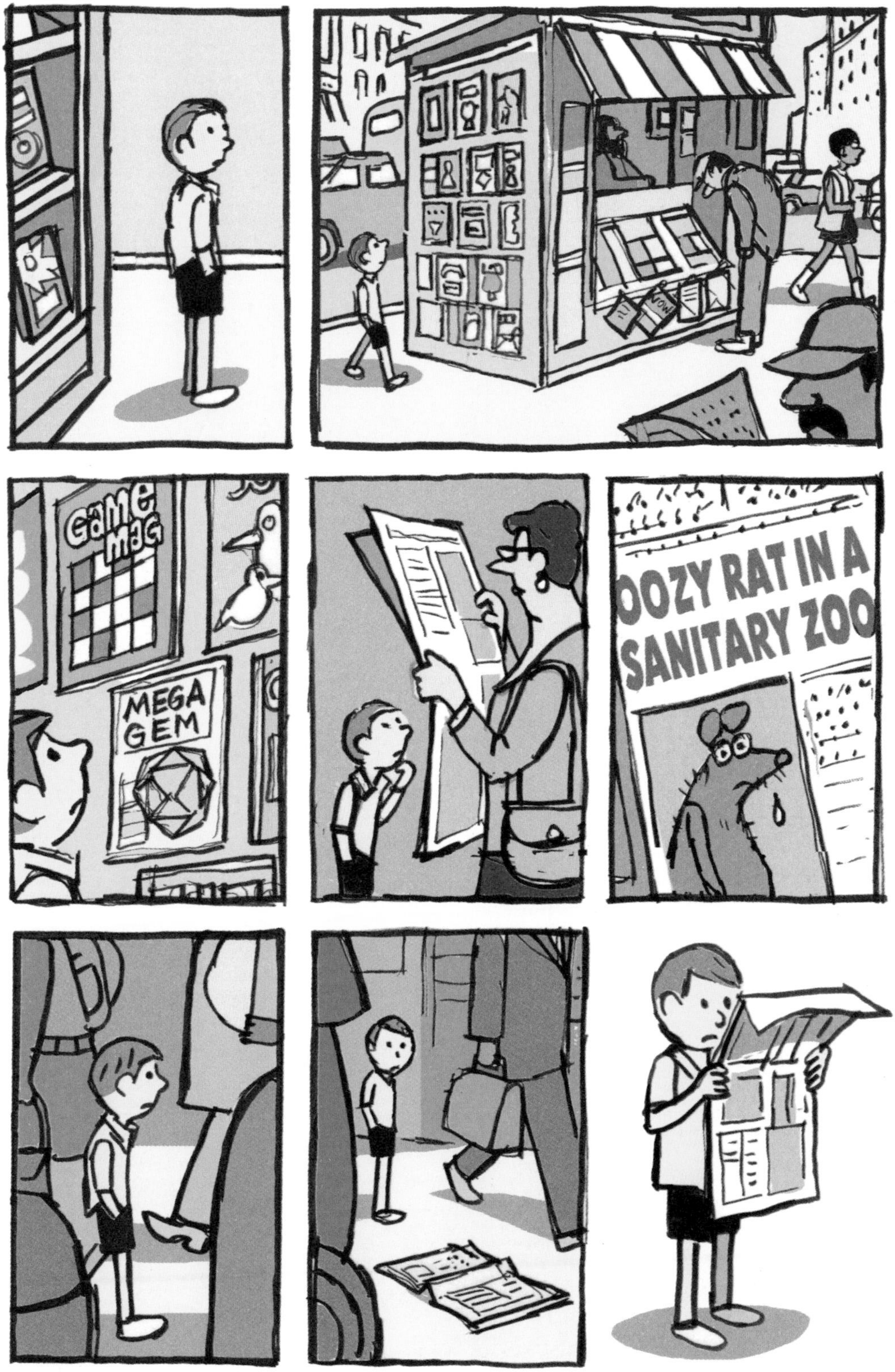
GAME MAG
MEGA GEM
OOZY RAT IN A
SANITARY ZOO

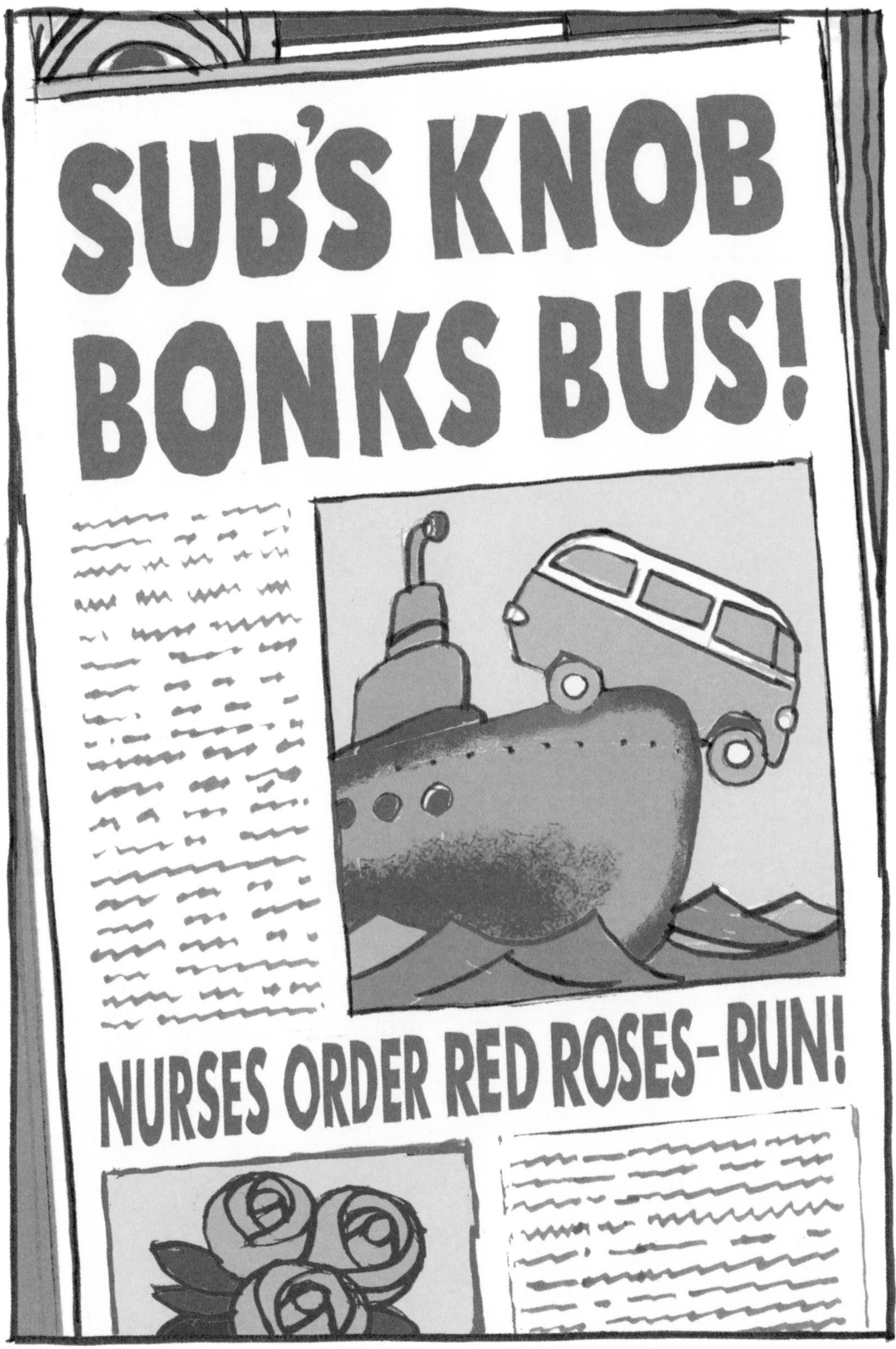
SUB'S KNOB BONKS BUS!
NURSES ORDER RED ROSES–RUN!

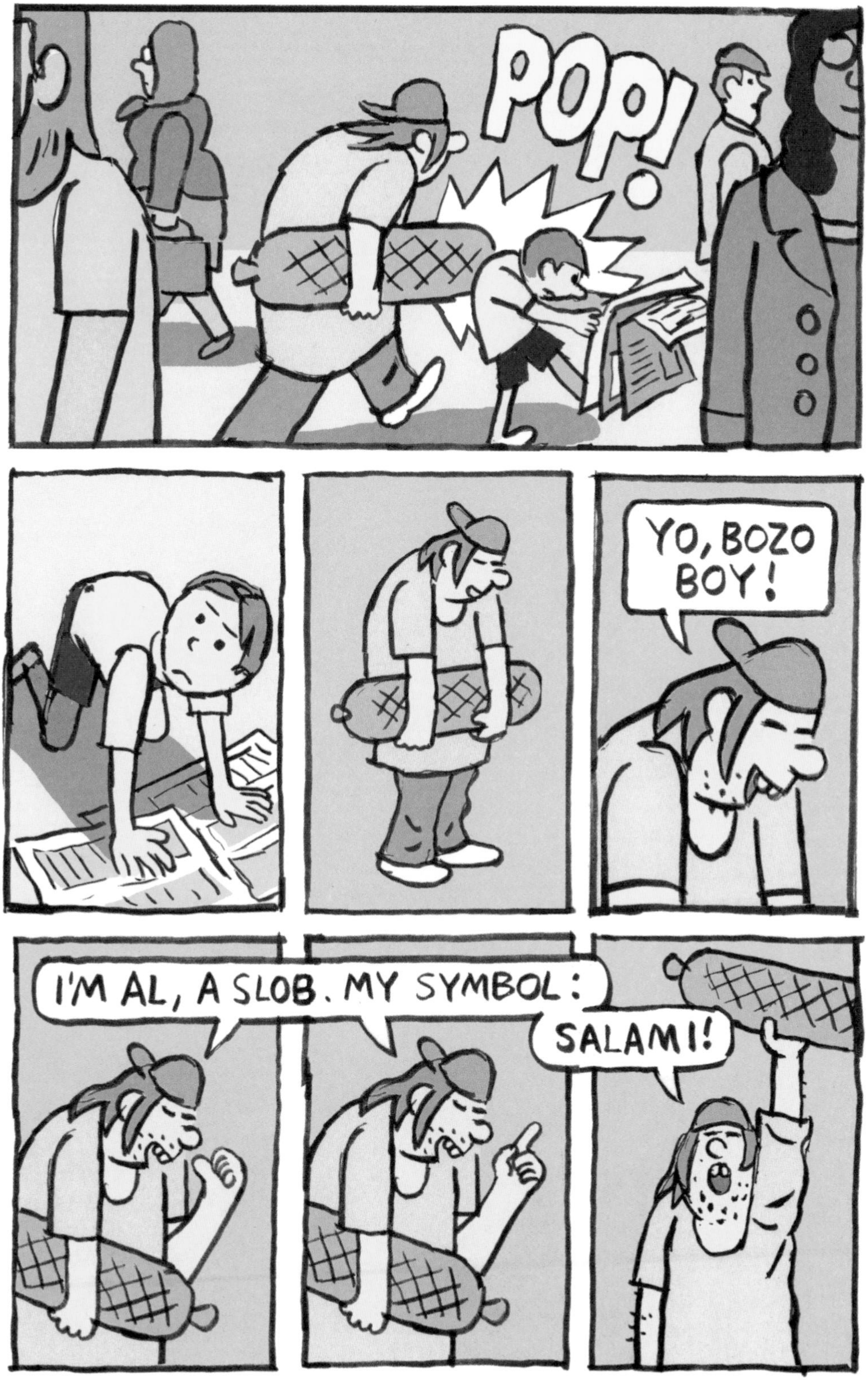
POP!
YO, BOZO BOY!
I'M AL, A SLOB. MY SYMBOL:
SALAMI!

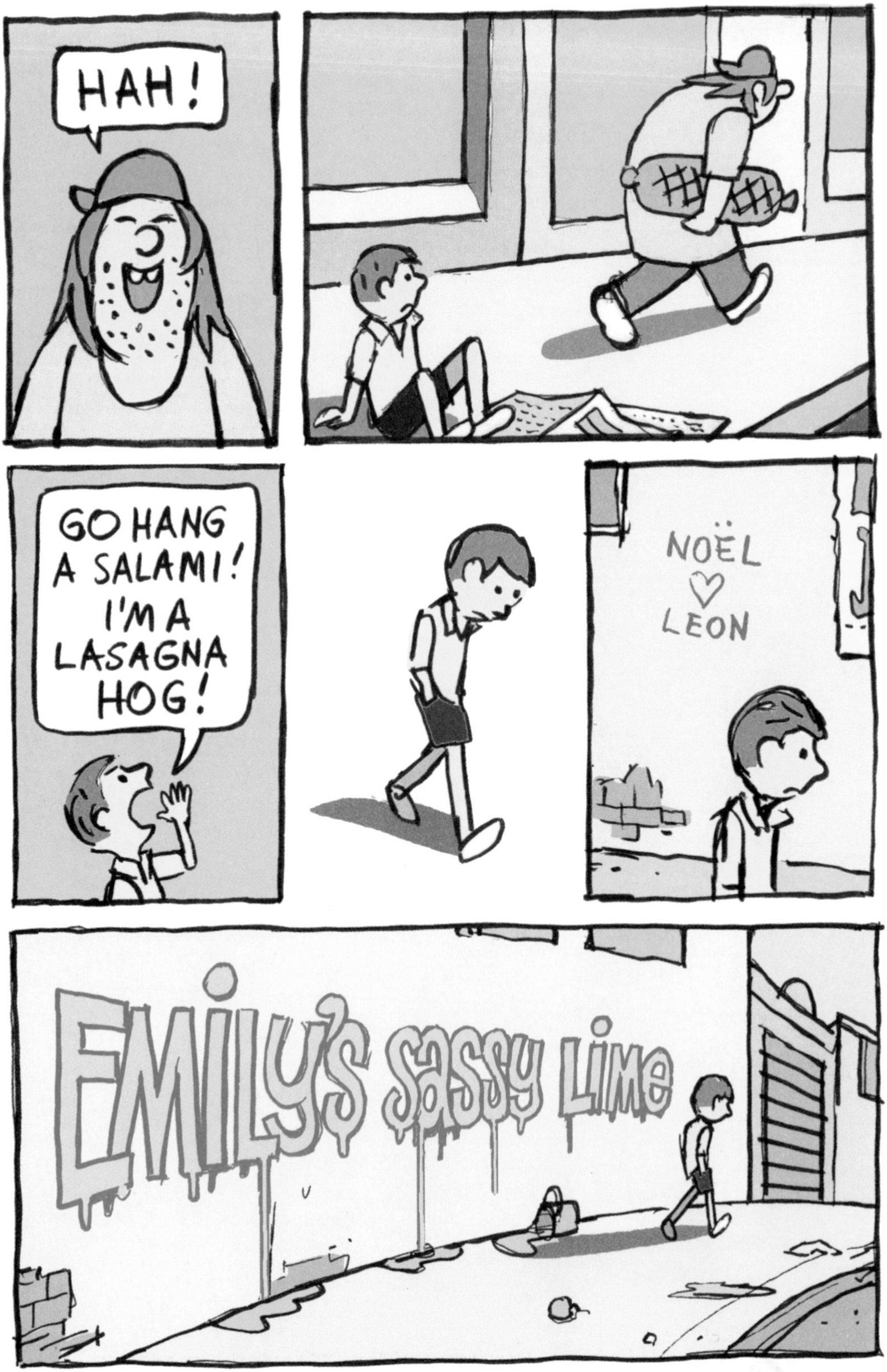
HAH!
GO HANG A SALAMI! I'M A LASAGNA HOG!
NOËL ♡ LEON
EMILY'S SASSY LIME

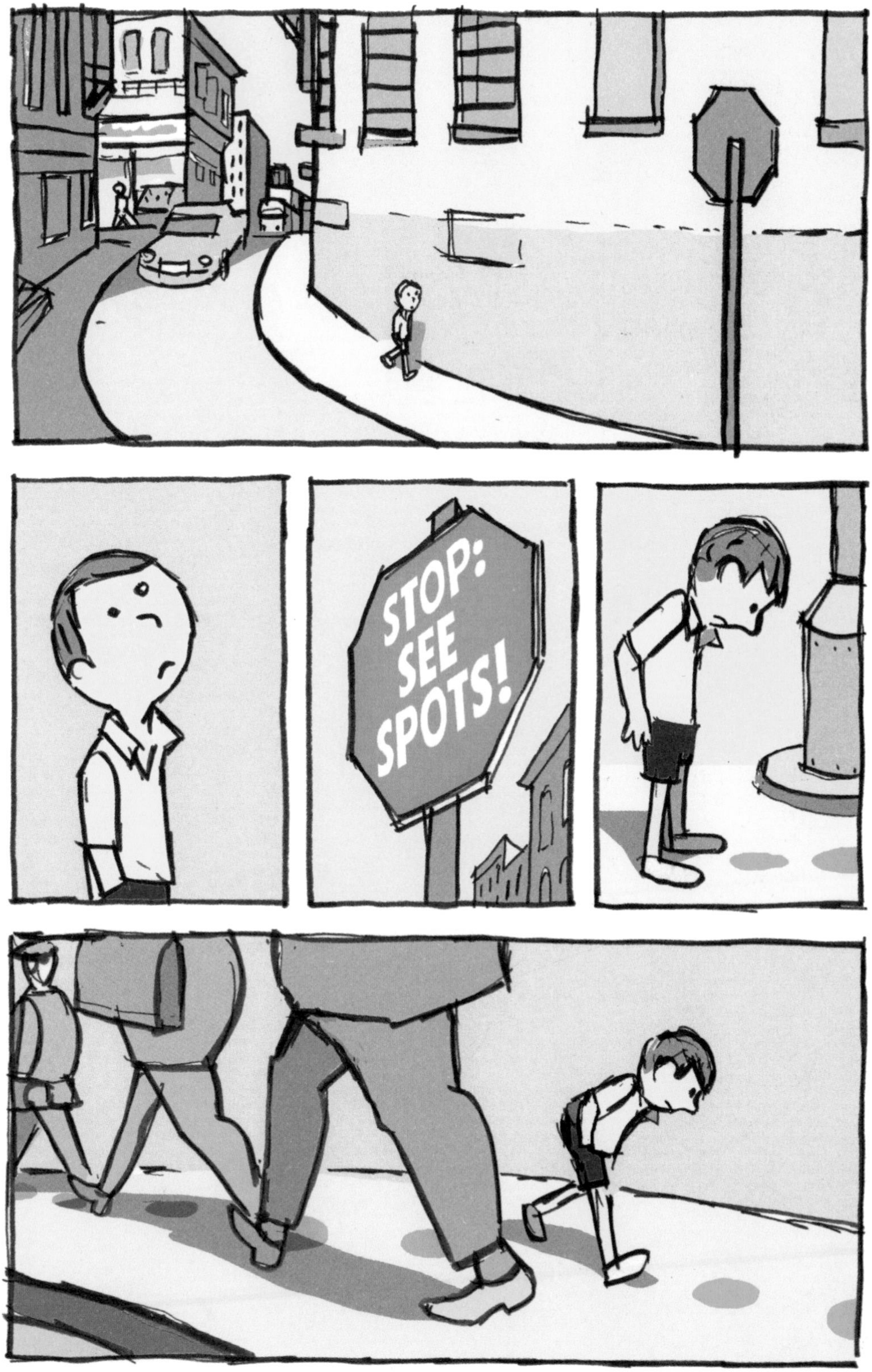
STOP: SEE SPOTS!

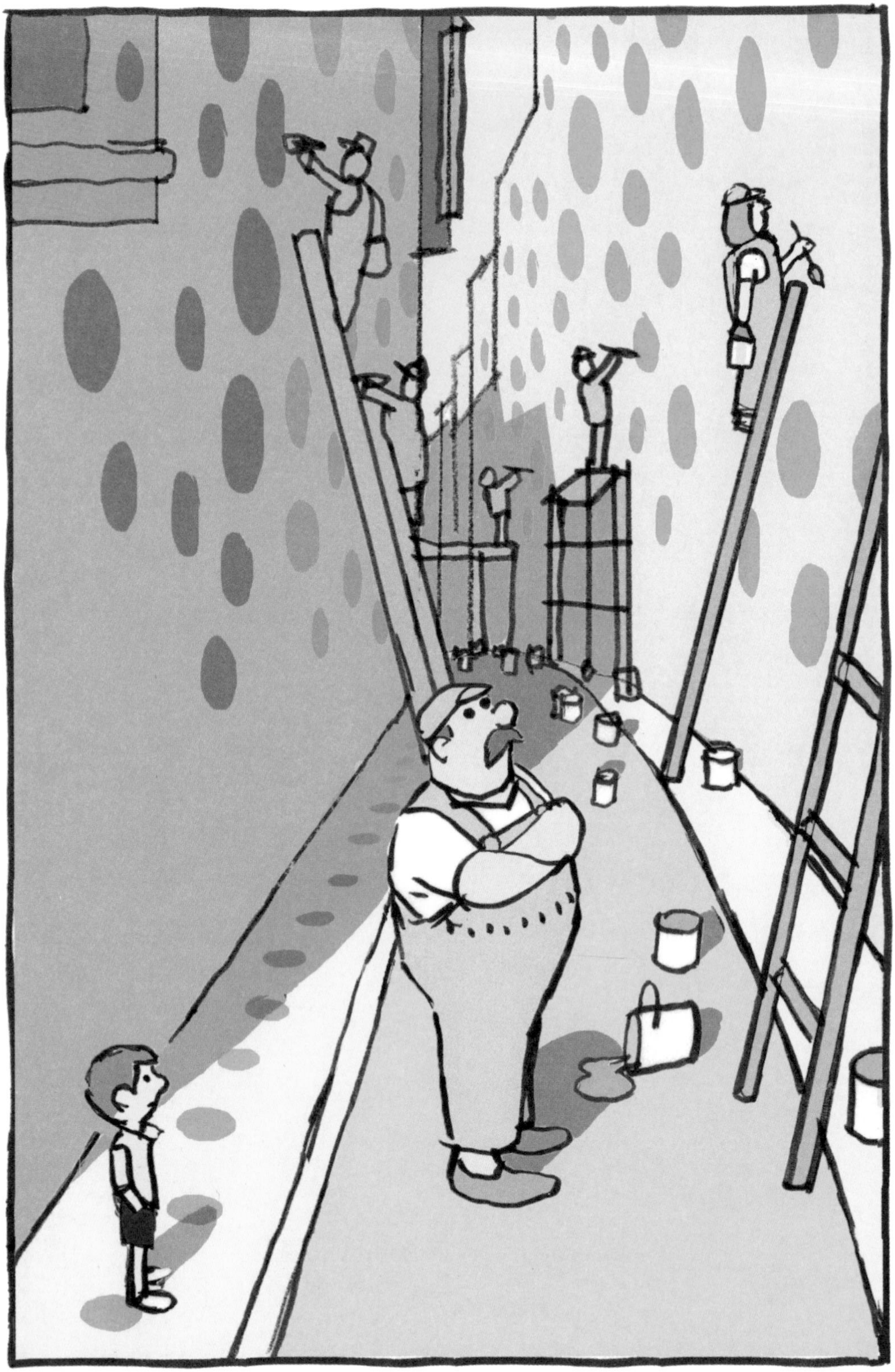

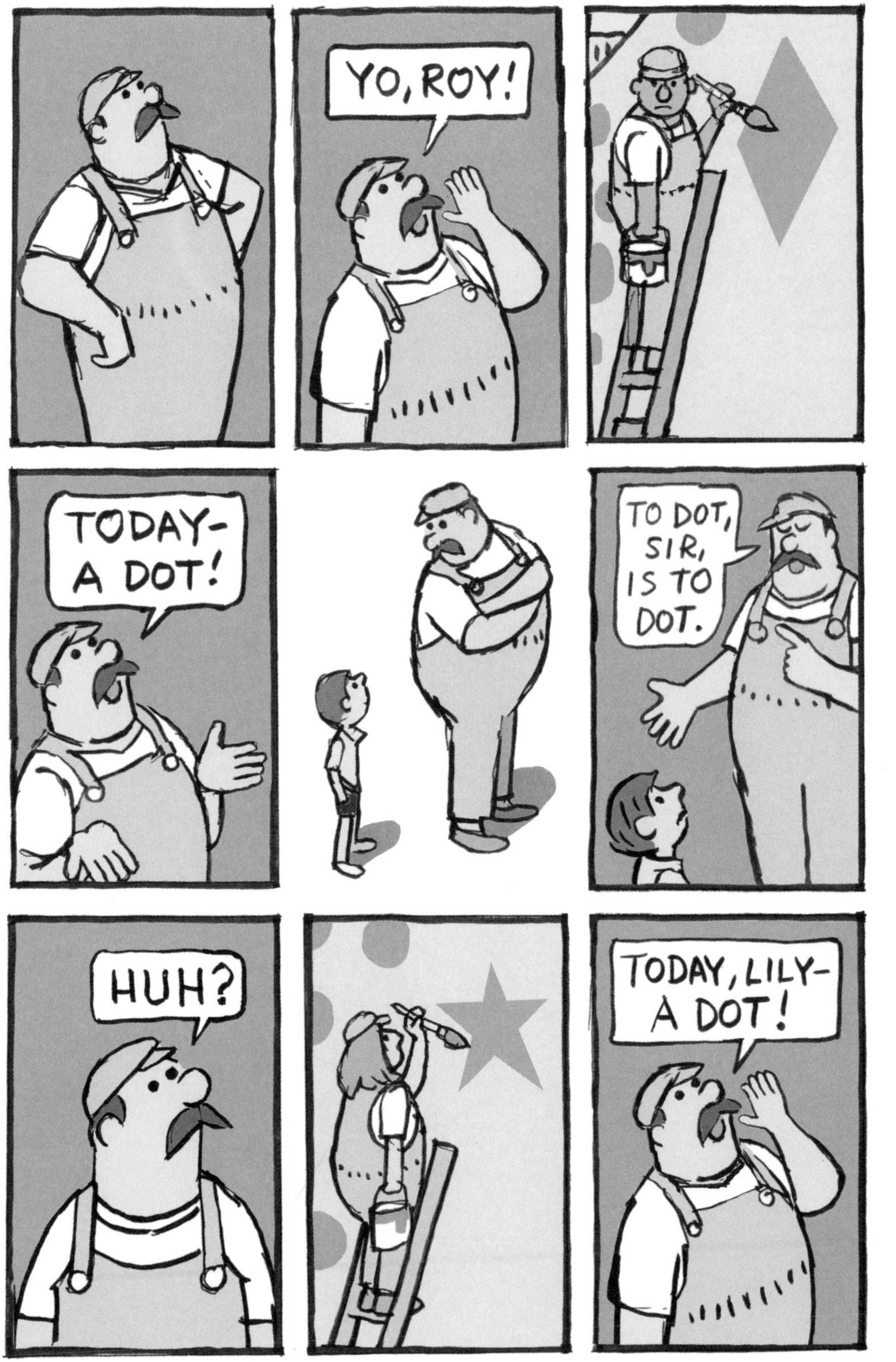
YO, ROY!
TODAY-
A DOT!
TO DOT, SIR, IS TO DOT.
HUH?
TODAY, LILY-
A DOT!

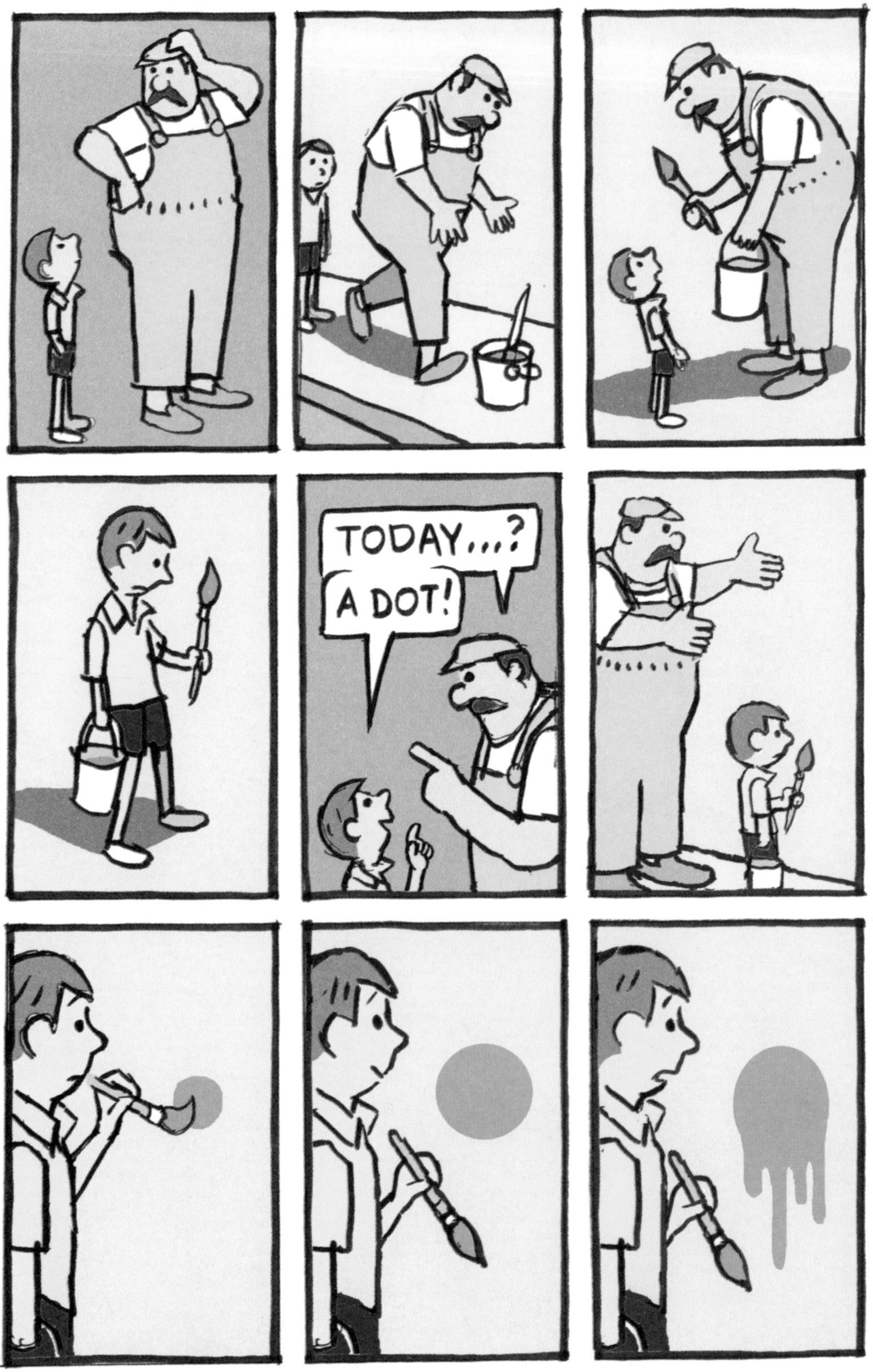
TODAY...?
A DOT!

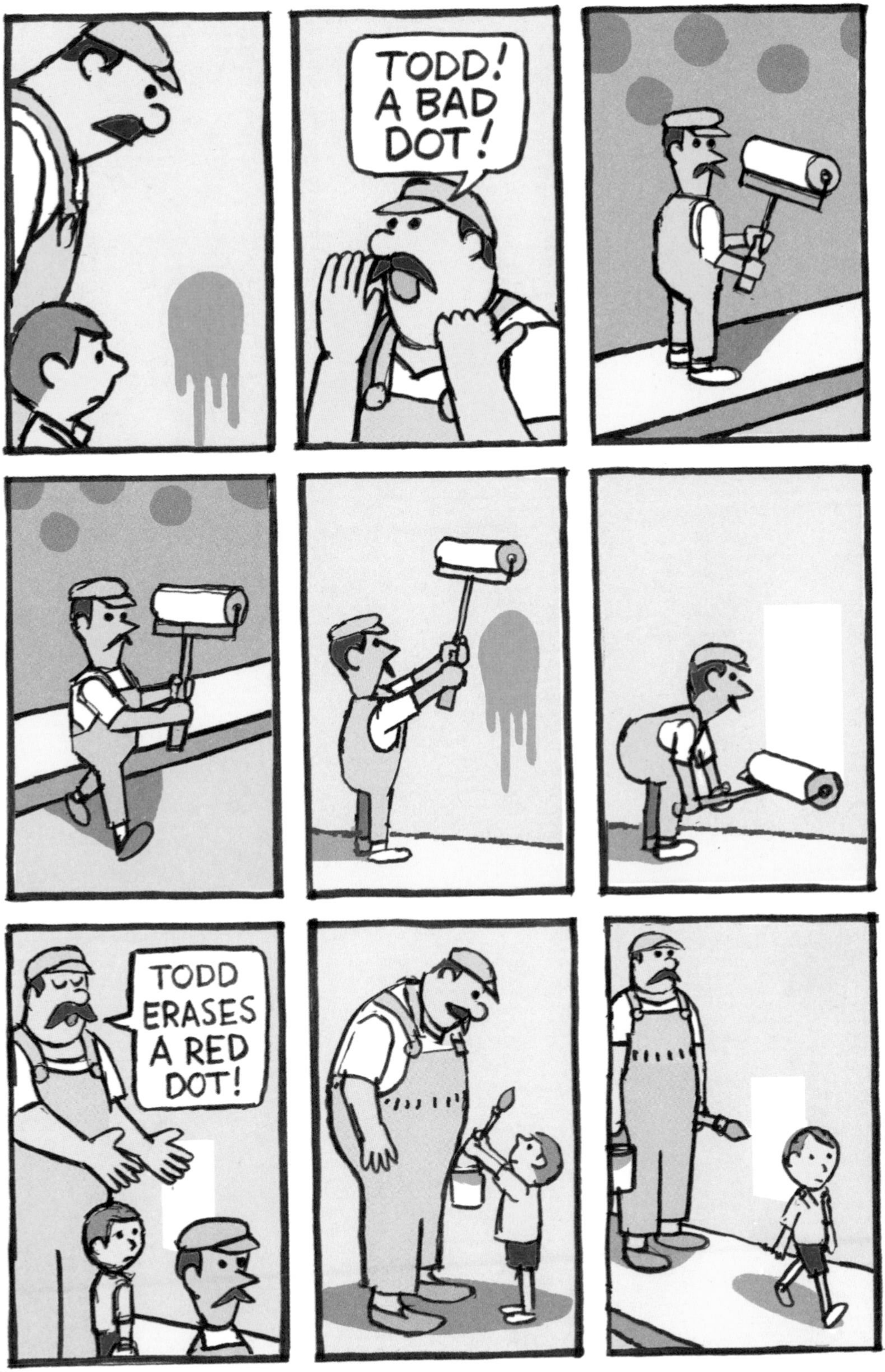
TODD! A BAD DOT!
TODD ERASES A RED DOT!

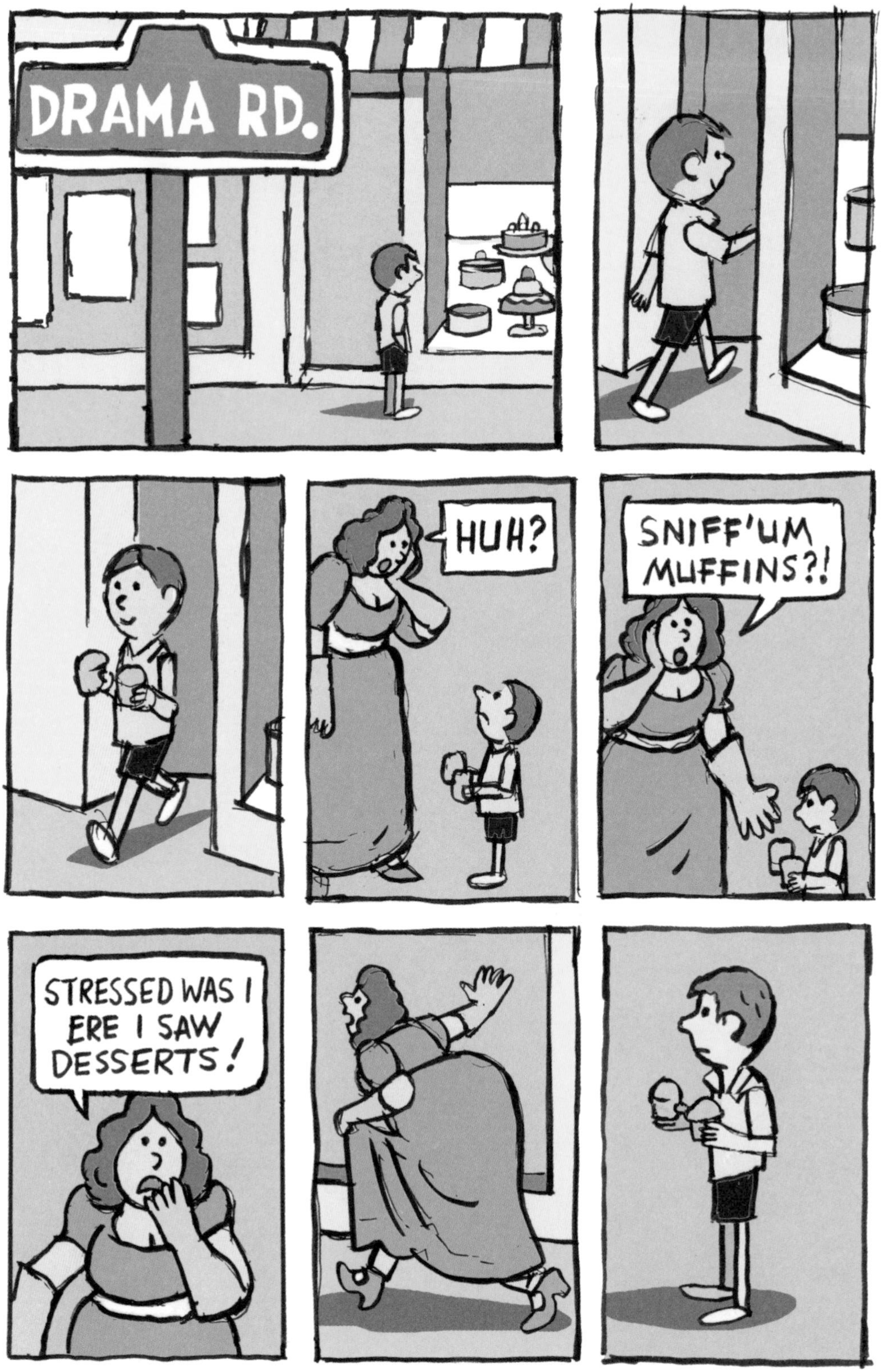
DRAMA RD.
HUH?
SNIFF'UM MUFFINS?!
STRESSED WAS I ERE I SAW DESSERTS!

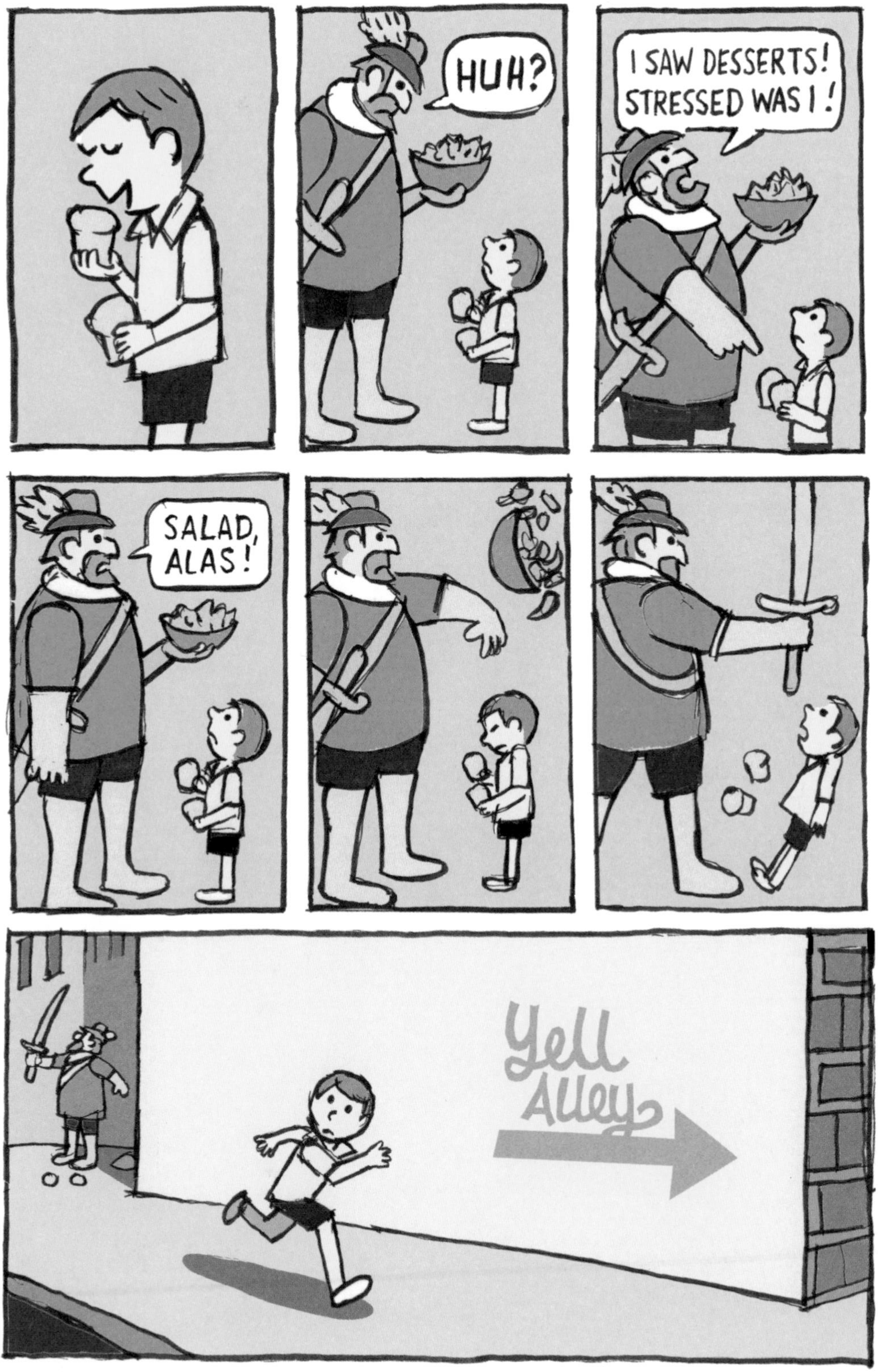
HUH?
I SAW DESSERTS! STRESSED WAS I!
SALAD, ALAS!
Yell Alley

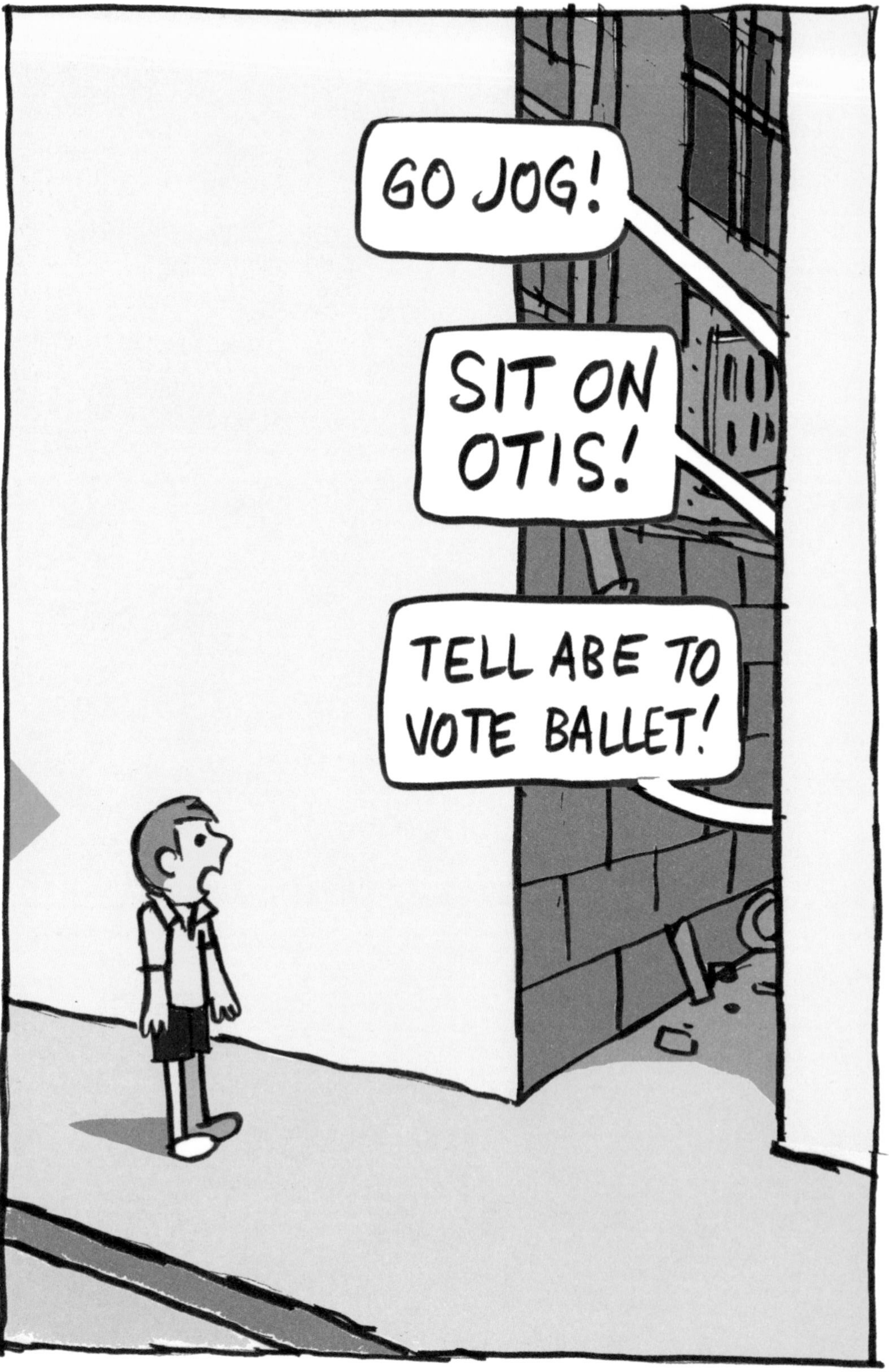
GO JOG!
SIT ON OTIS!
TELL ABE TO VOTE BALLET!

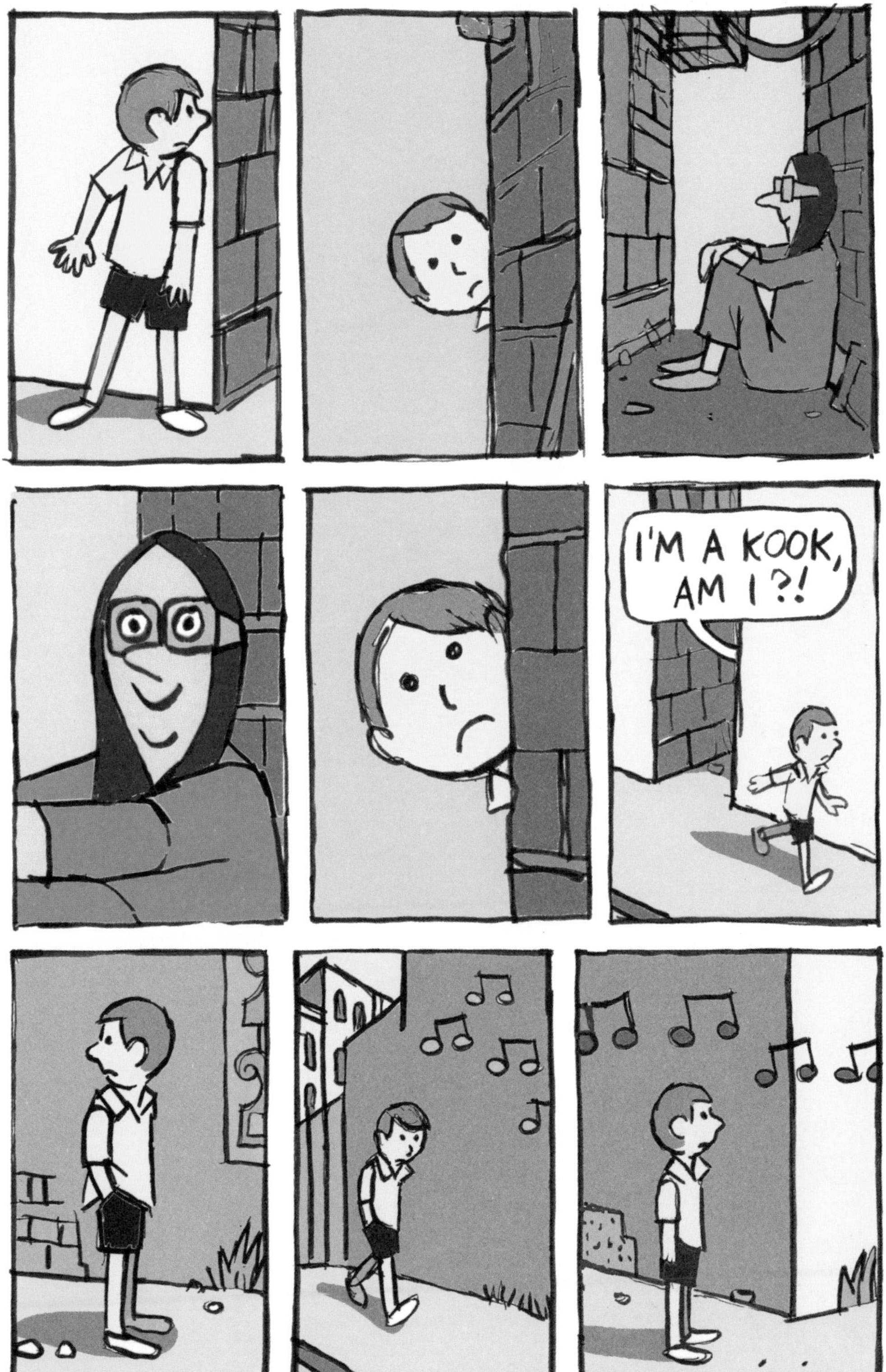
I'M A KOOK, AM I?!

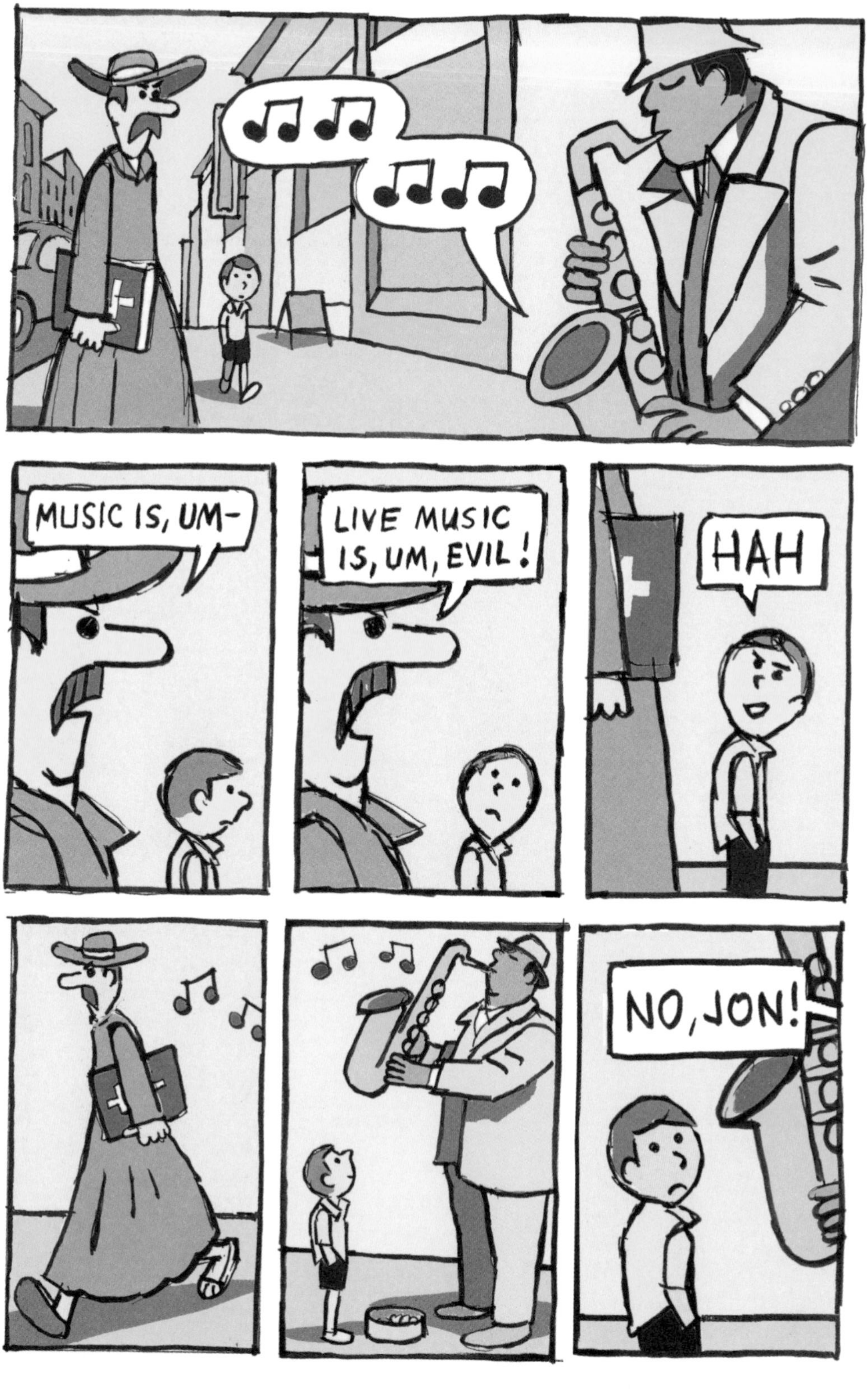
MUSIC IS, UM-
LIVE MUSIC IS, UM, EVIL!
HAH
NO, JON!

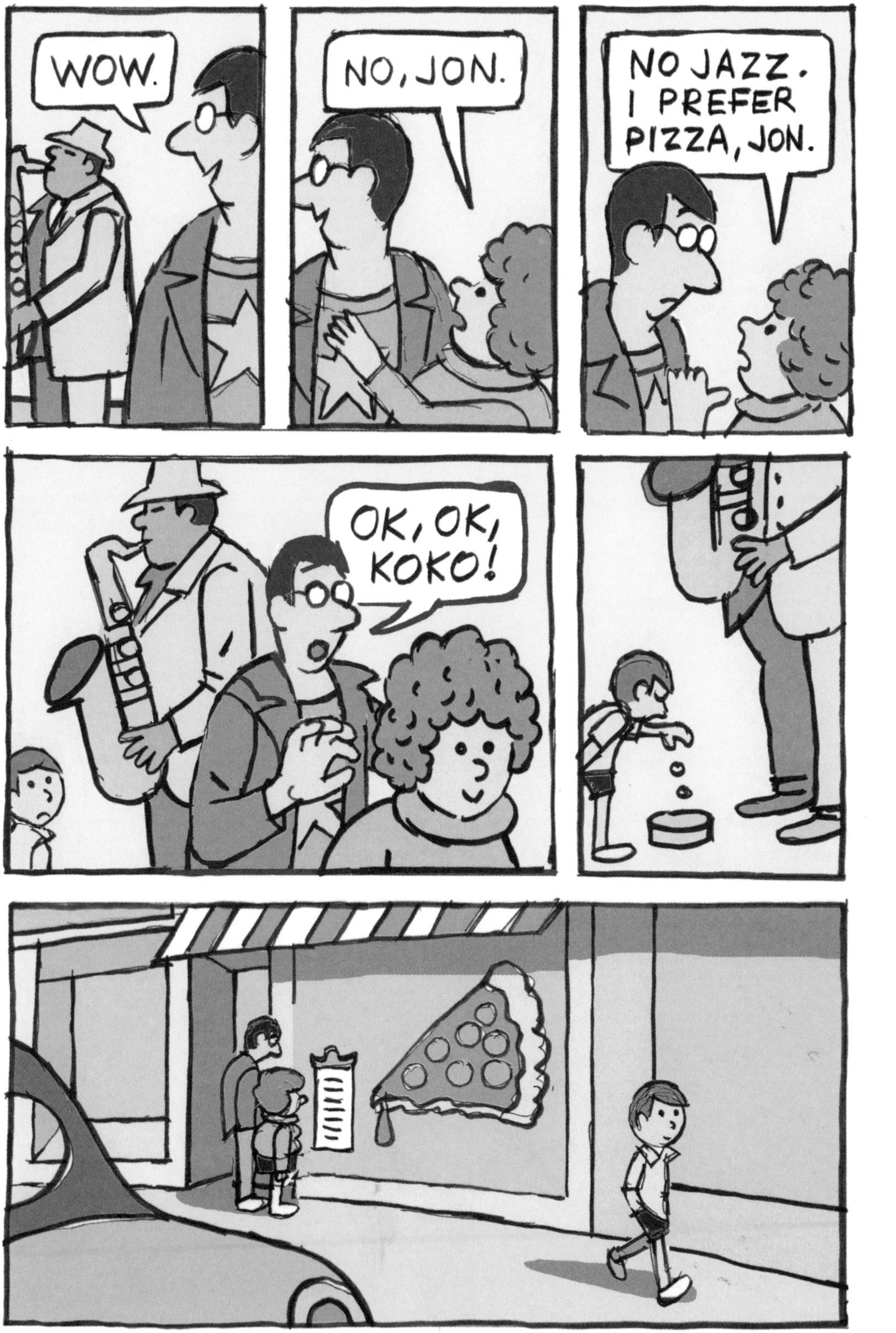
WOW.
NO, JON.
NO JAZZ. I PREFER PIZZA, JON.
OK, OK, KOKO!

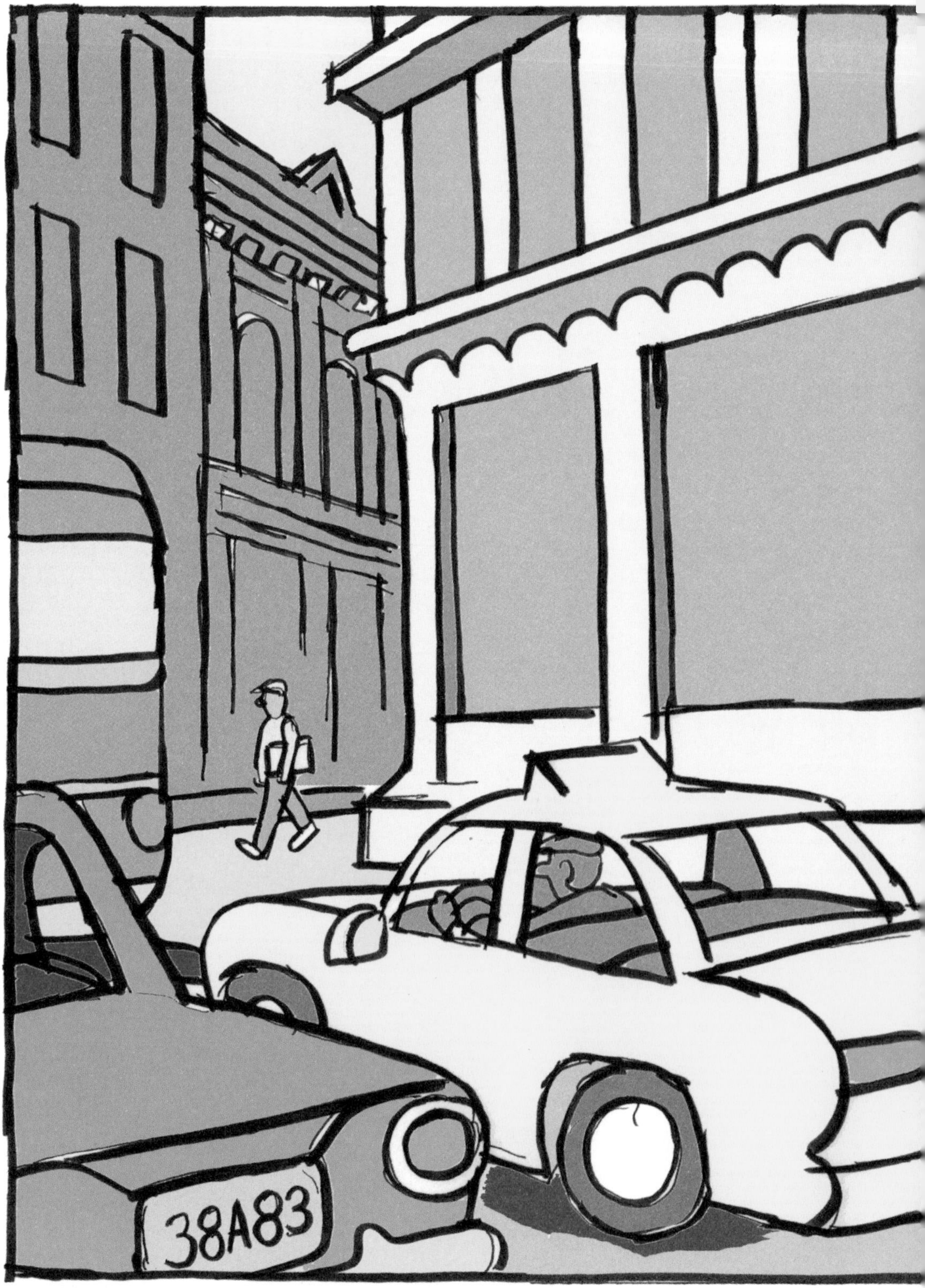
38A83

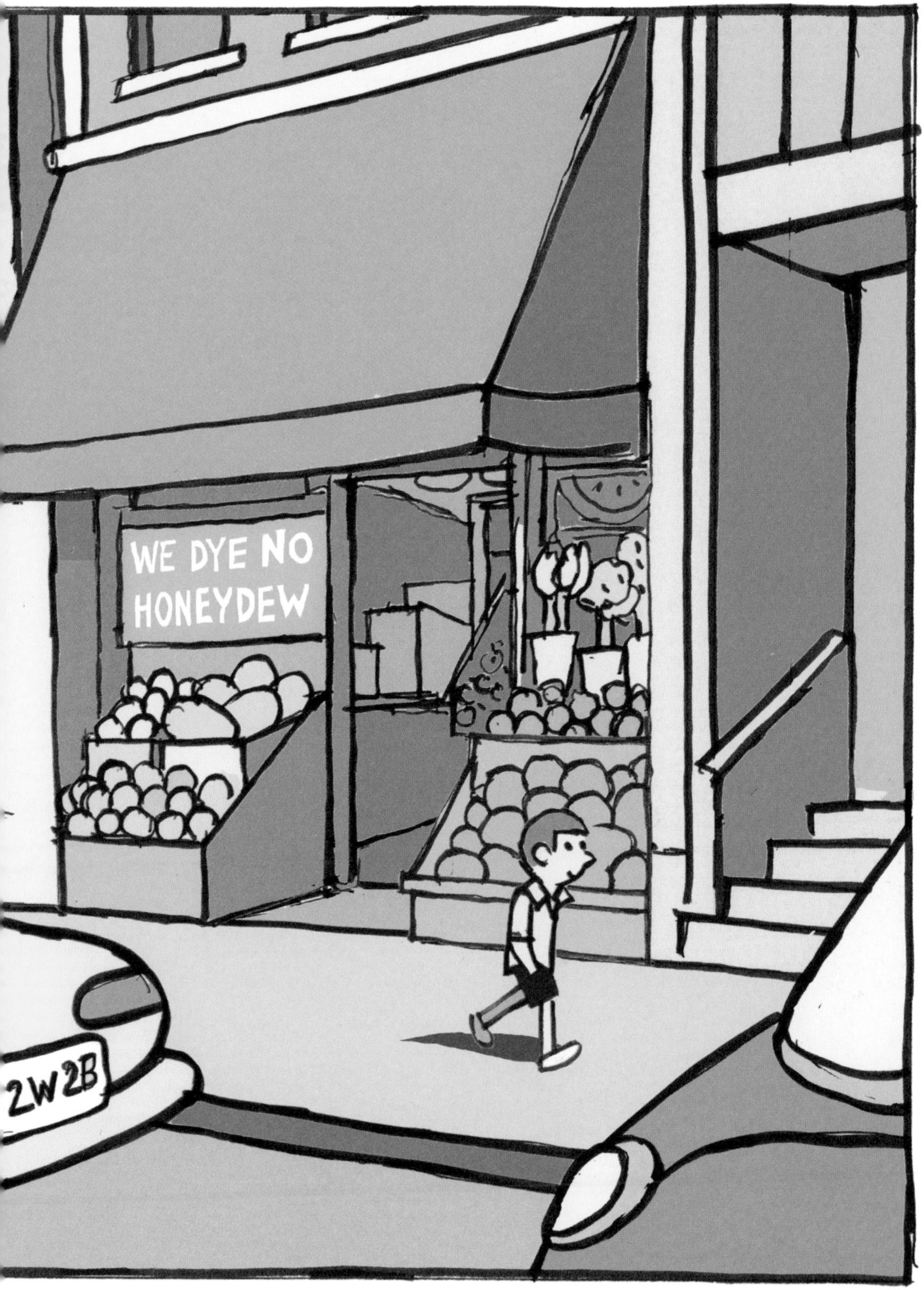
WE DYE NO
HONEYDEW
2W2B

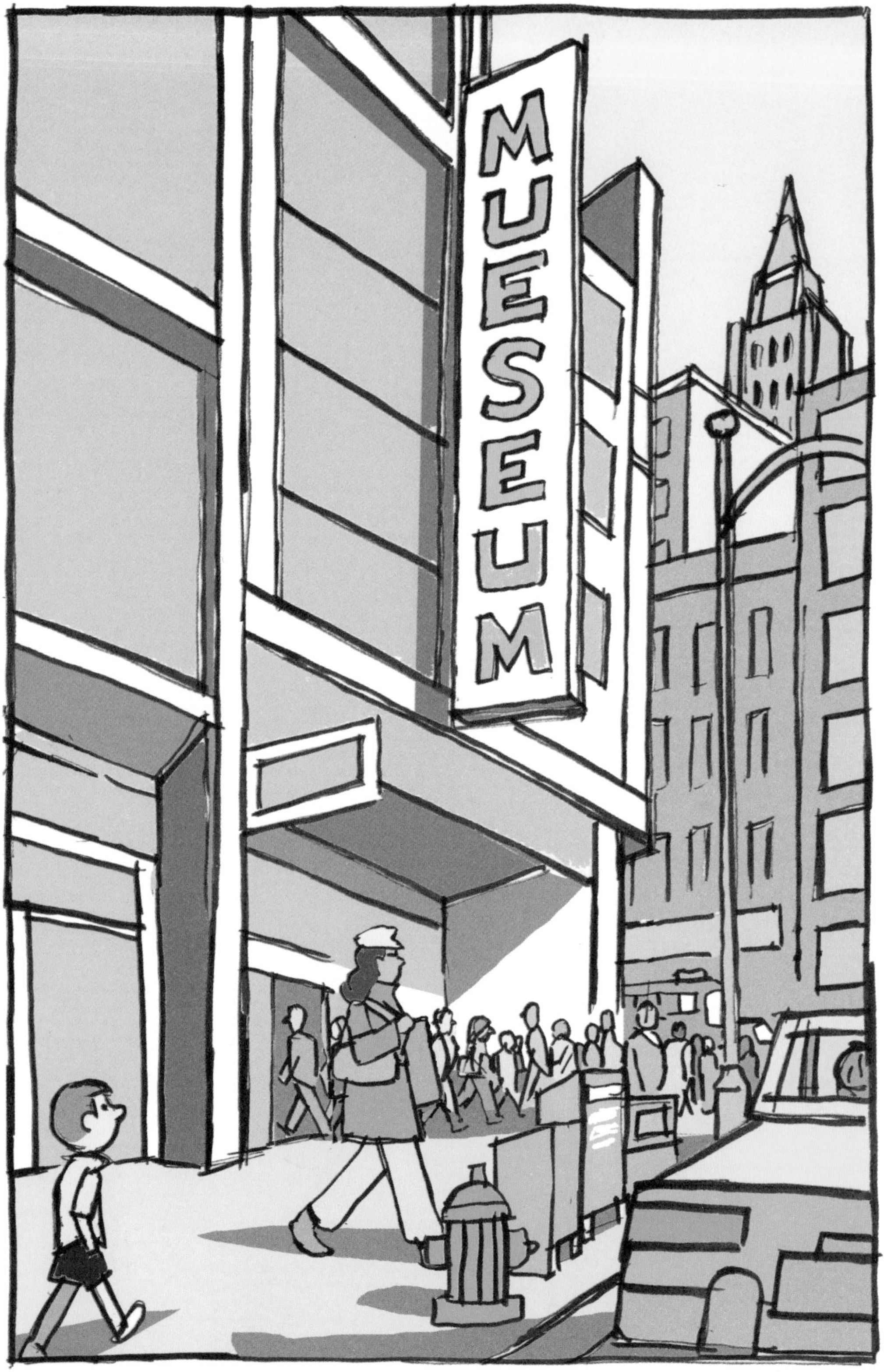
MUSEUM

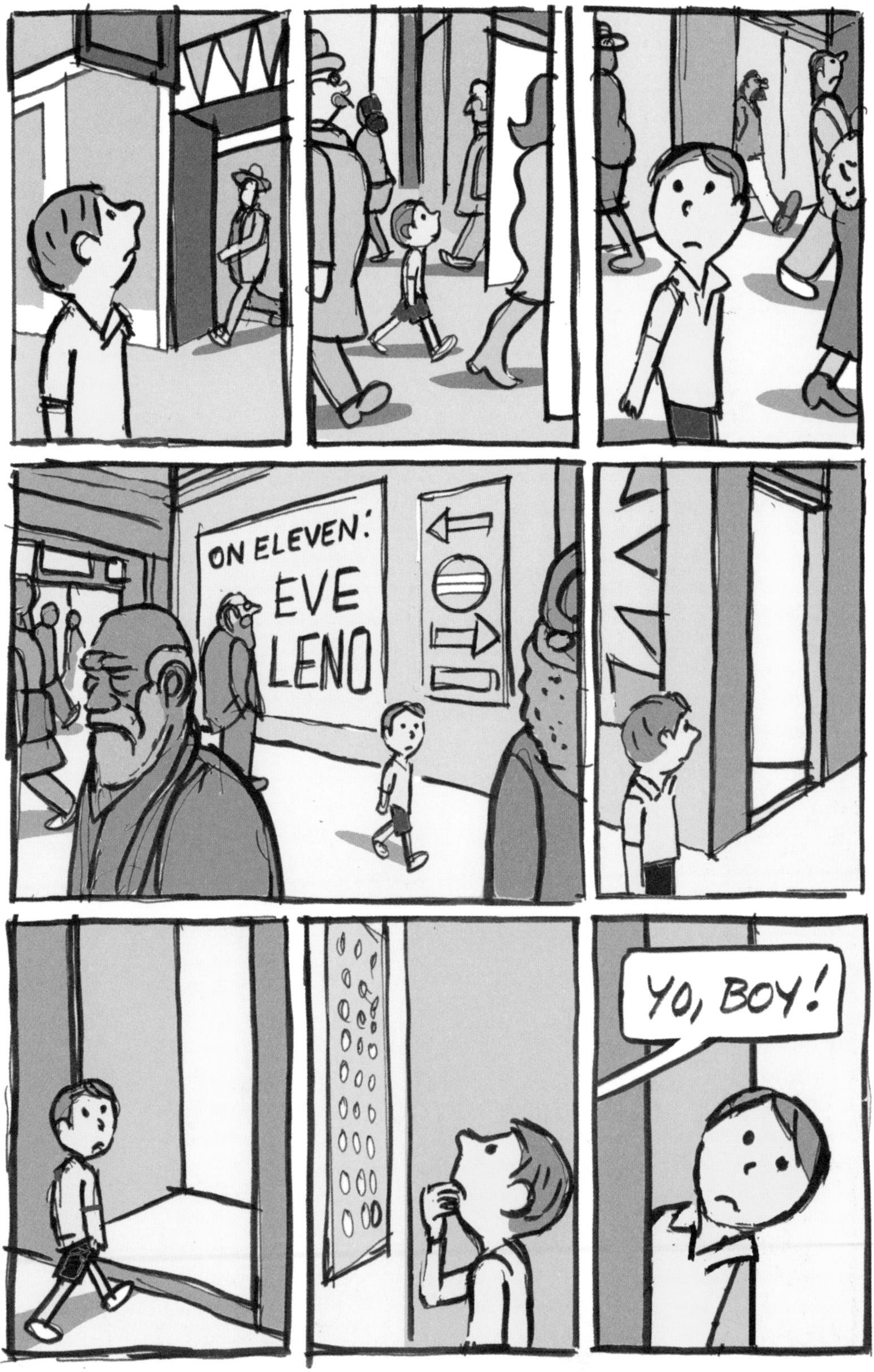
ON ELEVEN:
EVE
LENO
YO, BOY!

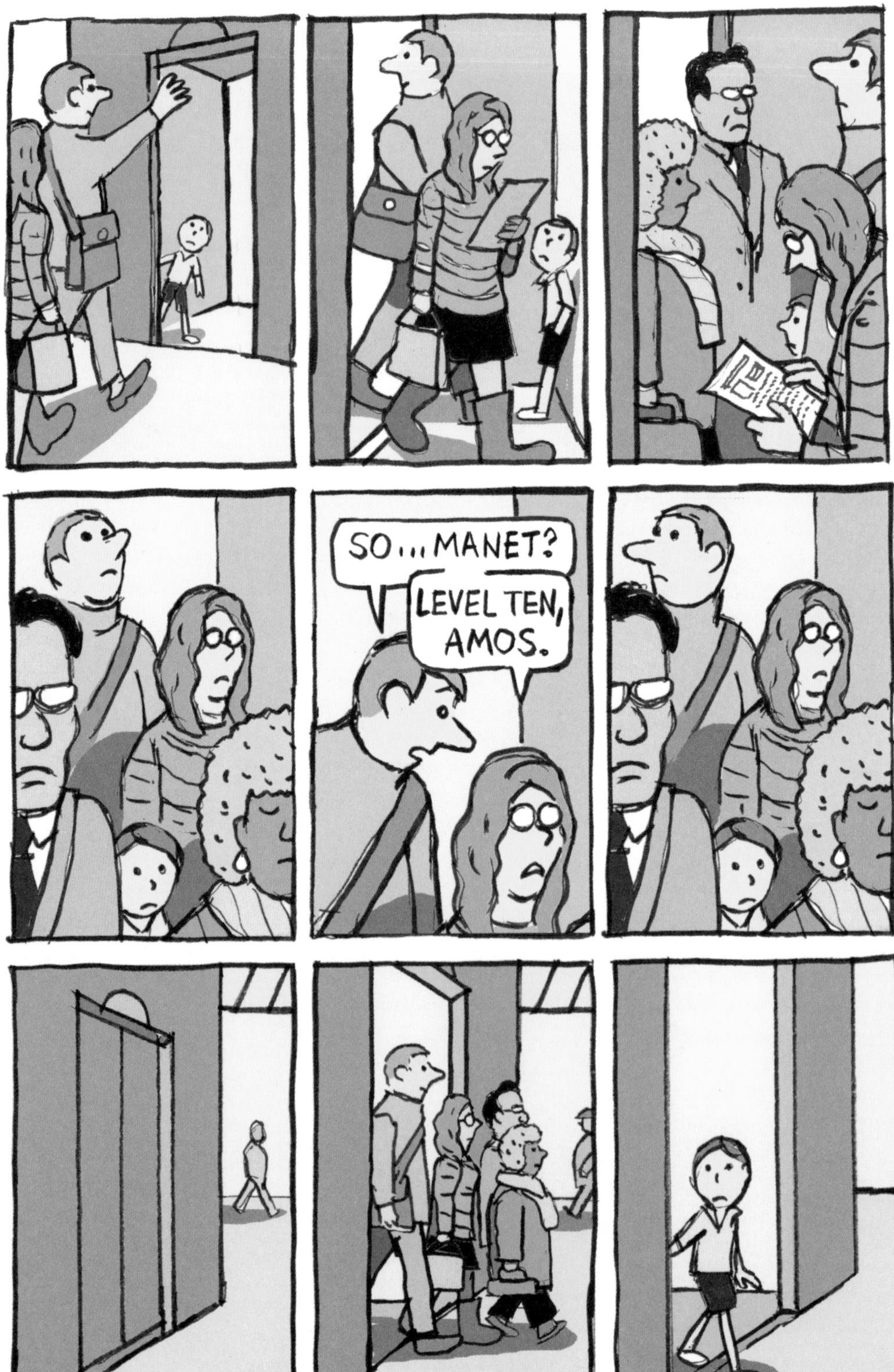
SO... MANET?
LEVEL TEN, AMOS.

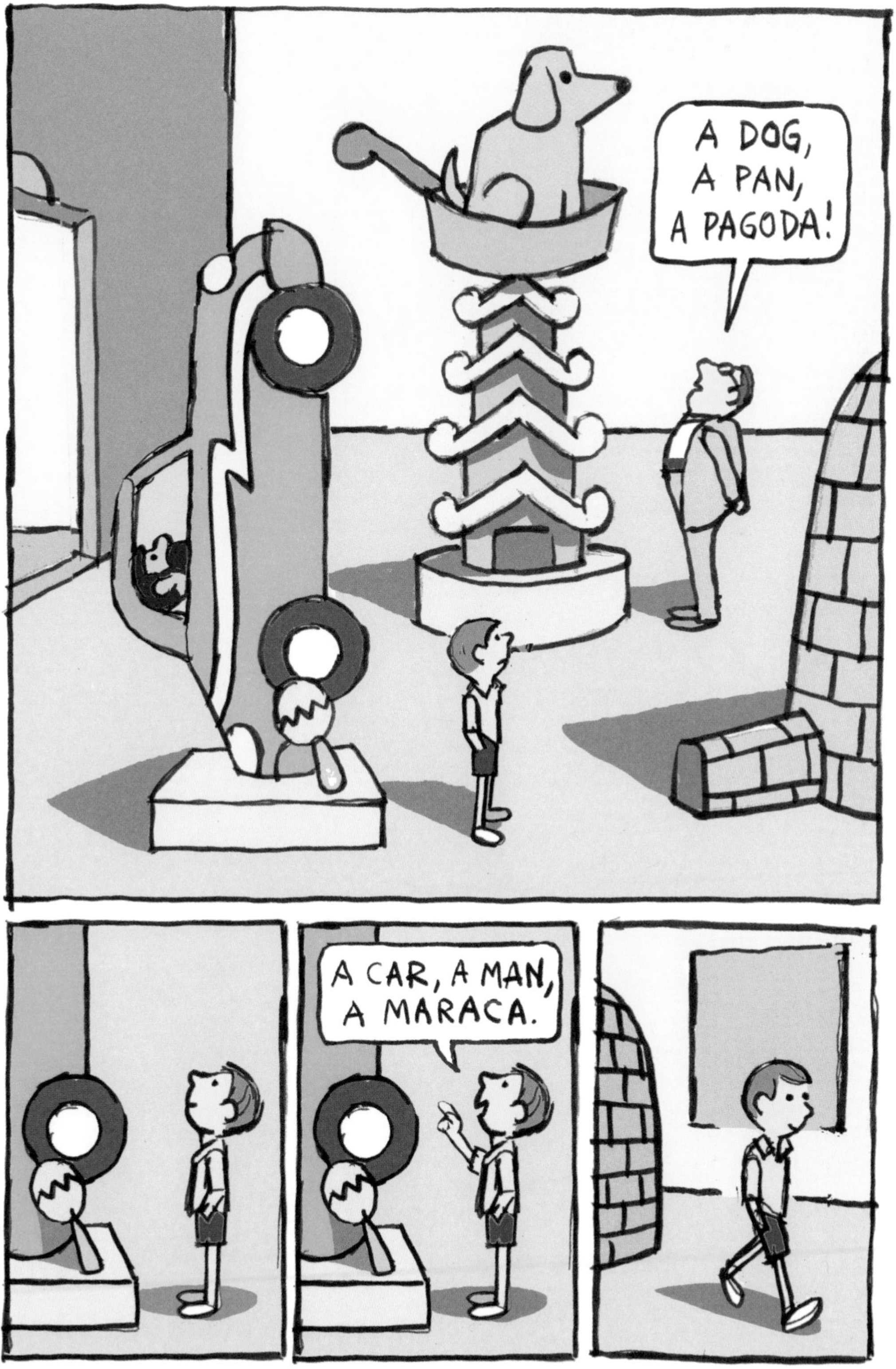
A DOG,
A PAN,
A PAGODA!
A CAR, A MAN,
A MARACA.

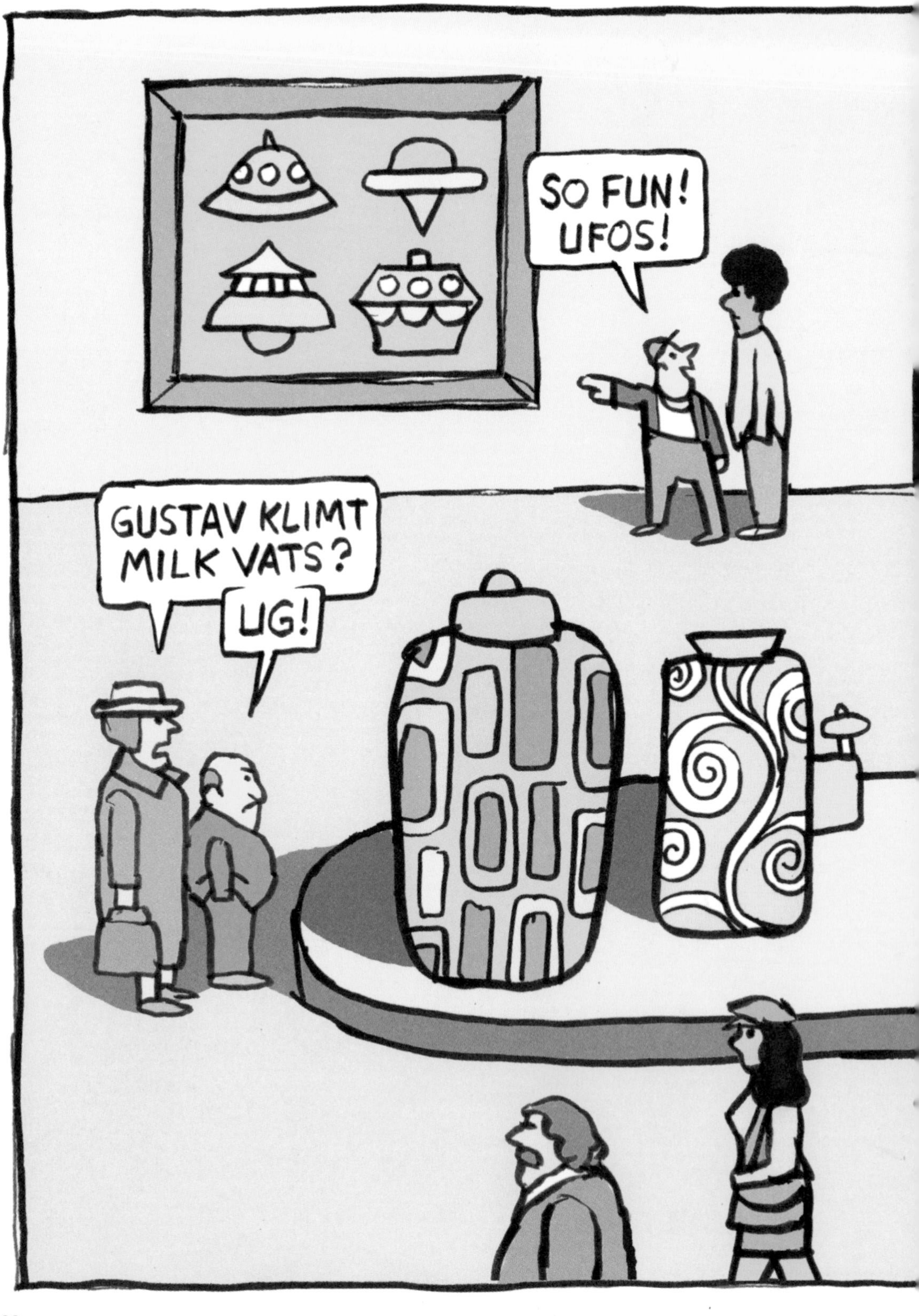
SO FUN! UFOS!
GUSTAV KLIMT MILK VATS?
UG!

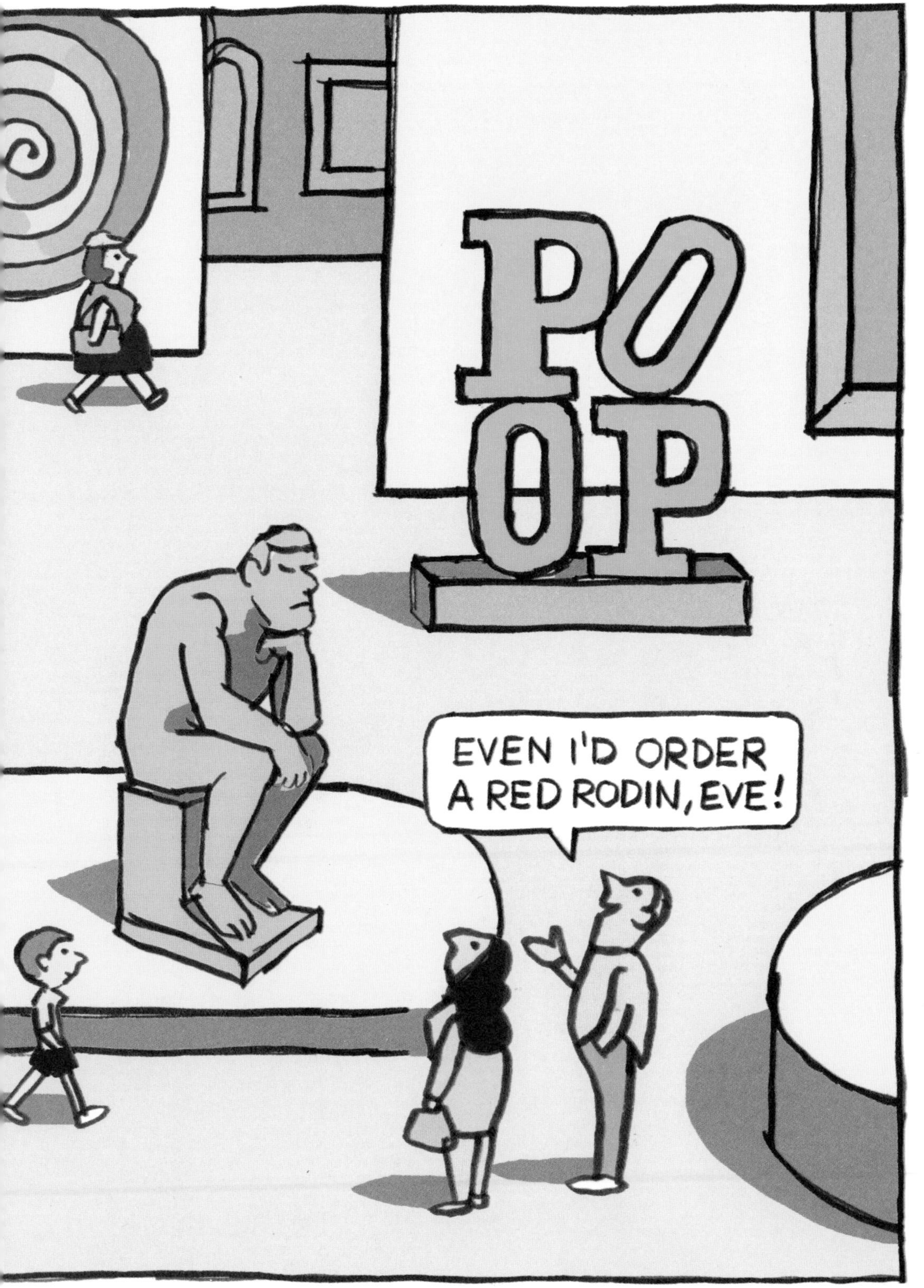
PO
OP
EVEN I'D ORDER A RED RODIN, EVE!

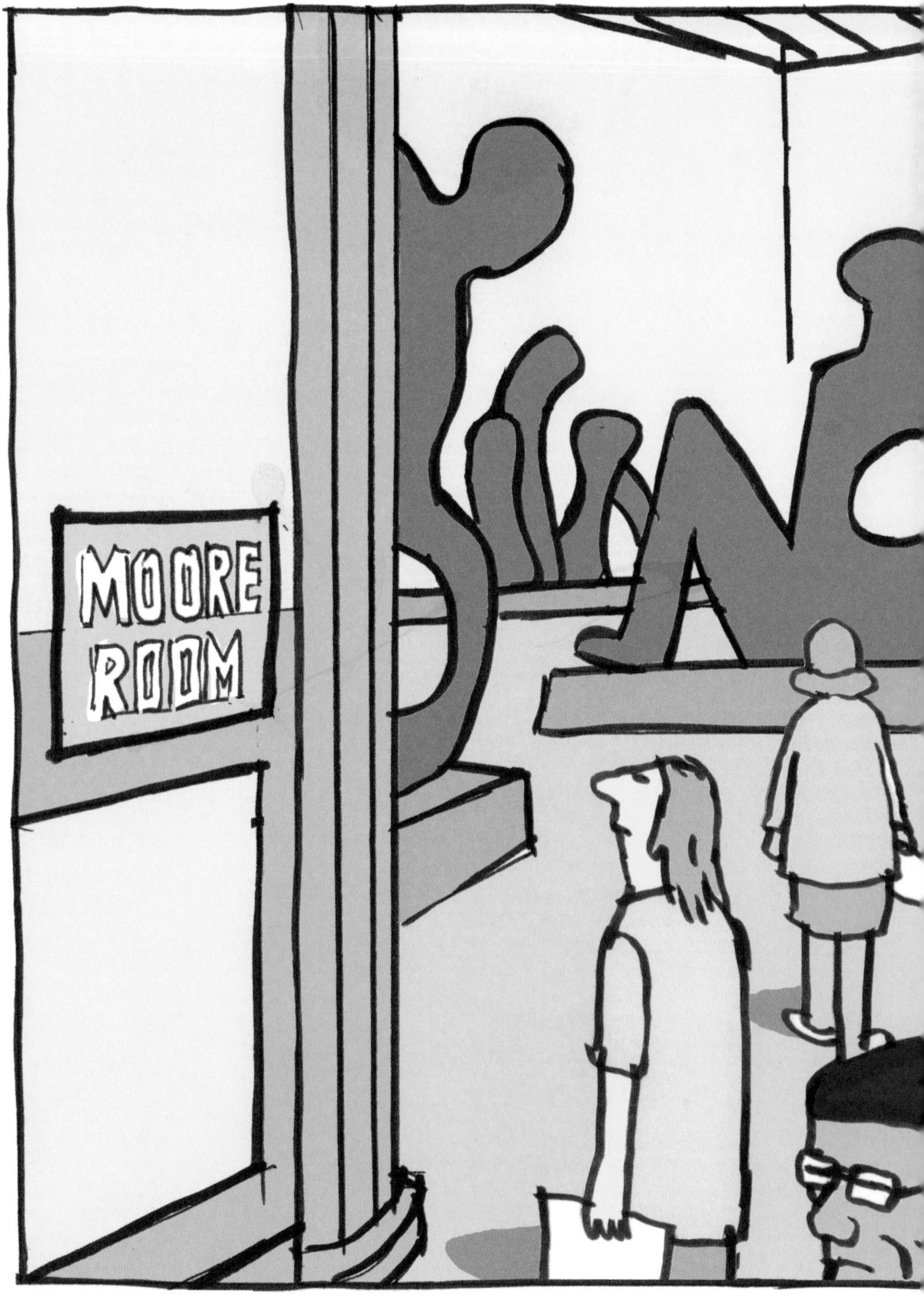
MOORE
ROOM

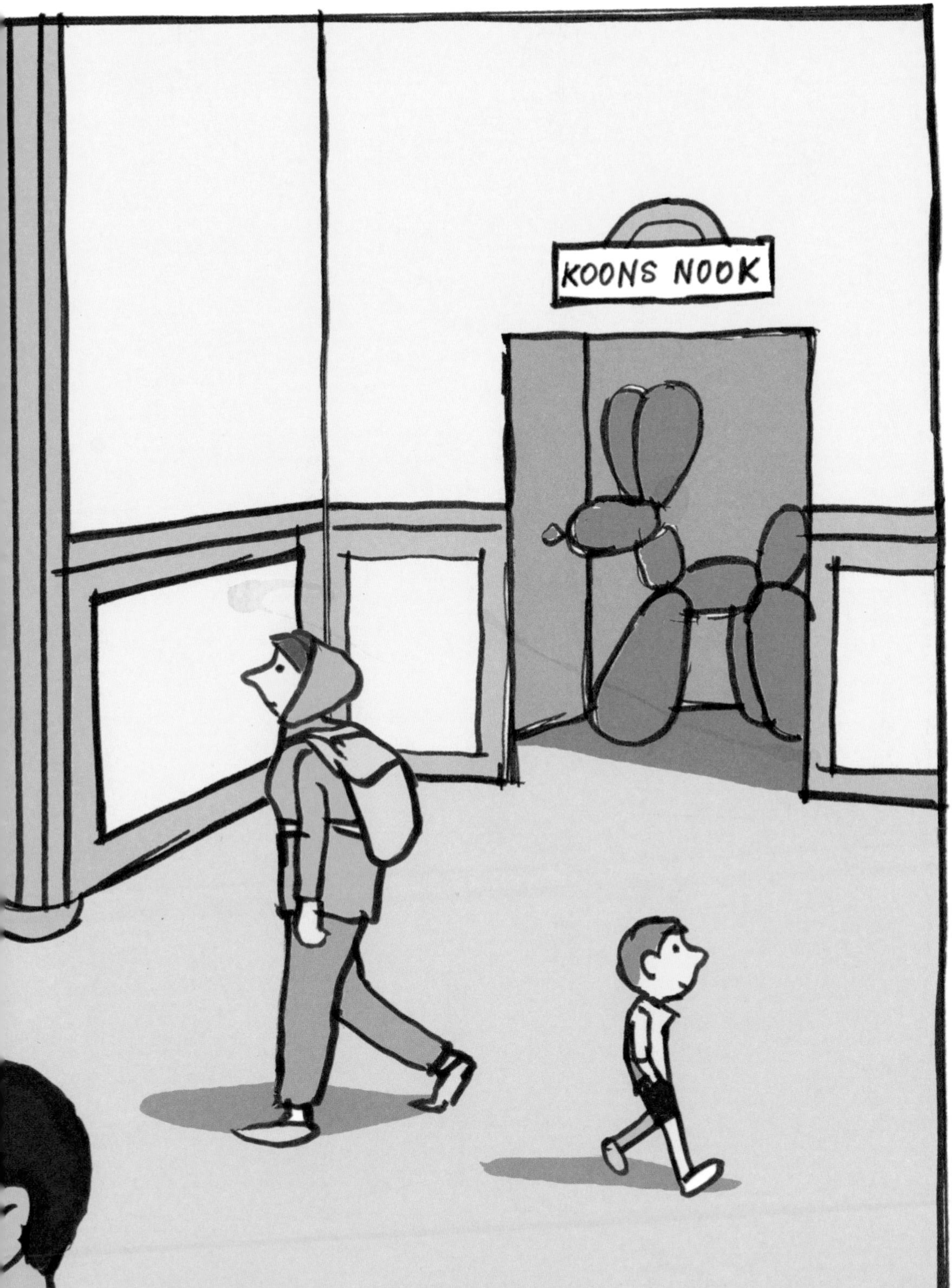
KOONS NOOK

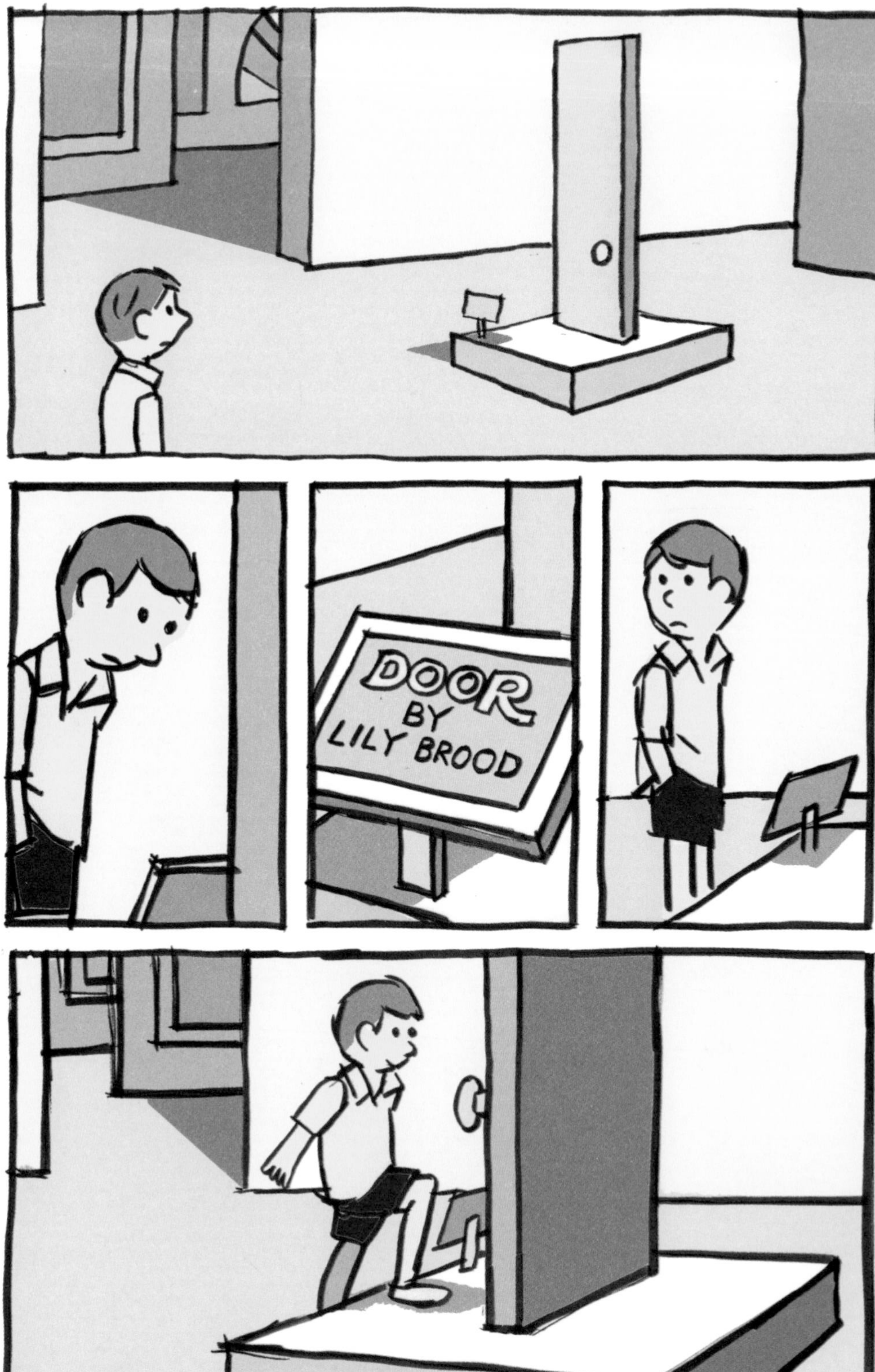
DOOR
BY
LILY BROOD

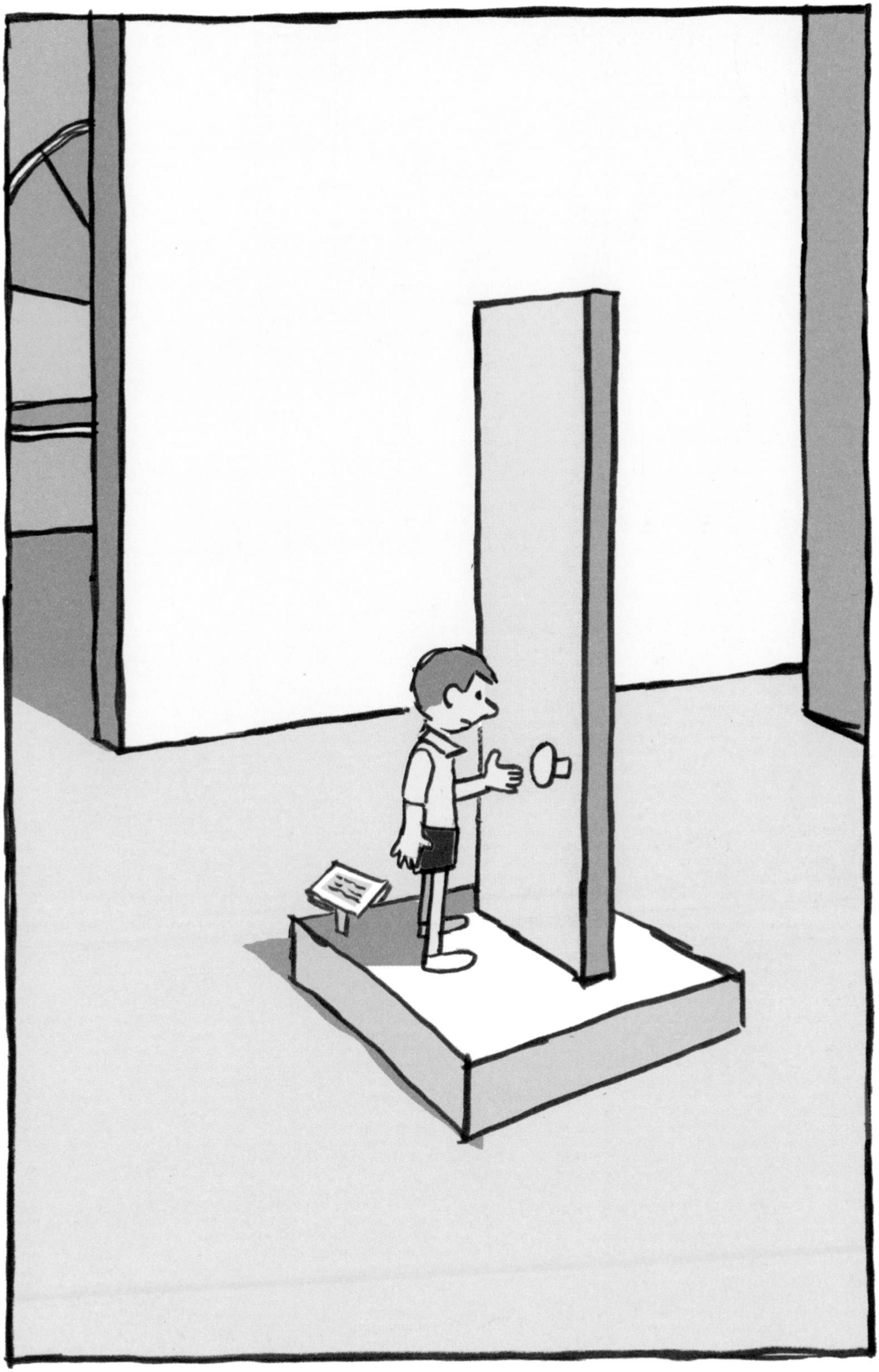

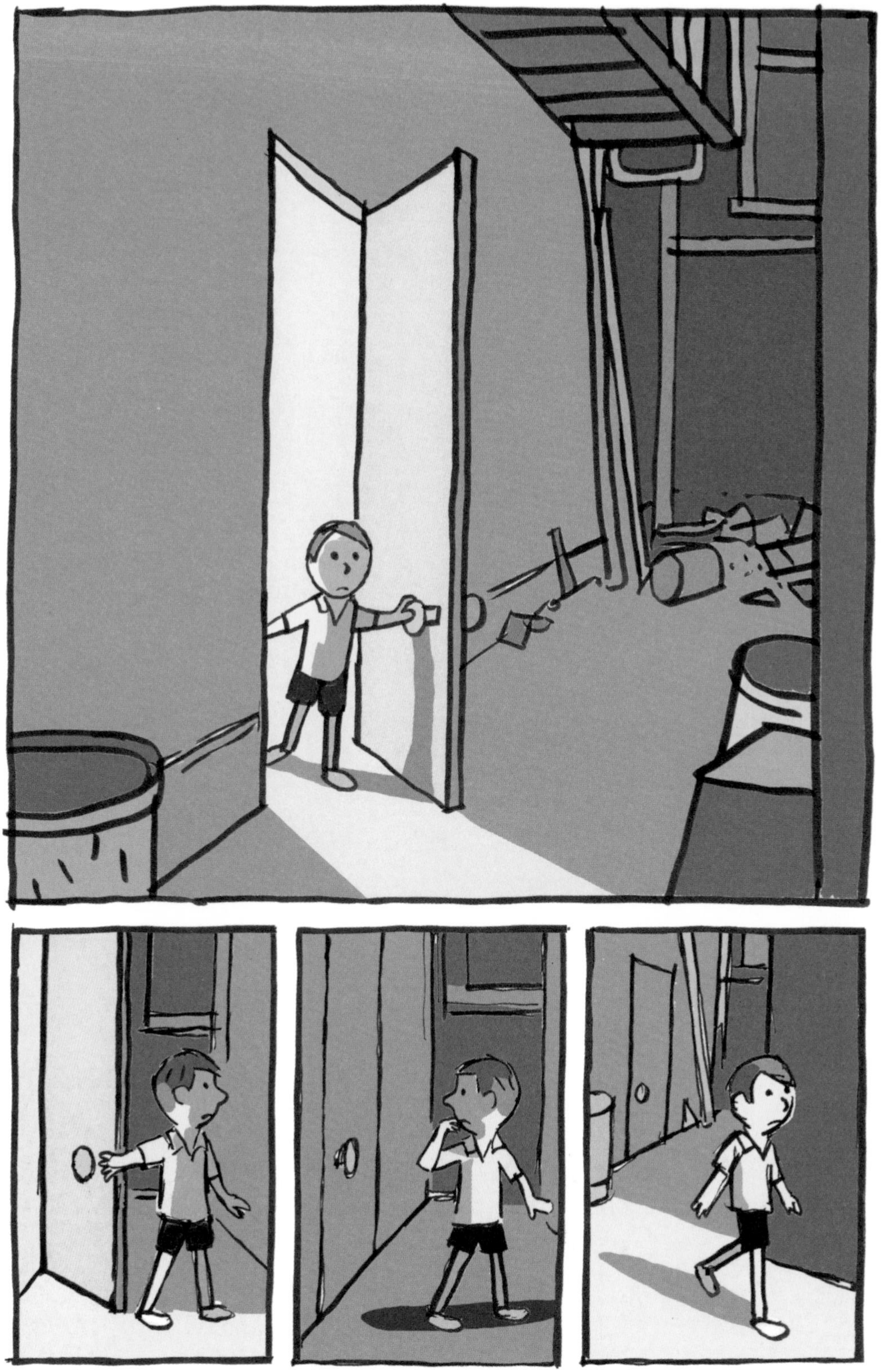

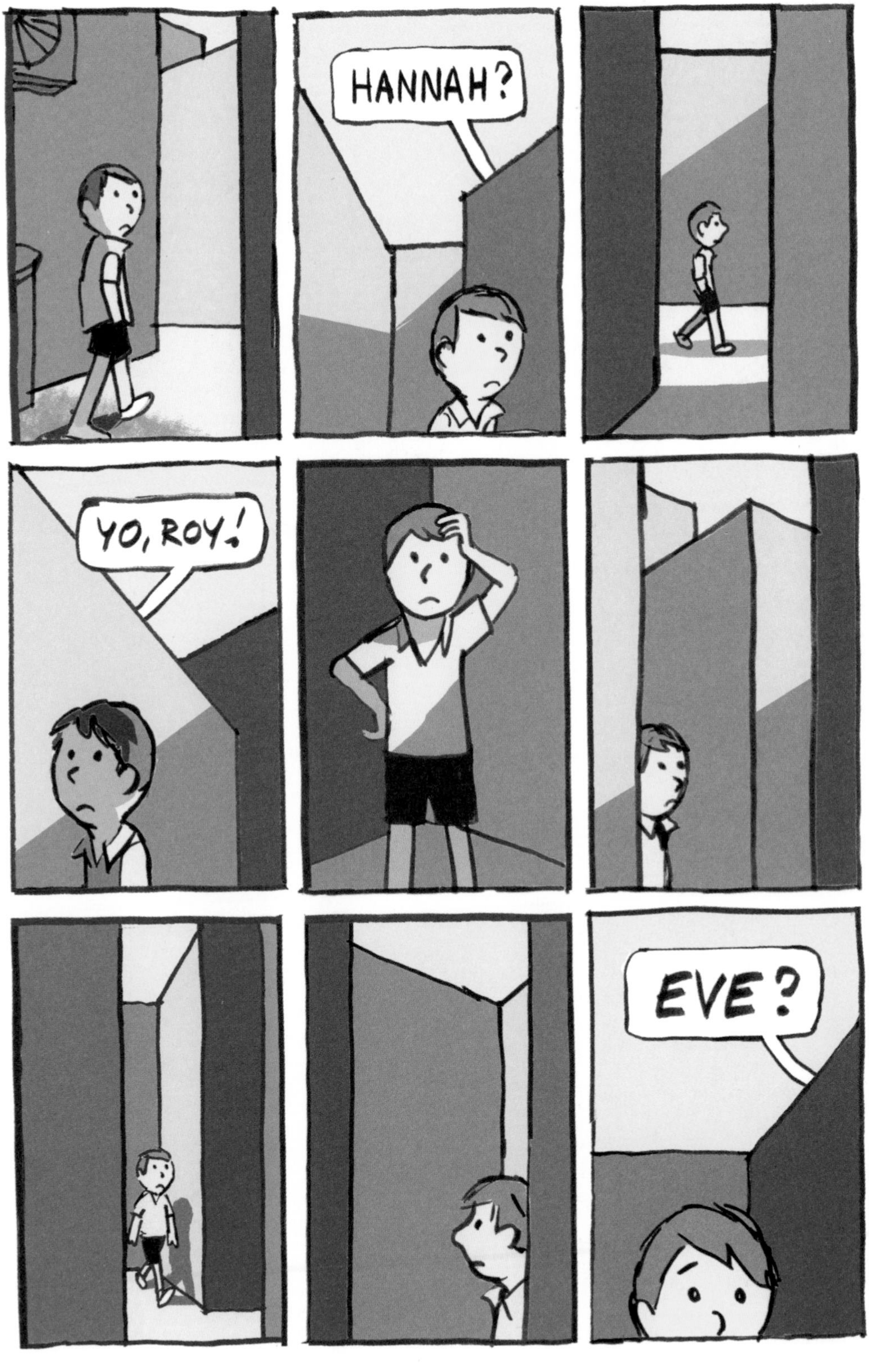
HANNAH?
YO, ROY!
EVE?

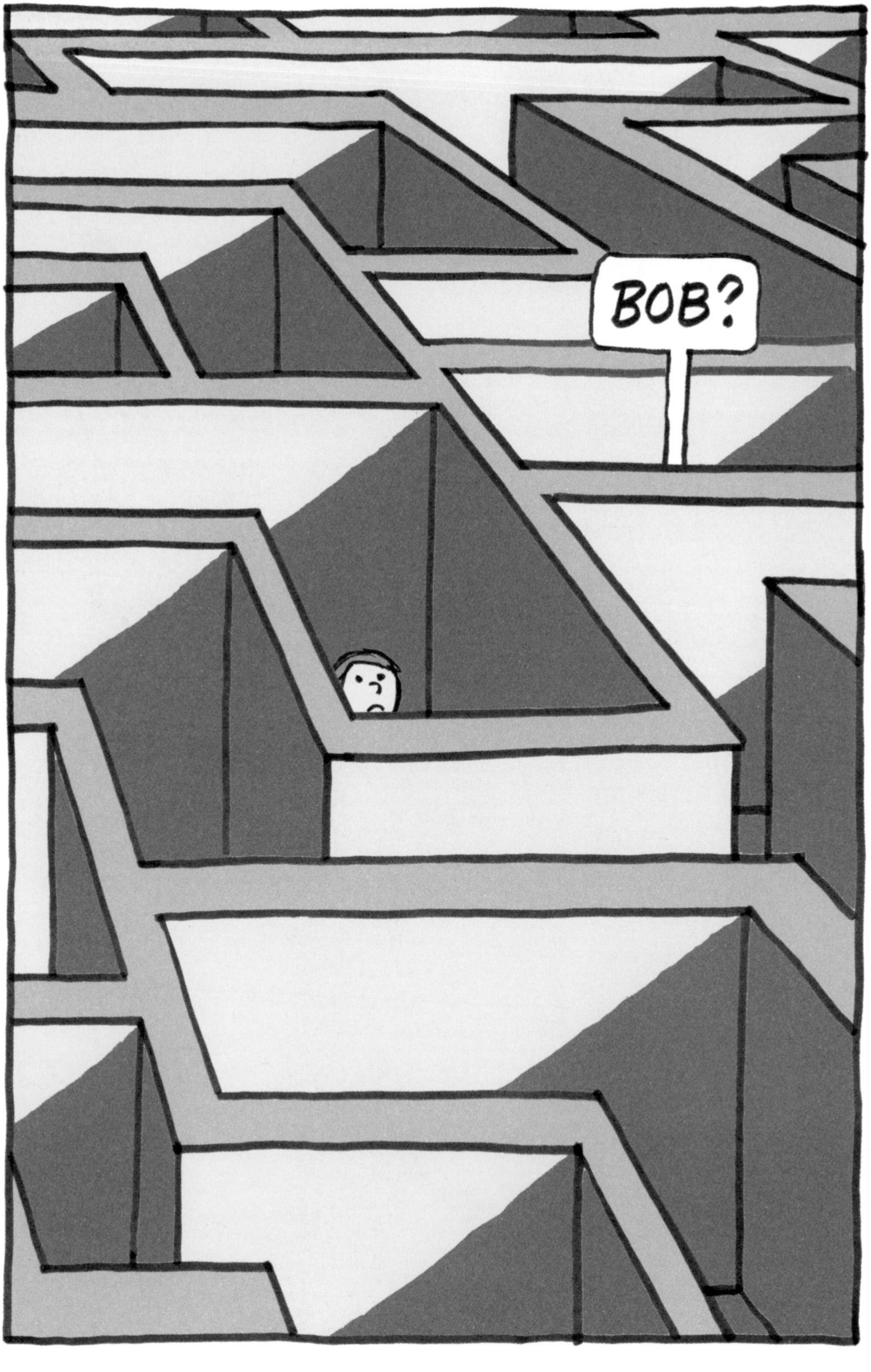
BOB?

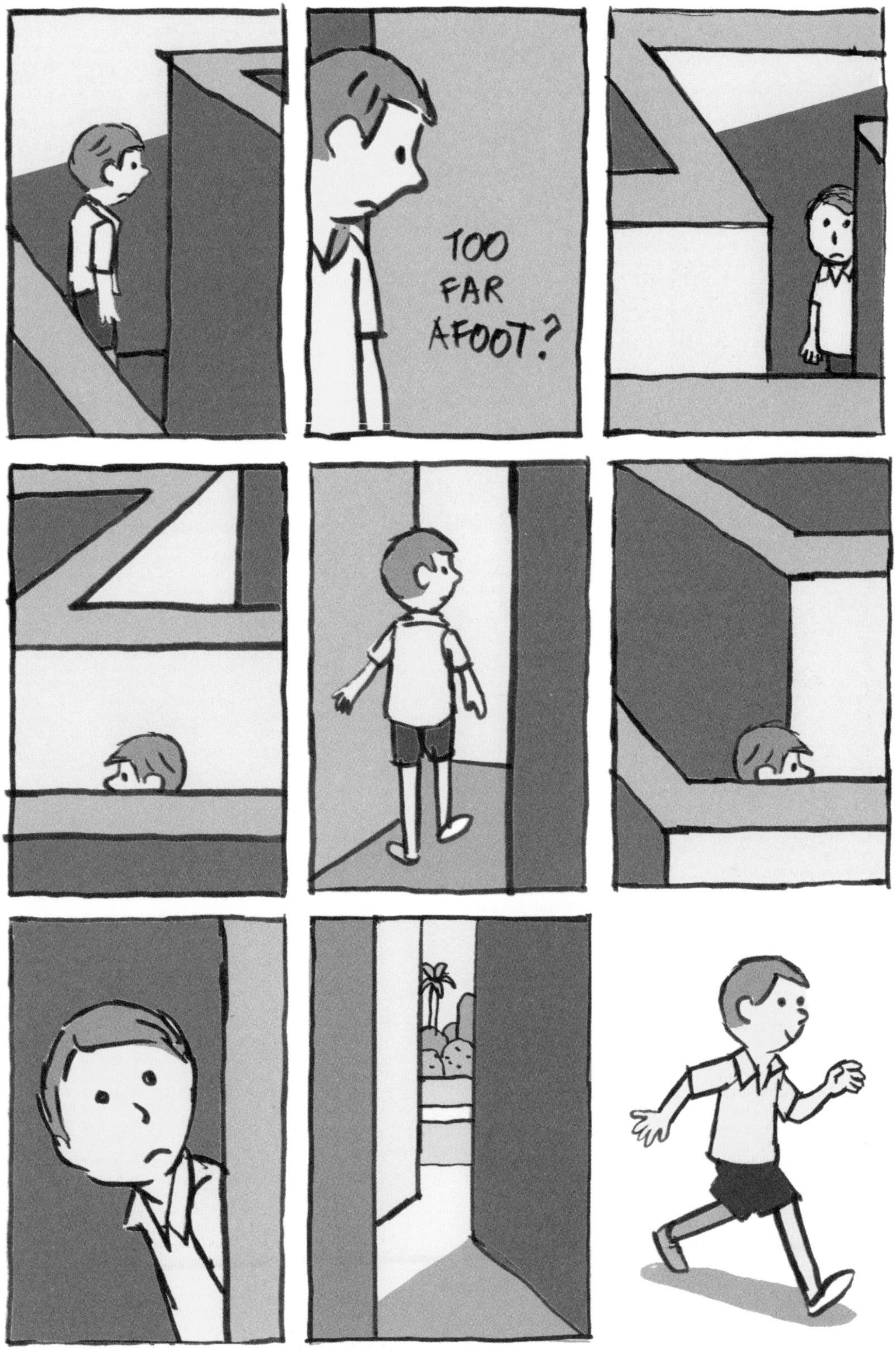
TOO FAR AFOOT?

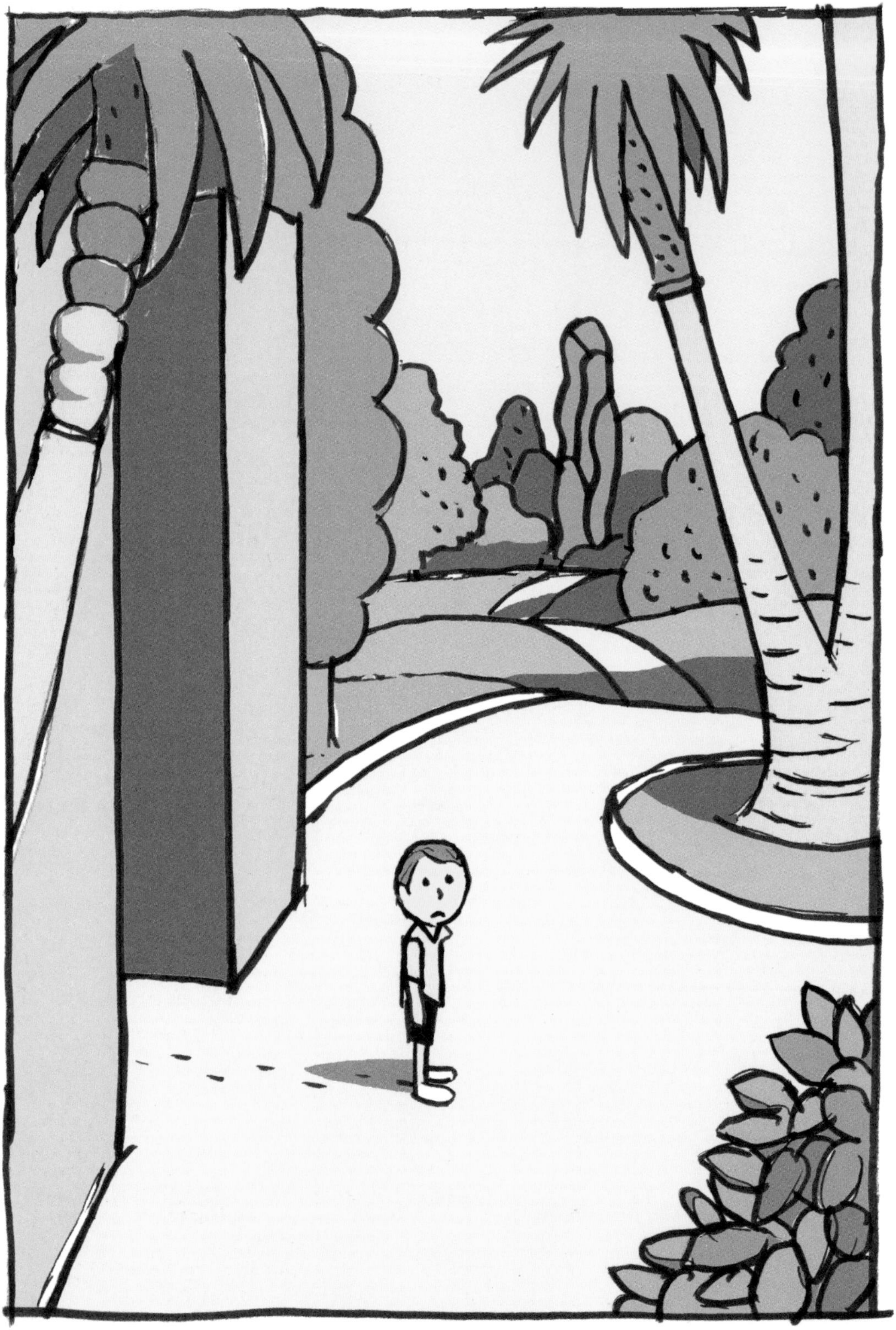

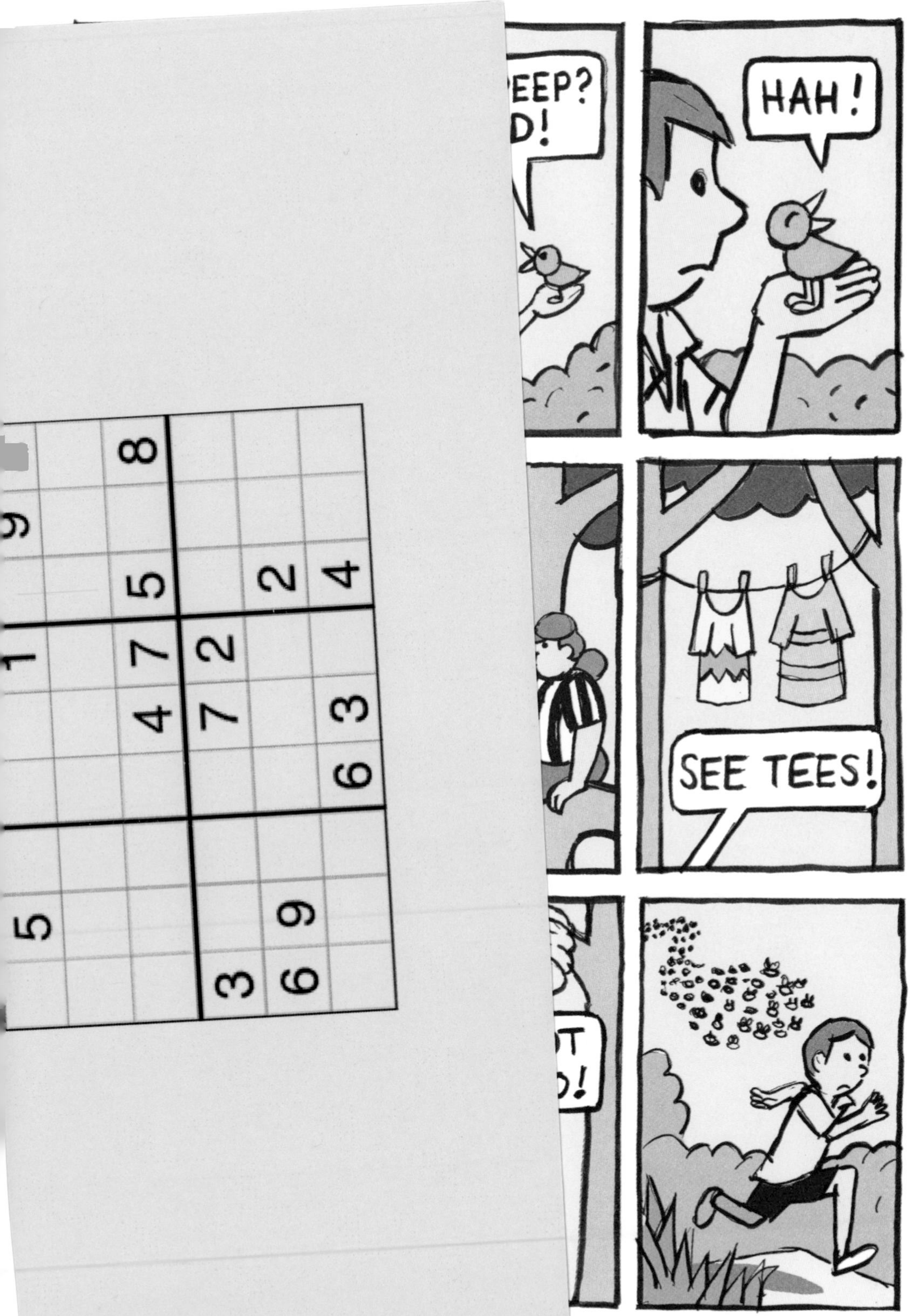
HAH!
SEE TEES!

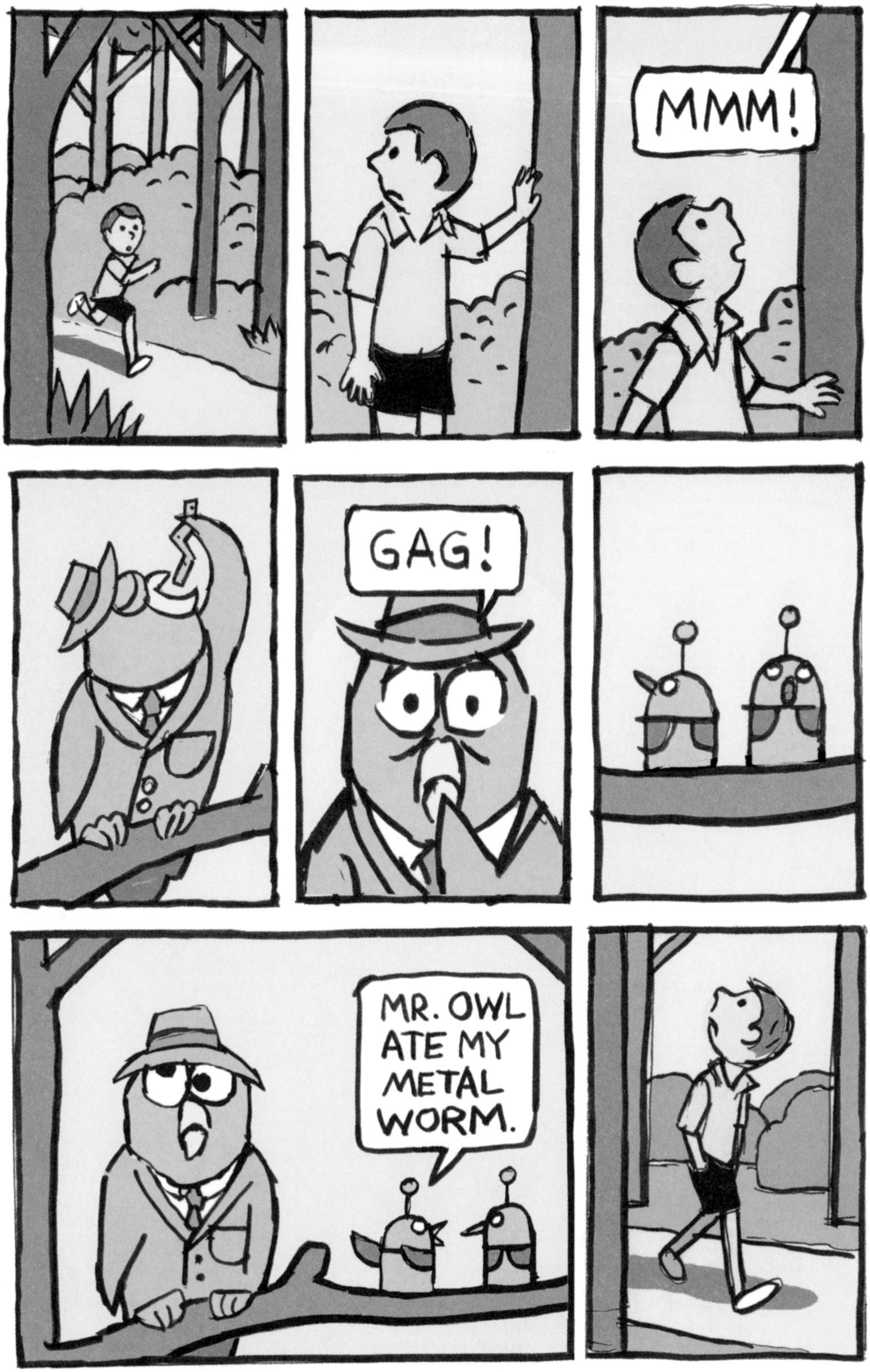
MMM!
GAG!
MR. OWL ATE MY METAL WORM.

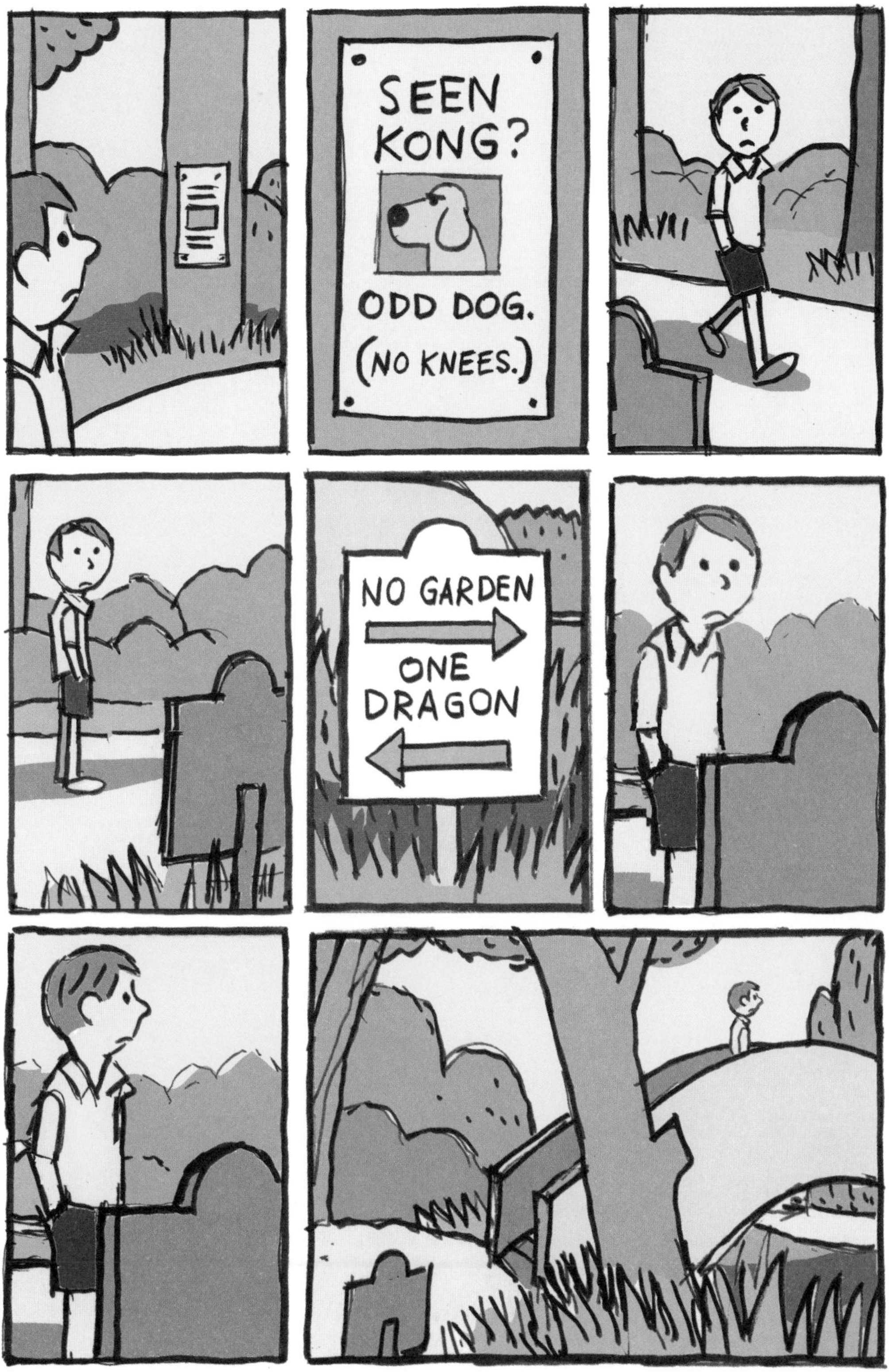
SEEN KONG?
ODD DOG.
(NO KNEES.)
NO GARDEN
ONE DRAGON

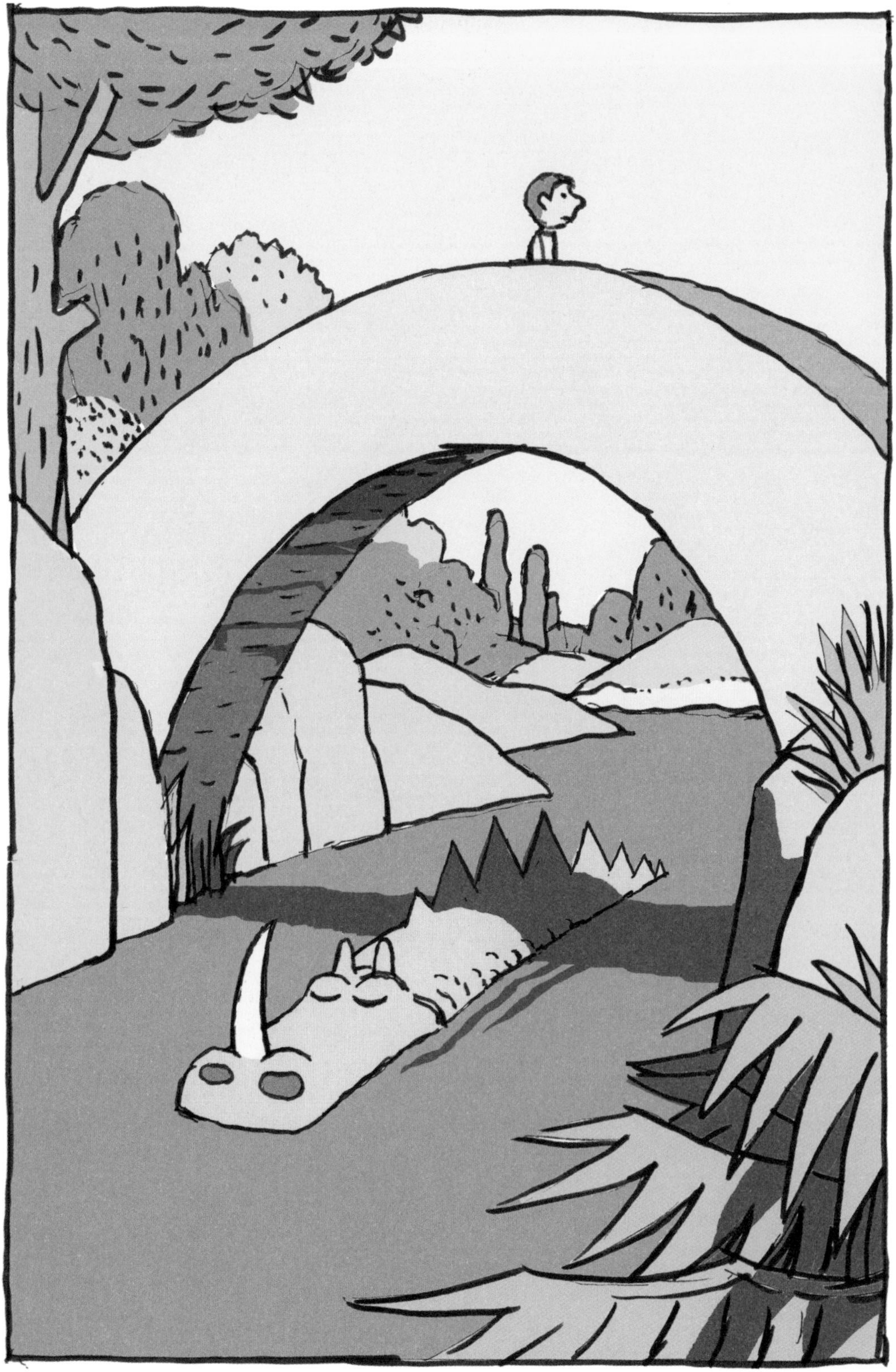

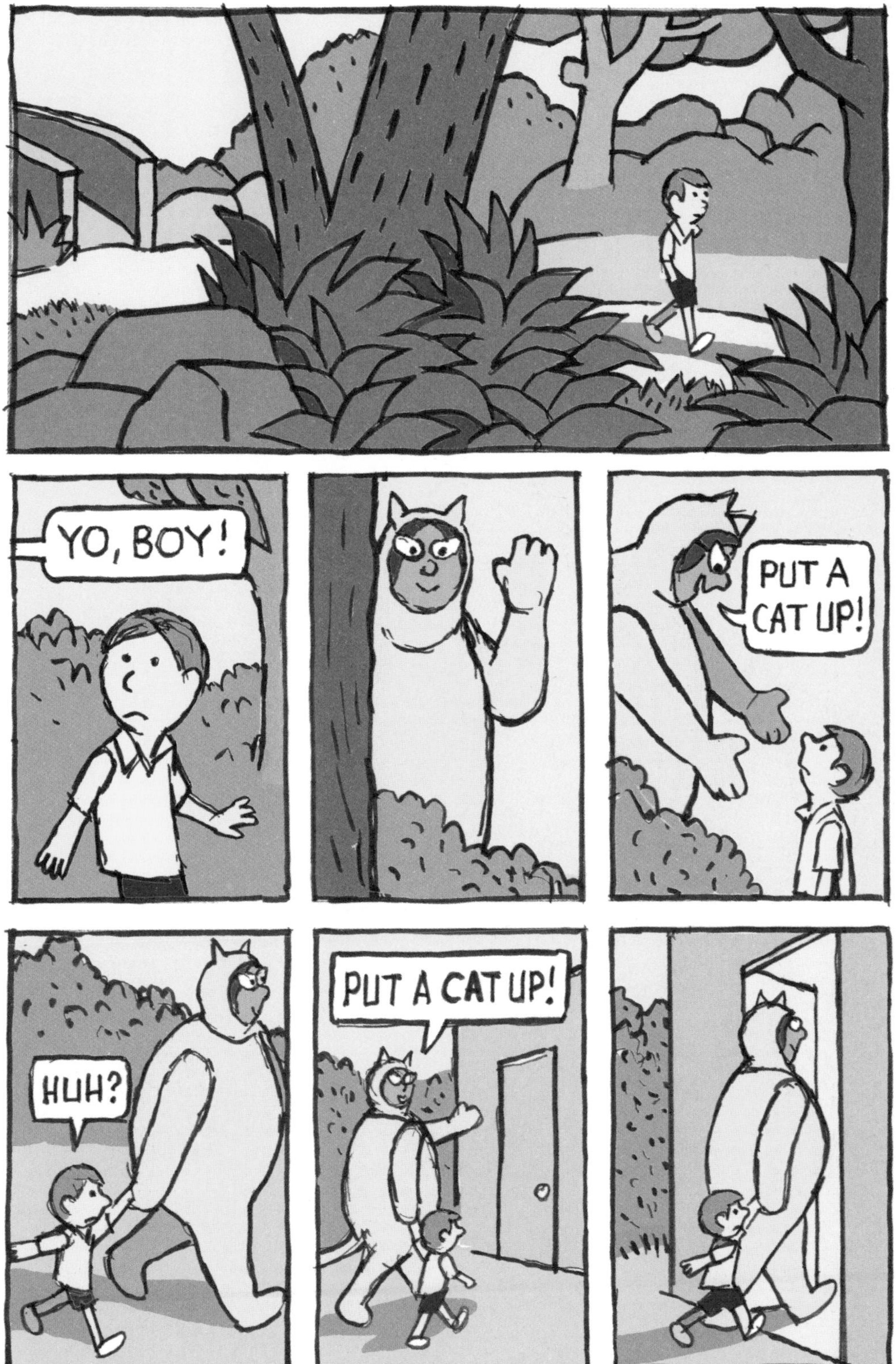

YO, BOY!
PUT A CAT UP!
HUH?
PUT A CAT UP!

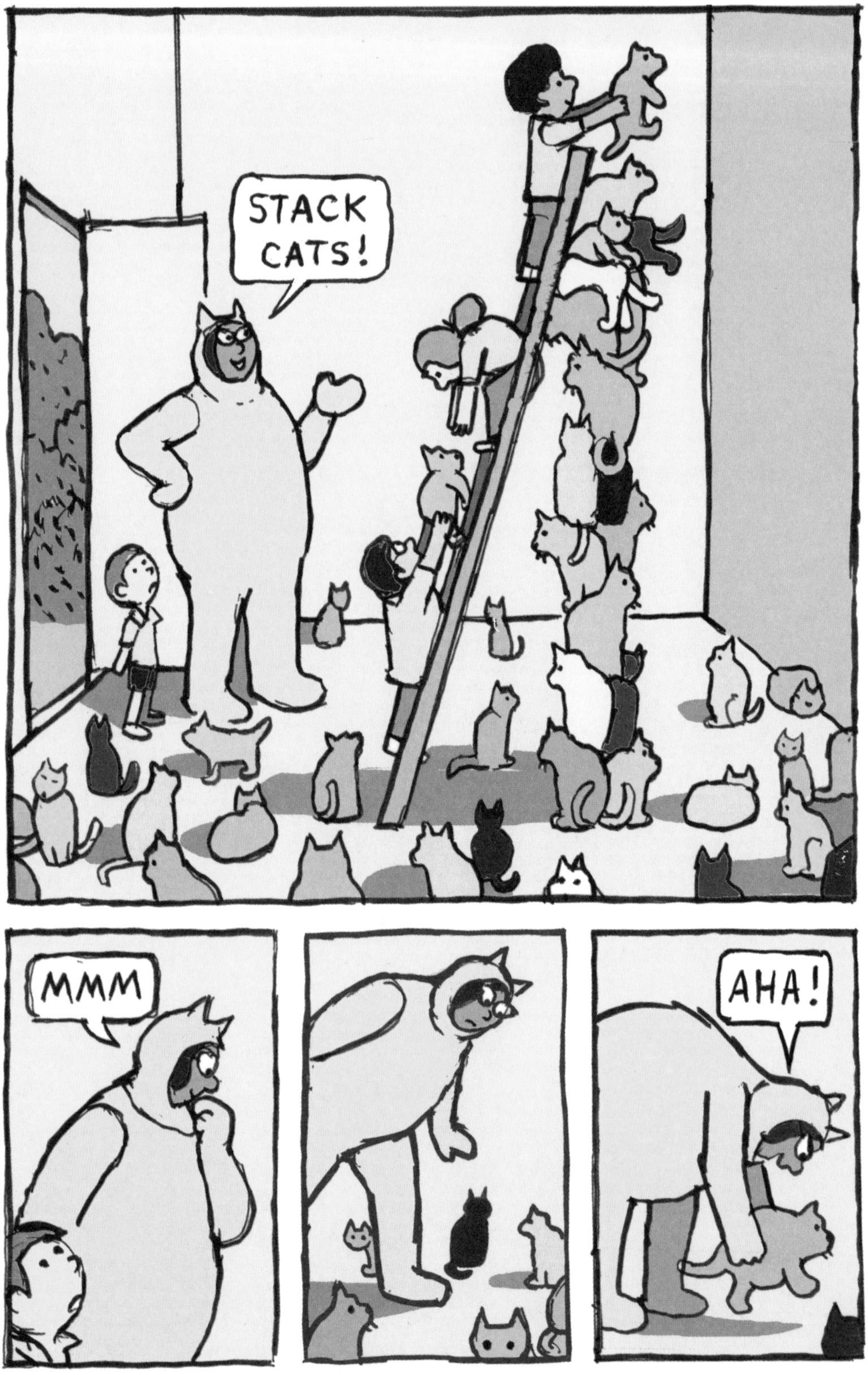
STACK CATS!
MMM
AHA!

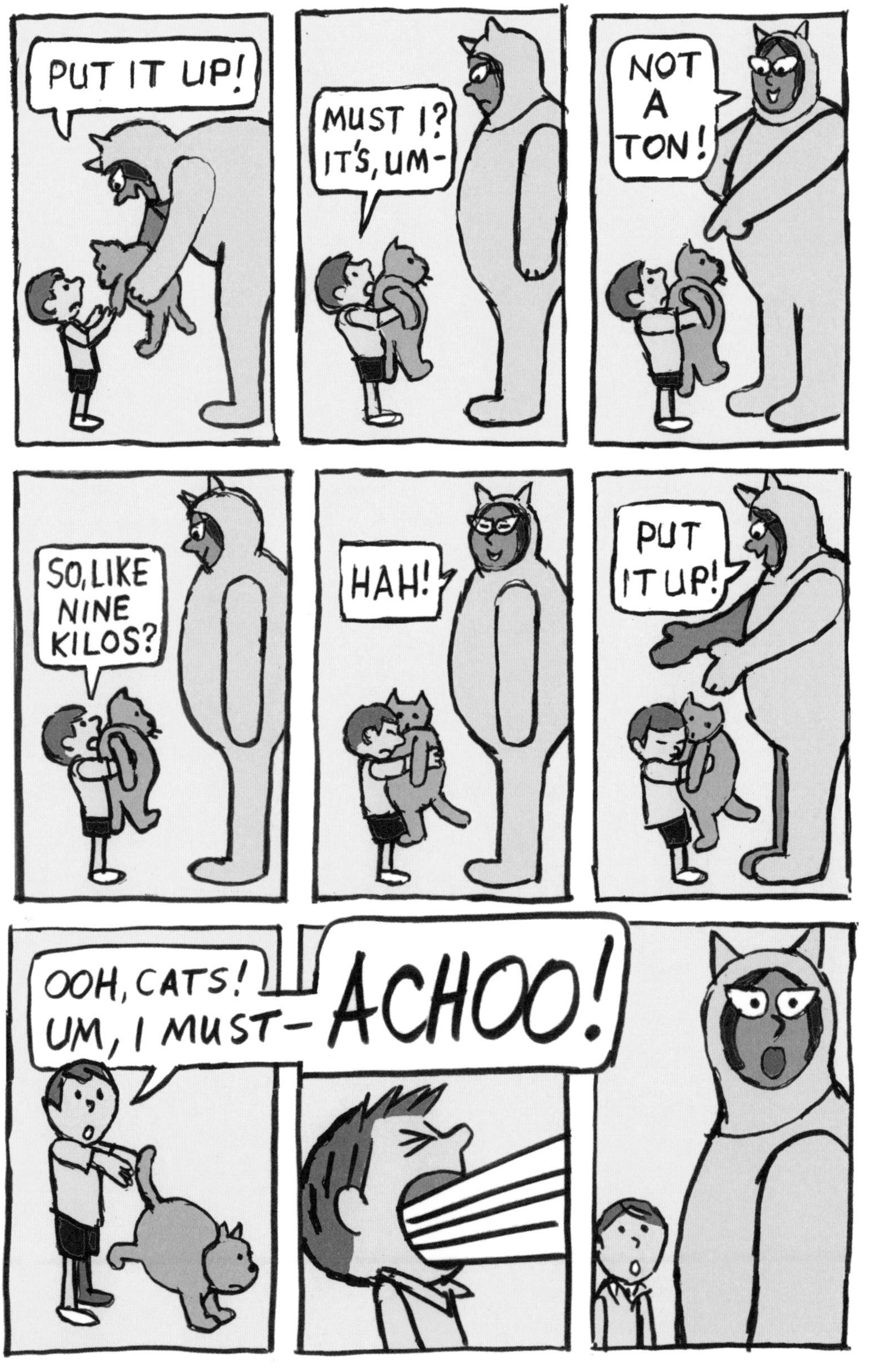
PUT IT UP!
MUST I? IT'S, UM-
NOT A TON!
SO, LIKE NINE KILOS?
HAH!
PUT IT UP!
OOH, CATS! UM, I MUST-
ACHOO!

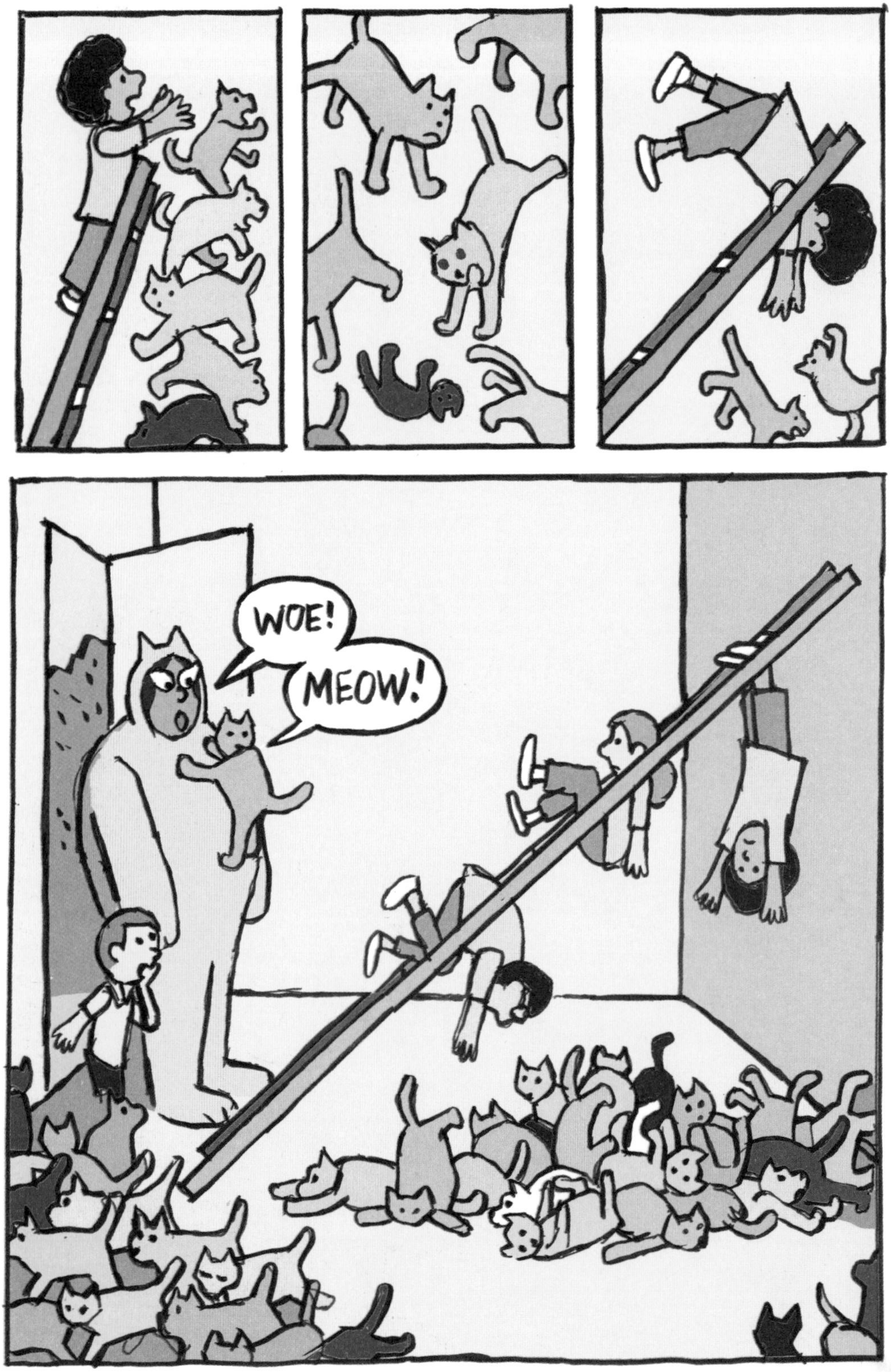
WOE!
MEOW!

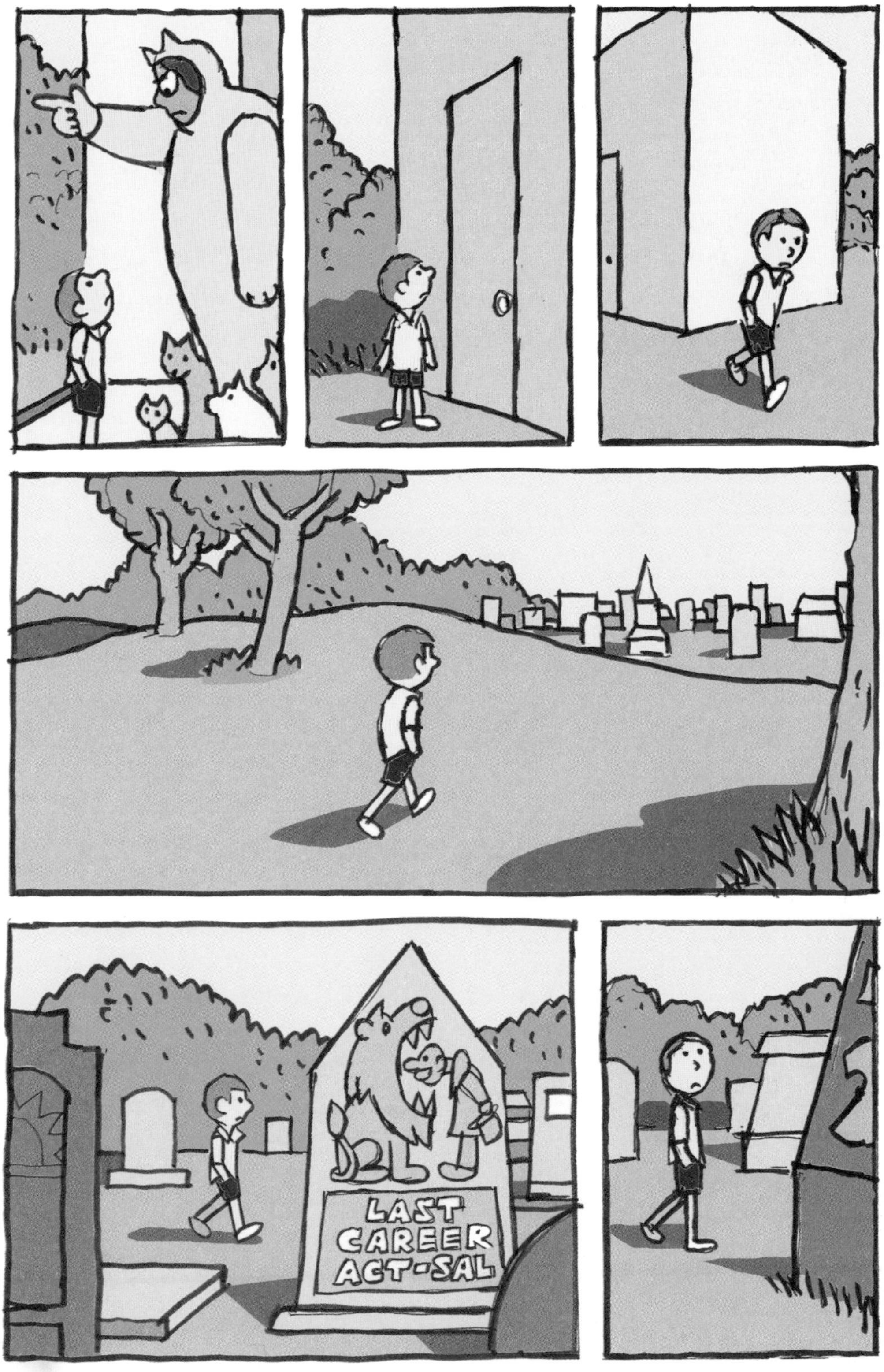
LAST
CAREER
ACT-SAL

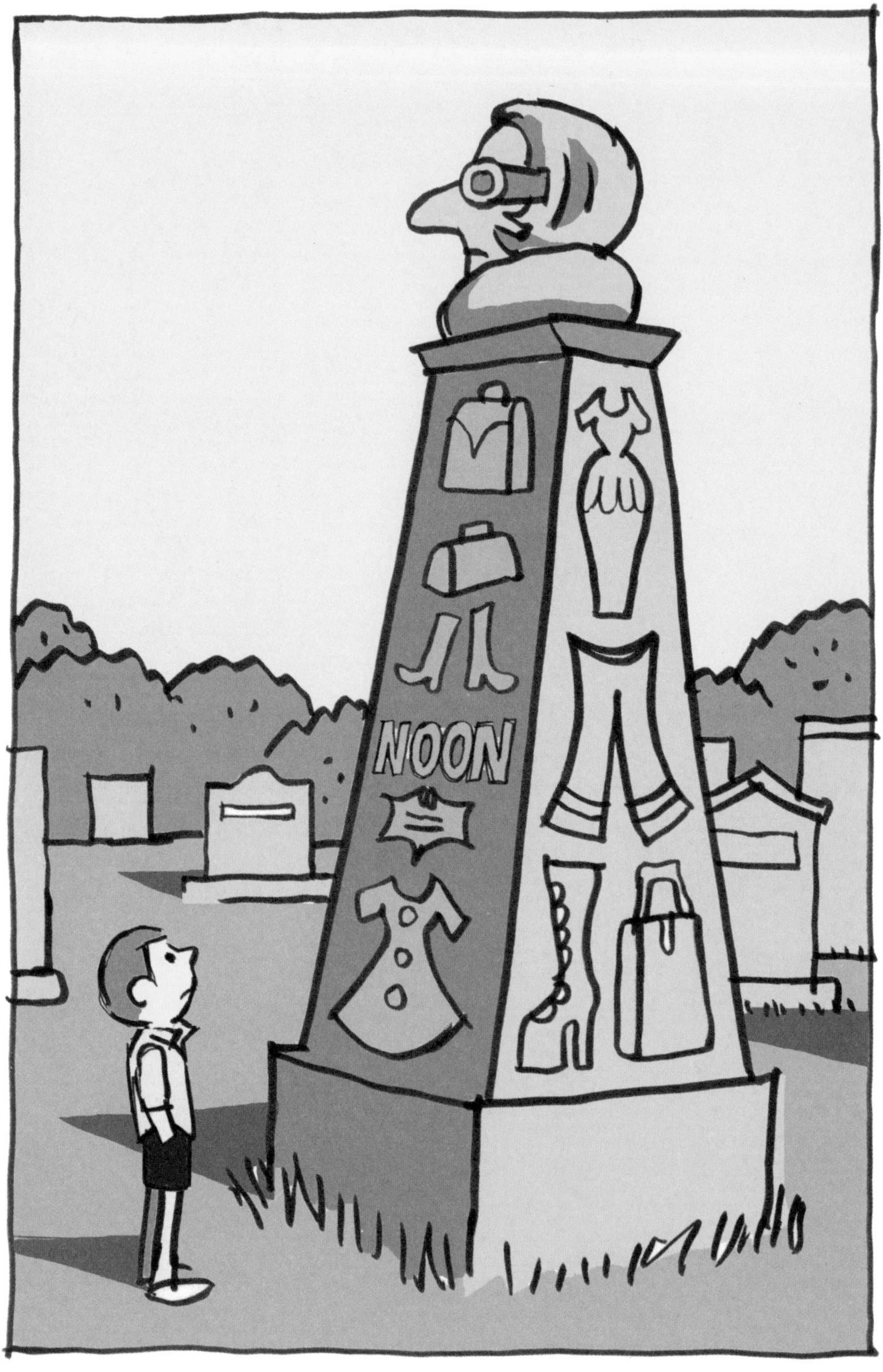
NOON

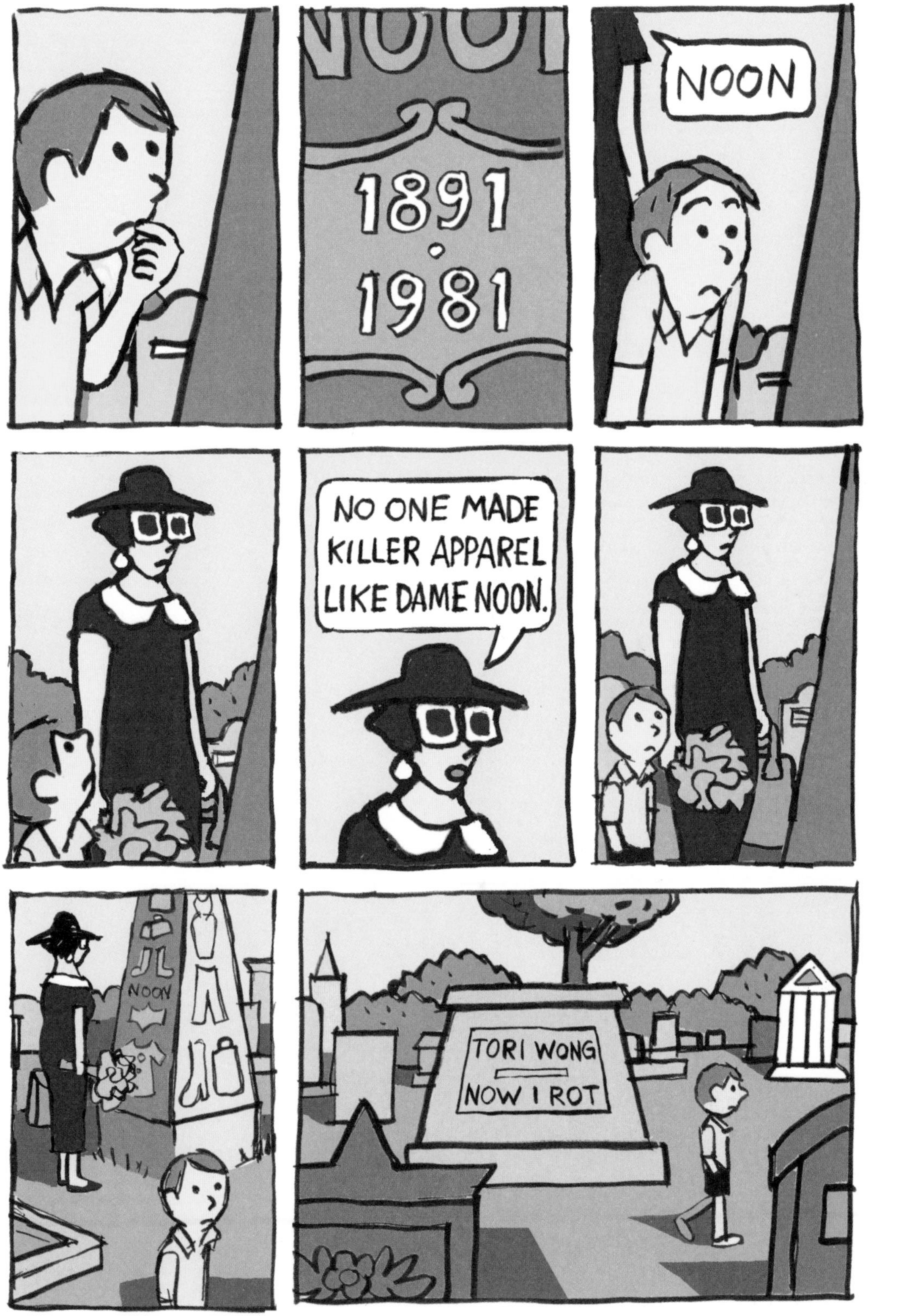

NOON
1891
1981
NOON
NO ONE MADE KILLER APPAREL LIKE DAME NOON.
NOON
TORI WONG
NOW I ROT

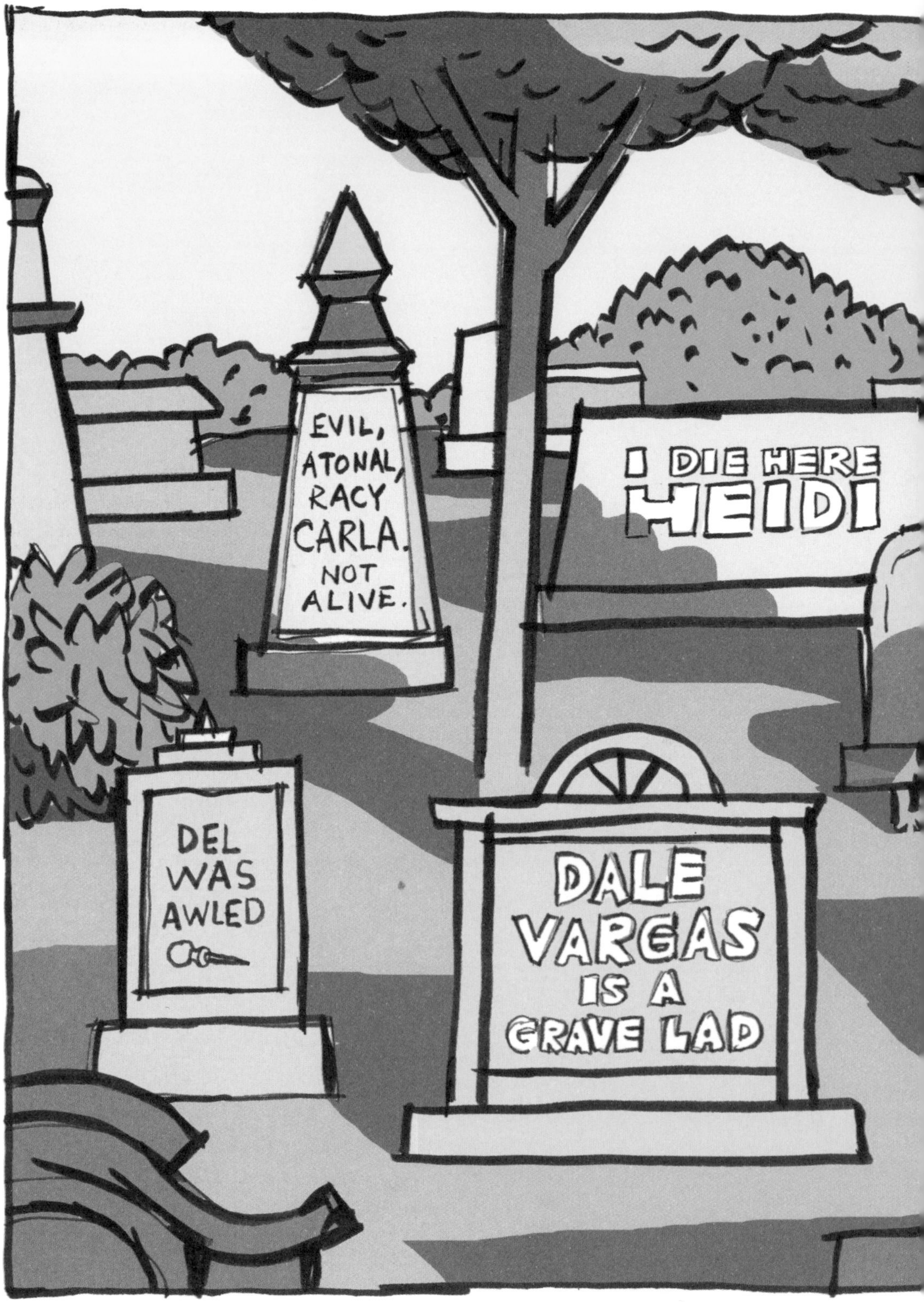
EVIL, ATONAL, RACY CARLA. NOT ALIVE.
I DIE HERE HEIDI
DEL WAS AWLED
DALE VARGAS IS A GRAVE LAD

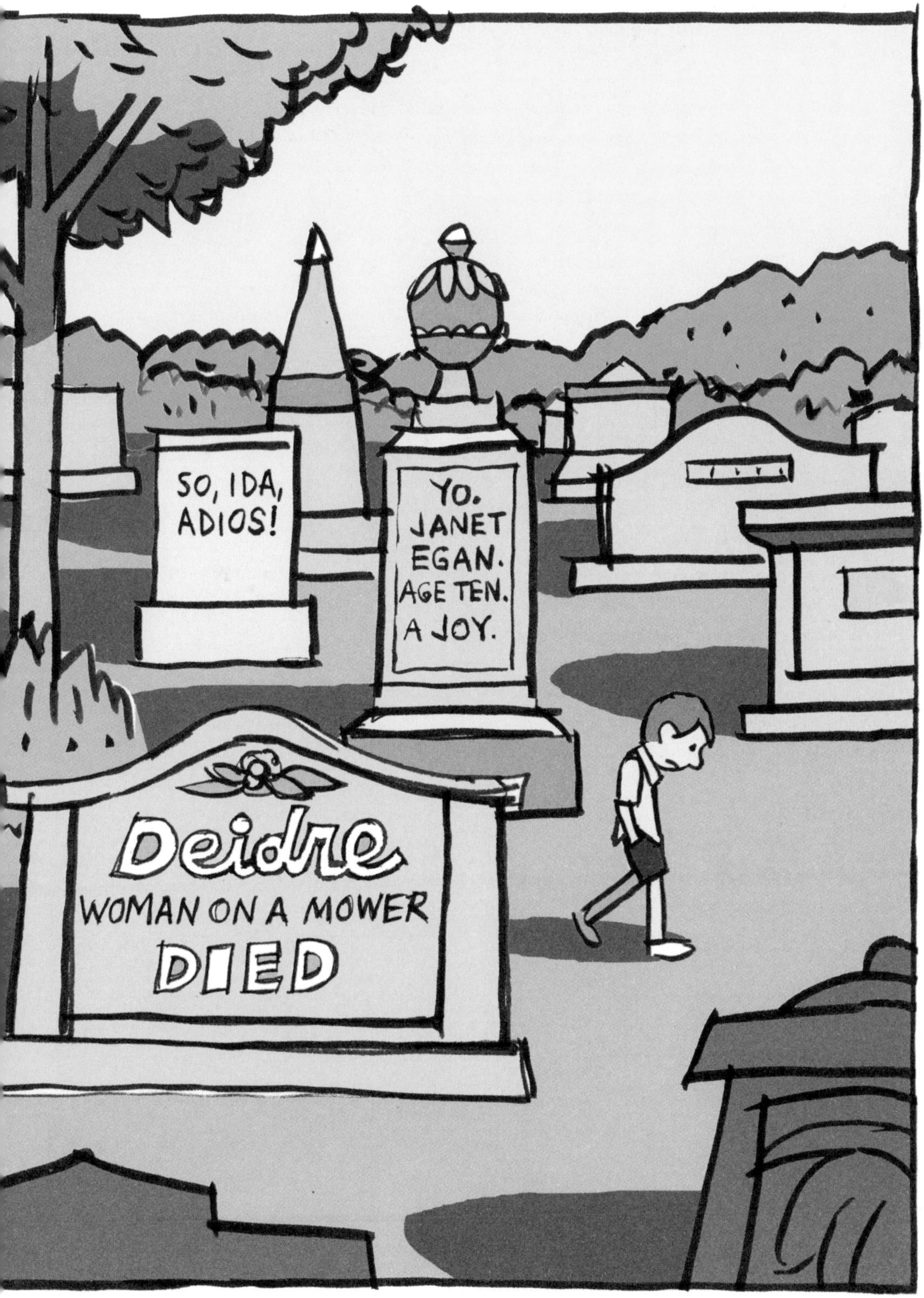
SO, IDA, ADIOS!
YO. JANET EGAN. AGE TEN. A JOY.
Deidre
WOMAN ON A MOWER
DIED

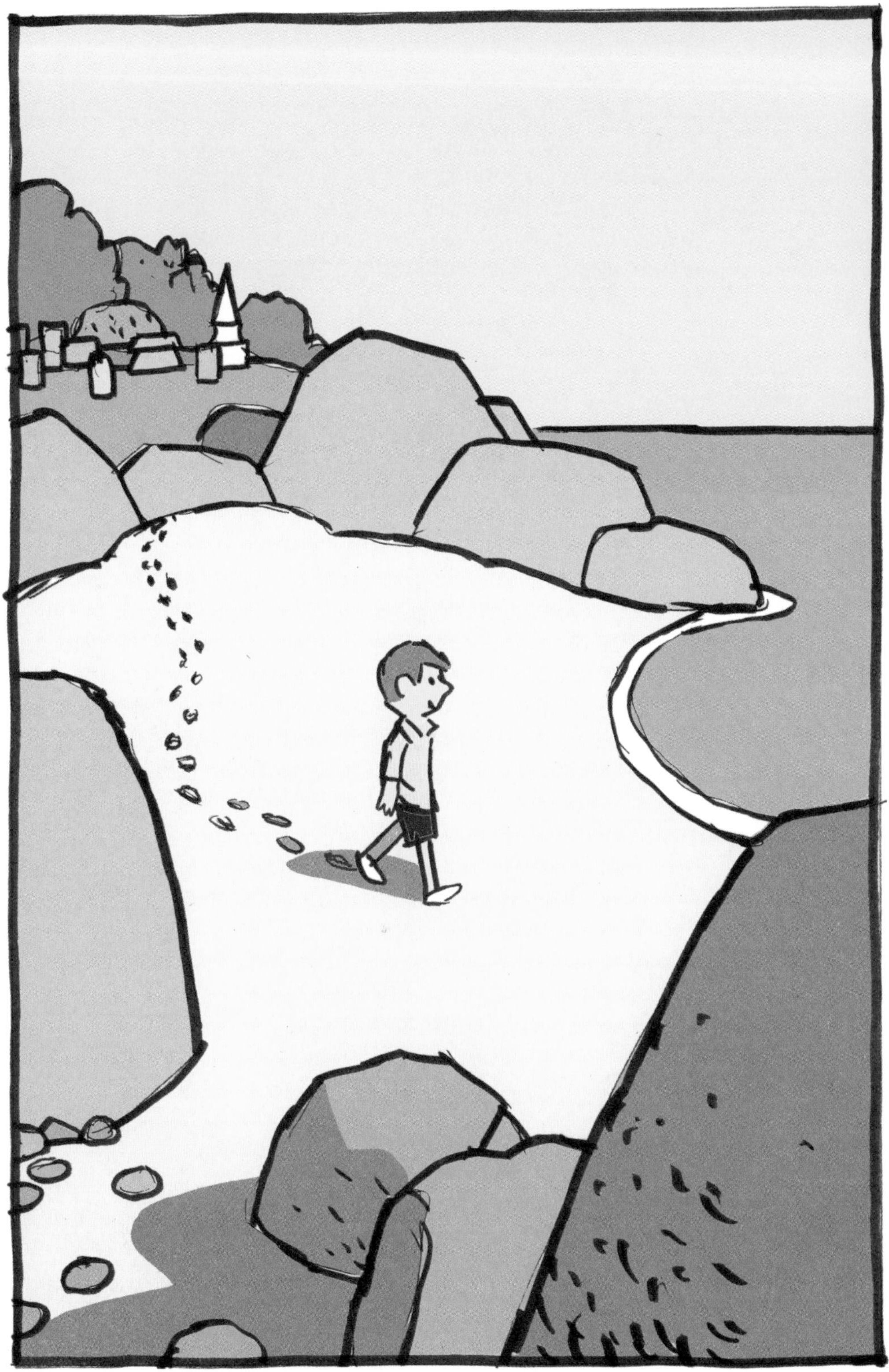

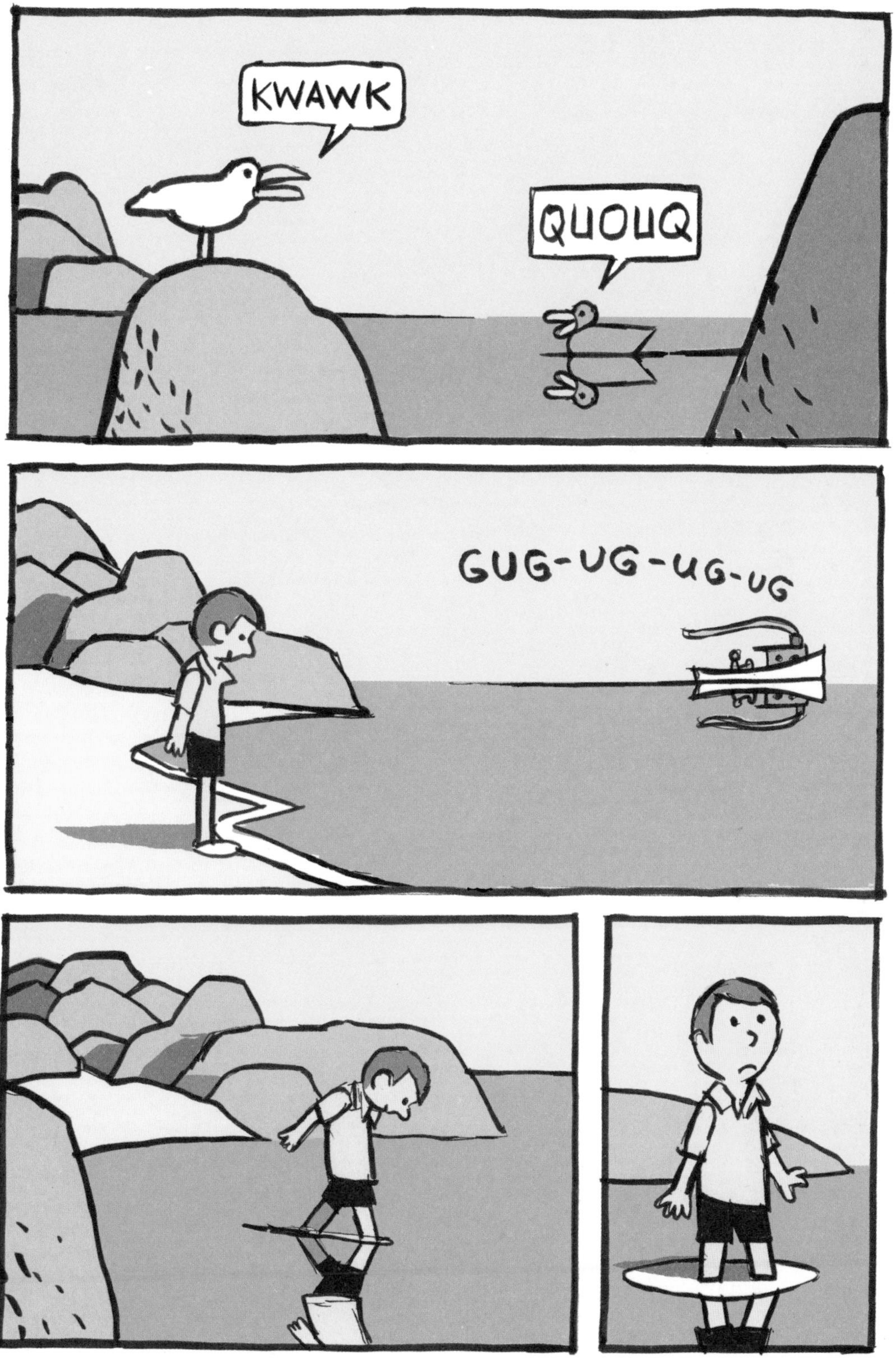
KWAWK
QUOUQ
GUG-UG-UG-UG

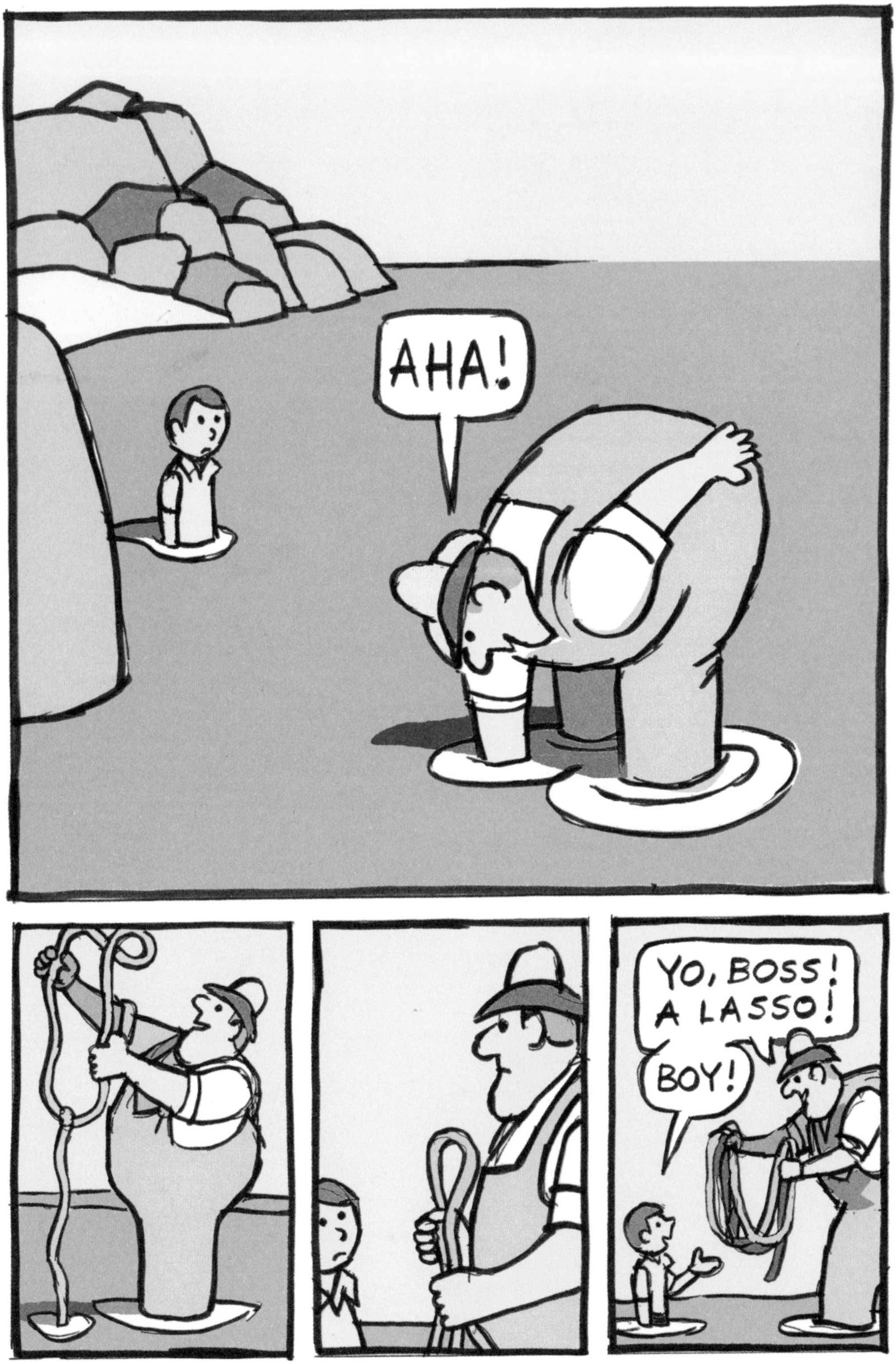
AHA!
YO, BOSS! A LASSO!
BOY!

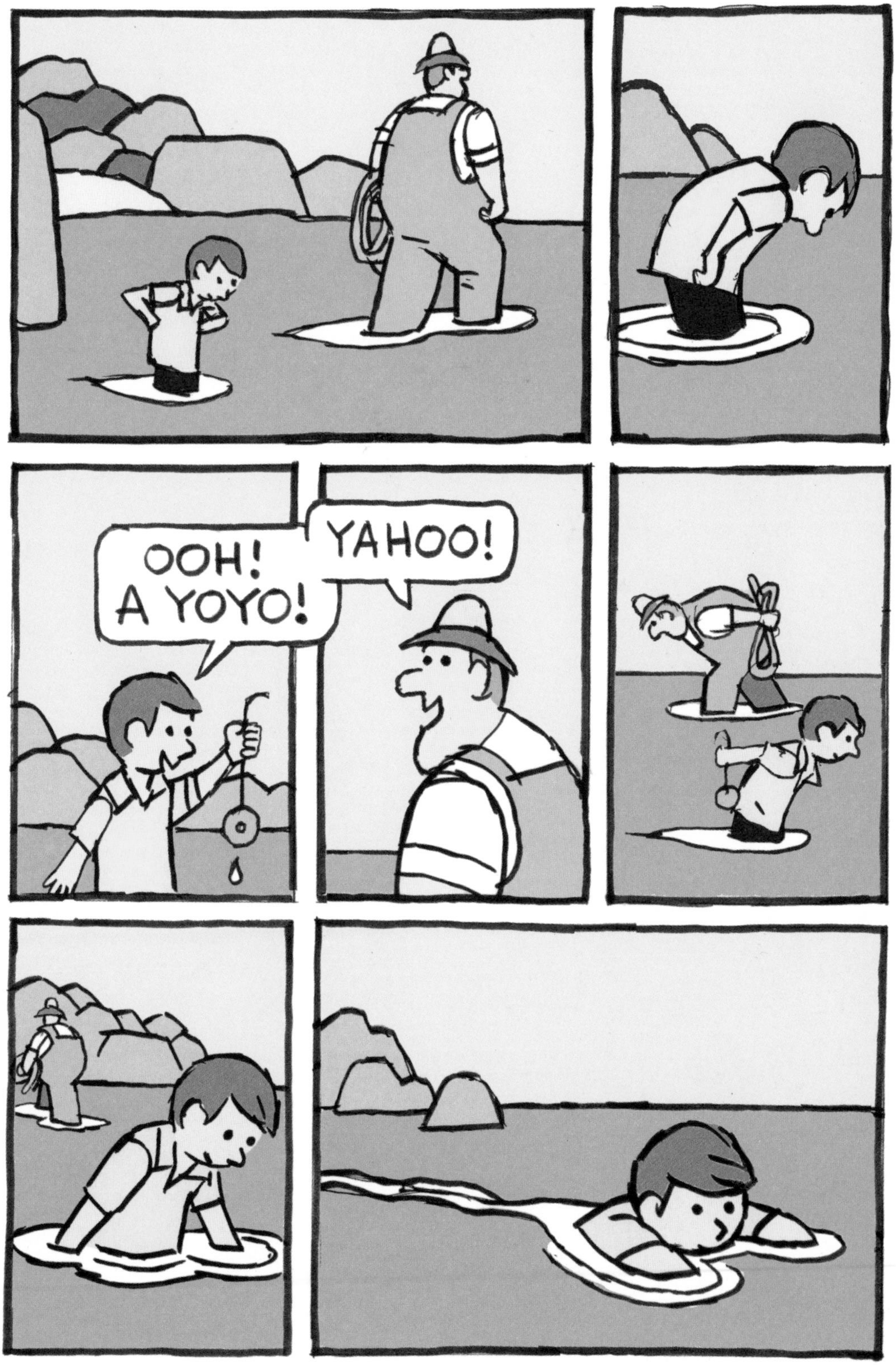
OOH! A YOYO!
YAHOO!

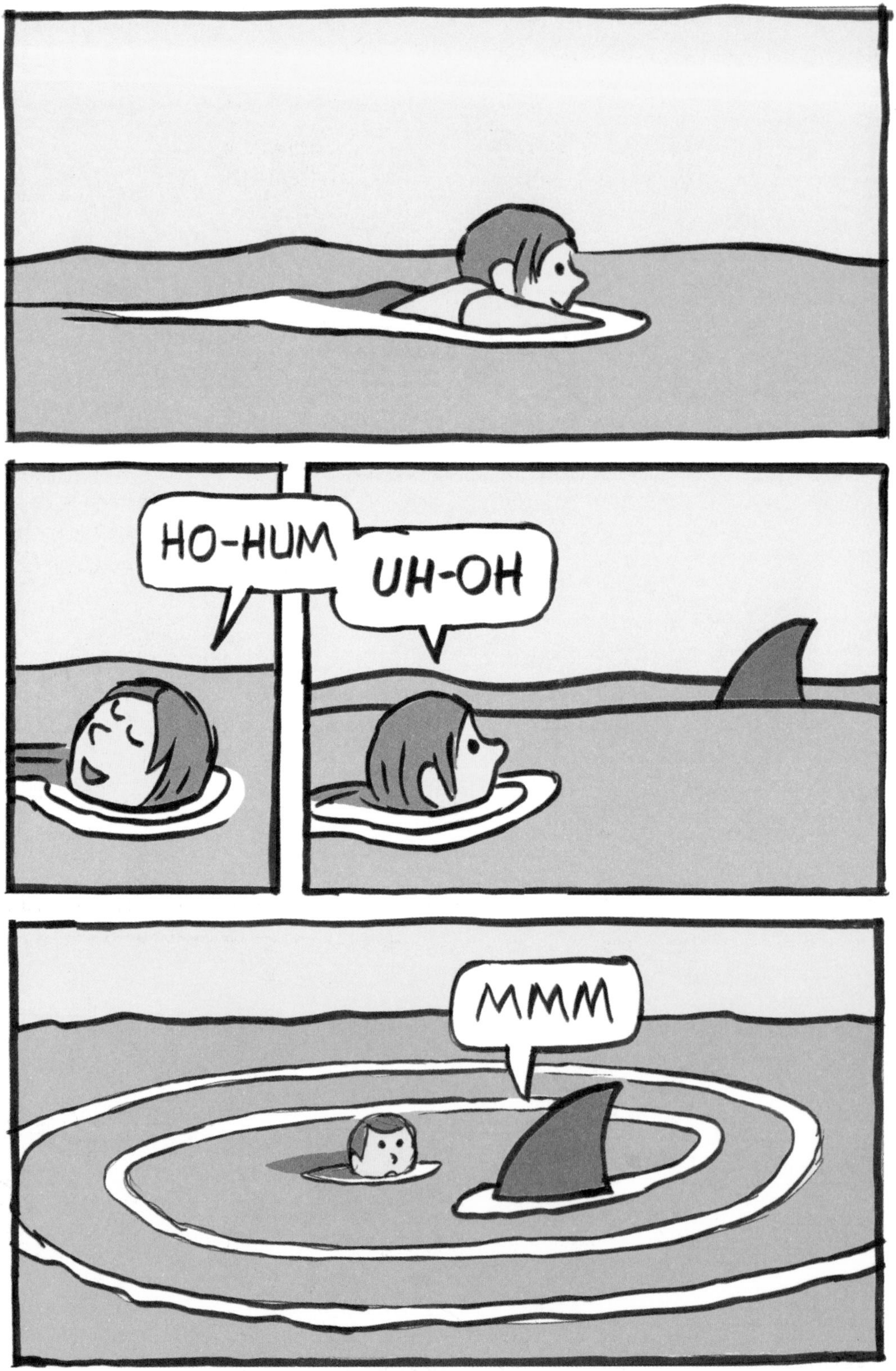
HO-HUM
UH-OH
MMM

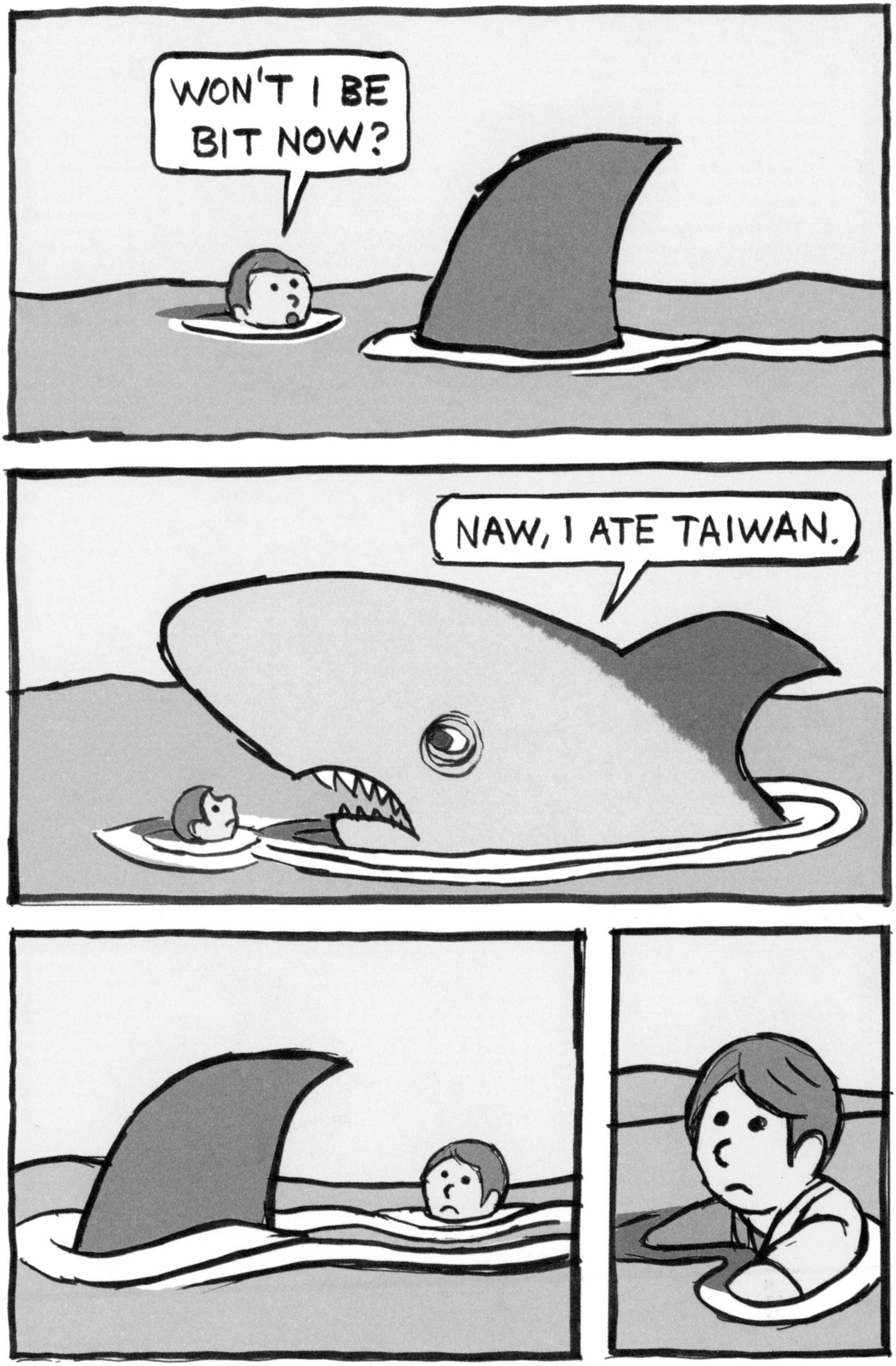
WON'T I BE BIT NOW?
NAW, I ATE TAIWAN.

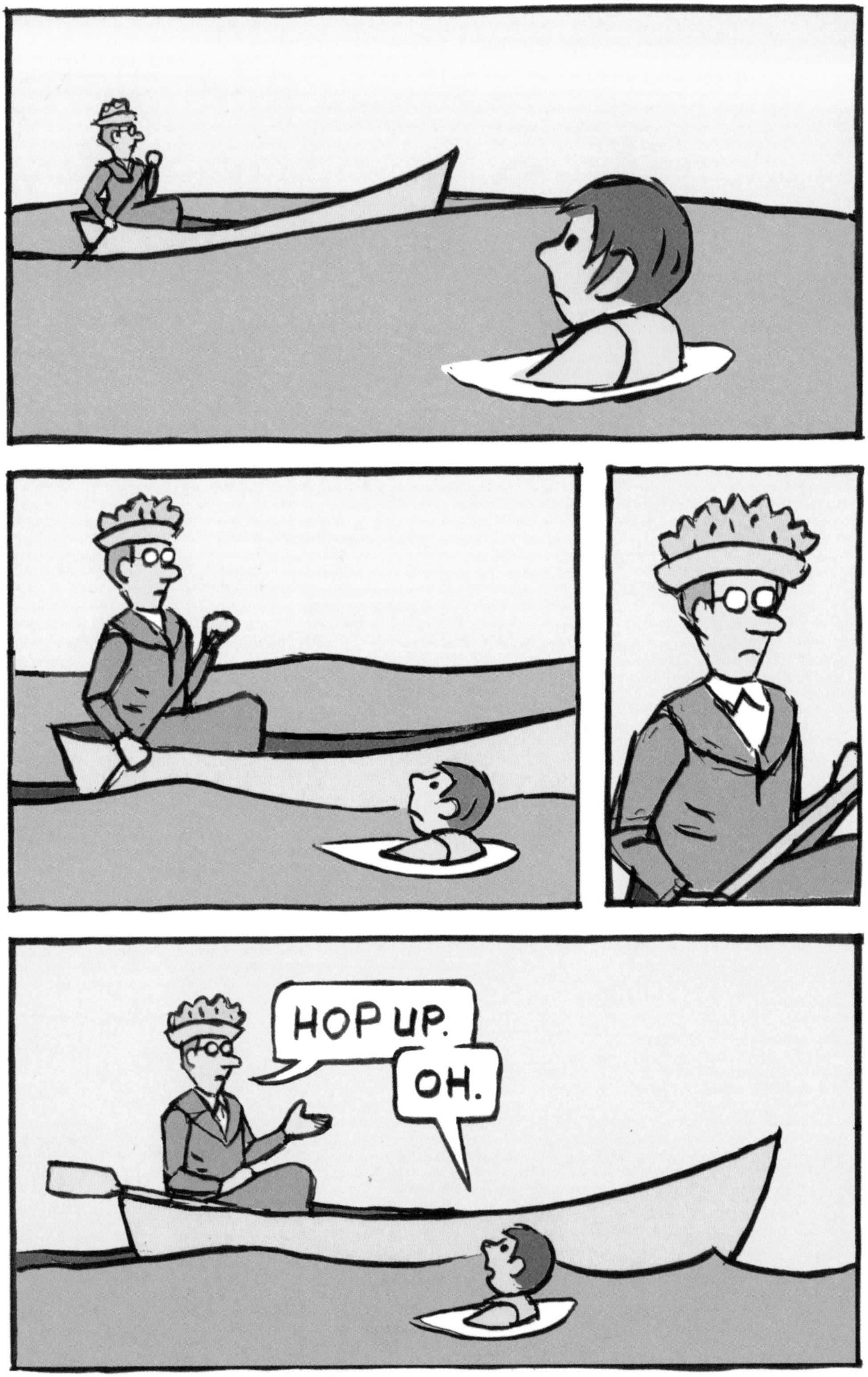
HOP UP.
OH.

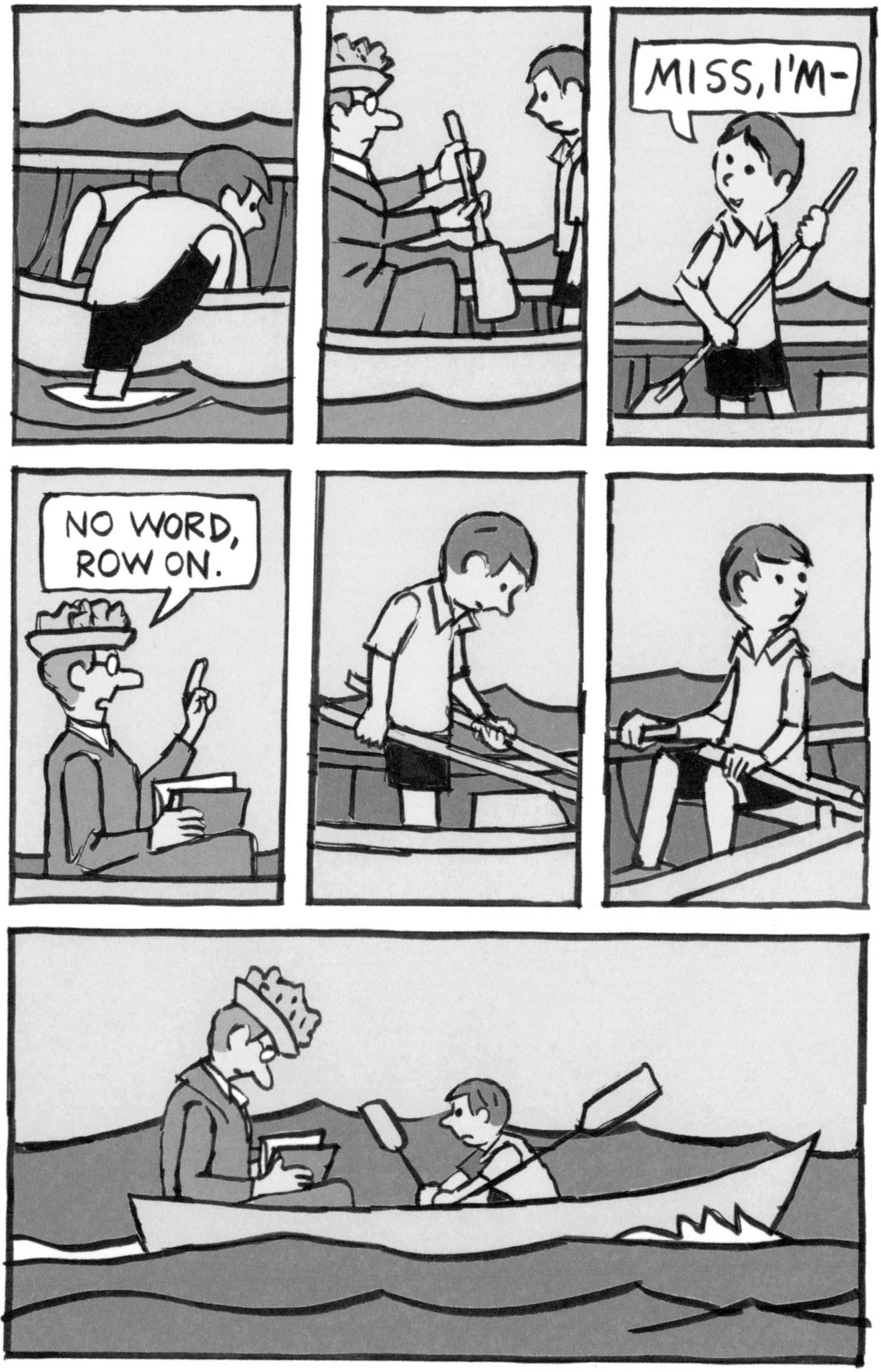
MISS, I'M-
NO WORD, ROW ON.

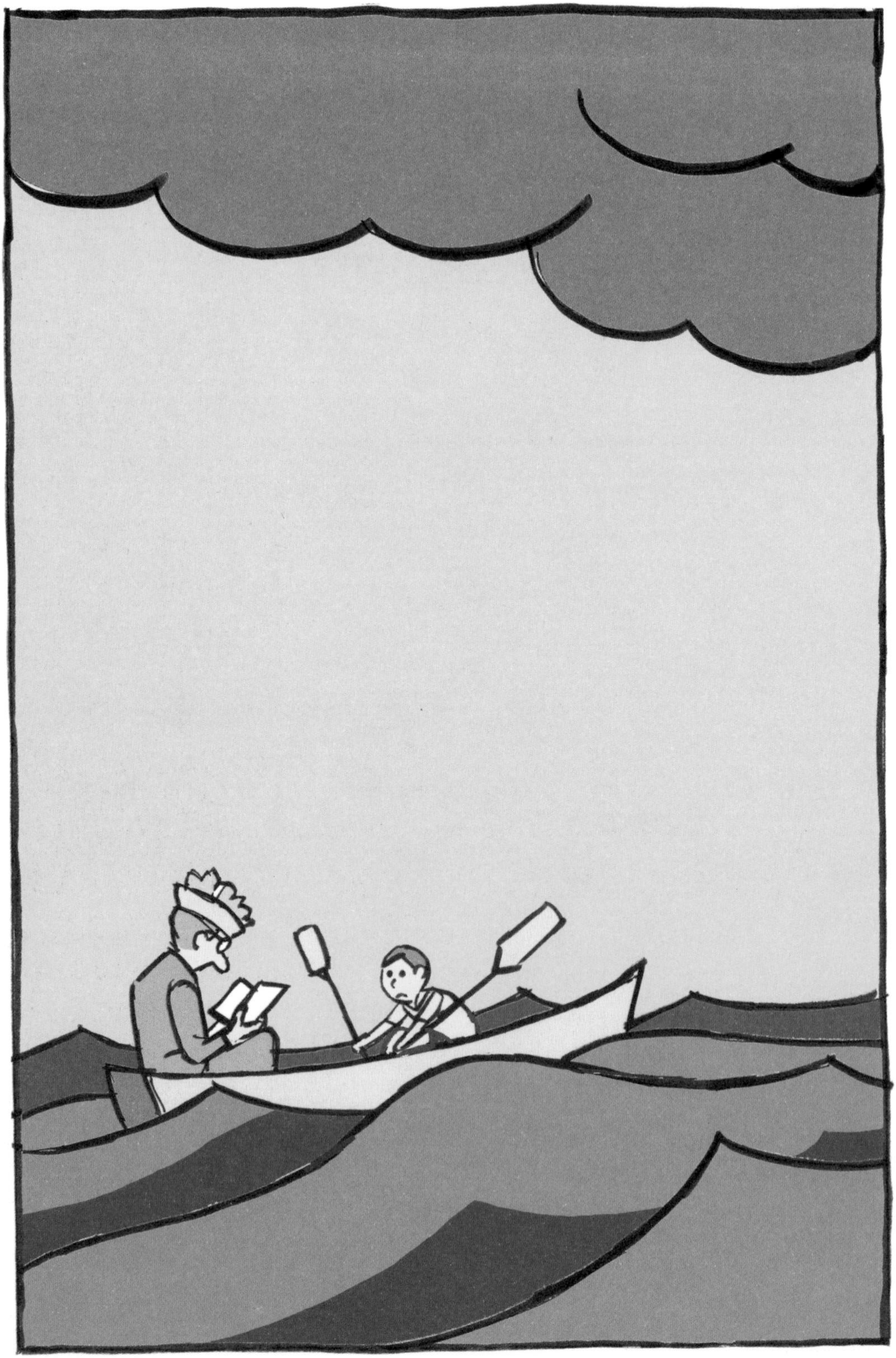

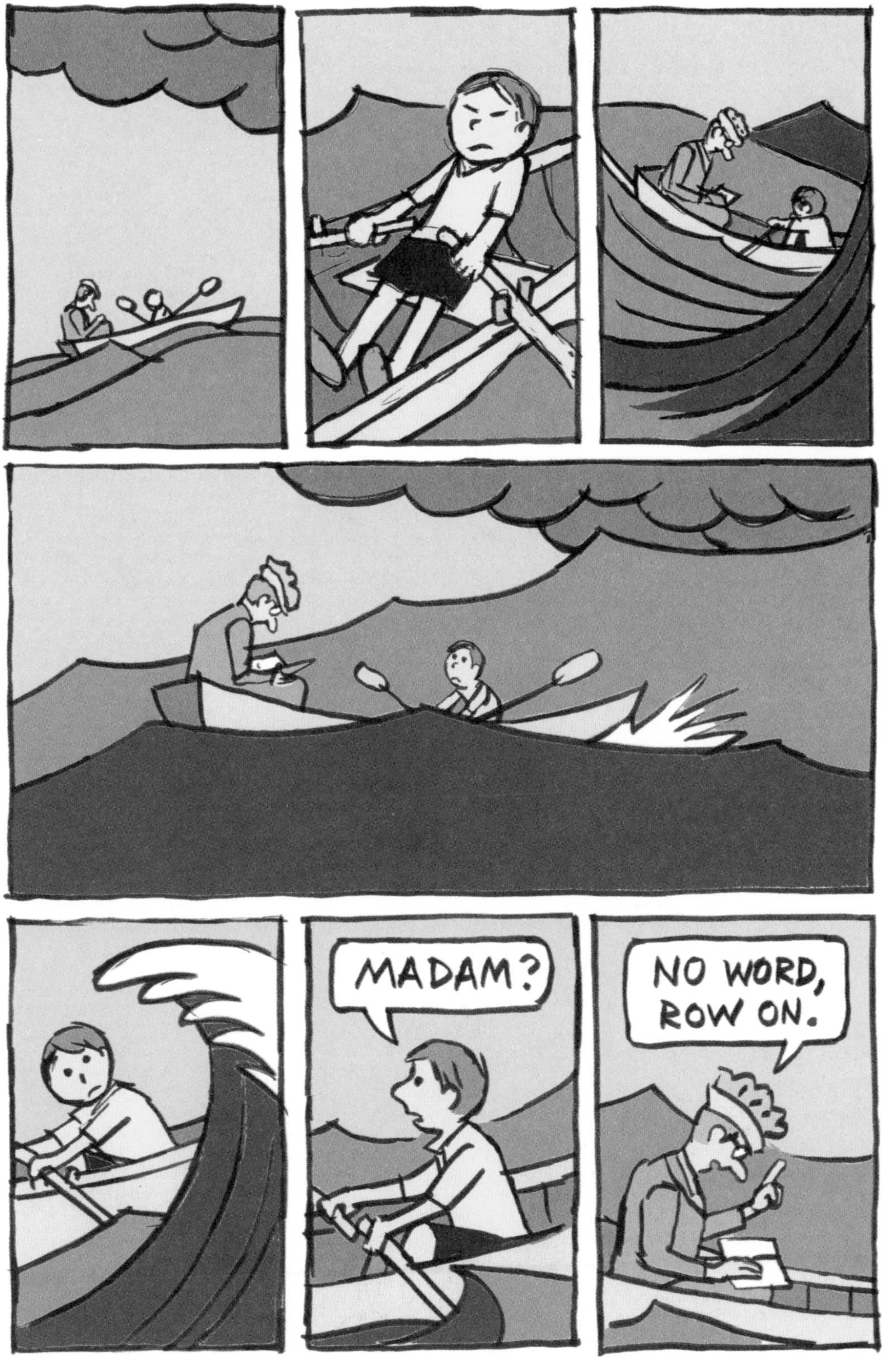
MADAM?
NO WORD, ROW ON.

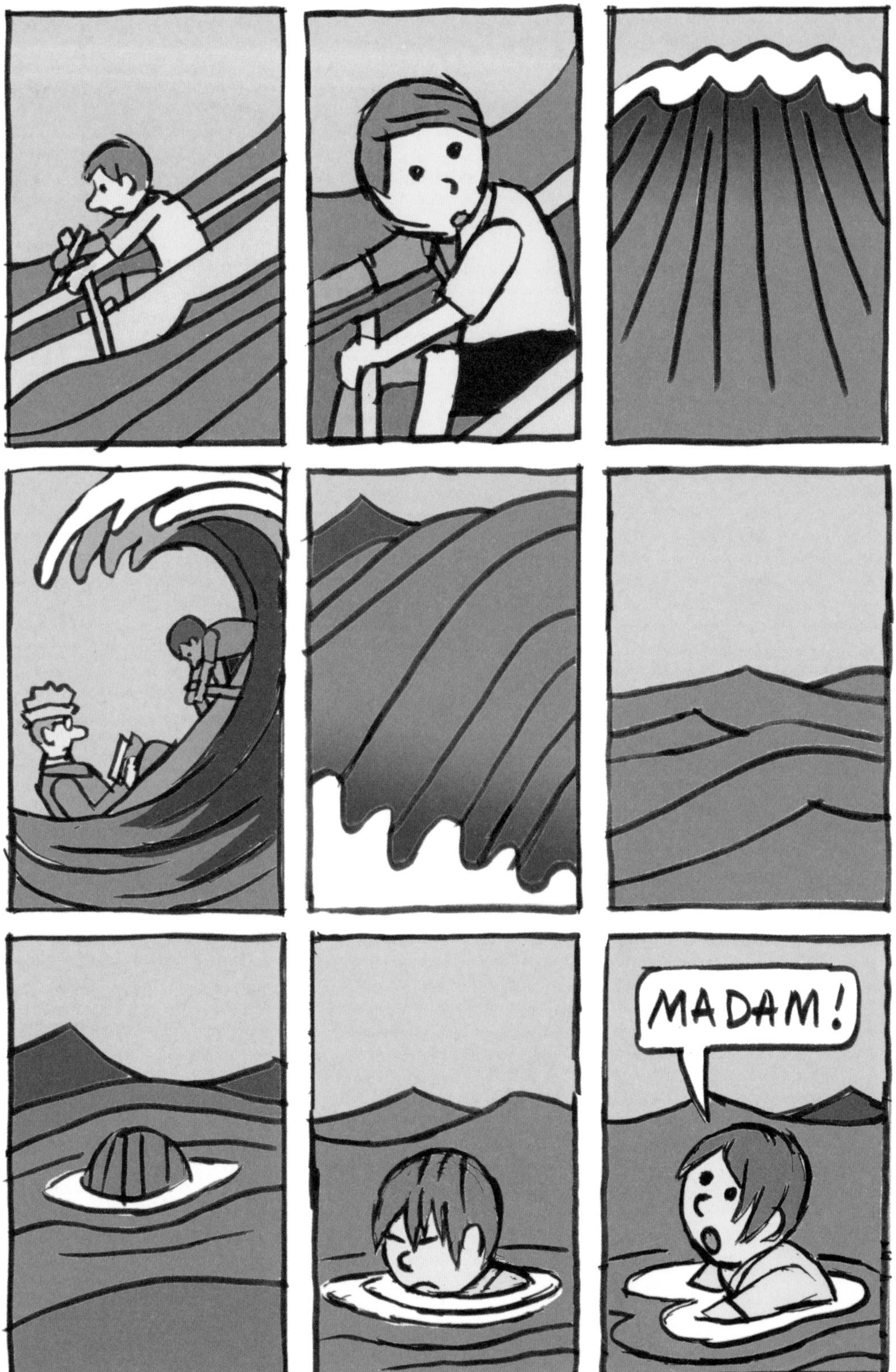
MADAM!

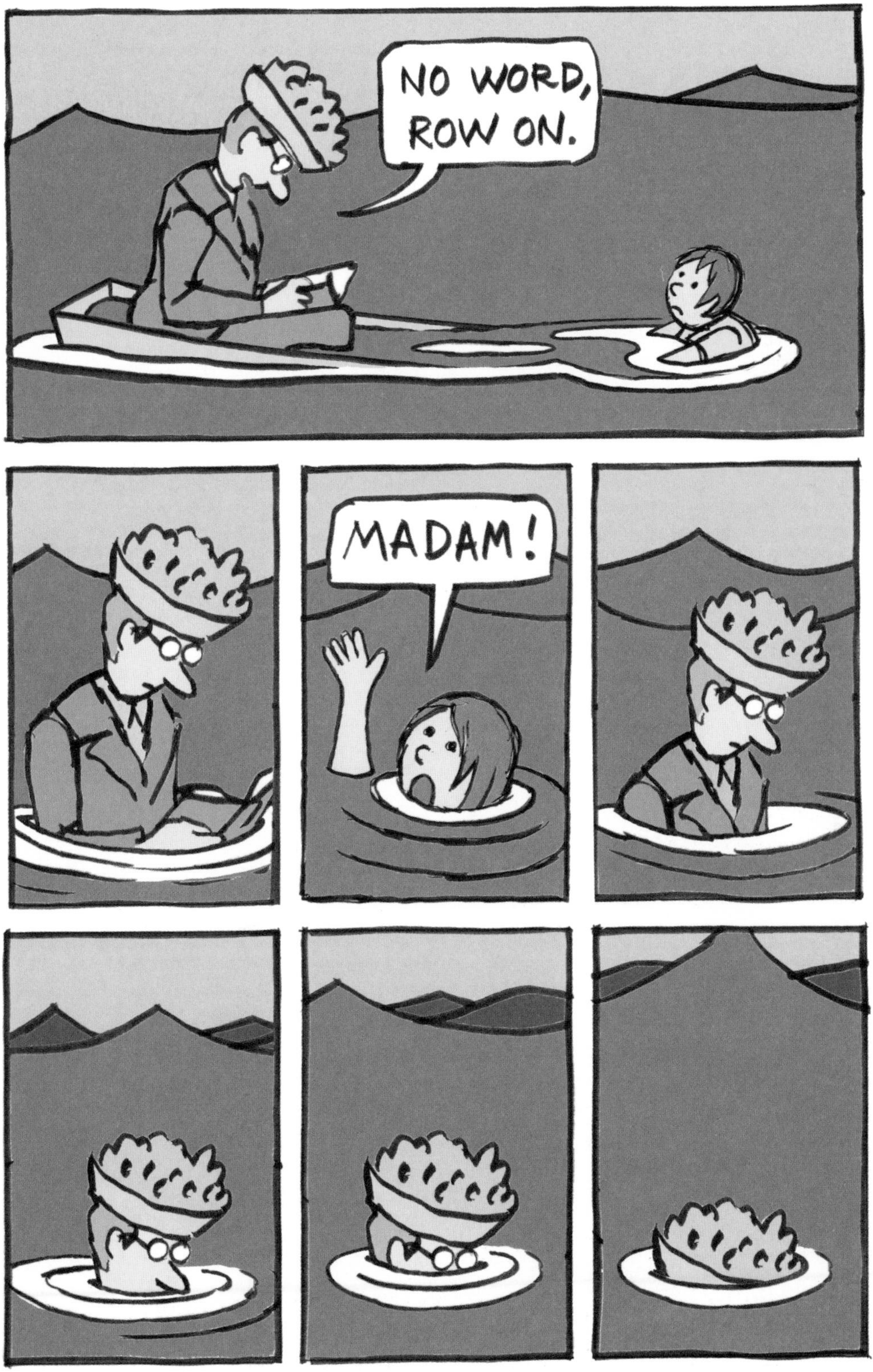
NO WORD, ROW ON.
MADAM!

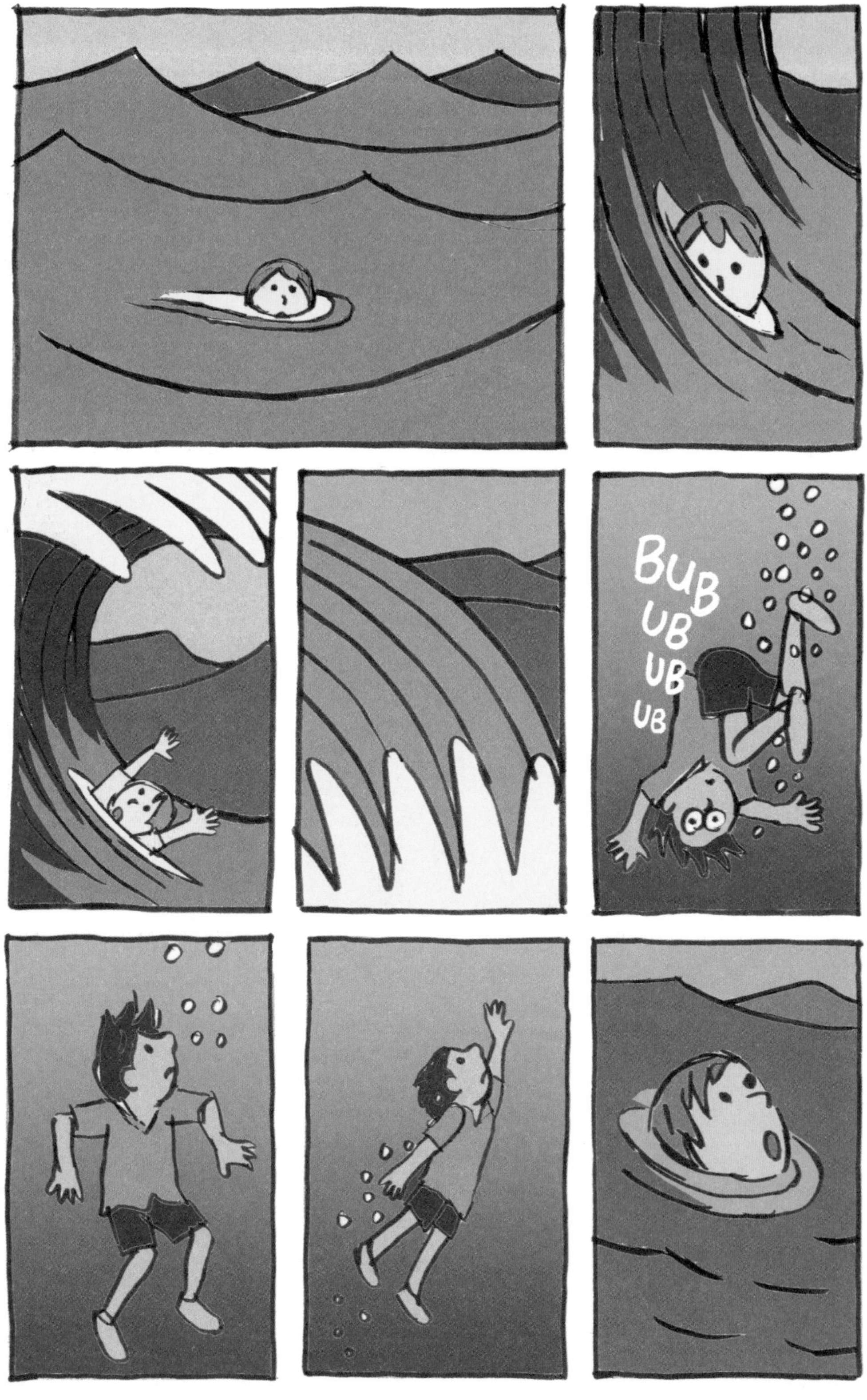
BUB
UB
UB
UB

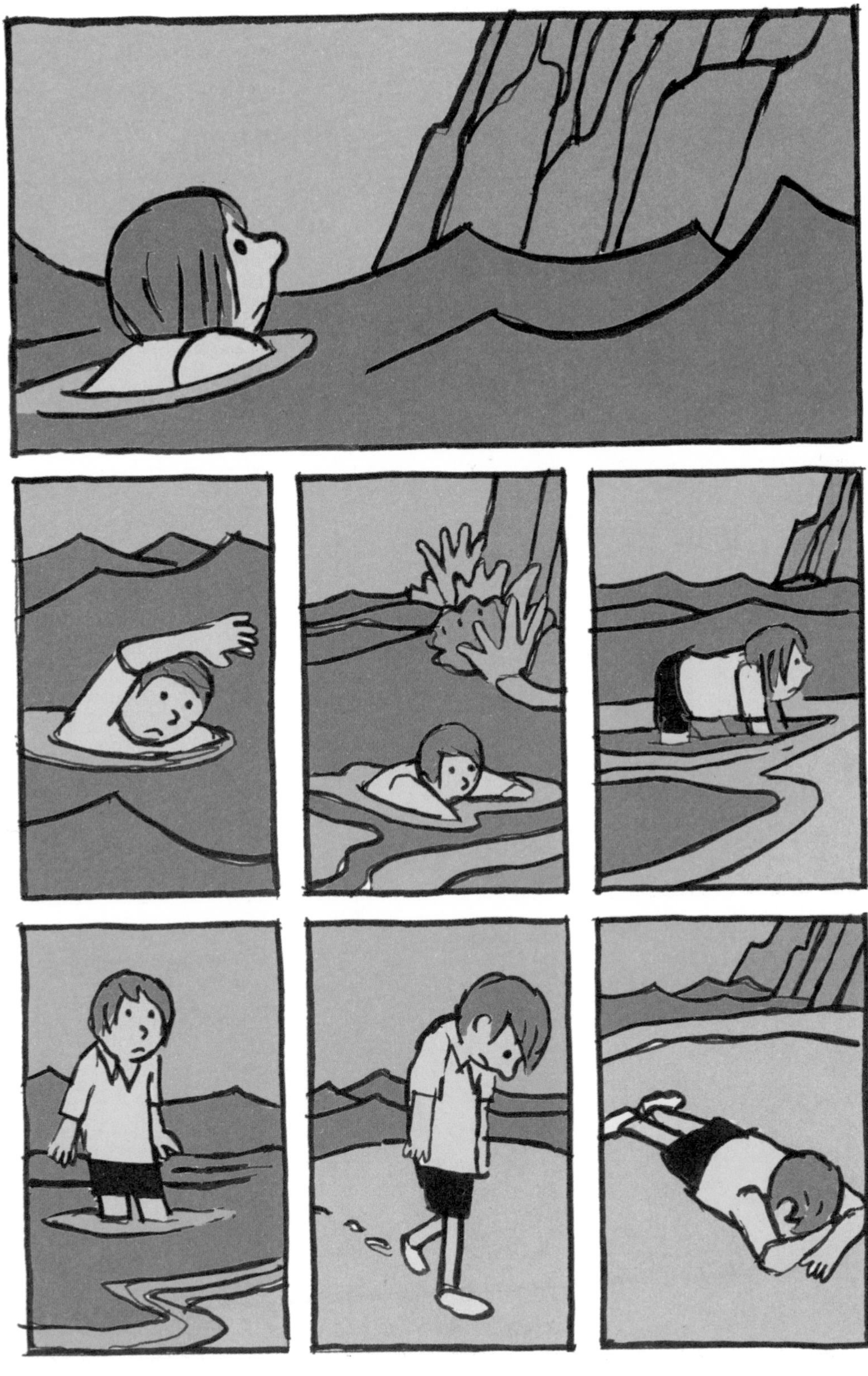

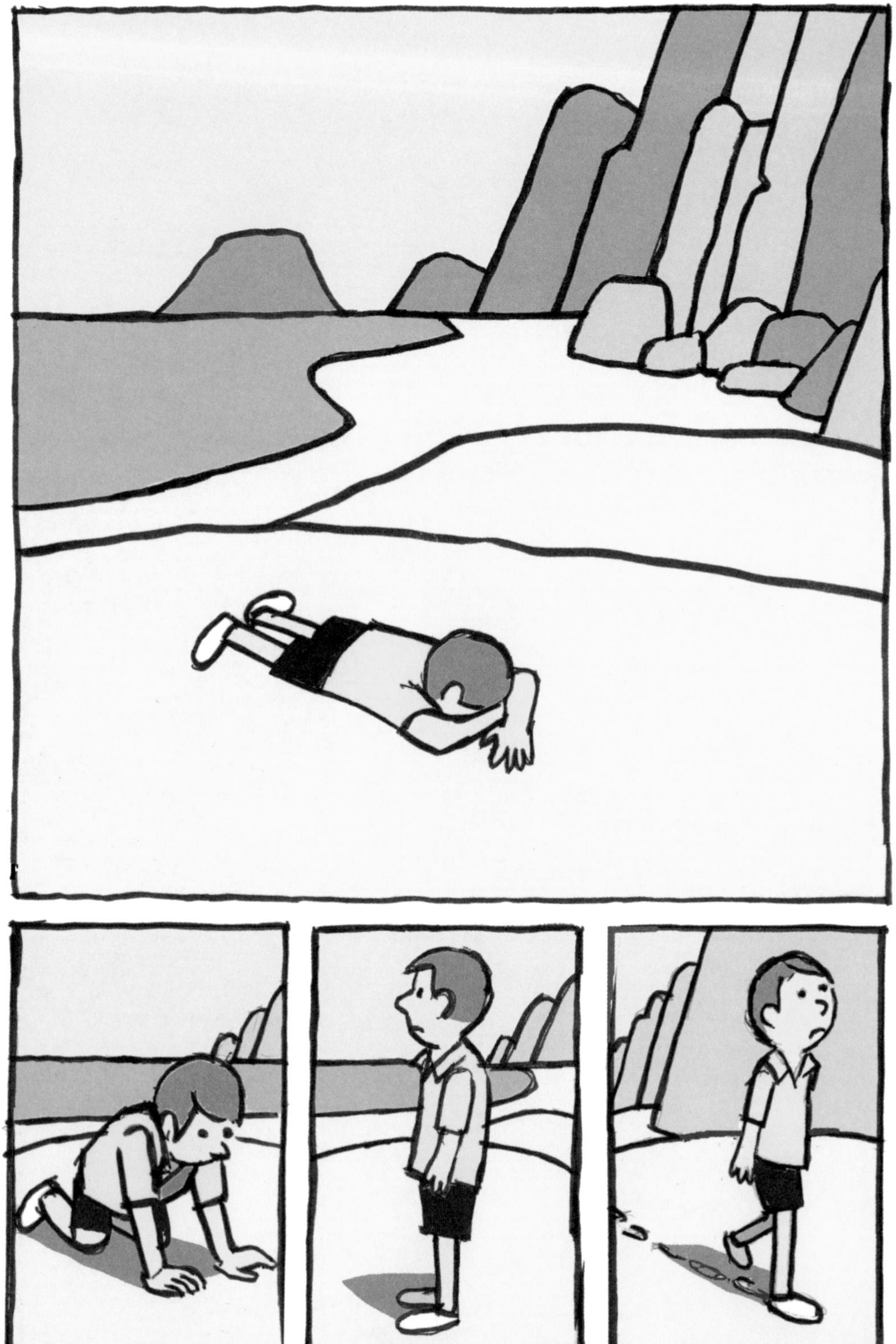

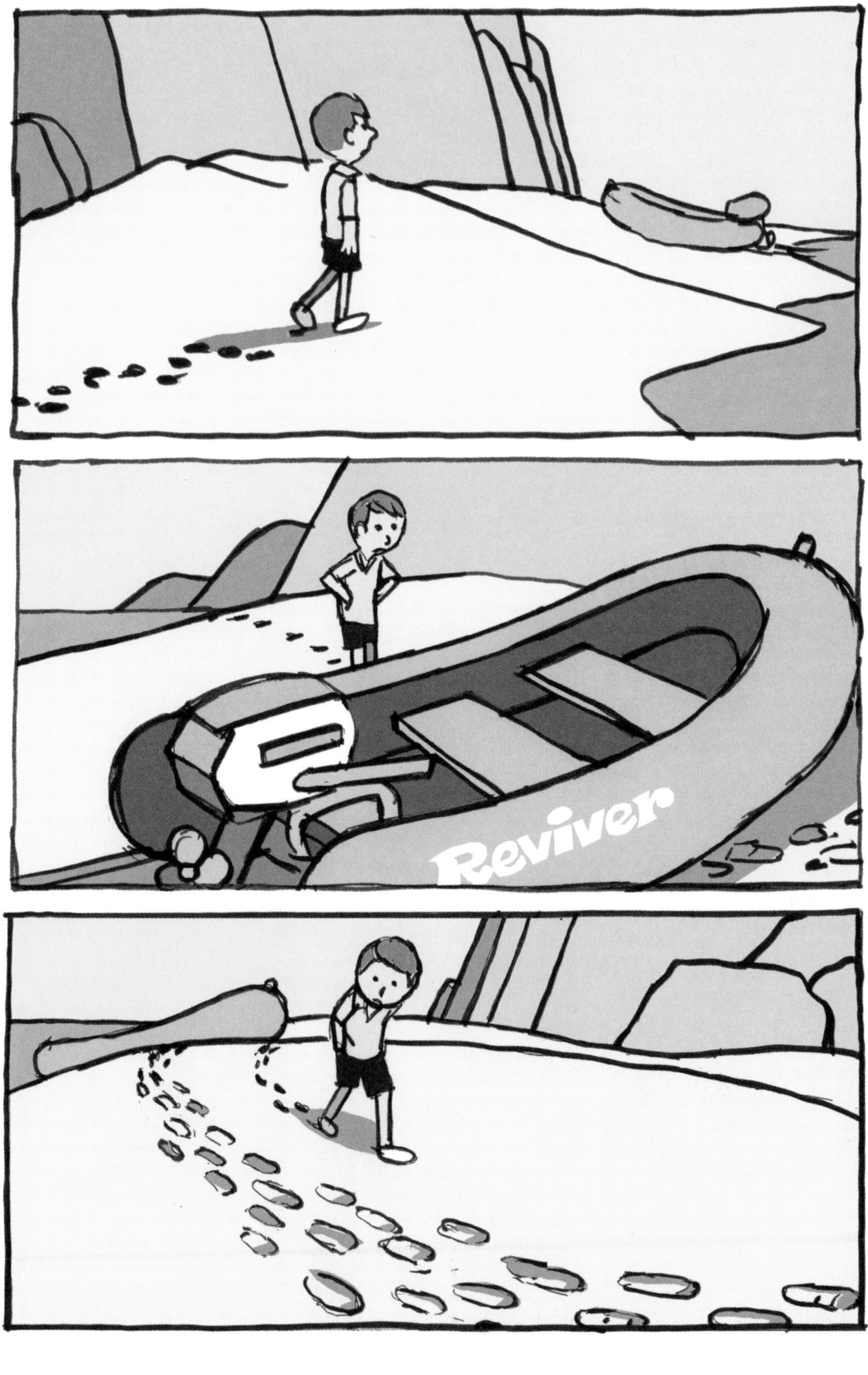
Reviver

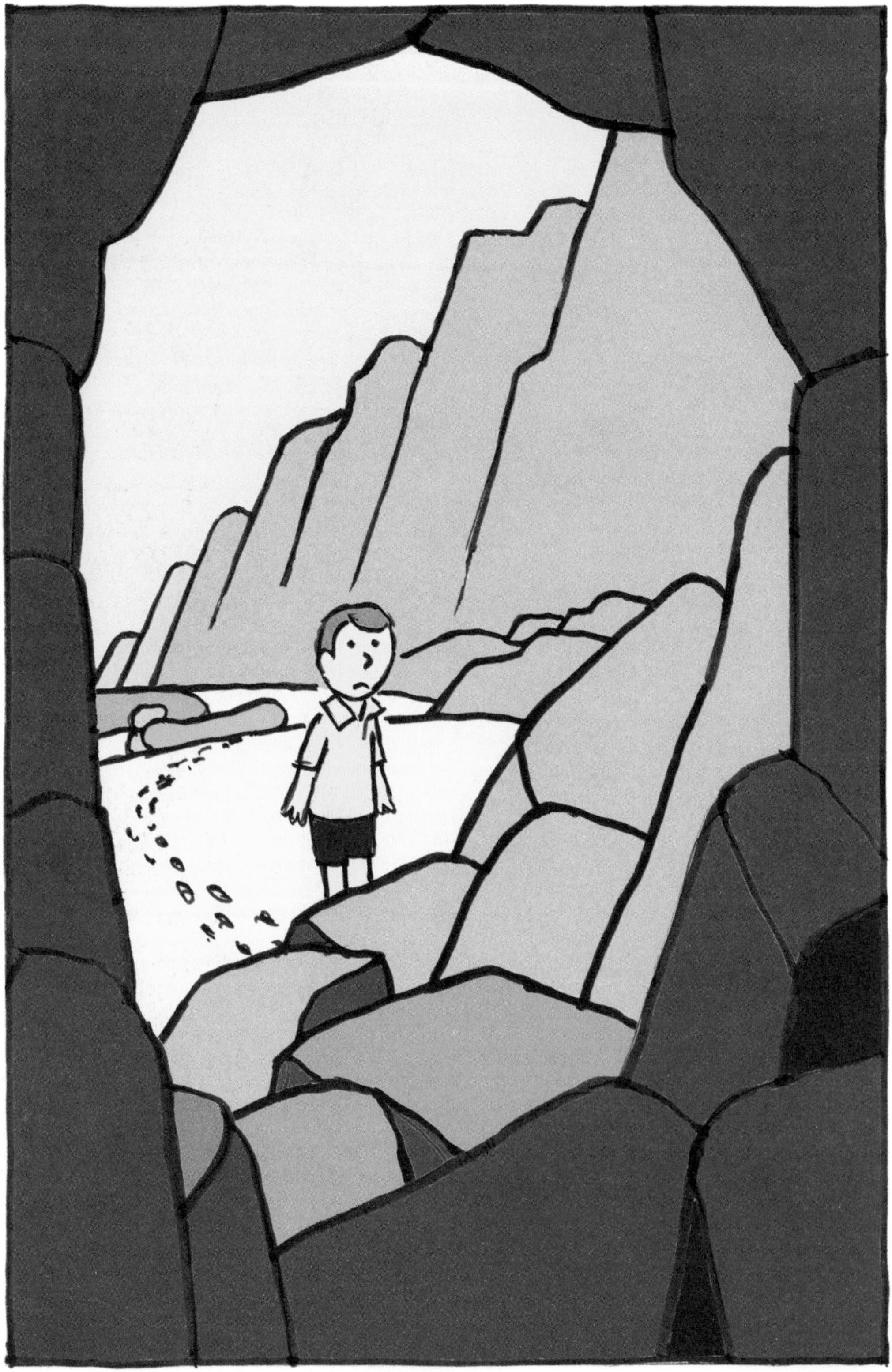

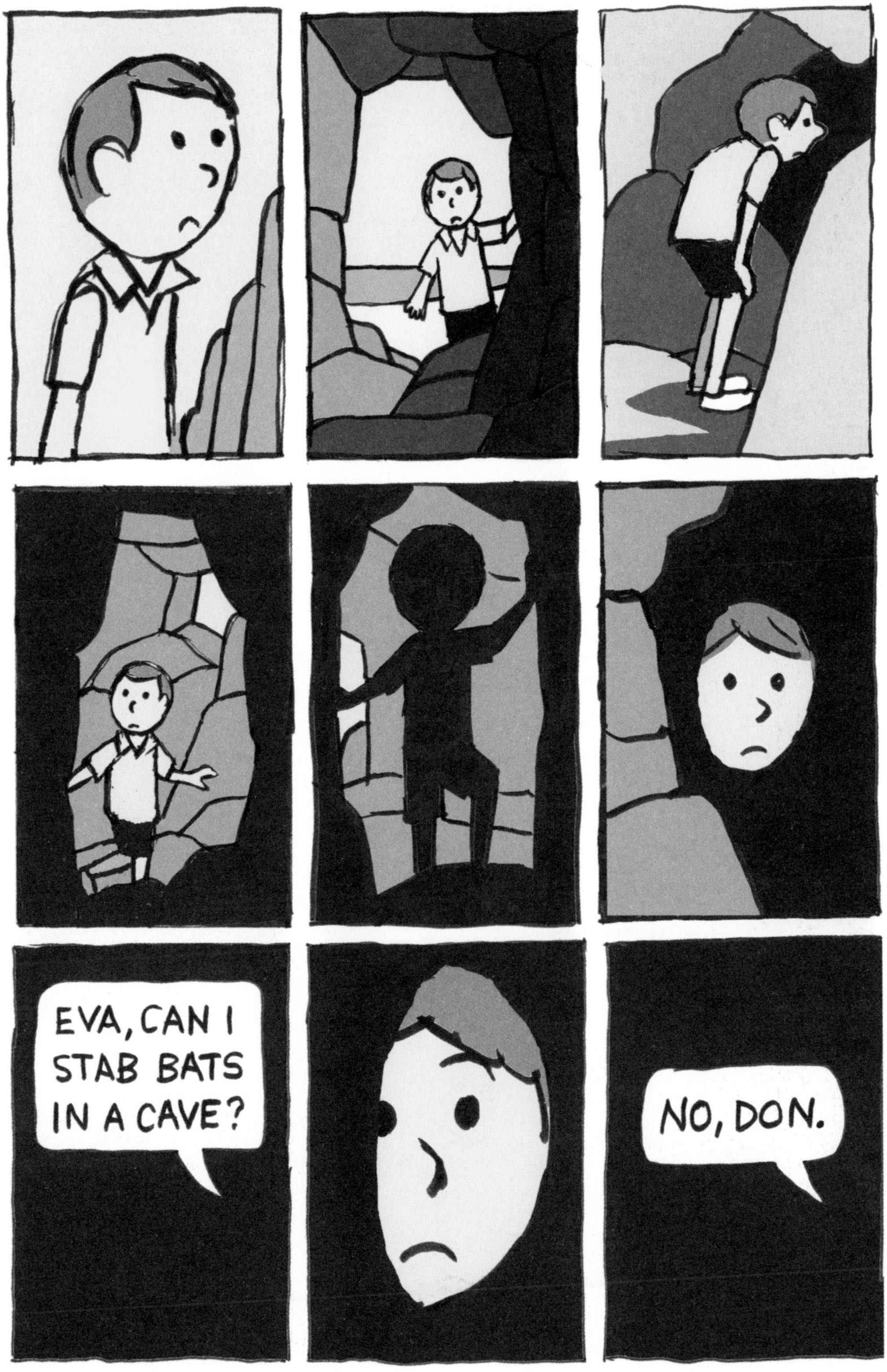
EVA, CAN I STAB BATS IN A CAVE?
NO, DON.

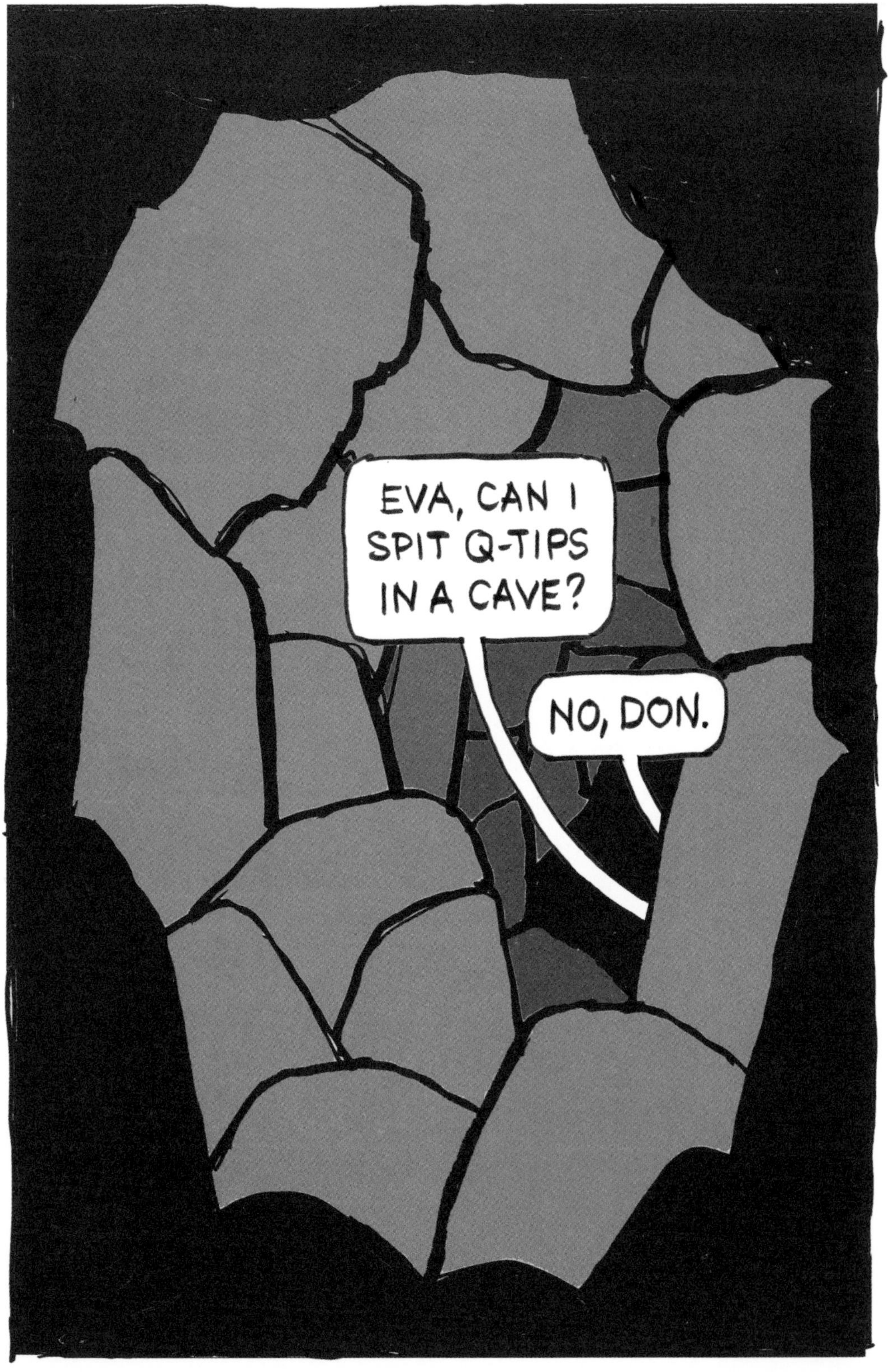
EVA, CAN I SPIT Q-TIPS IN A CAVE?
NO, DON.

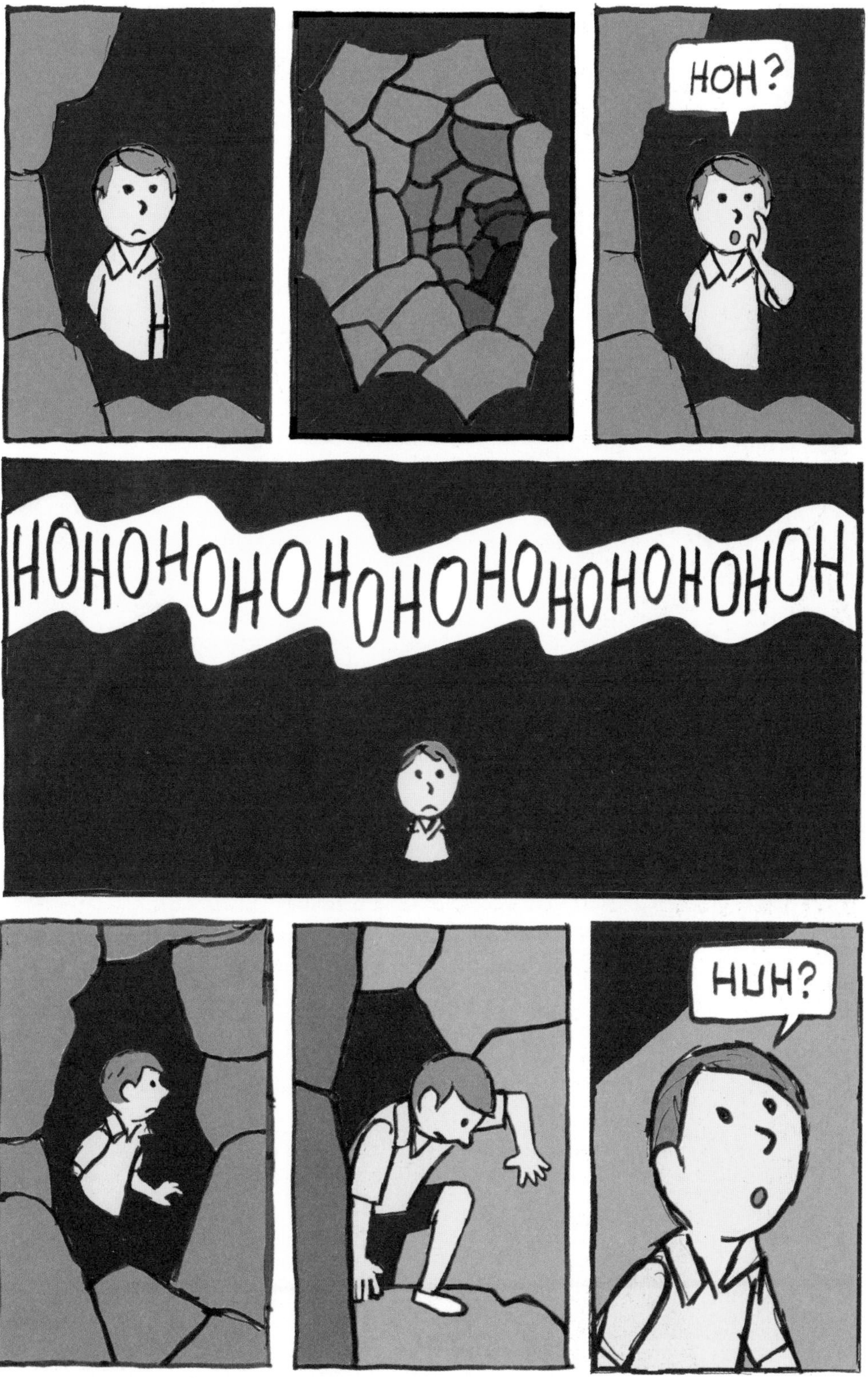
HOH?
HOHOHOHOHOHOHOHOHOHOHOHOHOH
HUH?

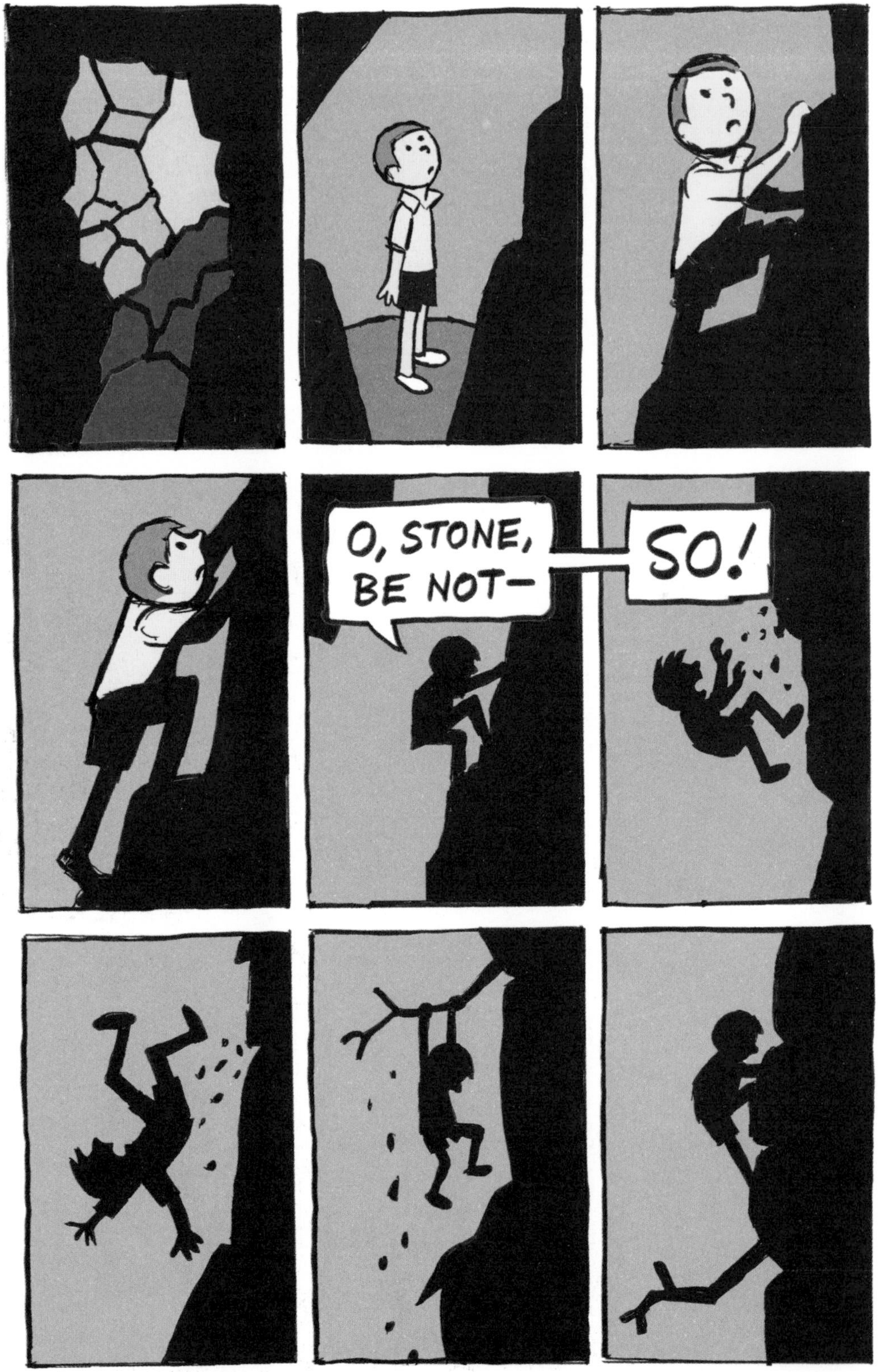
O, STONE, BE NOT—
SO!

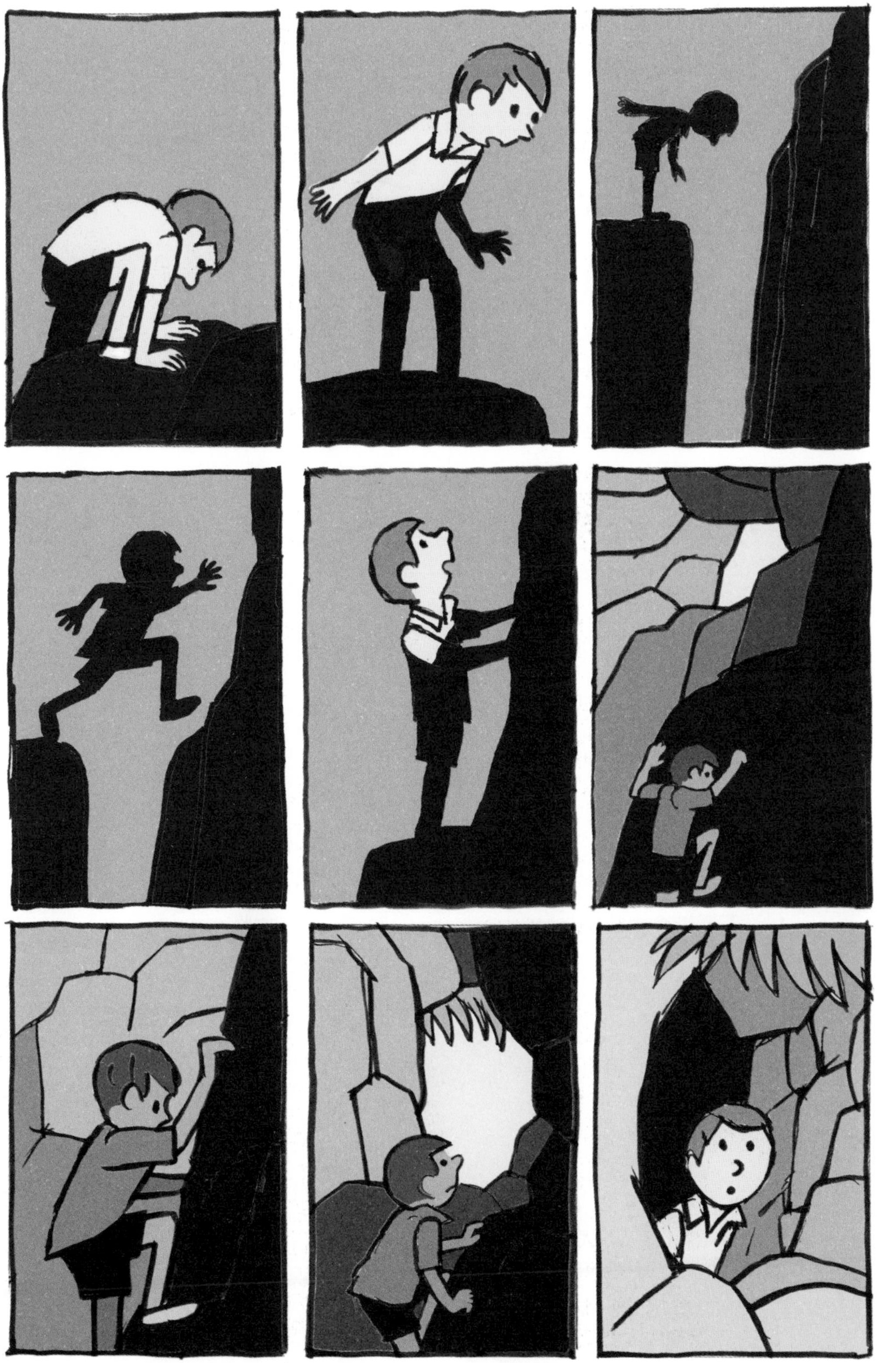

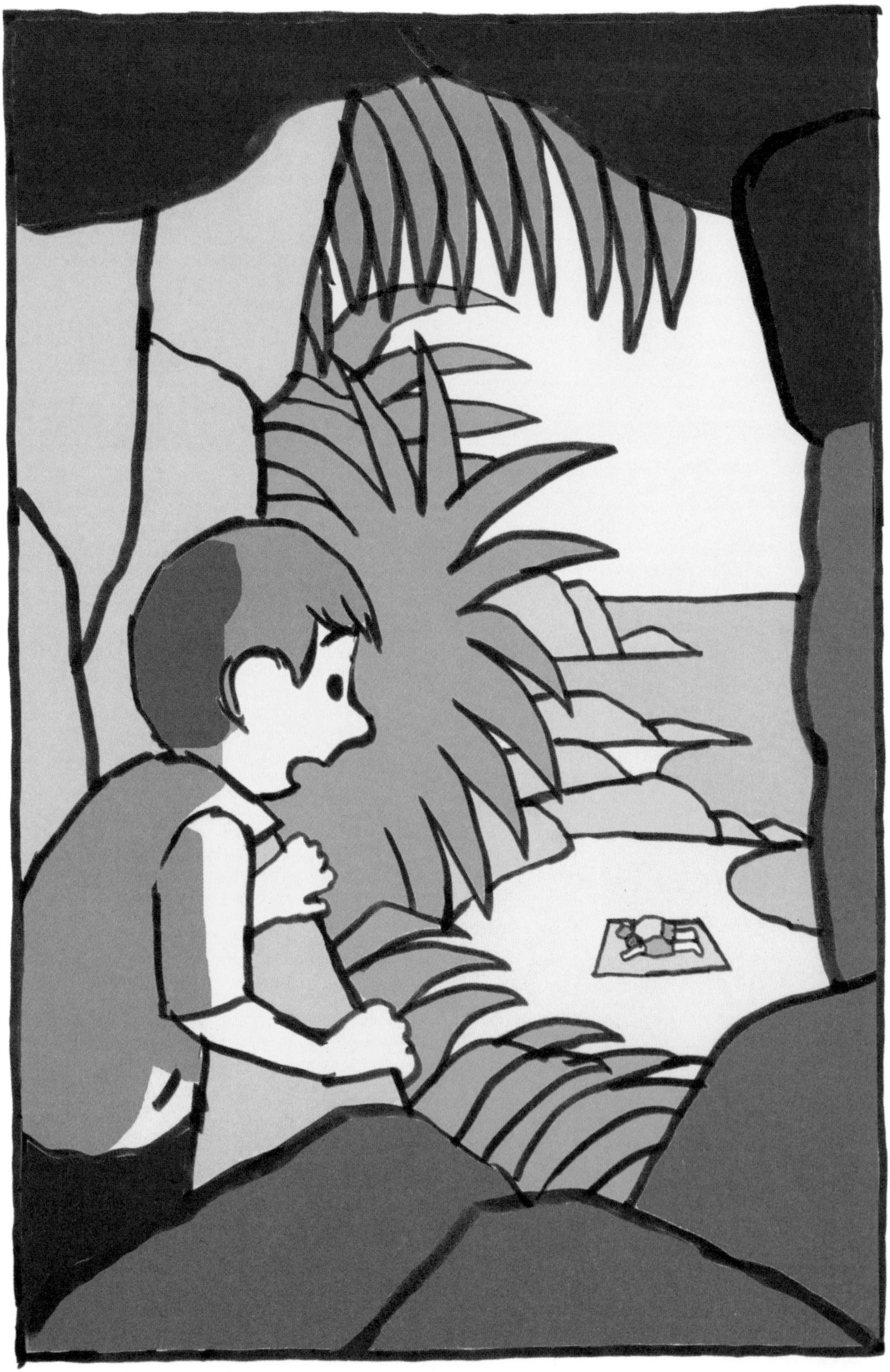

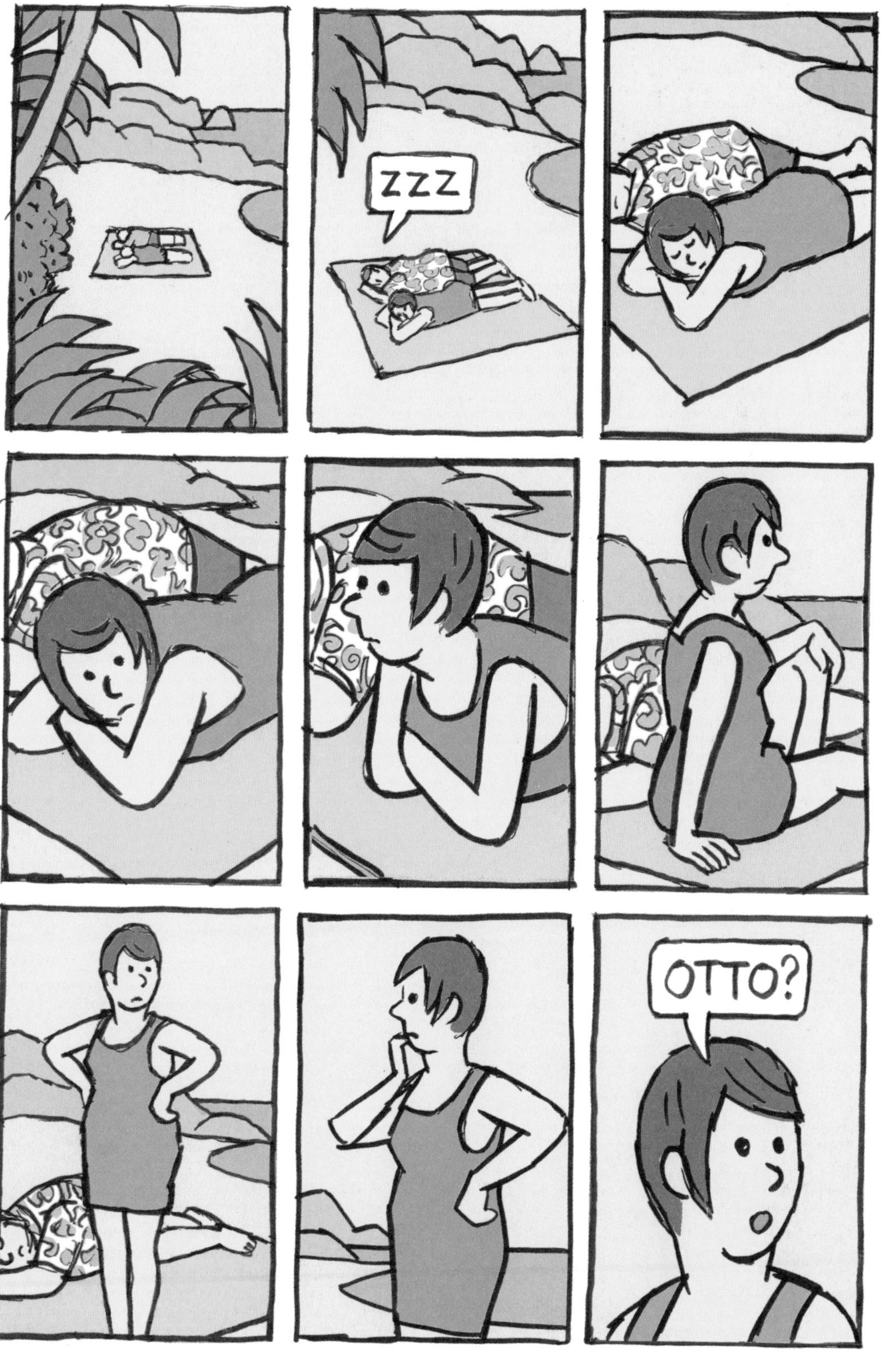
ZZZ
OTTO?

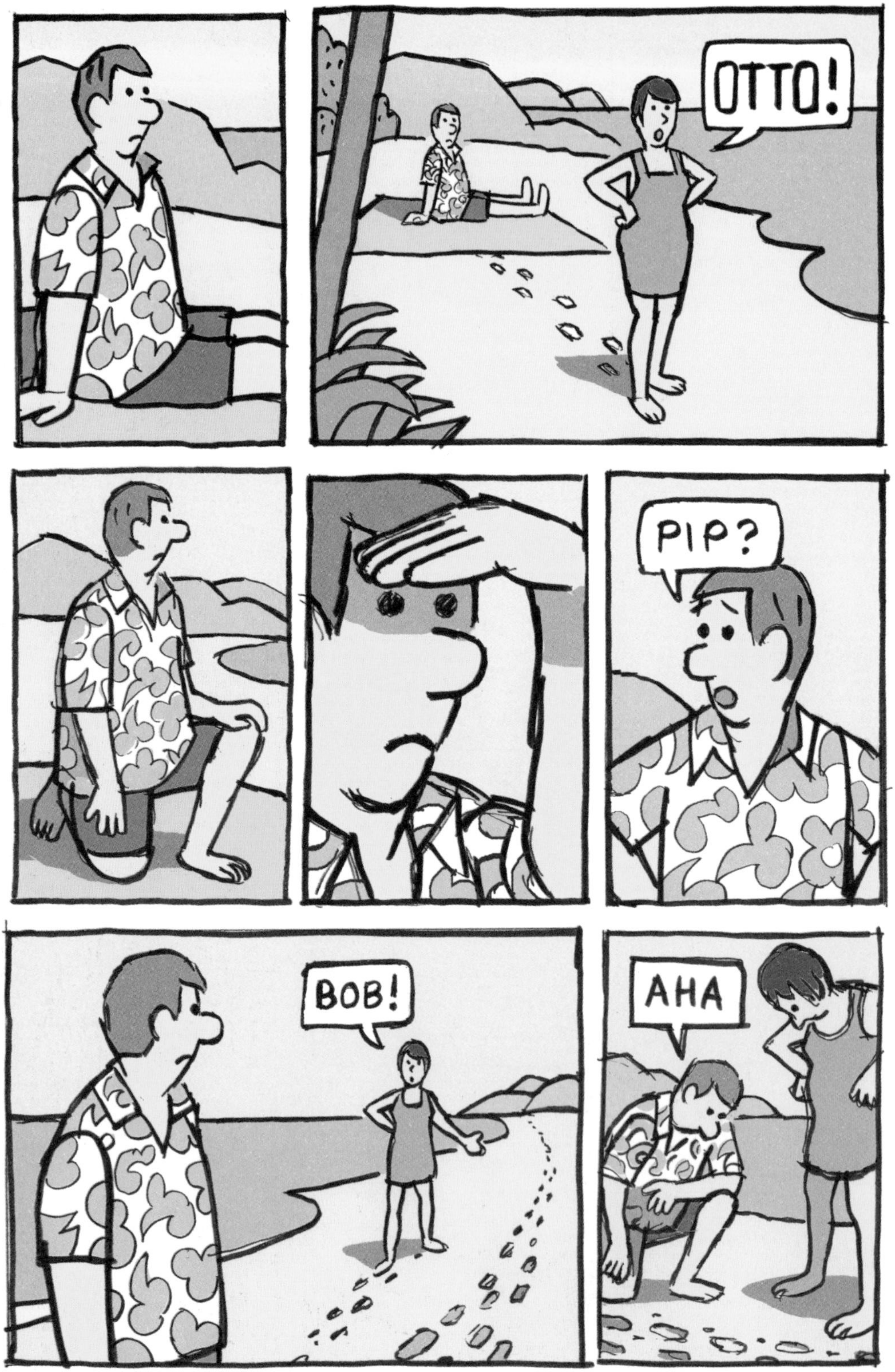
OTTO!
PIP?
BOB!
AHA

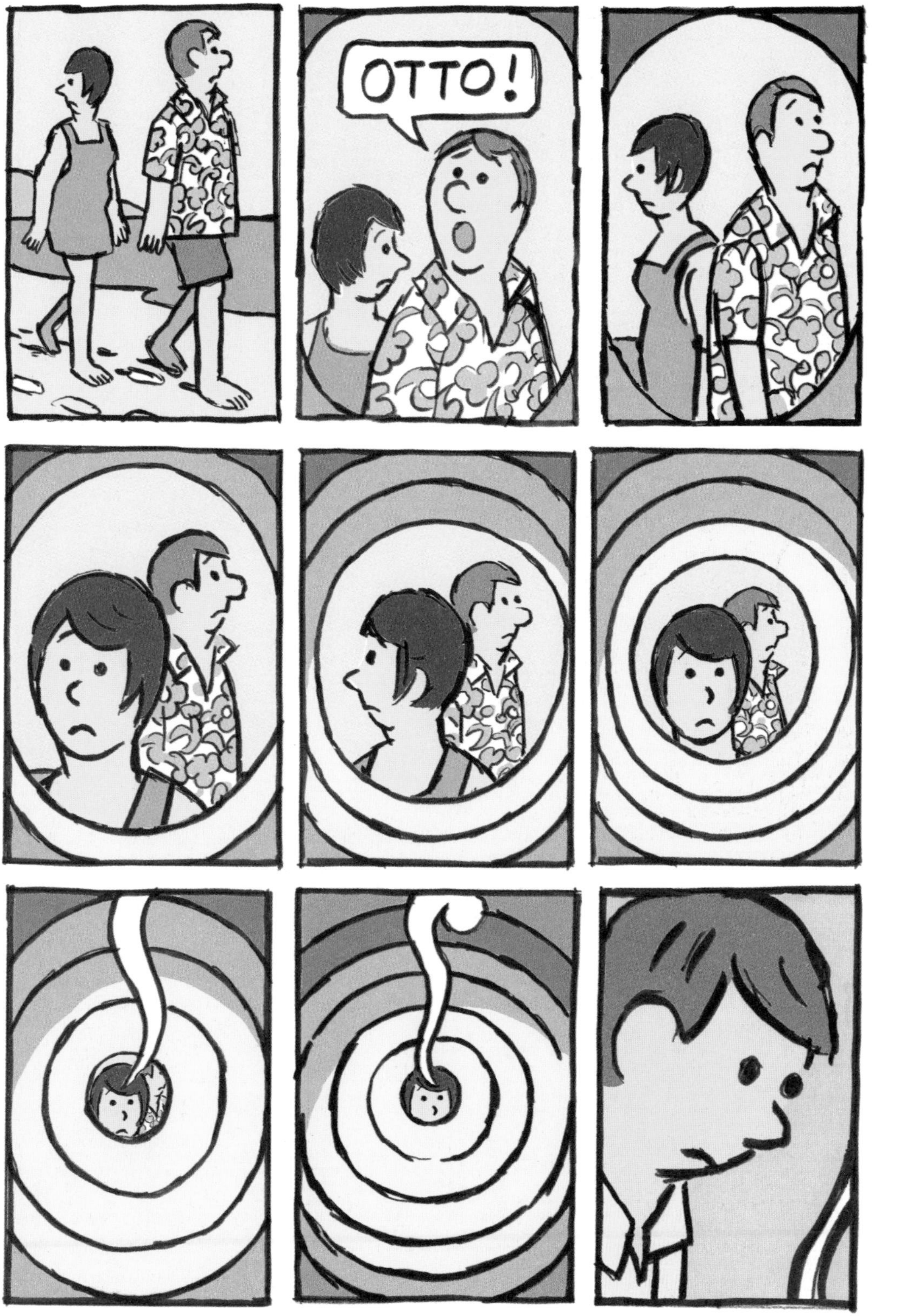
OTTO!

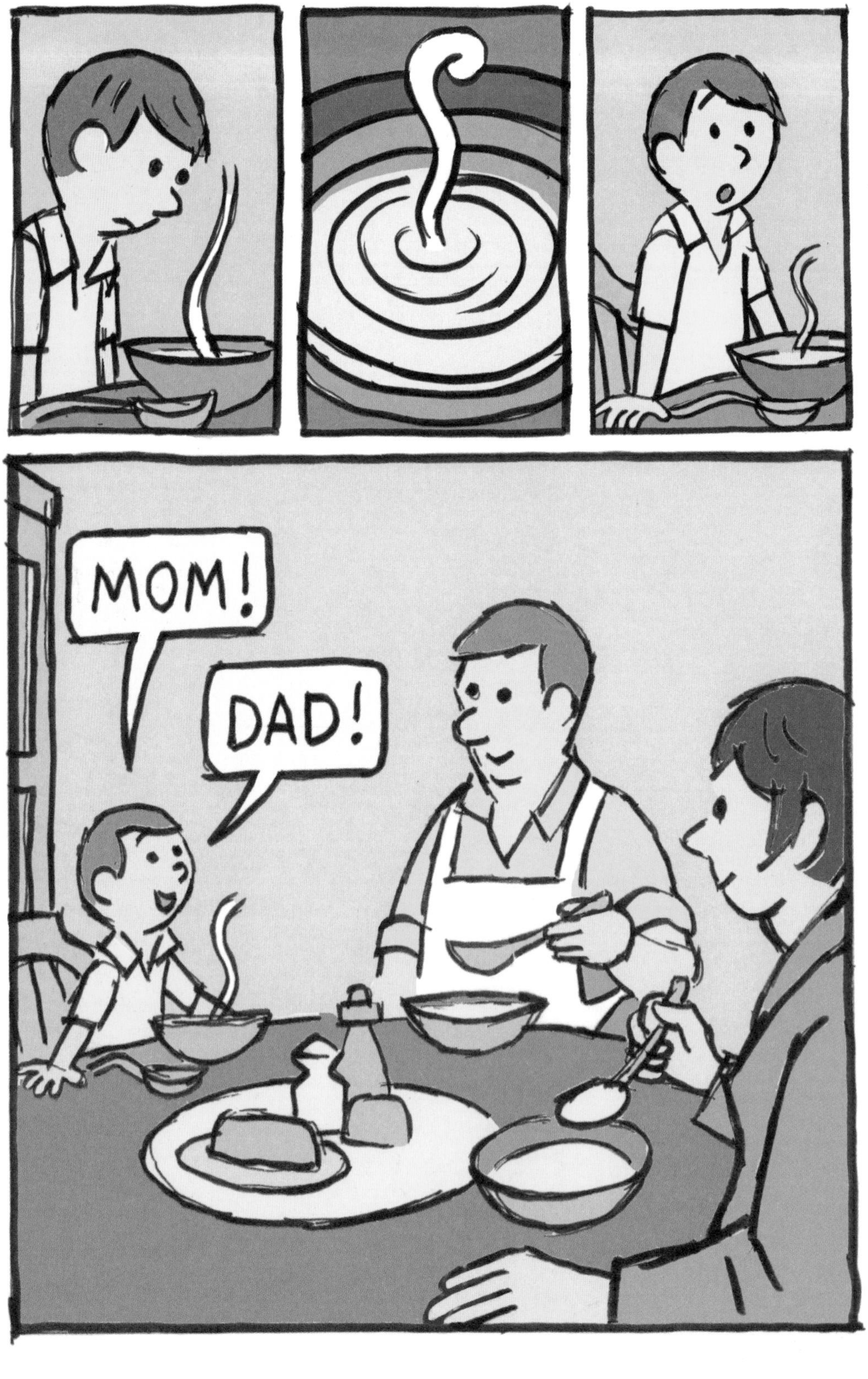
MOM!
DAD!

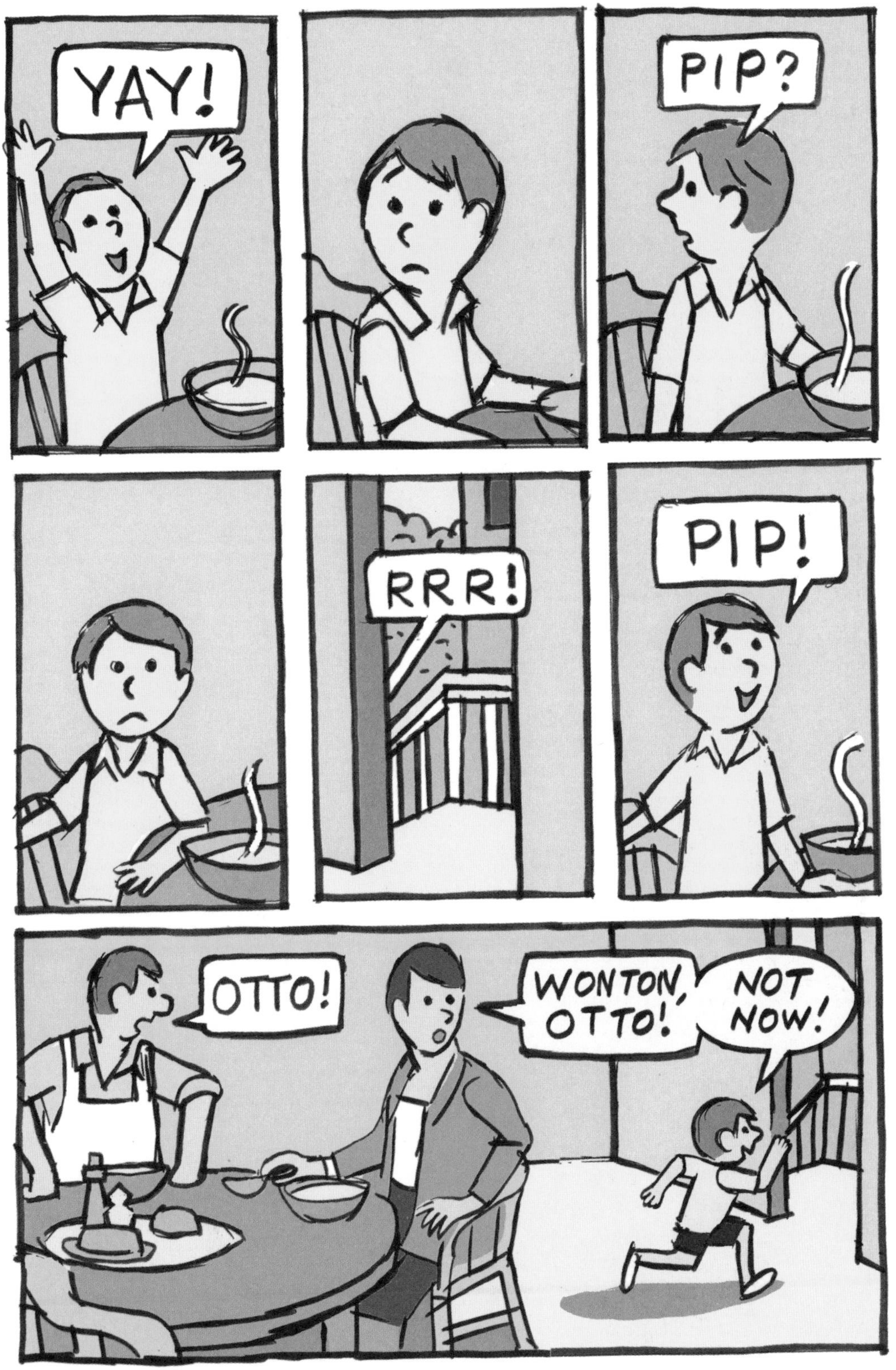
YAY!
PIP?
RRR!
PIP!
OTTO!
WONTON, OTTO!
NOT NOW!

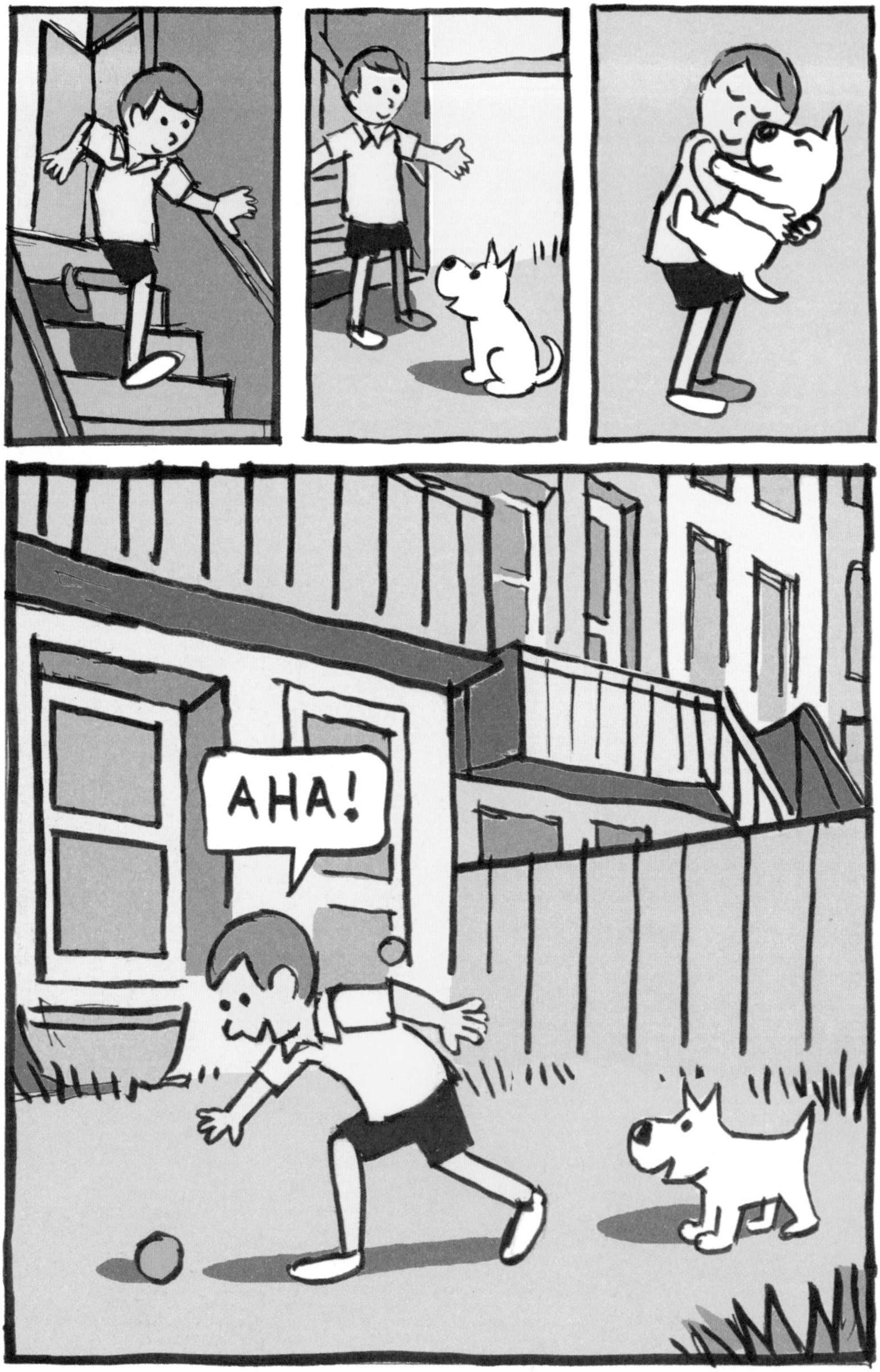
AHA!

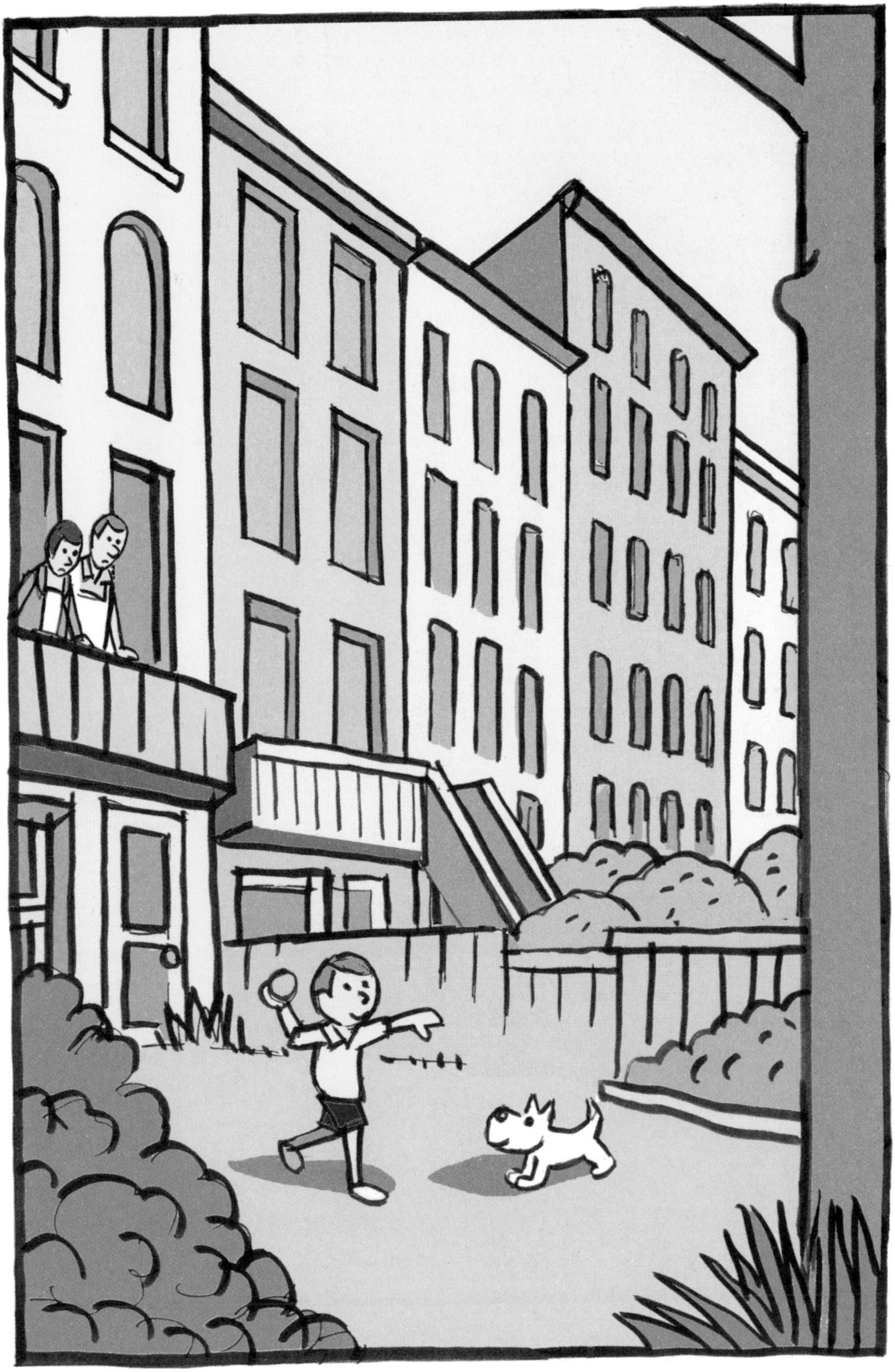

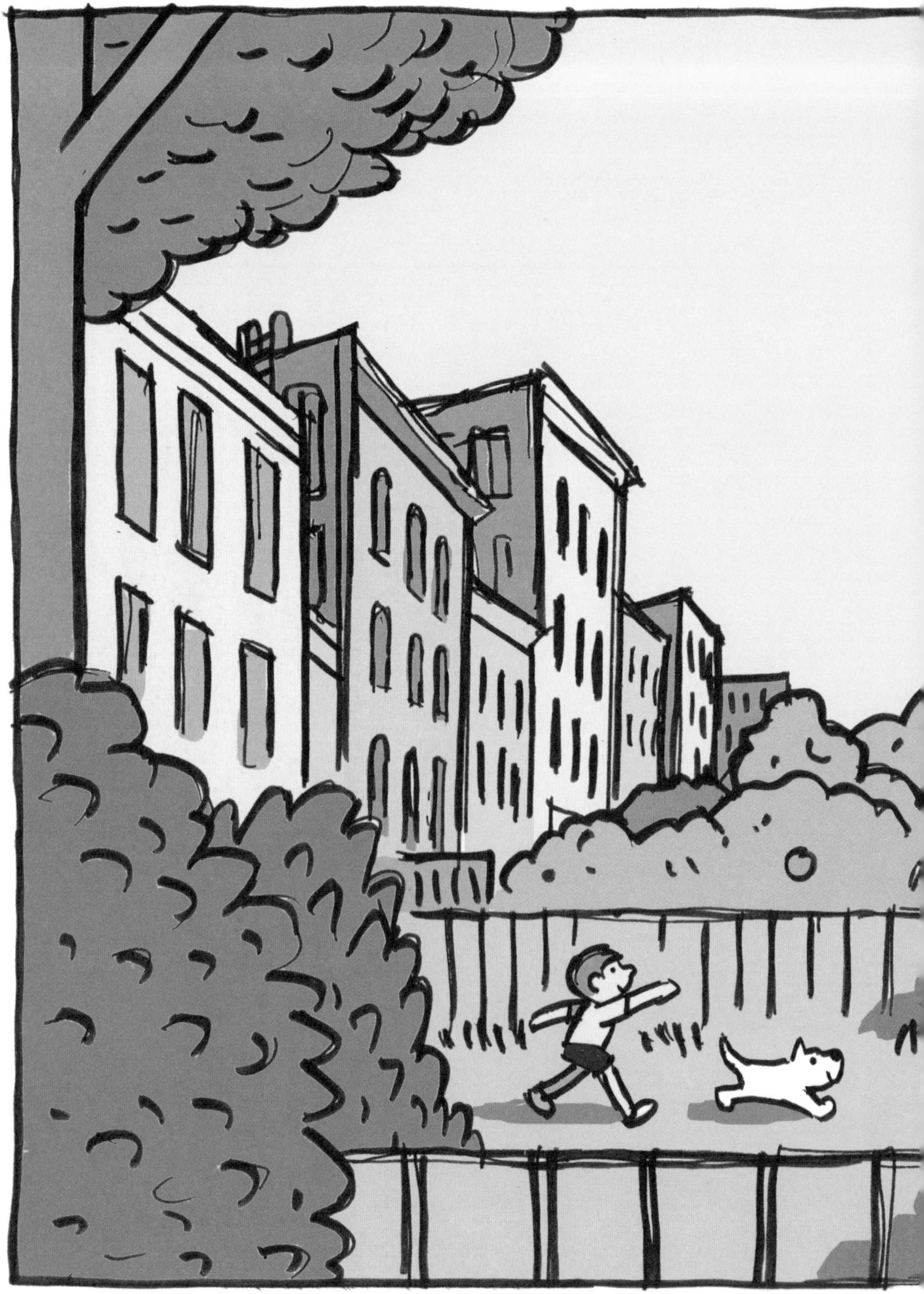

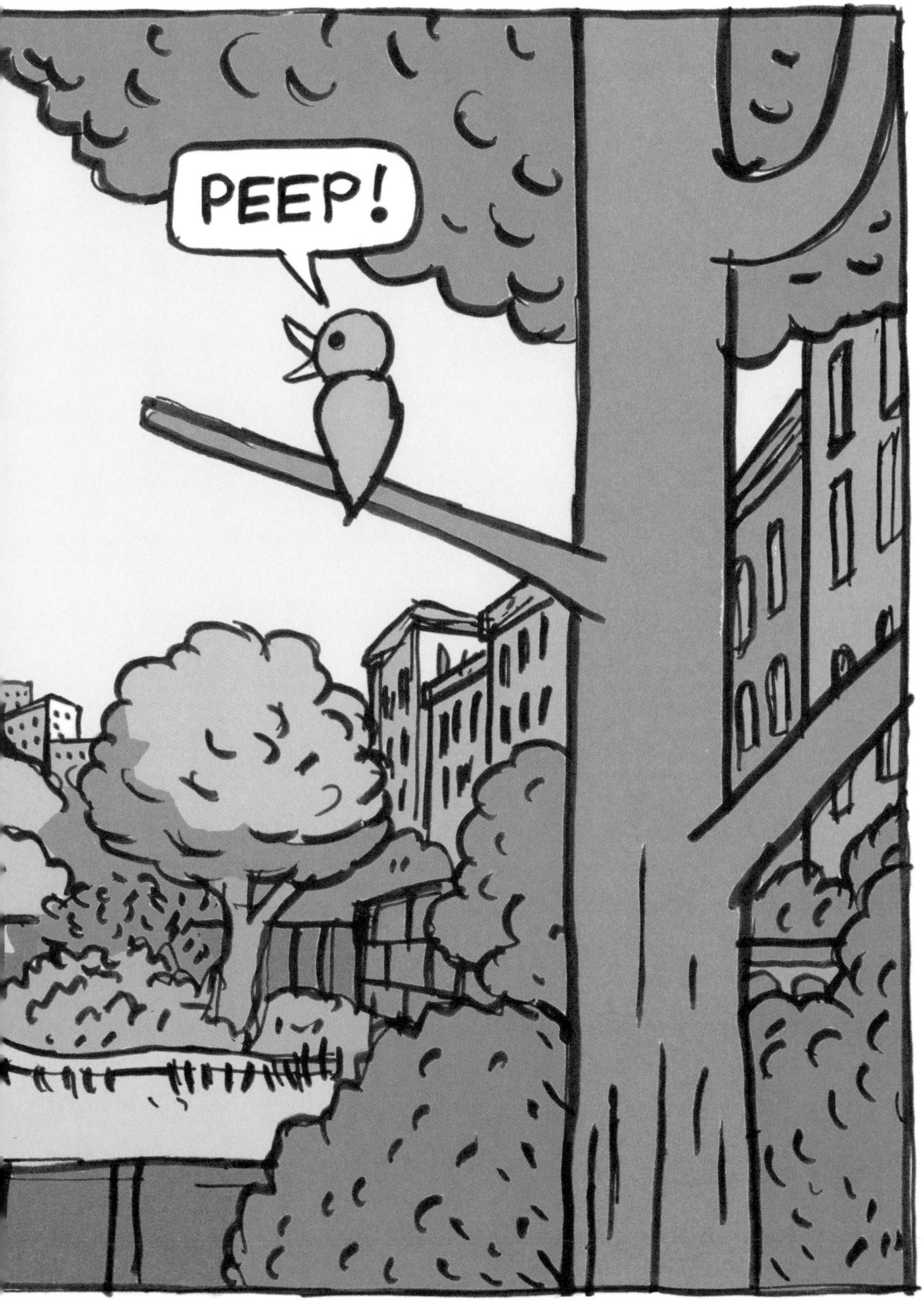
PEEP!